Island of Fog, Book 6

Chamber
of Ghosts

Chamber of Ghosts

by Keith Robinson

Printed in the United States of America
Published by Unearthly Tales on April 24th, 2013
ISBN-13 9780984390656

Visit www.unearthlytales.com

Island of Fog, Book 6

Chamber of Ghosts

a novel by
KEITH ROBINSON

Meet the Shapeshifters

In this story there are nine twelve-year-old children, each able to transform into a creature of myth and legend . . .

Hal Franklin *(dragon)* – The resident fire-breathing dragon can also belch flames while in human form, a talent he's beginning to find useful.

Robbie Strickland *(ogre)* – At three times his normal height, and with long, powerful arms, Robbie is a mass of shaggy hair and muscle.

Abigail Porter *(faerie)* – She regularly sprouts insect-like wings and can, if she wants, shrink to the size of her fellow faeries, a mere six inches tall.

Dewey Morgan *(centaur)* – While impressive in his half-equine form, Dewey is ashamed of his centaur roots for what they did to humankind.

Lauren Hunter *(harpy)* – This white-feathered bird-girl is discovering that her filthy, lazy harpy sisters can be manipulated into doing something worthy.

Fenton Bridges *(rare lizard monster)* – A large black reptile able to spit a stream of water that turns to glue, Fenton's kind is so rare he has no name.

Darcy O'Tanner *(dryad)* – As a wood nymph, she has the ability to blend into the background like a chameleon and influence plant life.

Emily Stanton *(naga)* – With the coils of a serpent, the land-dwelling naga are distinctly more human than the water-dwellers. Emily can be either.

Thomas Patten *(manticore)* – This redheaded boy spent six years in the form of a lion creature with a scorpion's tail, and is adjusting to human life.

Others include **Miss Simone the mermaid**, the Shapeshifter Program's leader; **Blacknail the goblin**, as grumpy as his pig-faced colleagues; **Molly the gorgon**, whose gaze is deadly even in her human form and must wear a veil at all times; **Blair the phoenix**, one of a rare breed of glorious birds capable of being reborn in a fiery blaze; and **Jolie the jengu** of the emotion-sucking miengu lake people.

Following the recent rebirth of a thousand-year-old phoenix, all magic in the region has been nullified and most of the shapeshifters are unable to transform. The village's source of power, energized *geo-rocks,* is dead.

To get around this problem, there's a place outside the phoenix blast zone known as Bad Rock Gulch where the shapeshifters hope to recharge their energy and bring back a wagon-load of working geo-rocks.

Deep in the mines is a super-charged cave. The mission is simple: to stay awhile in the famous Chamber of Ghosts . . .

Chapter One
Mountain Trolls

"Hey, Blacknail—are we there yet?" Molly the gorgon asked loudly. She was tall and thin, dressed in a gray robe with a heavy shawl around her shoulders. Curly black hair protruded from under her floppy wide-brimmed hat. A veil hung in front of her face, masking her features.

Blacknail, the grumpy goblin driver, shot her a withering glare and returned his attention to the front. Eleven passengers grinned behind his back—nine children and two adults, all of them shapeshifters.

Twelve-year-old Hal and his classmates had gotten to know Molly quite well recently, but they hadn't spent a lot of time with Blair. He was a plain-looking man with a thin face and pointed nose. His rather birdlike profile matched that of his alternate phoenix form.

Technically speaking, Blacknail was also a shapeshifter, though he remained a goblin at all times. It suited his dour personality.

A steep, rocky cliff loomed over them as they followed the meandering trail along the foot of the mountains. The giant, six-wheeled, steam-driven buggy rumbled along effortlessly, towing a covered wagon behind. Before long, they reached a gap in the cliff, and the goblin eased up on the levers. He wrenched the vehicle around to the right, turning almost ninety degrees to face the gap. It was a pass that led uphill then turned sharply to the left. Blacknail expertly steered the giant vehicle up the slope and around the corner, taking care to allow for the trailing wagon.

"Eastward Pass, I presume?" Molly declared.

Blacknail grunted in agreement. This was, he'd told them earlier, the only place to cut through the mountains. Abigail had immediately jumped in and questioned what people on the other side of the mountains called it. "Do they say Westward Pass?" she'd asked over and over. Finally, Blacknail had snapped at her to sit down and shut up.

They'd left their village of Carter a few hours ago, crossing open fields, endless rolling hills, some marshland, and eventually rocky, uneven plains. Now they faced a line of mountains running north to south, broken only by this narrow passage.

"I should have flown," Hal mumbled to Abigail. "Three or four hours in this buggy is only about an hour for a dragon."

"When will we be near Bad Rock Gulch?" Molly asked from behind her veil. She didn't *need* to wear a veil at the moment but kept it on just in case her magic returned unexpectedly.

"When we get there," the goblin snapped. "Look out for trolls."

Everyone leaned toward the nearest window. The buggy was now traversing a narrow ravine. Most of it was natural, but parts had been cut away or blown to bits with explosives to complete the route through to the other side. Blacknail had grudgingly explained that Eastward Pass was used by travelers of all kinds. Unfortunately, the popularity of the pass was bound to attract trolls.

Hal had never seen a troll before but had heard a tale or two about them. He watched anxiously, peering along the peaks of the craggy walls and into every shadowed nook and cranny. The pass was barely wide enough to fit the buggy through, but Blacknail drove fast, tearing along with only a few feet on either side. Dust and small rocks kicked up, showering the rickety wagon that bounced and rattled behind.

Once in a while, Hal spared half a thought for the wagon's occupant: another shapeshifter, seventeen-year-old Jolie. The jengu was literally half the woman she was, normally confined to a wheelchair but at the moment manacled to a bunk within her makeshift mobile prison. Nobody wanted to look upon her creepy face, nor hear what she had to say.

In fact, not one of them had even mentioned Jolie out loud. Fenton and Thomas, who had perhaps been closest to her before she'd shown herself to be a bad seed, had remained sullen and quiet throughout the journey. Dewey and Robbie, on the other hand, had talked non-stop— and from Robbie's constant nods and gestures, it was clear he often referred to his on-and-off girlfriend Lauren, who sat with Darcy and Emily in front.

Hal, as usual, sat with Abigail. "Hey," Robbie called to him. "If we run into trolls, I'll let the resident dragon take them on. Okay?"

Hal frowned. "Why? I thought you'd love a chance to bash a few trolls and impress Lauren with your ogre strength."

Lauren giggled, and Robbie scowled. "It's kinda awkward these days," he said, fingering his shirt. "I'd have to take my clothes off first, you know?"

"Yeah, I *do* know," Hal complained. "We all have the exact same problem."

It had been a week since the phoenix rebirth event. Everyone had received visions of the rare bird in its secret cave just moments before it had regenerated. Afterward, it was like the village and surrounding area had lost its vibrancy. The winter trees had never looked so drab. Even the air smelled stale. The entire region had been wiped of magic.

Hal, Robbie, Abigail and Emily had been in their old world when the phoenix had gone up in flames. They'd lost their magic like everyone else, but the effect on them had been temporary, and they'd regained their shapeshifting powers a few days later—partly because of the enchanted 'smart' clothes they'd brought back with them, which they'd inadvertently drained of magic. Now the friends were stuck with non-magical clothes like everyone else. It was *really* inconvenient having to undress before shapeshifting.

"I don't have a problem," Abigail said. "I cut holes in the back of my shirt for my wings, so I just need to take my coat off before I shift."

Beyond Eastward Pass, the forests, low mountains and coast lay outside the phoenix's blast zone. Magic remained there, unaffected by the rebirth. Of course, not everyone believed in magic, not even Miss Simone. *Especially* not her. As a scientist, she argued that 'magic' was just unexplained science. The word itself seemed to leave a nasty taste in her mouth whenever she spoke it aloud. After the event, she'd simply announced, "Our source of energy is gone."

In any case, geo-rocks were snuffed out. Dryads suddenly became visible in the woods. Large flying creatures like griffins found themselves floundering on the ground, their wings too small for their bodies. This also affected dragons to some extent, proving that magic was required to get these beasts airborne. The phoenix had, in one fell swoop, brought disarray to the land.

However, Miss Simone's concerns were a little more practical. "We can all survive without geo-rocks for light and heat," she'd told worried villagers. "It's how we used to live, after all. But there's no denying the convenience of portable energy to power our homes, and the laboratory in particular is suffering."

She and Blacknail had traveled outside the phoenix's blast zone to Bad Rock Gulch, the geo-rock mines in the east. They'd brought back a small supply of working rocks for the laboratory, thus restoring emergency power. But that supply was running low, and Blacknail was once more making the journey east to bring back a more substantial load.

Still, that wasn't why Hal and his friends, along with Molly and Blair, were riding with the goblin. "Just concentrate on your own mission," Miss Simone had told them. "We know it's possible to absorb the energy from smart clothes, but we have no working smart clothes left. So drain what you need out of the glowing walls in the mines. Get your shapeshifting powers back, persuade Jolie to take Emily's sickness away, and come home safe and sound."

"You're not coming with us?" Lauren had asked.

Miss Simone had smiled. "I actually like being plain and ordinary. People don't pester me as much. Oh, please say hello to Lucas for me while you're in Landis. It's a new moon, and the lycans are at their most human, so you'll be fine. Just don't stick around too long. No more than a few days. They start getting wolfish as the month goes on."

Wolfish, Hal thought for the umpteenth time, burning with curiosity.

When Blacknail announced they were halfway through the pass, he put on a bit of extra speed, and at one point the vehicle scraped noisily against the sloping rock wall to the left. *More repair work later*, Hal thought.

He was amused by the buggy's recent upgrades. Now it had an actual door in the side along with the windows. Half the roof was finished with new metal sheeting, thin but rigid; leather canopy stretched over the rest of the framework. The seats were the same—five rows of them with an aisle down the center, plus Blacknail's driver seat at the front. Even with nine children and three adults aboard, there was ample room, and they'd all spread out and thrown their sacks of clothes and overnight things toward the back.

Blacknail suddenly grunted and pulled back on the levers. The buggy lurched to a halt, throwing everyone forward out of their seats.

"Trolls," he growled, sounding really fed up. He slumped in his seat for a moment, then sighed and leaned sideways to open a slim compartment under the windshield to his right. He dragged out a bulky, heavy sack and headed for the door. "Stay put. Gonna buy our way through."

As he pushed open the door and climbed down the ladder, all the passengers stampeded to the front.

"There they are," Darcy exclaimed in a hushed tone.

Lauren let out a squeak, and Thomas said something under his breath.

"They look mean," Fenton said simply.

"And big," Dewey added in a small voice.

Hal, on tiptoes to see over his friends' heads, finally caught a glimpse of four gangly monsters slithering down the sloping walls just ahead of the buggy. They were vaguely similar to ogres only much thinner and a little shorter—but still enormous compared to Hal and his friends, at least twice their height. They had coarse gray hair and strangely oversized hands and feet that had clearly evolved to clamber up and down steep mountains. Ogres were dimwitted giants whereas trolls radiated a cunning intelligence. Fangs stuck up out of the corners of their mouths, and their eyes were so deeply sunken, their brows so heavy, that each of the four trolls appeared to be wearing a permanent grimace.

"Oh my," Emily said softly over the rumbling engine.

"Can't we just keep moving?" Fenton asked nobody in particular.

Darcy pointed high above, and everyone inched forward, jostling one another to press themselves against the windshield and look up. On the craggy peaks of the rocky walls to both sides, more trolls loitered—ready to lob boulders that would punch holes right through the roof.

"It's an ambush," Robbie said plaintively.

Down below, Blacknail walked around to the front of the buggy dragging his heavy sack. A troll came to meet him. Now Hal saw just how monstrous these creatures were. Ogres were friendly, if a little clumsy. These trolls, on the other hand, seemed willing and able to pick up the stout goblin and smash him against a wall. Three of them spread out across the pass and planted their feet, clenching and unclenching their fists over and over, while the fourth stood over Blacknail and scowled down at him.

The goblin said nothing. He simply dragged the sack forward, then stepped back. The troll tilted its head as if calculating the weight of whatever was inside. It bent, plucked the loaded sack effortlessly into the air, dangled it in front of its face, turned it upside down, and shook it violently. Ten dead chickens fell out, all fat and limp, feathers fluttering loose as they toppled onto the dusty ground. High above, the trolls let out a curious moan as if what they saw excited them. Even above the noise of the idling engine, the moan carried through the fabric part of the buggy's roof and filled Hal with dread.

The leader seemed unimpressed. It stared at the lifeless chickens for a long time, glared at Blacknail, and snarled something that Hal couldn't hear. He wished he could turn the engine off so he could listen to the conversation, but he dared not touch the controls.

Blacknail spread his hands and seemed to be arguing. Even though he was less than half the height of the troll, he didn't seem to care about his irritable personality coming through in his jerky hand movements.

The troll shook its head firmly, then pointed at the buggy and said something else. The goblin paused and craned his head upward to where the ambushers were ready to throw down a barrage of boulders. After a while, Blacknail returned to the buggy. He was out of sight for a moment before reappearing at the top of the ladder and entering with a terrible scowl on his face.

"Problems, Riley?" Molly inquired.

Normally, Blacknail would admonish her for using his old human name, but right now he was more concerned about the situation. "They ain't happy with ten chickens, especially as they're dead already. It was eight the other day, and they told me it would be ten next time I came through. So I brought ten. And now they've upped the price again. They want twelve now."

"They can't do that," Blair said shortly. "It's one thing to charge for passage, but to keep changing the price when they feel like it? That's not right."

"How do they have a right to charge us at all?" Abigail demanded.

"Because they live here," Blacknail snapped. "Think about trolls taking a shortcut through our village. After a while we'd want to charge them for it."

Abigail frowned. "Would we?"

"Never mind," Molly said, absently pulling at her hair. In her gorgon form, that hair turned into a mass of writhing snakes. "So what can we do? Do you have any spare chickens lying around?"

Blacknail barked a short, sarcastic laugh. "Yeah, I keep dead chickens stuffed in my pockets." He sighed heavily. "We either turn back, or . . ."

He looked squarely at Hal, then shifted his gaze to Robbie.

Robbie was quick to raise his hands. "Hal's got this."

"Thanks, buddy," Hal said. "I'll take care of it all on my own."

Abigail slipped her arm through his. "You don't need a giant moronic ogre. You can deal with these nasty trolls by yourself. Just fly around and breathe fire on them while Blacknail drives on."

There was a murmur of agreement. Hal looked around at a sea of faces that included one veil and a gnarled, grumpy goblin. Normally it would be very easy for an army of shapeshifters to chase the trolls away, but only four of them had magic right now. He threw up his hands in surrender. "Fine. When all else fails, send the dragon in. I see how it is."

"Attaboy," Blair said cheerfully. "Show 'em who's boss."

Fenton was a little more grudging. "If I could transform, I'd be out there myself dealing with them. But I can't, and you can, so quit moaning."

There wasn't much more to be said on the matter. Hal moved up the aisle and across to the open doorway, fingering his shirt and wondering where to undress in private—and also to dress again afterward. Not having working smart clothes was a real problem. He stood on the top rung of the ladder looking all around, aware that the trolls had now spotted him and were staring at him intently.

In the end he clambered onto the metal portion of the buggy's roof toward the front end. It was very thin, like tin, but sturdy enough as long as he stood near the edge. He steered clear of the temporary fabric stretched across the rest.

"Mind my roof!" Blacknail yelled from below.

Hal pulled a face at him as he wobbled precariously on his perch. He couldn't figure out how this was going to work but started removing his shirt anyway. He flung it down on the roof and awkwardly pulled off his shoes and pants. As he was doing so, the trolls stood there like statues, staring at him with obvious amazement and suspicion. The leader looked down at the ten dead chickens, then back up at Hal as if wondering if there was some kind of sacrifice on offer.

How many chickens am I worth? Hal asked himself as he slipped out of his shorts. He bundled the clothes neatly on the roof, grateful there was no wind within the narrow ravine. Feeling extremely vulnerable and embarrassed even in front of these shaggy, monstrous trolls, and praying that his friends wouldn't come to the open doorway and peer over the roof at him, he knelt in position and prepared to transform.

When he did so, the tin roof buckled under his weight even though he tried to perform his transformation in time with a leap into the air. It simply didn't work out well, and as he pushed off into the sky, wings beating hard, he looked down to see that he'd left a large dent in the metal and a tear in the fabric, through which Blacknail was shaking a fist at him. His clothes had tumbled in through the gap.

One thing at a time, Hal thought. *Trolls first, clothes later.*

The trolls were barking madly. It was the only way to describe their strange, frantic yells. Whether they were shouting at each other or simply screaming with fright, they were certainly making a lot of noise. Hal leaned into a dive that would take him straight toward the trolls atop the cliff.

Some of them scattered immediately, springing with amazing agility over the rocks and into narrow crevices. As they abandoned their posts, a few boulders toppled and bounced into the pass. Blacknail had stopped short earlier; if the buggy had been directly underneath, those boulders would have easily crushed a passenger or two.

This angered Hal. How dare these ugly brutes threaten his friends this way? What right did they have to demand payment for passage through what was the only direct route through the mountains? Whether the trolls called these rocks their home or not, travelers weren't bothering anyone by passing through.

He swooped around for another attack. This time he made sure to breathe a little fire toward the remaining trolls so they had no choice but to retreat. When the tops of the cliffs were clear, Hal landed on one side and folded his wings. He would stay right here and guard the ravine from above to make sure the trolls stayed away. The opposite side was only a short hop away; in fact, if any creatures reappeared, he could probably breathe fire across that distance without even moving. Eastward Pass was safe.

Blacknail had already started moving forward. The four trolls blocking his way had no choice but to move aside, and they were angry about it—and even more angry when the buggy's great iron wheels squashed some of the chickens into the dirt. Hal chuckled to himself. *That's where greed gets you, trolls—with less than you had to start with.*

At first it seemed his guard duty would be simple. All that changed when the leader troll leapt for the buggy's ladder and hung on. The creature reached through the open door and felt around, and several screams came from inside.

"Aw, heck, here we go," Hal muttered to himself, his words emerging as a guttural dragon grunt. He spread his wings and flexed his leg muscles, preparing to drop down on the moving buggy and deal with the troll.

He didn't need to because, at that moment, an ogre burst out of the buggy's roof, greatly widening the hole Hal had made earlier. Blacknail's wail of anguish was audible over the yells of the others. Robbie's roar then drowned out all other noise as he grappled with the surprised troll.

Robbie was bigger and stronger, but the troll was wily and fast. And there were three others rushing in to help. Their hoots and barks seemed to indicate excitement rather than fear—cries of joy as they leapt aboard to tangle with the ogre. Robbie, poking out of the fabric roof and balancing precariously, punched and kicked while the buggy bounced and jiggled under the enormous weight.

Trolls appeared on the clifftop on the opposite side of the ravine, popping up out of the crevices with a hungry look in their wild eyes. Hal realized immediately that he needed to stay right where he was, high above the battle, to keep his friends safe from boulders being tossed down—and to keep these trolls from joining in the fray.

He let out a savage burst of flames, letting the trolls know he was there and willing to burn them if they came too close. They barked and ducked. Others appeared behind Hal, and he swung around to deal with them, too. He could do this all day long if needed, but the trolls were already concocting another plan. They vanished, and Hal spotted them slithering through fissures, probably aiming to emerge farther along the slopes or within the ravine itself.

Hal hopped from perch to perch, following the buggy's progress through the pass. High up above like this was still the best way to guard his friends. He just had to trust that Robbie could take care of the invading trolls.

Abigail shot out from the hole in the buggy's roof, buzzing up and away. She'd thrown off her coat, and her faerie wings protruded through the back of her shirt. Hal breathed a sigh of relief for her but feared for the safety of the others. Robbie was holding his position on one side of the buggy, but only two trolls were interested in him; the other two were clambering around and trying to rip another hole in the roof at the back corner.

As Abigail buzzed near Hal's ear, he spread his wings and launched off his perch, catching Abigail's shouted "Go help them!" before he left her behind. He plummeted into the ravine and was on the buggy in seconds, his first target being the two trolls on the back corner. He snared one with his front paws, dragged it roughly off the roof, landed heavily on the dusty ground behind the moving vehicle, and catapulted back into the air, frantically beating his wings as he carried the howling troll upward.

Hal soared out of the ravine and looked for a decent place to drop the troll far enough away that its return to the battle would be seriously delayed. In the end he simply dumped his unwilling passenger on a random slippery slope, and the shaggy creature went skidding down out of sight.

One down, three to go.

Chapter Two
East of the Pass

There were still two trolls grappling with Robbie, and as Hal approached, the ogre toppled over the side and took the creatures and part of the roof with him. All three rolled in the dirt as the buggy rumbled onward. Jolie's lightweight covered wagon bumped past next, dragged roughly on its spindly wheels and just missing the scrapping trio.

That left one on the buggy, and it was busy clawing its way through the remaining piece of canopy at the rear, sending the passengers scuttling to the front. Hal thumped down on the ground and, as the buggy passed, he snapped at the troll's leg, catching it by the ankle. The shaggy monster barked angrily—and began hollering in fright as Hal yanked it backward and took off with his prey dangling upside down. Once again he soared high above the ravine and the surrounding hills. He slung the troll in an arc, and the creature spun through the air and hit a cliff face with a nasty thud. It fell away and landed on a rounded outcrop below, winded and barely moving as Hal swooped around and away.

To Hal's horror, three more trolls had appeared on the craggy peaks and were sneaking up on Abigail as she watched the fight below. He roared for all he was worth, and her eyes opened wide. She must have sensed something behind her because she spun and screamed as a troll leapt for her. She shot straight up, and the troll, finding nothing but air, almost ran straight off the edge.

Hal heated things up a little as he passed by, sending an arc of flames all around. The trolls scooted out of the way and snarled.

Robbie, left alone with the two remaining trolls—one of them the leader—seemed to be enjoying himself. Two trolls rolling about on the ground with even a young ogre stood little chance of success. And as Hal hovered overhead, the trolls spotted him and seemed to realize the game was up. They grunted and squirmed out of Robbie's fierce grip, then hurried away, one of them limping.

Hal resumed his guard duty above, hopping from one rocky outcrop to the next as the buggy sped through Eastward Pass. Jolie's wagon hopped and bounced behind, its occupant no doubt thrown all over the place.

Abigail buzzed around Hal's head, sounding like a giant hummingbird as she bobbed up and down. "I think we're being watched," she said.

Hal swung around to look. He sensed movement but was too slow to focus on it. Whatever it was ducked into a vertical crack in the side of a high-rising tower of rock. Another movement caught Hal's attention, and he scanned the slopes and peaks. There were clusters of boulders large and small that trolls could be hiding behind. Massive cracks laced the mountainside, most of which were deep and wide enough to squeeze into. Numerous tunnels, caves, and shadowed overhangs pockmarked the region, all potential hidey-holes for wary natives.

Hal left his perch and stomped over to a particularly deep-looking cave entrance where he'd seen movement a few seconds earlier. It was pitch-black in there and smelled weird, a bit like fruit that had gone bad. A long burst of flame lit his way, but he stopped short when he saw dozens of trolls cowering in the darkness. As his flames flickered bright and hot, most of the shaggy creatures shrank back into the shadows, but some of the smallest—clearly very young children—came forward to greet him with raised hands, apparently unaware of the potential danger of an invading fire-breathing dragon. But they were snatched back by snarling, protective adults and shoved into the darkest recesses.

Hal's breath ran out, and everything went black again. He breathed another long sheet of fire and saw maybe ten or fifteen adults, more slender in the limbs and with much longer body hair than the brutes he'd seen outside. Were all these females? Mothers? There were at least twenty infant trolls behind them, each with remarkably short fuzzy hair and big bright eyes.

With his nostrils wrinkling in disgust, Hal backed out of the cave. Something bothered him more than the smell, though—something he'd seen in the eyes of the young trolls in that brief instant when they'd rushed forward to greet him. Hope? Eagerness? They'd held out their hands toward him as if expecting food.

"What were you *doing* in there?" Abigail exclaimed, appearing nearby. She batted him lightly on the snout.

Hal gave a grunt and shrugged helplessly. Why did she ask him questions when she knew full well he couldn't answer in his dragon form?

"Come on," Abigail said, buzzing around behind his head and dropping onto his back. "Catch up with the others."

More trolls peered at them from behind rocks as Hal soared into the sky and surveyed the area. Eastward Pass was a long, jagged crack through the otherwise unbroken line of mountains, probably the result of an earthquake that had ruptured the land long ago. The buggy was two thirds of the way through by now. Hal scanned the area, seeing occasional trolls scampering about on the cliffs. He flew low and bellowed to make it clear he was still around.

His bellow was half-hearted, though. As fearsome as these trolls were, Hal realized they weren't so much greedy as hungry. The males were always out and about hunting for food, but feeding such a large clan—or perhaps several clans—must be tough. What did they feed on when they weren't negotiating with passers-by for a relatively small payment of chickens?

And straight away the answer literally jumped out at him. A brown sheep with curved horns leapt in fright as he swooped low over a rocky slope. As he circled around to study it, more sheep darted away with sure-footed agility. So there *was* food in these mountains. It was just hard for trolls to get hold of.

A sudden, powerful urge took over Hal. If he'd thought about it for longer than half a second, he probably would have changed his mind and left the sheep alone. But dragons were hunters, after all. Sheep, goats, boar, deer, wildebeest—he was *supposed* to hunt these animals. Abigail screamed at him to stop, but he was already on top of the creature, his claws digging into its torso and eliciting a strange cry as he lifted it into the air.

A second later, he felt a jolt of shock at what he had done.

He flew with the animal dangling and squirming while his passenger yelled in his ear to let the poor thing go. He didn't, though. He was certain the sheep was already mortally injured from his powerful claws. It would probably die slowly even if he returned it carefully to the slopes and let it stagger away. Since it was already too late, Hal stuck to his plan, though he felt awful about it.

He returned to the cave of trolls and hovered a few dozen feet above, beating his wings furiously to stay in one place as the sheep hung limply from the grip of his hind feet. Trolls crept out of hiding places and stared up at him.

Hal dropped his kill. It bounced on the slopes and wriggled feebly. Seconds later, at least fifteen male trolls rushed in and leapt on it, working together to put the poor sheep down quickly and efficiently.

It was both horrifying and gratifying to see this violent frenzy. There was nothing pretty about surviving in the wild, whether it was trolls leaping on an injured sheep or a dragon plucking one from a mountainside—or even a human catching a rabbit in a snare and cooking it over a fire. But it was necessary, and when the death of one innocent sheep meant feeding a family of starving trolls . . . well, there was something gratifying about that. It was certainly no worse than sitting down to a meal of beef or pork at home.

Hal told himself this as the males dragged the carcass into the cave without sparing him another glance. The trolls' ambush had failed, but they appeared reasonably satisfied with their gift. A big fat sheep would go a long way.

With no desire to wait around, Hal left them behind with their fresh dinner.

* * *

He flew out of the mountains to the east just in time to find Blacknail's buggy trundling from the pass onto a flat, open plain. They had made it through with no further trouble from the trolls. Robbie, in his ogre form, was gamboling alongside the buggy, keeping pace with Jolie's trailing wagon.

The scenery had changed. The rocky mountains were behind them, and Blacknail headed across the plain toward a nearby forest and the glittering ocean beyond. The trees would be bright green and vibrant in the summertime, but since winter was fast approaching, what leaves remained were brown and brittle. Still, it was all far more cheerful than the desolate region and craggy mountains they'd just passed through.

The sea sparkled brightly when the sun popped out from behind ominous clouds. It was a breathtaking sight, and Hal felt a thrill of excitement—but half a minute later the clouds shifted again and a shadow fell, and suddenly everything was drab and depressing. What a difference a bit of sunshine made!

When they left the plain behind, the road meandered through increasingly grassy hills on its way down the slopes to the forest. There was no sign of a village, but Hal caught sight of several trails of smoke rising up through the trees. Chimneys? If those trails of smoke pinpointed the lycan village, Hal estimated another twenty or thirty minutes of travel for the giant six-wheeled buggy.

Astride his back, Abigail was silent. Hal could almost feel her simmering anger. Or perhaps he was imagining it. In any case, he remained in flight for the rest of the journey, circling around and around and taking in the scenery while Blacknail and his friends headed down the road toward the forest.

Just before they disappeared from view among the trees, Hal decided to join them. It was hard work trying to land in dense woodland, and besides, he didn't want to drop into the lycan village unannounced.

The clothing problem came up as he landed on the side of the road just ahead of the buggy. Hopefully his friends would throw his clothes down to him so he could change in private. He waited there as the steam-huffing vehicle rumbled closer. Blacknail's small goblin face peered out the front window, surly and scowling as usual. What was left of the fabric roofing was flapping around in the breeze, with various structural supports sticking upward at weird angles from where Robbie had burst out in his ogre form.

The buggy slowed and stopped, its engine grumbling as a hiss of white steam puffed out from underneath. Faces appeared in the windows. The door opened, and Molly leaned out. "Are you joining us?" she yelled. "Want your clothes?"

Hal gave a frantic nod. Robbie simply shrugged and grunted.

"I'll get them," Abigail said, and she rose off Hal's back and flew to the buggy. She eventually emerged with a bundle of clothes in her arms. To Hal's surprise, she buzzed off with them into the woods. When she returned again, she grinned and pointed. "I've dropped them on the road ahead. If you hurry, you'll have time to get dressed before we catch up."

With a giggle, Abigail zipped back inside the buggy. The door closed, and a second or two later the vehicle began moving again.

Hal and Robbie hurried along the curving road into the trees. They found their clothes piled on a tree stump to one side. Rather self-consciously, they reverted to human forms and dressed quickly.

When the buggy caught up, the boys clambered inside and gaped at the damage to the roof, which hung in tatters. Blacknail gave them both a long, heated glare before turning to the front and shoving the levers forward. The buggy lurched, and Hal almost fell down in the aisle. He found his seat next to Abigail as Robbie happily began to explain what it was like fighting trolls.

"They're so *weedy*," he said with a sneer. "But when there's a few of them, they cling on like . . . like clinging things, and they're hard to shake loose. But I had them under control. I didn't need Hal's help."

"You're welcome," Hal said.

"It was yanking on your ear," Darcy said with a giggle. "You looked so annoyed, like you were about to blow."

"It was a good scrap, though. Did you see how . . ."

As he rambled on, Abigail turned to Hal. "Why, Hal? That poor sheep!"

He sighed. "I don't really know. I just had an urge. I'm a dragon, remember? Normally I don't give in to those urges, but seeing those sheep like that . . . And I wanted to feed the trolls. I wouldn't have grabbed the sheep otherwise. I just thought the trolls would like it."

"You thought the trolls would like it?" she said incredulously. "After they attacked us like that? You wanted to give them a *little treat* for being so mean?"

"That cave on the mountain was full of starving kids," he protested. Seeing the slight change in her expression, he laid it on a little thicker. "Little baby trolls, Abigail, all fluffy and cute, with big round eyes, holding their hands out to me as if I had some food for them. It was pitiful."

Abigail chewed her lip and frowned, and Hal knew he'd won her over. He returned his attention to Robbie, who was just finishing his tale of heroism.

". . . and I threw it off like it was a rag doll. They're really pathetic. They *think* they're tough, but trust me, they're not. They're like ogre wannabes."

"You're so brave," Lauren said, batting her eyelashes at him. She giggled and whispered in Darcy's ear, who laughed out loud.

Robbie's face reddened. He clammed up and stared out the window.

"Not far now," Molly called from the front, twisting around in her seat. "Listen up, guys. Lucas will be our guide. If Lucas wasn't here, we wouldn't be either. The village of Landis is not one most people dare to visit. The people are kind of . . . well, angry is putting it mildly."

"Angry?" Fenton repeated. "What about?"

Molly reached up to scratch her nose behind her veil. "Maybe not angry so much as hostile. They just don't like visitors. They don't like themselves all that much, quite honestly. And this is a *good* time of the month. The moon is new. We'll stay a few days at most, then head home. We don't want to be here when the moon waxes. The fuller the moon, the meaner these people get."

Abigail's hand slipped into Hal's. When he looked at her, she was wide-eyed and tense. Everyone else had gone quiet, too.

"So why are we visiting them?" Emily asked, her voice sounding scratchy. She was beginning to look pale again, her sickness never-ending. "Why can't we just go on to Bad Rock Gulch and ignore the lycans?"

"Because, my dear, the lycans own the mines. Or rather, they own the land the mines are on. The lycans have lived in these parts for centuries. It was only a couple of decades ago that the goblins gained permission to start mining. This area is rich with energy, one of the richest spots in the world, so naturally Bad Rock Gulch has become one of the primary mines for geo-rocks. But since it's on the lycans' land, we have to ask their permission before visiting, and especially before taking away a large supply of rocks."

Blair nodded furiously. "Goblins mine there all the time, but that's a standing arrangement. Even so, extracted material is checked by the lycans as it leaves the mine to make sure it's within the maximum allowance. So—"

"Maximum allowance?" Abigail blurted. "Why on earth is there a maximum allowance? Don't we all want the same thing? Don't we all want powered lighting and heating in our homes?"

With a snort, Blair said, "Believe it or not, young lady, the answer is no. Although the lycans look human, they're really not, and they have no interest in powered lighting or heating like you and I. They'd prefer to close the mines and send everyone on their way, and live their lives without outsiders traipsing around their land. But there's too much pressure from other communities, so rather than risk a war, they allow the mining but insist on certain rules—the main one being a limitation on the mining output."

Molly nodded. "They're very protective of their resources. You'd have to be a lycan to understand why. Mostly it's superstitious nonsense. They're rather like the centaurs in that respect. But we're not just here to take home a wagonload of geo-rocks. Our mission is much more important. We need to regain our magic, and being in close proximity with the source of the energy should help us achieve just that. With luck, Jolie will get her healing powers back, and Emily will be cured once and for all." She reached out and patted Blair's hand. "And you, my friend, are going to help me with my experiment."

"Yeah, yeah, whatever," Blair muttered.

Hal and Abigail glanced at each other with excitement. Recently, Fenton had fallen victim to Molly's gorgon death-gaze, and he'd turned to stone. But, shortly after, he'd come back to life thanks to the thousand-year-old phoenix's rebirth, which had somehow nullified the gorgon's spell. And if it could be done once, it could be done again—by Blair, the resident phoenix shapeshifter. "Think of all my accidental victims!" Molly had exclaimed. "You can wake them all!"

Blair wasn't convinced, though. He doubted he would ever possess the kind of power needed to revive calcified people.

The way ahead grew darker as the canopy of trees thickened. There were dead leaves everywhere, in some places almost completely covering the road, and many of the trees were bare. The long summer season had given way to a very fast and sudden fall, and winter was just a week or two away.

"I'm hungry," Robbie said.

Abigail groaned. "What is it with you being hungry all the time? We just had lunch a few hours ago!"

"We'll eat later," Molly said. "Maybe we'll be invited to supper. In any case, we'll be heading over to the mines in Bad Rock Gulch this evening."

"Tonight?" Darcy said.

"In the dark?" Lauren added.

Robbie leaned forward. "I've got news for you, Lauren: it's dark in the mines *all the time.*"

She shot him a hurt look, but Robbie scowled and shook his head.

Hal whispered to Abigail, "What's going on with those two?"

"Girls," Abigail said mysteriously, and left it at that.

Hal wasn't done. "Come on, Abi, shed some light here. Does she like him or not? What's her deal? He doesn't say much, but he's pretty fed up."

Robbie chose that moment to sigh deeply and look down at the floor.

"Lauren's confused," Abigail said finally. "She likes Robbie until he puts his foot in it and says something really dumb or acts like an idiot. He's kind of thoughtless sometimes, and that puts her off." She grinned at him. "See, you're cool and smart and nice, and when you mess up, well, it's sort of cute."

"Cute?" Hal repeated, appalled.

"When Robbie messes up, he's kind of embarrassing. Lauren likes him when he's sweet and nerdy—her words, not mine—but can do without the times when he turns into a moron."

Hal frowned. "You mean when he turns into an ogre?"

"No, when he turns into a *moron*. This has nothing to do with him being an ogre. He's fine when he's an ogre. It's when he turns into a moron that she has trouble with."

Hal pondered that for a moment. He had to admit that Robbie had moments when it seemed like he'd left his brain and manners at home. At times like that, even Hal got annoyed with him. Still, he was who he was. "He's a good guy. He's saved my life a few times. I don't care if he acts like a moron sometimes."

Abigail squeezed his hand. "And that's why I like you, Hal. You just seem to have a way of knowing what's right. You're loyal and brave. A little clueless sometimes, but you get there in the end. I'm way smarter than you, but I'm sure you know that already."

Hal loved that they could talk to each other this way without awkwardness. They were just comfortable being together. One thing nagged at him, though. Holding hands was commonplace between them, as was hugging. But there was something Hal had yet to do, something he felt sure Abigail wanted from him and had resigned herself to waiting on.

Why couldn't he kiss her?

It was like he had some kind of hang-up over it, and worrying about it only made it worse. If he could only break through his invisible barrier and *kiss her*, just once, without thinking about it, without making a big deal out of it . . .

As the darkness of the woods pressed in, Hal steeled himself, thinking that this was it, this was *really it*, he was going to do it. Her face was right there by his. It would be so easy to snatch a kiss. He just had to *do* it.

He swallowed. His lips were suddenly bone-dry. He licked at them, certain that Abigail was aware of what he was building up to do. *Do it*, he told himself furiously. *Right now! Kiss her! NOW!*

Abigail sat up straight and looked at him with a frown. "Are you all right?"

"W-what?" he sputtered. "Why?"

"You look pale. And you're licking your lips. Are you ill?"

The moment fled, and Hal nodded weakly, his breath escaping with a long, shuddering sigh. "Feel a bit sick, yeah."

"Okay, people," Molly called. "We're here."

Flickering lights appeared in the gloom ahead, and all thoughts of smooching fled Hal's mind as a new sense of anxiety crept over him. They were really here in Landis, the village of the lycans.

The village of *werewolves*.

Chapter Three
Lucas and the Lycans

Although it was still mid-afternoon, everything was so dark in the forest that it might as well have been dusk already. As they drove into the village, the trees thinned to reveal the gloomy daylight and its oppressive clouds above, yet there were lamps lit everywhere, hanging from posts. An enormous fire burned brightly in the center of the village. Stone-walled cottages with straw-thatched roofs were crammed closely together everywhere they looked, with no obvious routes between them. The ground was somewhat muddy and covered with orange and brown leaves.

Blacknail slowed. The road ended at a sign that read LANDIS in sprawling handwriting. Rather than standing by the side of the road and inviting visitors in with a welcoming arrow, or hanging overhead as part of a grand, impressive entranceway, this particular sign literally stood in their path and seemed to indicate the end of the trail. Hal imagined a hidden meaning: *Stop. Turn around and go away. This is our place, not yours.*

"Nice," he murmured as the engines died. After several hours of constant rattling, rumbling din, the sudden silence was almost eerie.

"There are people by the fire," Abigail said, peering through the mud-flecked glass. "Is there a party or something? Why are they staring at us like that?"

The public bonfire in the middle of the village was surrounded by men, women and children, all silent and staring, obviously distracted from whatever festivities they were involved in.

Molly cleared her throat and stood. "I see Lucas. He's coming to meet us. Let's step down and wait outside. Stay together, okay?"

One by one they descended from the vehicle amid a cloud of white steam that drifted in the afternoon breeze. Half-bare trees loomed over them, their leaves blanketing the otherwise muddy ground. The silence was eerie.

A very tall man limped toward them. He wore a drab gray shirt tucked into dark, baggy pants. His scruffy boots were caked in wet mud. "Molly," he called, and Hal was instantly struck by how deep his voice was.

The man was immense, easily six and a half feet tall. He was long-haired and unshaven, and his eyebrows needed a trim. When he reached Molly, the two embraced tightly and stayed that way for several seconds without moving or speaking. After they separated, the man turned to shake Blair's hand.

"Been a long time," he rumbled.

Blair nodded, looking up at the man with obvious respect. "I don't know how many years. You look . . . hardy."

Lucas raised a bushy eyebrow. "Hardy? You mean ugly?"

"No. *Weathered*." Blair pulled himself loose from the man's grip. "Strong grip, calloused hands, terrible body odor. I see they've been working you hard."

"Nothing like a good day's work," Lucas said, a grin forcing its way across his face. He slapped his thigh. "Even with a busted leg."

Hal wondered why the man didn't just transform and heal himself . . . and then remembered how, when shapeshifters grew older, serious injuries failed to mend properly. Felipe the dragon was the same, with severe burns along his flank.

"As for you, my friend," Lucas went on, looking Blair up and down, "a weak grip and soft, delicate hands just as always." He sniffed sharply. "And you say I have a terrible body odor? Have you smelled yourself lately?"

When he turned to Blacknail, the goblin screwed up his face in what appeared to be a grin. Lucas reached out, and the two grasped hands with obvious warmth. Neither said a word even though it was clear they were good friends. Or had been once upon a time.

A second later, Lucas turned again to Molly and studied her veiled face. She reached out and touched his cheek, then patted one of his broad shoulders before gesturing toward the village. "How's the mood around here today?"

Lucas shrugged. "Fair. There's a party tonight."

"For our benefit?"

Again, Lucas raised a bushy eyebrow. "Seriously? Nah, a couple of young 'uns got married earlier."

Molly clapped her hands together. "Oh, so this is a wedding reception! How nice." Her tone changed suddenly. "We're not intruding, are we?"

"Nah. Well, yeah, but that's nothing new. It'll be all right. Just get the chief's blessing and hightail it outta here."

"We can't stay for supper?"

Lucas looked pained. "You want to *eat*? Here?"

Molly sighed. "Well, if not, at least get us something to take with us to the mines. We plan to stay all night."

He considered this for a moment. "I might be able to pilfer a few things for you. Let's head over and see the chief. Don't invite yourself to the party, though. It'd be bad enough *without* ale and wine flowing. You know how it is."

Molly nodded. "Maybe the children should stay here. I'll speak to your chief alone, and we'll head to the gulch after you've nabbed us some nibbles."

Surprisingly, Lucas shook his head. "Chief wants to see all of you. Well, he doesn't *want* to see *any* of you. He just *needs* to. For his peace of mind."

With that, he turned and limped back toward the village, gesturing for them all to keep up. Molly started to follow, but Blair caught her arm. "What about Jolie?" he asked, jabbing his thumb toward the covered wagon.

"She's not going anywhere," Molly said. "She'll be fine."

"But the chief wants to see *all* of us."

"Jolie doesn't count. Come on."

She and Blair hurried after Lucas, and the rest shuffled along in single file with Blacknail bringing up the rear.

"What's with the limp?" Fenton called to Molly.

She turned and, even through her veil, it was obvious she was giving him a withering look. "Lucas got into a fight years ago."

"With werewolves?" Fenton asked—apparently too loudly, for Lucas halted and swung around. The man's face quickly darkened.

"*Never* say that around here. These people are *lycans*. Werewolves are shapeshifters, and these people aren't shapeshifters. Not in the way you think, anyway. Calling them shapeshifters to their faces will get you killed."

"Sorry, I just meant—"

"Fenton, *shh*," Darcy hissed at him.

Everyone lapsed into silence, and Lucas resumed his awkward march into the village. Toward the center, there were fewer trees and more open sky, and the field ahead was thick with lush grass. The bonfire raged twenty feet tall, and Hal could feel the heat coming off it before he got anywhere close.

Just about every man, woman and child was lean and mean with an unusual amount of hair on their faces. The men especially had thick, shaggy eyebrows and impressively long manes as well as excessive hair on their forearms. Many had beards to complete the picture. Even the women seemed unable or unwilling to keep their eyebrows trimmed.

Rather stiffly, Lucas led the group around the perimeter of the field while the party remained on pause. Heads swiveled, brows furrowed, and lips drew back. Hal couldn't remember ever feeling quite so unwelcome.

As if the world had come to an abrupt halt, a musician waited with his fiddle raised to his chin and his bow resting on the strings. Numerous couples were frozen like statues in mid-dance, clasping hands and waists. Many were sitting on the grass with plates of finger food, all of them glaring at the visitors. Apart from the crackling of the enormous bonfire, the silence and tension was palpable, and Hal felt that his every grassy footstep could be heard across the village.

Once they were out of the field, Lucas turned into what might be called a street between several small cottages. Behind them, the sudden squeak of the fiddle marked the end of the hostile pause, and suddenly there was noise all around as people resumed their dancing, eating, and talking.

A cottage loomed ahead. It stood out among the rest—larger and grander, with five burly men loitering outside. They closed in as Lucas approached, their faces showing distaste.

"Chief wants to see 'em," Lucas barked.

The guards, if that's what they were, growled and grudgingly moved aside for him. Hal noticed that they barely left room for him to pass between. They stuck their faces toward Lucas as he turned sideways and slipped through the gap, then snarled at Molly, Blair, and everyone else that filed past. When it was Hal's turn, they looked down on him from what seemed an incredible height—easily seven feet—and sniffed continuously as if they detected a really nasty smell in the air. *They're like dogs*, he thought. *Wait, no—I mean wolves.*

Lucas rapped noisily on the cottage door. It opened seconds later, and Hal heard mutterings from within as the group waited. Lucas stepped inside, followed by Molly and Blair. *We'll never fit in the living room*, Hal thought as he watched his friends enter.

As it turned out, the living room was huge. The wooden floor was dark and stout, filthy from years of grime and dirt. The room smelled of sweat. As his friends fanned out, Hal pushed forward to see a man sitting in a rocking chair, using a shiny knife to whittle away at a wooden object.

The only sounds in the room were the crackling of a fire in the hearth and the continuous scraping of a sharp blade on wood. Tiny slivers fluttered down to the floor, amassing in a pile at the man's feet. When he shifted in his seat, it creaked under his massive frame. His dark brown hair was long and tied into a ponytail. His beard was overgrown and shaggy, his eyebrows thick and black. Eventually he looked up. Unlike most of the other lycans Hal had seen, this one's eyes were pale green and startling. "So," he rumbled.

Lucas gestured first to Molly, then everyone else. "So here they are. You wanted to see 'em. A couple of old friends, a bunch of kids, and a goblin."

Hal had forgotten about Blacknail. The goblin stood to one side, his grumpy expression rivaling the lycan chief's.

Molly nudged Lucas and cleared her throat. He stared at her blankly for a moment before his puzzled expression cleared. "Oh, right. Molly, this is the chief of the village, Nathaniel. Chief, this is Molly. She's a gorgon."

"I guessed," the chief growled, studying her veil with obvious suspicion. "So you're in charge, gorgon?"

"Molly," she said firmly. "And yes, I suppose I am."

"Well, *gorgon*, do I need to explain the rules?"

She placed her hands on her hips, and next to her, Blair sighed and covered his face with one hand. "Well, *lycan*, I suppose you'd better."

"Molly," Lucas warned quietly.

Nathaniel stared at Molly for a long period, his eyes narrowed. His knife glinted as he slowly turned it in his hands. He took it by the handle and pointed its sharp end toward her. "You'll address me as Chief. Any more attitude from you, lady, and I'll throw you on the fire. Are we clear?"

If Hal could see Molly's face, he would expect that she was slowly turning purple with rage. Luckily, her veil merely quivered. After a long, drawn-out pause, her hands dropped to her sides. "Clear," she said quietly. "*Chief.*"

Nathaniel gave the smallest of nods and eased back in his rocking chair. It creaked noisily again. "The rules are simple. You want extra rocks from our land? Fine—you get one wagon. But only because of this *problem* you have." He sneered at them all, showing surprisingly even white teeth. "Get this straight. One wagon is a three-month supply. I'm giving you a whole extra wagon's worth out of the goodness of my heart. That's your lot. If you haven't got your sparkle back by the time that lot runs down, that's your problem, not mine."

"Did he say *sparkle?*" Abigail whispered in Hal's ear.

"Understood," Molly said dully. "But I feel I should point out—"

"She understands," Lucas interrupted loudly. He shot her a sideways glare. "She's spent so long on her own that she's forgotten her manners. What she means to say is *thank you*, Chief, for your generosity. Right, Molly?"

Molly simply sighed heavily.

Nathaniel leaned forward in his chair and waved his knife at them all. "I don't like outsiders. If it weren't for the mines, you wouldn't be allowed on our land. But here you are, traipsing around our woods, stinking up the village . . ."

He sniffed the air in a slow, deliberate way, and grimaced.

"Get out of my house. I don't want to see any of you again. And be warned. Make yourselves scarce before the half-moon. That's when we start hunting. Don't be anywhere close."

Lucas turned and began ushering everyone from the living room. Hal caught glimpses of pale faces as he and his friends left. Blacknail looked furious.

Outside, the guards stood quietly, leering at them. They said nothing at first, but then one of them made a comment that stopped Lucas in his tracks. "Why don't you go with them, shapeshifter? You're not one of us. You never were."

Lucas stepped up to the man and shoved his face close. He was two inches shorter than the brutish guard and had to peer up at him. "I'm more lycan than you'll ever be, Wesley. Do I need to remind you *again?*"

Something was happening to Lucas. His shoulders were bulging under his shirt, and his hair was growing longer. Tufts sprouted from his face as his nose and jaw began to stretch forward into a blunt point. The deep, rumbling growl that emitted from his throat caused Molly and Blair to step back in a hurry. Likewise, Hal and his friends shuffled sideways in case a fight broke out.

The one called Wesley refused to budge, and he visibly trembled with anger. He wasn't changing the way Lucas was. "Two weeks," Wesley hissed. "Full moon. You and me, shapeshifter."

"Suits me," Lucas snapped. His transformation had now halted, but his furry face was decidedly inhuman and his ears quite a bit longer than before. And he was now taller by at least three inches, suddenly looking down on his opponent. "You want to wait for the full moon? Fine—but you know I'll still be bigger than you. You know it, and *they* know it." He jabbed his finger at the other guards, who quietly looked away. "You want to tangle with me, Wesley? Wait for the full moon if you need to, when you're *big and tough*, but I'll still pound you into the ground and tear you to shreds."

Lucas slowly shrank back down to size. Then Wesley was able to look down on his enemy one last time before uttering a snarl and turning away in disgust.

The tension lifted immediately, and Lucas led the group away.

They headed back through the village the way they had come in, around the field where lycans again paused to stare at them. Hal decided he hated this place and all the people in it. What an unfriendly lot they were.

Molly wasn't impressed either. "If I'd had my powers," she said, walking alongside Lucas, "that chief of yours would be a statue by now."

"If you'd had your powers, we wouldn't be here," the man retorted.

"Are the women just as hotheaded as the men?" she asked. "Honestly, I don't recall your people ever being quite this hostile."

The enormous buggy lurked in the trees ahead, and Lucas limped toward it. "This is a bad week," he admitted. "You think you're the only village to come here asking for extra geo-rocks? You're not. When you get your sparkle back, things'll settle down. Until then, the chief is just trying to limit the output from the mines. If he let you go in and take whatever you want whenever you want it, there'd be nothing left in no time. It has to be taken in moderation."

"Why?" Abigail suddenly asked.

Lucas ignored her. "Hey, goblin—get that machine fired up and wait while I go grab some food." He abruptly turned and disappeared into the trees.

Blair looked bemused. "Where's he going? To kill a sheep or something?"

He winked at Hal as they all continued on to the buggy. Once aboard, they waited a minute until Blacknail climbed in after them and stomped to the front. He lifted the lid of a large container and peered inside—then slammed it shut. "All dead," he muttered. He glared suspiciously at the shapeshifters. "There were brand new rocks in here. Got 'em just the other day. Shoulda lasted weeks. Them rocks are dead, and the one powering the starter underneath is dead as well. You're sucking the life out of 'em."

"Now, hold on a minute," Emily exclaimed, and promptly started coughing.

Darcy took over. "First of all, we can't help it. If we're really 'sucking the life' out of your geo-rocks, well, it's just meant to be. Second, don't forget you're a shapeshifter too, Blacknail."

"Yes, *Riley*," Molly said with a sudden laugh. "Nice one, Darcy."

Blacknail drew himself up, his face reddening. "Me 'n Simone brought a bunch back the other day without a problem. All you lot together are like a giant sponge." He grimaced and headed for the exit. "I'll be back. Gonna have to start this contraption the hard way."

Everyone pondered the problem while he was gone. Hal couldn't help remembering the small geo-rock he'd carried around in his pocket when he'd been stuck in his old world with Robbie, Abigail and Emily. They'd all lost their powers, but only temporarily, like a brief short in their magical circuitry rather than a complete drain. They'd soon recovered with the help of bundles of fresh, magical smart clothes in the lighthouse, some of which they'd brought back with them. But whereas the rock had rekindled its energy, the enchantment in the smart clothes had died, their life 'sucked out' as Blacknail would say.

"I wonder if we have our powers back," Dewey said. He looked like he was contemplating the idea of shifting into his centaur form—which would be a mistake. Even if he had absorbed enough energy from the geo-rocks to shift, his former smart clothes would still be ordinary and easily ripped apart.

"I don't *feel* any different," Darcy said. She was staring at her hands, turning them over and over as if trying to make them invisible.

"Nor me," Lauren said. "Except maybe . . . a tingle?"

"That's pins and needles," Abigail said.

Lauren shook her head. "No, I feel a little tingling in my toes. I wonder if it's magic? Maybe not enough to transform with, but *something*."

Steam suddenly began puffing out from under the buggy, and the engine rattled while they all sat there waiting for Blacknail's return. He eventually climbed the ladder—with Lucas right behind him.

"Got some food here for you," he said gruffly. "Let's go."

Blacknail turned the buggy around and started off through the woods as everyone marveled at the amount of fresh-baked rolls Lucas had stuffed into a single sack. In the very bottom was a massive hunk of cheese, easily as big as Hal's head.

"I love bread and cheese," Robbie said happily, practically salivating.

"What a tremendous spread you've laid on for us," Molly said, rolling her eyes. "Really, Lucas, you shouldn't have gone to all this bother. Your chief was so pleasant to us, and here we are leaving the village half an hour after we got here, with a lovely meal of bread and cheese for us to eat later in a cold, dark cave. I feel so . . . *welcome*."

"It's your lucky day," Lucas said, a grin working its way onto his face.

The lycan seemed impressed by Blacknail's vehicle, and before long the two of them were deep in conversation. It was hard to tell who scowled the most.

They headed back the way they had come and turned onto an equally narrow road that cut through the trees. Branches hung low, often scraping along what was left of the roof and sometimes catching under the framework so that it pulled and twisted further. Much of the material snagged and ripped free, and Blacknail's bitter complaining increased tenfold.

Soon, though, they left the dense woods, exiting at the coast. Conversation halted while they all stared out the windows at the sea. The buggy trundled down a slope and cliffs rose all around. The beach was just a narrow strip of sand running alongside endless jagged rocks. None of it was very pretty, but Hal realized this was the first time they'd visited the coast in Miss Simone's world.

He had a vision of virus survivors—*scrags*—hiding among the rocks. He shook his head and asked Lucas a question while he had the chance. "So was that your full transformation back there?"

Lucas raised one of those bushy eyebrows. "Nowhere near it, kid."

There was a silence. Then red-headed Thomas spoke up. "So how come you can transform and they can't?"

"Because I'm a shapeshifter," Lucas said, and glanced toward Molly. He seemed oddly uncomfortable with the questions.

"But they're werewolves," Fenton blurted. He reddened. "Sorry. I didn't mean to say that. It's just . . . well, I don't understand why—"

Lucas gave a grunt. "Explain to them, Molly."

"*You* explain," she protested.

With another grunt, Lucas stared out the window at the sea. "Lycans are in a constant state of change. They're recognizable as human during a new moon—when the moon is barely a crescent, like right now," he added, glancing around. "As the month goes on, the moon waxes." He pursed his lips and spoke more slowly. "That means the moon gets bigger and fatter and—"

"They're kids," Molly told him, "but they're not imbeciles."

"Ah, right." Lucas cleared his throat. "Well, the moon gets bigger, and the lycans change. They slowly turn into something far more than human—huge creatures, seven feet tall, part human and part wolf, very big and strong, and really, really vicious. You don't want to be around during their full-moon phase two weeks from now. In fact it's best to stay away even at the half-moon phase when the urge is too strong and they start hunting. If they don't go out hunting, they'll turn on each other. By the full moon, they often *do* turn on each other. Many a savage death can be attributed to that wild phase." He shrugged. "As the moon wanes, they slowly revert to human."

"But you can change instantly?" Thomas persisted.

Lucas nodded. "I'm a shapeshifter. I can be entirely human, or I can be a lycan. I tend to stay in my lycan form, which at the moment is—" He spread his hands. "Well, you can see for yourself. See, when I'm in lycan form, the phase of the moon determines what I look like. But unlike all the others in the village, I can advance to full-on wolf any time I want, which makes me a werewolf. Or, during a full moon, I can switch to a gentler phase if I prefer . . . but it's really difficult. The full moon is a powerful thing. It's like being swept along by a tide; you just kind of go with it unless you struggle really hard and break free."

"A werewolf," Fenton repeated, his eyes shining. Lucas glared at him, but this time Fenton didn't bother retracting his use of the forbidden word. He simply blathered on without pause. "There are so many legends of werewolves, but the stories must be based on shapeshifters like you, not the lycans themselves."

Lucas nodded. "Lycans would never leave their packs and go off to another world. Not alone, anyway. Shapeshifters would, though. I've heard about the early shapeshifter programs where men bred dragons and monsters as pet bodyguards. The lycans were a pretty desirable choice back then."

Molly snorted.

"They were," Lucas snapped. "Lycan shapeshifters—*werewolves*—were common. And some of them escaped into the other world, which is why there are legends there. The pull of the moon is hard to resist. As much as the shapeshifters tried to be normal people, they couldn't help turning once a month."

"So technically you're a werewolf," Fenton persisted. "Not a lycan. Miss Simone called you a lycan, but actually—"

With a snort of exasperation, Lucas threw up his hands. "Call me what you want. People are always getting it wrong anyway."

"Well, I'm glad we don't have to be around them anymore," Lauren said. "We don't, do we, Molly? We don't have to go back to Landis, do we?"

Molly shook her head, her hat bouncing. "No. We're done with Landis now. Now it's on to Bad Rock Gulch. We need to stay long enough to get our powers back and force Jolie to cure Emily. Then we'll head home with our geo-rocks."

Sounds easy, Hal thought.

Chapter Four
Bad Rock Gulch

While the buggy rumbled along the beach toward Bad Rock Gulch, Lucas turned to Molly with a frown. "So what's the deal with this Jolie girl you mentioned? She's the prisoner in that wagon back there, right?"

Everyone automatically looked out the back of the buggy. The wagon was in a sorry state after its arduous journey being dragged relentlessly this way and that. The wheels wobbled, and the whole thing teetered like a drunken giant.

"I'll bet she's feeling pretty sick," Hal said.

"I hope so," Abigail said stiffly.

Molly explained the situation to Lucas, during which she pointed to Emily right when the girl happened to be coughing violently. To everyone's horror, a small dribble of blood glistened on her chin.

Molly's veil masked her expression, but her upright jerk made it clear she was shocked. "Emily! You're—" She broke off and rushed to her. "Has this happened before? Have you seen blood before?"

Emily was pale and shaky as she touched her chin and drew her fingers back to study the blood. "N-no. This is . . . new."

"How do you feel?"

"Sore," Emily admitted. She clasped her chest. "I hurt. You know how your throat hurts after coughing a lot? It's like that, only much worse."

Lauren and Darcy crowded and fussed over her, but it was Fenton who pointed out that she only had to transform as before.

"I could," Emily croaked. "But it seems I have to transform more and more often to hold this sickness back. I'm afraid the sickness is . . . starting to win."

"What exactly is wrong with her?" Lucas asked bluntly.

Molly patted Emily's hand and answered. "Pulminary-something. I'm not good with medical terms."

"Idiopathic Pulmonary Fibrosis," Abigail offered. Everyone looked around at her, and Lucas's eyebrows shot up. "It's like her lungs are filling up with gunk, making it hard for oxygen to make it into her bloodstream."

Lucas let out an exclamation and turned to Molly with a dumbfounded expression. "How does a kid know that stuff?"

"Her mother's a doctor. I guess all that medical stuff has rubbed off on her." Molly patted Emily's hand again, raising her voice as if the patient had suddenly gone deaf. "Don't worry, dear. We're on track with our plan. We'll stay at the gulch and absorb some magic so we can transform again."

"How will that help?" Lucas asked with a frown. "She said transforming isn't helping anymore."

Molly jabbed a finger toward the rear of the buggy. "That's where Jolie comes in. Her people, the miengu, have the ability to heal others. Once she gets her powers back, her first job is to cure Emily—like she should have done in the first place."

The rumbling journey continued a while longer. The mood was decidedly more somber than before as Emily tried hard not to make a fuss and ended up making herself worse. Every time she started a coughing fit, a silence fell as everyone looked to see if she was spitting up more blood. If she was, Emily hid it well by holding a handkerchief to her mouth and not letting anyone see.

"I used to think she was a do-gooder," Abigail murmured in Hal's ear. "A teacher's pet. Always finishing tests early and getting the best grades, organizing things and expecting everyone to follow her instructions . . . She was a real pain. Now I think she's amazing."

Hal had to agree. Emily had been through a tough patch lately, fighting to stay on top of it without complaining and whining. If anything, she'd downplayed her illness a little too much, making them all assume she was coping just fine. And now she was coughing up blood.

Emily transformed back and forth a few times to ward off the disease, her self-healing abilities kicking in. As always, a little color returned to her face, and she perked up a few notches. But they all knew this was a temporary fix.

The sun was already descending toward the horizon when they arrived, a tiny sliver of a crescent moon rising to join the very first of the evening stars. The days seemed so short now. As Blacknail shut off the engine and steam puffed up past the windows, they all grabbed their bags and jammed in the aisle in their hurry to exit. Once outside, they stood and looked around in slowly mounting awe.

It was hard to see at first, but the bare, rounded hills in these parts were glowing orange. The beach petered out here, and the rest of the coast was made up of rocks that stuck up along the base of the curious mounds as if trying to keep the hills from sliding into the sea. The mounds were tallest near the water's edge where the waves crashed and frothed. Farther inland, the smooth rock flattened into massive plateaus.

"What a strange place," one of the girls piped up.

Hal nodded absently. If the sun were lower, if it were the middle of the night already, the orange glow would be much more obvious. "I bet the hills look really cool at nighttime," he said, "especially from above."

"The hills are alive," Abigail said. "Is this the gulch?"

Lucas nodded and stepped up onto a boulder so he towered above them all. He breathed in deeply, clearly savoring the vigorous ocean air. "Somewhere over that way," he said, pointing inland, "is a ravine. A big split between the hills. That's Bad Rock Gulch, so-named because of the amount of magic in the ground. Being superstitious, the lycans are convinced the rock is evil. They'd prefer it if everyone would just go away and leave it alone. Anyway, the mines are below the hills. There's a side entrance to the mine in the gulch, but we normally use the beach entrance because it's easier to pull wagons up to."

He jumped down, winced, and hobbled off up the last stretch of sand to a massive cave. Endless tracks led in and out—a mess of footsteps and wheel marks. Two enormous wooden wagons stood to one side. Loitering in the cave entrance were a couple of tall men with long hair.

Hal groaned. More lycans.

"Lucas, wait," Molly called after him. She was carrying two bags, one full of food. "We need to get Jolie out of her wagon. She needs to come in with us—she more than anyone, actually. But she doesn't have legs."

The look on Lucas's face was almost comical. "No *legs*? Well, obviously. You said she was one of the miengu. They're mermaid types, aren't they? Of course she doesn't have legs. She has a tail."

"Ah, but Jolie is special. She's a shapeshifter."

"So . . . she *does* have legs," Lucas said.

"No. Right now she's stuck in her fishy form."

"So she has a tail."

A smattering of murmurs caused Lucas to frown and look around.

Molly tried to explain. "No tail. No legs. No nothing. Just a stump." She moved closer and spoke quietly. They were standing fairly close to the wagon and Jolie could be listening right now. "So if you carry her up the beach," Molly finished, "then we can use her wheelchair in the tunnels."

"No," Lucas said. "The tunnels aren't that smooth or level. In some places they're downright treacherous. And there are steps. I'll just carry her."

"Fine. Hold on a second." She stepped around to the front end of the wagon where it was hitched to Blacknail's buggy. The goblin sat on the sturdy coupling, looking bored. "If all goes well," Molly said, "Jolie won't need to be locked away for the return journey. You can unhitch her wagon and leave it here."

"Trust me, I'm gonna," Blacknail said as if that were perfectly obvious. "We're towing *rocks* back home, not some two-faced uppity princess fish-girl. I'm gonna unhitch it and grab one of those open wagons yonder."

"Well, I'll leave you to arrange that, then," Molly said.

As she hurried around to the tail end of the wagon, Hal and all his classmates tore after her, suddenly eager to see how Jolie had fared on her bumpy journey. He felt a sense of glee that she had been thrown around but at the same time hoped she hadn't knocked her head and been seriously injured.

Nobody had any love for Jolie, that was for certain. *It's just her way*, Hal thought sadly, remembering how she'd reveled in the fear and panic she'd generated throughout her stay at the village—Dewey's nervousness when she'd persuaded him to read a terrible poem in public, Hal's fright as she'd grabbed his dragon wing mid-flight and nearly caused him to smash into the ground, the terror of two innocent boys when she'd convinced Thomas to pounce on them in his manticore form, and of course the dread and suspicion of the entire village when Abigail had mysteriously disappeared leaving only a bloody handprint. Jolie's 'way'—the way of the miengu—was to feed off strong, preferably negative emotions. It gave them a buzz.

The hideous creature had done something even more insidious, though. In her guise as a beautiful cripple on crutches, she'd sucked a disease right out of a terminally ill patient and miraculously saved her life—and passed that same disease to Emily without anyone knowing. The disease had to go *somewhere*, she had later admitted.

"Let me go in and unshackle her," Molly said as she dumped her bags and climbed the short flight of steps to the narrow door. She threw back the squeaky bolt and pulled the door open. It was dark inside, and silent.

Hal moved closer, straining to see in through the doorway. As usual, Fenton moved in front of him, and Hal found himself staring at the back of his head of short, spiky hair. Irritably, he jostled alongside him to get a better view.

"We've arrived, Jolie," Molly said, now framing the doorway and blocking the view. "How was your journey?"

There came a muffled retort, and Hal smiled. Angry and uncomfortable was fine as long as Jolie wasn't badly hurt. Emily needed her.

Molly turned and motioned for Lucas to come and help. He leapt up the steps, making the entire wagon jiggle. He had to duck to enter.

"Come *on*," Thomas complained when a few minutes had passed.

"She's probably putting her face on," Fenton said wryly.

Then Molly descended the steps, and after her came Lucas, holding aloft a blanketed bundle. Everyone stared in silence.

The size of the bundle was disconcerting in itself. In a freak accident that many suggested she fully deserved, Jolie had been severed below the waist as she swam through a portal just as it winked out of existence. She'd been magically cauterized in a way that allowed her body to continue functioning without pain, though she longed for the return of either her tail or legs.

And it was this longing that had sealed the deal as far as the mission was concerned. Nobody knew whether magic could somehow heal her. It seemed ludicrous to think that she could grow another tail, yet if there was any place in the world with enough magic to make such an impossible thing happen, it was here at Bad Rock Gulch where energy shone out of the hills themselves.

Privately, Hal didn't believe there was any hope for her. Shapeshifters could heal . . . but *half a body*? He doubted it. She would just have to deal with life in the lake without a tail. Or life on land confined to a wheelchair. He wasn't sure which would be preferable, but he was certain—as was everyone else—that she would never again be a whole person.

Lucas stamped down the steps, and Jolie's long black hair flopped from side to side. That hair had once been thick and lustrous. Now it was greasy and so thin that patches of her pale head could be seen here and there.

She twisted her head around to peer at them all as Lucas shouldered past. She was hideous—thin and drawn, her eyes tiny and black and sunken into her skull like she was a living corpse. Her teeth were uneven and rotten, her ears floppy and pointed. Her skin was strangely translucent, blotchy and glistening like she had just emerged from the water.

"Hi, Hal," she crowed as she was swept past. "Hello, my dear Thomas. And little Dewey! Written any poems lately?" Her tone changed as she came face to face with someone almost as pale as her. "Emily," she added stiffly.

Emily managed to croak a reply without coughing. "Jolie."

Lucas was already limping up the beach to the cave entrance, so any further interactions were cut short. A good thing, too, for she had already left a sour taste in everyone's mouths. Molly and Blair followed closely behind.

"Oh my," Abigail murmured. "And to think you had a crush on her, Hal."

"I did not," Hal retorted. Still, for a moment he recalled Jolie's extraordinary beauty at the height of her enchantment. "But it goes to show just how much her people need magic. Without it, they're kind of . . . well, *nothing*."

They were all padding up the beach toward the cave entrance when the ground began to shake. Everyone stopped at once. Abigail flung herself on Hal as the tremors worsened. The deep, ominous rumble shook him to the core, and his legs felt like jelly as the sand shifted and bounced around his feet.

"Just a quake," Lucas called back over his shoulder. He had stopped along with everyone else, but simply to keep his balance rather than out of fear. "There have been a few lately. They're getting worse, I reckon."

His voice sounded oddly muffled and faraway as the rumbling grew louder. Rocks broke free from the overhanging cliffs and thudded down onto the sand. The lycans in the cave entrance retreated backward into the darkness, while Hal and his group remained at a safe distance from it.

Then the noise died away. The quake was over apart from a few echoing aftershocks and a continuing trickle of debris from the higher ground. Lucas turned to face them, swinging Jolie around as though she were a sack of potatoes. "Come on," he said shortly.

"Is it safe in there?" Blair asked, voicing everyone's concern.

Lucas resumed marching, easily carrying Jolie despite his limp. "Nothing to worry about. This region is funny like that. We get quakes from time to time."

Hal remembered that the area surrounding the Labyrinth of Fire was equally temperamental. They'd driven around massive cracks in the baked ground on their way to the village of Louis.

When they entered the cave, the two lycans nodded to Lucas but growled at the visitors. Apparently they'd been sent to show their faces as a small reminder of who owned the place. They glared with distaste as everybody filed past.

"They'll be off home shortly," Lucas whispered once they were inside.

The cave was small with two tunnels leading off. Lucas ignored the first and led them into the next. It was rigged with stout wooden supports, and lanterns hung all along its length. The ceiling was high, no doubt to make the tunnels suitable for the lycans. Since the goblins had built these mines, it must have frustrated them to no end having to put in extra work just for the sake of their tall wolfish hosts, who probably hardly bothered to venture inside anyway. Had it not been for them, the short goblins could have built the tunnels half the height.

It was surprisingly warm inside. Lucas strode along, not bothering to explain how that was so. He wasn't a very good tour guide. Molly had been here before, though, and she filled in the blanks. "Hot springs, mainly," she said. "The bedrock is riddled with cracks, and hot water comes bubbling up from deep below the earth. You know about geothermal warming, don't you?"

Everyone said yes, that Charlie Duggan up in Louis had told them all about it. Simple cold rainwater trickled down through cracks in the rocky ground and, deep below Earth's surface, was superheated by red-hot magma—or perhaps by the friction of tectonic plates rubbing together, the same plates that were causing the earthquakes. In any case, the boiling water, under great pressure, rose back up through the cracks, eventually making it to the surface in the form of hot springs. Sometimes these springs were comfortably hot, and others dangerously so, depending on whether the water had time to cool as it rose. Sometimes the water was so hot it steamed out of the earth as searing gas. What had always fascinated Hal was the fact that all this hot water bubbling out of the ground was the same water that had rained down hundreds, sometimes *thousands* of years earlier. It was mind-boggling.

Lucas nodded. "Yeah. Bad Rock Gulch isn't anywhere near as exotic as the Labyrinth of Fire, but it has its moments. See, here's a hot spring."

It turned out to be a fissure in the right-hand wall, at the bottom of which a pool of clear water bubbled and steamed in a bowl-shaped recess. Oddly, there was a wooden ledge fixed to one of the fissure walls, positioned just a few inches above the water.

"If anyone wants to try it," Molly said, resting her bags at her feet, "go right ahead. Just sit on the seat and dangle your feet in. It's wonderful."

Darcy immediately threw down her own bag, kicked her shoes off, hiked up her knee-length skirt, and gingerly stepped into the pool. She let out a cry as her toes touched the water. "It's so warm!"

Laughing, Molly pointed to a vertical thin bronze pipe fixed to the rock wall. It led down into the pool. "It would be much hotter if it wasn't cooled with cold water directly from the hills above. This pool is just a tiny outlet for a steaming river running deep below the mine."

Darcy edged into the pool until she was standing in the middle, then sat on the seat. There she eased back against the wall and let out a sigh. "This is fabulous. The water's lovely, and it's swirling around my toes."

"Believe it or not," Molly said, "the goblin miners enjoy this a lot. They kick their dirty, smelly boots off and sit in here during breaks."

"Wonderful," Darcy said. "I'll stay right here. You guys go on."

"I want to try," Lauren said—but at that moment Lucas gave an exasperated snort and glowered at her. "Um . . . later," Lauren added sheepishly.

The tour continued, with Darcy hurrying to catch up. The tunnel started bending to the right and dipping downward. The slope grew steeper until it became a set of roughly hewn steps. It must have taken ages for the goblins to carve them into the rock itself. Hal marveled at their industriousness. Nothing seemed to stop them; they just got it done.

"Do they bring geo-rocks out this way?" Robbie asked, walking up front with Molly. "Must be a real slog."

"No, they have a conveyor belt," she told him. "There's a network of tunnels down here, and Lucas is going to take you through some of them so you can see the goblins at work. Then we'll move on to the famous Chamber of Ghosts."

Lauren let out a squeal. "Did you say *ghosts?*"

As the tunnel descended, the lanterns abruptly ended as they neared a sharp bend. There was a patch of darkness there, but it was clear that a larger source of light shone just out of sight. Lucas turned the corner first, then Molly and everyone else. Darcy and Lauren were giggling at the creepiness of it all, though Hal found nothing creepy about these tunnels. Normally he didn't much care for tunnels, but these were fascinating to him.

When it was his turn to round the corner, his mouth fell open, and he almost stopped dead at the sight of so much energy in the walls. "Holy cow!"

Chapter Five
Goblins at Work

They all felt a curious tingle of energy as they headed down the sloping tunnel. Light flooded the place, an orange radiance from the rock walls that reminded Hal of the Labyrinth of Fire, only these walls were cool to the touch.

The farther they walked, the more noise they heard—clinking and clanging, numerous hammers chipping or pounding away at the rock somewhere ahead. Right now, though, all Hal saw was more of the same long tunnel, neatly squared off and braced with timber struts, wide enough for broad-shouldered goblins and tall enough for lycans.

Everyone stopped to peer at a particularly bright patch of wall on their left. It looked like some kind of illuminated liquid was moving deep inside the rock, again reminding Hal of flowing lava. "It's moving," he whispered.

To his surprise, Molly heard him. "Yes, it is. Lucas? You know far more about this than I do."

Lucas sighed, and Jolie sagged in his arms. "Well, this is what geo-rocks look like in their rawest form, at least here in *these* mines. The walls weren't always glowing like this, though. All the hot spots were deep underground. The goblins dug these tunnels while the rock up here was cold. Before it sparkled."

"There's that word again," Abigail remarked.

"If the goblins tried to dig through this rock now, they'd blow the place up. The sparkle you see inside the rock is in liquid form and highly volatile. The stuff creeps around the hills, leaking in, expanding . . . Nobody knows where it comes from or how it's formed. It's just there."

They all watched, mesmerized, as the mysterious glowing substance moved sluggishly deep inside the wall, easing along in tiny, jerky movements, like a frozen stream that was beginning to thaw. "It's like blood," Abigail said.

Robbie snorted, but Molly seemed to agree. "I've only been here once before, but I always thought it was like being inside the body of a gigantic beast. I imagine there to be a heart beating within these hills, pushing blood around its enormous arteries."

"Eww," Lauren murmured.

"Let's move on," Lucas said impatiently.

As they continued their journey, the noise of mining activity increased. They rounded a gradual curve and emerged into an enormous cavern, the source of the din. Teams of goblins were spread out all over, banging away at the walls, but before the group could take a look around, Lucas led them to a nearby tunnel on their right. Along the short, dark passage were wheelbarrows filled with glowing geo-rocks. At the end, a small cave was lit up with oil-filled lanterns.

"Drilling room," Lucas said. "You might as well see what goes on in here."

Four goblins were working at tables, each with a single rock secured to his workbench in a vise. Above each vise was a contraption made of wood and iron, with a bunch of pulleys and levers. A single long drill bit pointed downward at the secured geo-rock. Hal watched a goblin casually turn a wheel, which spun the drill bit extraordinarily fast. When a lever was pushed forward, the drill bit descended, cutting easily into the geo-rock and boring a tiny hole.

Everyone winced, but the goblin had clearly done this a million times before. He narrowed his eyes and, still turning the wheel, eased the drill bit deeper. He bent to peer closely, nudged it just a little farther, then finally let go of the wheel and released the lever so the drill sprang back up and slowed. Hal breathed a sigh of relief—and sucked in his breath again as the goblin shifted the geo-rock sideways a couple of inches to repeat the process.

"Deadly work, this," Lucas rumbled, clearly awed. "A few have exploded in the past. That's why the stock is kept out in the tunnel. But this work is necessary. The drill-holes are so rods can be inserted later—to draw out the power."

He tossed Jolie in his arms until she was turned around the other way. Flexing his free arm with obvious relief, he pointed to a conveyor belt that disappeared into the wall through a narrow passage about two feet in diameter. The belt moved slowly and continuously, apparently powered by an engine somewhere.

"All the geo-rocks leave through this room. They're drilled and sent up the belt to a cave at the surface near where we came in. Saves carting the rocks up in barrows." He abruptly turned to leave. "This way."

Back in the huge cavern, the noise was deafening. Lucas led them to the first team of workers—two goblins hammering away within a large recess in the wall. The tour group paused to watch.

The goblins hardly seemed to notice they were being studied. They chipped at the wall, which was pockmarked with glowing smudges. Some were bright and near the surface; others were dim, buried deep.

"See how the energy is solid here?" Molly said loudly as the goblins worked. "Lucas, explain."

The lycan again hoisted Jolie into a better position, clearly tired of carrying her. "What's to explain? The sparkle here has settled."

"Explain what they're doing," Molly said over the din of the hammers.

Lucas rolled his eyes. "They're digging, woman!"

"But not all miners dig geo-rocks out of the walls," she argued.

"Well, true." Lucas scratched his nose and pursed his lips. "Normally geo-rocks just kind of naturally break loose and lie around in tunnels waiting to be collected like a load of golden eggs. But this place is different. Bad Rock Gulch is highly active. And these goblins are crazier than most."

Fenton gave a snort. "They'd have to be."

Suddenly defensive, Lucas drew himself up straight and swung Jolie around as if using her to point at the walls. It was hard to tell how she felt about that since her sunken eyes and twisted mouth were already set in a permanent grimace. "This stuff is stable. When it stops flowing—when it breaks apart and solidifies into individual lumps like this—then it's okay to work with. The miners could wait years for geo-rocks to work loose on their own, but they're speeding up the process by chipping away at them. Sometimes they can blast into the walls with dynamite and dislodge them, but mostly they work *around* them with hammers."

The goblins were carefully excavating the wall, chipping off great chunks of cold rock and leaving what looked like glowing protuberances. One goblin was farther along than the other, deftly cutting into the stem of rock that held his prize in place while the debris built up around his ankles. A few minutes later, the nugget broke off. The goblin knelt and tapped at it with a smaller hammer and chisel, turning it slowly as he did so to round it off. Then he brushed it down and threw it into a wheelbarrow full of similar geo-rocks.

"He makes it look so easy," Darcy said.

"That he does," Lucas agreed.

The goblin looked startled, apparently noticing his audience for the first time. He grunted and returned to work on another deeply buried nugget.

There were about fifteen other teams of goblins around the cavern doing the exact same thing—extracting nuggets from the walls and tossing them into wheelbarrows. Hal would have got bored after the first few, yet these goblins did this all day long, every day, probably five days a week. There were alcoves everywhere, some so close together they had joined into one. Hal imagined the cavern slowly growing over many years of hard work.

"There are other chambers like this," Lucas said. "This entire hill is riddled with natural fissures and tunnels. The goblins have turned it into the biggest mine in the region. And the energy stems from the Chamber of Ghosts."

"Stop mentioning ghosts," Lauren complained.

"Show us!" Robbie chimed in, shooting her a look of defiance.

Lucas moved on through the vast domed room. There were plenty of tunnels to choose from, each leading to another chamber or cavern, though one was marked with the word OWT in scrawling white paint. "That's the exit," Lucas explained shortly when Hal inquired about it. "Can't you read? Leads out to Bad Rock Gulch."

He led them to a lonely tunnel on the far side where nobody was working. With a shiver of anticipation, Hal shuffled along it with his friends, grateful for the faint illumination within the walls. Gradually, the drilling and hammering noises receded until the only sounds were multiple footsteps on the rock floor. There were wooden supports all the way along, but Hal had to wonder if they would actually help in the event of a roof fall; surely the colossal weight of all that rock would snap the supports like matchsticks!

Although he was excited to see the famous Chamber of Ghosts, he couldn't help thinking it would just be more glowing walls. What else could there be?

The tunnel went on and on, twisting and turning, narrowing in places before widening again. Lucas explained to the group in his rumbling voice that most of the goblin-made tunnels followed natural crevices and passages through the hills. "They just widened 'em. Took years. Okay, watch your step—we're going down a steep bit now."

It was so steep that steps had been cut in the smooth floor. Hal marveled at how the floor itself was glowing now, along with the walls and ceiling. It wasn't a strong glow, just a dark orange, but it was the liquid kind, moving sporadically through the rock under their feet like blood through veins.

Pumped from the heart, Hal thought. *Is the Chamber of Ghosts the heart of these hills?*

As they descended, several gasps from up ahead drew Hal's attention. He craned his neck to see past everyone in front of him and caught a glimpse of dazzling orange light.

The walls, ceiling and floor brightened as the floor leveled off, and they all turned the corner into another cavern—the famous Chamber of Ghosts itself. The silence was palpable as they fanned out and looked around in awe. Even Lucas, who had surely seen this place several times before, seemed mesmerized.

The roughly circular chamber had a fairly low ceiling, no more than a dozen feet high, but had the footprint of three small houses. Not only the walls but also the floor and ceiling were glowing strongly here. Numerous thick columns of rock seemed to hold the ceiling up when in truth they were simply stalactites and stalagmites joined in the middle, formed long after the creation of the chamber. They glowed, too. Everything in this room did.

But the main focus of the chamber was its centerpiece—a bizarre rounded lump about eight feet across and six feet high that was too dazzling to look at directly. Hal squinted and shielded his eyes, trying to get a good look. The mound pulsed with energy and motion as though its surface was transparent and the interior was filled with a weird life form—like an upside-down glass bowl stuffed with wriggling jellyfish. It was both fascinating and creepy. A network of fat veins and capillaries zigzagged off across the floor in all directions.

"The core," Lucas said softly, his voice strangely amplified. "The heart."

Hal mentally nodded. *The heart.*

Lucas moved closer to the core and turned to face everyone. Jolie twisted in his arms, trying to peer over his shoulder at the centerpiece as he spoke. "As far as we know, this place is perfectly safe to visit.

Nobody has reported any ill effects from being here. That said, people don't normally stick around for long. It's pretty and all, but some say it messes with your head after a while. So be warned. You still thinking of staying awhile?"

Molly nodded. "We'll stay as long as we need to get our powers back. Then we'll be off with our payload."

"Well, just know that the goblins work until dusk. After that they lock the gate, and the mine will be empty. Even I don't have a key to get you out."

He looked around as if seeking something, then shrugged and bent to put Jolie on the hard rock floor. When he stepped back, she eased up on her elbows, reclining there as though she were basking in the sun— only without legs. The effect was disconcerting. The raggedy dress she'd been given, though long, clearly defined where her torso ended; the rest of the material draped flat on the glowing floor, eerily illuminated.

Her face twisted into a grimace. "Is the magic working yet? You're all staring at me. I must be back to my former glory already, yes?"

Immediately everyone turned away in a fit of mumbles and embarrassed coughs. The walls suddenly became a subject of intense interest—anything that diverted attention from the hideous Jolie creature.

Molly, Blair and Lucas spoke quietly amongst themselves while Hal and his friends dropped their bags and wandered around the chamber. Even with the walls glowing this brightly, the surfaces were only lukewarm. *So definitely not lava*, Hal thought. As he touched a wall, he felt the slightest tingling sensation. Was that . . . magic? Lucas called it 'sparkle,' but in any case it was pure energy running through the walls.

With growing excitement, Hal's doubts about this place faded away. He was certain they would all regain their powers by absorbing the energy around them. How long it would take was anybody's guess. Hours? Days? He shook his head. No, not days. Surely no more than a few hours at most.

"It's making my hair stand on end," Abigail whispered. She had both hands planted firmly on the wall surface, her fingers splayed. Her hair wasn't really standing on end that he could see, but she had goose bumps on her arms.

Thomas and Robbie were standing with their backs to a wall, arms and legs wide, their heads touching the hard rock. Fenton seemed lost, looking around as if he didn't know what to do with himself. Lauren and Darcy had gone off to the far side, their excited voices carrying easily through the chamber. Emily and Dewey had approached the core itself; he was helping her sit because she looked pale and shaky. As she collapsed against the mound, leaning back on its rounded, gently sloping surface, she closed her eyes and gave a heavy sigh.

Since nobody was helping Jolie, she had rolled onto her stomach and was wriggling awkwardly across the floor, dragging herself along, her dress trailing behind. Molly, Blair and Lucas stopped talking and turned to watch her. Then, either out of pity or guilt, Molly went to help.

"I can manage!" Jolie snapped at her, her voice cracking like a whip and echoing throughout the chamber. Everyone quit talking at once and a silence fell as she continued wriggling. "Keep your filthy gorgon hands off me."

Although veiled, it was obvious Molly was shocked at the rebuke. She shook her head and moved away, returning to Lucas and Blair.

Ten seconds later, Jolie made it to the core. Panting, she twisted around and got herself into a sitting position similar to Emily's. The two girls were mere feet apart, and they stared at each other in silence for a long, awkward moment. Then they each turned away, their postures suggesting an intense dislike of each other.

"Well, I'm outta here," Lucas said finally. "You won't see me again. Get your sparkle back, get your rocks, and go home. Don't stay in these parts more than a few days, a week at most. You don't want to be around when my people start getting itchy for the hunt. They might decide a bunch of kids will make a good dinner."

Molly clicked her tongue. "Lucas, really—"

He grinned somewhat humorlessly. "I'm kidding. Sort of. We won't eat you for dinner. We're not cannibals. But seriously, when the urge to hunt takes over, the distinction between man and beast starts to blur. I'm just saying you don't want to stick around, okay?"

"We heard you the first time," Blair complained. He looked a little ashen even in the chamber's orange glow. "You always were a savage, Lucas, even at school. Always running around terrorizing us . . ."

47

Lucas clapped the smaller man on the back and made a play of baring his teeth at him. Then he laughed and gave Molly a rough hug before limping out of the chamber, holding his thigh as he went.

"All right, everyone," Molly said loudly. "Let's all gather around the core and get comfortable. The quicker we draw out its magic, the better. We have no idea how long this is going to take."

"But we're not thinking of *sleeping* here, are we?" Lauren said, coming into view around the mound. "I mean, we have no blankets or pillows."

"Oh, the goblins will have all that stuff," Molly said. She held up the sack of food Lucas had provided. "Along with dinner. But it's early evening yet. Let's just sit awhile."

They all sat with their backs to the core, spreading out around it and shuffling until they had found reasonably decent places that didn't have lumps protruding painfully into their backs. Hal and Abigail sat within reach of one another, but somehow he ended up near Jolie as well. He sighed. In a game of musical chairs, he almost always dropped out first because he lacked the fighting urge to win. It was the story of his life, allowing others to pile in first, forever ending up at the rear of a group . . . and now here he was with the least desirable seat. He caught Jolie staring sideways at him, and he looked away.

Meanwhile, the energy tingled through his clothes and warmed him.

Blair grumbled something unintelligible, and Molly's frustration was clear even though she was around the other side of the core. "Blair, *please* change the tune! Have some faith in yourself. Do you really think you know everything there is to know about shapeshifters?"

"Pretty much," Blair said. "About myself, anyway."

"Really? When you showed up in the village and performed your phoenix rebirth in front of everyone, didn't you say it was a 'new trick' you'd picked up? Something you didn't know you could do?"

"Well, yeah. It's one thing turning into a phoenix, but burning to death and being reborn in my own ashes is something else."

"And yet you did it."

Blair shrugged. "So?"

"So you learned something new about yourself. And did you know that such a dazzling display of blue flames, sparkling energy, and spectacular regeneration could cancel out the effects of my deathly

48

gorgon gaze? That a phoenix could bring Fenton and other petrified souls back to life?"

"No," Blair admitted.

"Neither did I." Molly sighed heavily. "Blair, I've spent years trying to undo my magic. Some of my victims deserved to be turned to stone for one reason or another, but most didn't. I've lost count of the number of times someone—or something—has looked upon my unveiled face and *wham!*—calcified in less than two seconds. When Simone brought me Abigail's little glass faerie ball, I felt sure it would tell me how to undo my magic, the same way it taught Orson how to fly after all these years of being grounded. But it never did. And do you know why?"

"No, but you're going to tell me," Blair murmured with a sigh.

"Because the information was not stored in my brain. That little faerie ball can retrieve lost memories, but it can't retrieve what I never knew in the first place. So it was a great surprise to find out that Fenton came back to life right after that phoenix blew itself up."

Blair said nothing. There was a long silence, and at last Molly spoke again, more softly this time.

"Whether you like it or not, Blair, you're going to get your magic back, and I'm going to calcify a few rodents, and you're going to perform your wondrous rebirth trick and bring those rodents back. And if that works, I'll take you to some of my past victims and give them their lives back."

"Do you know how tiring it is to—" Blair started.

"Don't want to hear it," Molly interrupted. "Honestly, kids, Blair is such a big crybaby. Always was. Back when we were in school, he would bawl whenever he fell and scraped his knee. I remember—"

"Ignore her," Blair exclaimed. "She's making it up. Never take a word she says without a pinch of salt. She's just jealous because my grades were better than hers. And because I'm better looking—*ouch!*"

Everyone laughed as the sounds of a scuffle echoed around the chamber.

Darcy spoke up. "Molly, was your school like ours? I mean, on a remote island somewhere?"

"What? No, no, nothing like that. Actually, our school was in the middle of beautiful countryside. It was miles from anywhere, yes, but we weren't cut off from civilization like you were . . ."

She started describing the school and the vast plot of land all around. There had been other buildings, too—a large house on a hill overlooking the property, an enormous barn, and various small offices and cabins, all of it owned by one very rich man. Hal grew bored very quickly as she started describing everything in detail, and evidently Fenton did, too, because it wasn't long before he interrupted.

"You promised to tell us about the ghosts. I don't see any."

"I don't want to know," Darcy said plaintively.

"It's true that people have reported seeing ghosts in this chamber," Molly said. "What's strange is that goblins never have, nor lycans. Just humans."

"Oh, great," someone muttered. It sounded like Lauren.

Molly laughed. "Superstitions, that's all. This place is really strange and beautiful, and we don't understand it—and whenever there's something we don't understand, we're afraid of it on some level, and fear leads to irrational thoughts and behavior. People see things that aren't really there. In fact, the very idea of ghosts inspires ghostly encounters. So don't worry about it. You won't see any ghosts despite the fanciful name of the place."

There was an unhappy grunt from Fenton, but most of the group sighed with relief. "Are you sure?" Lauren asked. "Definitely no ghosts?"

"I promise," Molly said.

Chapter Six
Absorbing Magic

"Not sure I feel any different," Thomas said grumpily. "I can't transform yet. What about the rest of you?"

"Oh, for goodness' sake," Darcy said. "We've only been sitting here five minutes. Give it some time."

"Actually," Molly said, "we should all make a point to try shapeshifting once in a while. Not too often in case we deplete our powers before we're rejuvenated, but perhaps every hour?"

It was funny how she had latched onto the idea that shapeshifting powers could be drained to nothing if used too early in the recharging process. Hal, Abigail, Robbie and Emily had come to the same conclusion during their mad dash in the virus-stricken world. They had slowly absorbed magic from their clothing and had been afraid to try and shift until they were 'completely ready'—whatever that meant. Hal had talked to his parents about this, and his dad had suggested it was like starting a car that had not been used in a long time. "You just need enough juice to turn the starter motor," he'd explained. "If it's not charged enough, you'll drain it flat and have to charge it awhile before trying again. But once the engine's running, the battery becomes self-charging."

This explanation had stuck in Hal's head ever since. It had taken days for he and Abigail to fully shift. Until then, they'd only managed partial transformations. But once they'd absorbed enough magic and were able to shapeshift properly, they became 'self-charging,' able to shift back and forth without a problem.

"We could just watch Jolie," Emily said, sounding tired. "If she starts looking normal again, we'll know her enchantment is returning."

"*You* can watch Jolie," Fenton said. "I can't see her from here. Good job, too. Let me know when she doesn't look like something I spat out."

There were a few chuckles at this, but mostly silence. Looking sideways, Hal noticed that Jolie was motionless, staring into space, the only movement being the gentle rise and fall of her chest. Either she wasn't taking the bait or she was preparing for a retaliation later.

After fifteen minutes, Robbie sighed. "I'm bored. Is there a bathroom in this joint, or shall I just use one of these walls?"

"You'll have to walk all the way back up to the top," Molly told him firmly. "Ask a goblin. And please don't get lost."

"How come *he* gets to wander around and we have to sit here on this hard floor?" Lauren demanded.

"Because he doesn't need to be here, doofus," Fenton said. "He doesn't need any more magic. Quit your whining."

"I'll come with you," Hal said, getting to his feet. "Abi?"

She looked up at him. "Excuse me? You want me to go to the bathroom with you both? Really?"

"Well, no—I just meant—"

Abigail grinned and climbed to her feet. "You're so easy to tease."

The three of them headed for the chamber exit. They looked back at Emily to see if she was coming with them, but she was clearly too weary and sick to move. They left the group behind and headed up the tunnel's sharp incline with its brightly glowing steps.

"Emily's not looking so good," Hal muttered. "I hope Jolie gets her magic back soon."

"Do you think she'll grow new legs?" Robbie asked.

Abigail snorted. "Don't be ridiculous."

The tunnel felt cold now that they'd left the subtle warmth of the chamber's core. It was a long walk back uphill to the enormous cavern where the din of workers greeted them. They approached a lone goblin who was having a break and munching on roasted nuts. "Which way's the bathroom?" Hal asked.

The goblin scowled at him and jerked a thumb over his shoulder. "Tunnel next to the drilling room. Second right."

The bathroom was nothing more than a small, dark cave at the end of a short tunnel, lit only with a couple of lanterns. It smelled awful. There were various holes around the edges, and in those holes were hot, bubbling pools of water. Hal knew the pools themselves were probably sanitary; they carried away any mess and provided a never-ending supply of fresh water. But that didn't mean the goblins were careful with their aim.

"I'll leave you boys to it," Abigail said with a grimace. "Have fun."

Hal hurried after her. "I don't need to go. But at least we know where the bathroom is. We'll wait outside, Robbie."

"Uh, right," Robbie said doubtfully.

Hal and Abigail walked back into the corridor. There were other small rooms, and they peered into them to find a pantry and what looked like a rough dining hall with tables and chairs. There was a storage area, too, with shelves full of sticks of dynamite, rolls of fuse wire, and more ordinary things like large jugs—and blankets. "Shall we grab some?" Abigail wondered aloud.

The blankets looked weighty. "What if we cart a ton of blankets all the way down to the chamber and find we don't need them after all?" Hal argued.

"We're supposed to be staying the night," Abigail countered. "Are you willing to come back up here again to fetch them?"

"Someone else can," Hal retorted. He won the discussion simply by refusing to grab any. As they lingered there, waiting for Robbie, he caught Abigail looking at him. She smiled and turned away, and he narrowed his eyes. "What?"

"Nothing."

He frowned. "Tell me."

"Nothing," she insisted. "Can't I smile at you without being interrogated?"

He pursed his lips. Either she was amused by him or she had something on her mind. Or she was just smiling at him for no apparent reason. Or maybe she was expecting something from him. That was probably it. She was pretending not to look at him but kept glancing his way.

Luckily, Robbie returned shortly after. He looked disgusted but relieved. "I needed that," he said bluntly.

"Did you do a number one or a number two?" Abigail asked.

"None of your business."

"I hope you washed your hands."

"Shut *up!*"

When they returned to the Chamber of Ghosts, everyone was silent and still. Molly placed her hands together by the side of her face to indicate that everyone was asleep and put one finger to where her lips would be behind her veil. "Shh."

The three of them returned to their places. Hal sighed. This was going to be a long night, and he didn't even need to be here. Maybe he and Abigail could just go outside. Then again, it was probably much warmer in here than outside. He returned to his place against the core, immediately wishing he'd brought some blankets after all. He avoided Abigail's eye as she whispered, "I told you so."

Still, the silence was so complete, and the core so pleasantly warm, that he started to feel the pull of sleep despite the lack of blankets. It was way too early for bed—heck, the goblins were still working!—but night and day were irrelevant in the confines of the tunnels under the hill. Maybe it was best to just fall asleep right here and now . . .

"Hal," Abigail whispered.

He jumped. "Mmm?"

She spoke so softly that he could barely hear her. He shuffled sideways to where she was reclining. "What?"

"I said, why don't you ever kiss me?"

He froze. "Well . . . I want to," he said awkwardly. "I just . . . I . . ."

"You just what?" She looked at him earnestly. "Sometimes I don't think you like me all that much."

"I do!" he said, and winced as his voice carried around the chamber.

After a pause, Abigail put out a challenge. "Then show me."

This was it, Hal realized. *The moment.*

He leaned closer. Her face was inches away, so close he could count the freckles on her nose and see his reflection in her eyes. He puckered up. He could do this. He'd practiced on his hand. It was *easy*.

She closed her eyes and waited.

He glimpsed movement and looked around. He saw nothing untoward, but he suddenly had the feeling he was being watched. He turned to see if Jolie was watching him. She wasn't. Over Abigail's shoulder he saw Dewey's feet around the curve of the core. There was nobody watching, and yet . . .

"What are you waiting for?" Abigail whispered.

She had opened her eyes again and didn't look very happy.

"I thought I saw something," Hal said weakly. "Never mind. Let me—"

This time they both caught movement out of the corner of their eyes. They snapped their heads around to stare at the nearest glowing wall. Something shifted there. The bright orange glow dimmed as if something passed in front of it, a momentary silhouette, or a shadow. Yet it was plain there was nobody around. The wall was so bright that there were no places to hide.

"Did you see that?" Abigail whispered.

"Yeah," Hal replied in an equally low voice, grateful he wasn't going crazy.

They sat and watched the distant wall for a while longer. Eventually Hal shrugged and said quietly, "I guess we're imagining things." He licked his lips. "Uh, where were we?"

"You were about to kiss Abigail," Jolie said loudly, making them jump.

Hal swung around. Jolie was still facing away, apparently asleep. But as he stared at her, her head slowly turned, and she returned his stare with her awful sunken eyes and sickly grin.

"Go on, Hal," she urged. "You can do it."

Her voice was so deliberately loud that everyone woke at once. "What's that?" Blair started. "Did somebody say something?"

"Did we fall asleep?" Molly asked, surprised.

Hal glared at Jolie, furious—not so much because everyone was now awake and alert but simply because she was so mean. He didn't really care if anybody found out he and Abigail were smooching, but there was no reason for Jolie to be so ugly about it. He remembered that she had good hearing and vowed to stay well away from her when he wanted a private moment with Abigail.

Jolie's voice had a rasping quality about it as she giggled and milked the moment for all it was worth. "Sorry to wake you all, but Hal was about to kiss Abigail—finally! He's busy puckering up over here. Come on over and watch."

"Oh, shut up, Jolie," Molly snapped.

Not surprisingly, Fenton and Thomas both came tearing around the core. They skidded to a stop in front of Hal and Abigail and stared down at them, their faces alight with excitement. "Go for it, Hal," Fenton said. "Right on the mouth."

"Gross," Thomas said with a grimace.

His simple one-word comment infuriated Hal. He leapt to his feet and pounced on the red-haired boy, gripping him by the shirt and pushing him backward as he yelled in his face. He wasn't quite sure what he said—the words streamed out of his mouth too fast to recollect. But he stopped mid-sentence when he realized the top of his head was pressed against the rock ceiling and Thomas was dangling from his reptilian-clawed grip.

Hal blinked and took stock. He was still in human form—sort of. His arms and body were thick, dark green, and armored, and his shirt was in tatters because of his increased size. His legs were human, and he was relieved to find that his pants were intact. Something was wrong with his face, though. He'd grown a snout, and his final words had come out as a rumbling growl.

There was a silence behind him. Thomas's face was inches from his. The boy was wide-eyed. Slowly, Hal lowered him to the floor and stepped back. As Thomas straightened his shirt, Hal reverted to full human form, shrinking down until his ruined shirt almost fell off.

He turned to face his friends. Every one of them was standing there staring at him, some shocked, others simply puzzled. Molly's veiled expression was impossible to read, but she had her hands planted firmly on her hips.

"Hal Franklin," she said sternly. "What on earth got into you?"

"Nothing," he mumbled.

"Apologize to Thomas, then."

"Sorry."

Abigail climbed to her feet. "Hal was just watching out for me. Thomas made a stupid comment and nearly got his head bitten off. *He's* the one that should apologize." She shot the boy a stern look, and he looked sheepishly at his feet. "So be warned, Jolie," she added. "If Hal's willing to do that to a friend, think what he'll do to *you*."

Jolie said nothing. Her ugly smirk was gone, though.

"How long have we been asleep?" Darcy said, rubbing her eyes. "Feels like hours. Can anyone transform yet?"

There was a comical moment when most of the group stood there frowning and glancing down at themselves. Then a collective sigh went up. "Nope," Dewey said. "Nothing."

"All right, then," Molly said. She pointed at Hal. "Take a walk. Go get us some blankets and pillows. Since we're all falling asleep already, it makes sense for us to get comfortable."

"I just went for a walk," Hal protested.

Abigail took his arm. "Come on, Mr. Bad-Tempered Dragon. We don't need to be here anyway."

As he and Abigail left the chamber, the rest once again settled down around the dazzling core.

"Thanks for looking out for me," Abigail said from behind him on the steps. "But don't do that again, okay? I don't want any, uh, *accidents* just because an idiot says something you don't agree with."

"I don't know what came over me," Hal said, amazed. He fingered his tattered shirt with dismay. Had his mom packed another in his sack? He'd have to check when he got back. "Thomas just—well, what he said—"

"Wasn't worth the bother," Abigail insisted. She gave him a gentle shove from behind. "Let's go and sit by the hot pool."

They traveled the long, winding route back up to the gigantic mining cavern where droves of goblins toiled, then across to the far side where they'd first entered. They followed the tunnel, climbed the steps, and at last came across the strange alcove with the bubbling, steaming water. It had taken maybe fifteen or twenty minutes in all, and they were eager to sit down and rest. They kicked off their shoes and waded in to sit on the bench with the water lapping all the way up to their knees. Abigail sighed and closed her eyes. "Lovely."

It would have been nice to sit there awhile, but just a few minutes later three weary goblins came along, filthy and sweating. They were deep in conversation until they stopped in front of the pool and found it occupied. "Clear out," one said rudely. "This ain't for a bunch of kids."

"Uh, okay," Hal said. Disappointed, he and Abigail splashed out of the pool and allowed the goblins in. As they grunted and made themselves comfortable, more goblins showed up. It looked like they were done for the day.

Hal and Abigail returned to the cavern. The place was emptying. Many of the goblins were exiting through the tunnel marked OWT. Hal and Abigail headed for the storage area and grabbed what they could carry. There were no pillows, just neatly folded blankets, and Abigail ordered Hal to hold out his arms so she could stack them up on him. Then they headed back to the Chamber of Ghosts.

They'd been gone forty-five minutes or more, and everyone was sound asleep again. Hal suspected the core had something to do with that—some sort of sleep-inducing magical effect.

Rather than wake the others, Hal and Abigail quietly distributed the blankets around the core so they were within reach if anybody needed them. Then they spent a few minutes arranging a few for themselves, working in silence. One rolled-up blanket made a suitable extra-long pillow they could share, and two more served as a mattress to protect them from the hard floor.

In a shockingly short amount of time, Hal began to feel sleepy again. "This rock thing is making us drowsy," he whispered.

"I know," Abigail said. "It worries me a bit. What if we fall asleep and never wake up? Does that ever happen, do you think?"

"Does anyone normally fall asleep in the first place? I'll bet most visitors walk around for a while and leave."

After a pause, Abigail sat up. "If that's true, then I'm afraid to go to sleep. I think someone should keep watch just in case."

Hal sighed. "Well, you go to sleep," he murmured. "I'll stay up for a bit."

"No, you go ahead. I'm too nervous now." She patted his arm. "Go ahead. I'll wake you when I'm tired."

Hal couldn't help thinking that Molly should have been the one to think about keeping watch. Or Blair. Or Lucas for that matter. It was up to the adults to look out for the safety of Hal and his friends, wasn't it? Unless there really was nothing to worry about. Maybe he and Abigail were just being overly cautious. Lucas had clearly said that the chamber was a safe place.

He drifted off in no time.

* * *

"Hal," Abigail whispered in his ear. She shook his shoulder gently until he roused and blinked awake. "Hal, wake up. I keep seeing something."

He struggled up onto his elbows and looked around. "That shadow again?"

She nodded. "Looks like the same shadowy figure but in different places around the chamber. I think there are lots of them."

"Lots of *them*?"

"Yes—them. Whoever they are."

Hal rubbed his eyes and frowned when he looked down to find his shirt in tatters after his earlier tantrum. "You think they're people?"

"Yes. In the walls."

They stared hard around the chamber trying to spot another shadowy figure. It seemed that whenever they tried too hard, the shadows went into hiding.

"Well, I guess they're the ghosts Molly was talking about," Hal said after a while. "As long as they stay in the walls, I guess we're safe enough."

Abigail nodded and lay down. "Your turn to keep watch," she murmured.

"Already? How long was I out?"

She shrugged. "An hour or two." She looked sheepish. "I might have dozed off at some point. Sorry."

Hal climbed to his feet and walked past her around the core. All his friends were sleeping soundly, hopefully absorbing magic, *recharging*. Darcy and Lauren, Fenton and Thomas, Robbie and Dewey, all flat out on the floor . . . and Molly and Blair, who were sitting up with their heads lolling to the side. Very few of them had bothered with or even noticed their blankets.

Molly's veil was dangling at a potentially dangerous angle with her head to one side like that. If she jerked, it could slip sideways and reveal one of her eyes. If she'd absorbed enough magic, and if she happened to wake in that moment, someone could quite easily be turned to stone.

He quietly approached her and reached out to make an adjustment. As his fingers touched the fabric, Molly's head lifted, and she appeared to be staring at him from behind her veil. Her hand moved to tug on it, but her action seemed automated as if she did that several dozen times a day. In seconds, her head lolled again and she was sound asleep.

Hal wondered if Blair would be able to nullify the effects of a stoning as Molly hoped. If so, it could change her life. She'd probably insist that he stay with her forever just in case she needed him!

He'd almost walked full circle. Emily was there, flat out, and Jolie was buried under a blanket nearby with just her black hair sticking out. Hal paused, listening. Emily's breathing was ragged. He knelt closer, suddenly worried. Could she die in her sleep because she was neglecting to transform and heal? He shook her gently. "Hey. Wake up and transform."

She stirred. Her lips were parched, and she had horrible shadows under her bloodshot eyes. She looked awful. When she eventually gazed up at Hal, he saw no recognition in her expression. Her breathing was even more ragged and harsh, and way too shallow.

"Em," he said softly. "Can you transform? You need to heal. Go ahead, shift for me before it's too late."

Her brow creased slightly, the only visible sign that something was going through her mind. Was she looking at Hal? He moved sideways, but her gaze remained locked and unmoving, blind to his presence. He snapped his fingers in front of her face, and she didn't even blink.

Really worried now, he shook her roughly. "Hey," he shouted, uncaring if he woke anyone up. "Emily! Come on, wake up."

He struggled with her, lifting her up off the floor into a sitting position. Her head lolled, and she almost flopped over sideways.

Hal yelled for help.

Chapter Seven
The Sickness

Molly climbed unsteadily to her feet and swayed drunkenly as she came to see what was wrong. Others stirred while Hal breathlessly explained that Emily was slipping away. "She's not listening! Look at her—she's having a hard time breathing, and she's staring into space. Make her wake up, or she'll die!"

By the time Molly got a response from Emily, everyone was crowded around adding their voices of encouragement. Emily started blinking and frowning. Then she focused on Molly. "Wha . . ." she mumbled.

"Time for you to change, girl," Molly said loudly, gently patting Emily's face. "Come on, now. Transform for us."

Emily shook her head. "Too tired," she rasped.

Hal turned to Jolie, who was peering out from under her blanket and a mop of black hair. "Do something," he snarled. "Take her sickness away."

"Yes, Jolie," Molly said sternly. "If you have any magic in you at all, you need to use it on Emily."

Curiously, Jolie looked a little different, not quite so hideous. Either Hal was getting used to seeing her ugly mug . . . or she was absorbing magic and regaining her powers of enchantment. She had a long way to go, though. "I'm not ready," she said. "Besides, we need something to dump the sickness into. An animal."

Hal mentally kicked himself. Of course! He stood up. "What do you need? I'll go get it right now."

Jolie shrugged. "Something bigger than a rat or bird. A pig would be great. A cat or dog would do."

Darcy gave a cry. "No way! We can't go killing cats and dogs!"

Jolie rolled her eyes. "But a pig's okay? Well, whatever it is, it needs to be big enough to absorb the sickness—otherwise the sickness will spill out."

There was a clamor of voices, a number of suggestions as to what might be acceptable to receive Emily's terrible sickness, but Hal tuned them out. What was the point in listing a bunch of possibilities unless he could actually *find* something nearby? He raised his voice above the babble. "I'll be back as soon as I can. Robbie, come with me. We can both look."

He shot Abigail a parting look. She nodded, smiled back, and joined Lauren and Darcy with the patient. "Hurry back!" Molly called, her voice echoing up the tunnel as Hal and Robbie dashed away.

They said nothing all the way up the steep incline, nor during the jog along the winding tunnel to the mining cavern. Hal rushed in first, ready to interrogate the goblin workers about the local wildlife. But of course it was empty. The workers had gone home.

"Typical!" Robbie snapped.

They hurried onward up the tunnel, passing the hot pool and finally arriving at the entrance cave. There they found a sturdy gate blocking their exit. Hal threw himself on the bars and rattled them. "You've got to be kidding me!" he yelled.

His heart pounding from their mile-long jog, they both hunted around for a way to open the gate. Clearly it was built to keep out more than just the average man. It didn't open on simple hinges but instead slid upward into the cave roof like a castle's portcullis. A locked iron box was fixed to the wall outside the gate. There was probably a switch in there, but it was well out of reach. The mine was a fortress, and there seemed to be no way of escaping.

Hal turned to Robbie. "I hate to break stuff, but . . ."

Robbie nodded. "I'm way ahead of you." He began shedding his clothes, and when he started on his pants, Hal turned away. Seconds later, a stooping ogre stood there under the low ceiling.

The giant lunged at the gate. It rattled noisily but refused to budge. Robbie tried again, this time stuffing his fat fingers through the bars and yanking them to and fro. The gate buckled and twisted bit by bit.

It occurred to Hal that there *must* be some way to open it from the inside as well as the outside. Now that he was backed up away from the gate, he found a metal box fixed to the wall opposite, just like the one outside, only this one had no lock on it. He pulled the door open and found a simple switch marked OPEN and CLOSE. Feeling rather stupid, he reached for it—but just then Robbie let out a roar and pummeled his way through the gate. It was so badly twisted now that

Hal knew it would never slide up into the ceiling. He quietly closed the box.

The ogre guffawed as he ducked through the gap in the gate and lumbered out onto the beach. Hal hurriedly undressed, transformed, and went after him, tucking his wings in as he squeezed through.

Freedom! He launched into the air, surprised at how high the moon was. It was the middle of the night. Surely it had only been a couple of hours since the goblins had left for the day? . . . but Abigail had admitted to dozing off during her watch duty, so they all might have slept several hours more.

As Robbie lumbered around, Hal flew in circles looking for something—anything—that might be suitable for Jolie. But chancing across a random animal right when he needed one was asking too much. They should have thought about this earlier. He cursed first himself, then Molly and Blair. *They* were the ones who should have thought about this earlier. They were the adults, weren't they?

After several hopeless flights up and down the beach, Hal ventured over the hills. They were spectacular, all lit up as though the entire region were a giant volcano waiting to erupt. The rocky hills went on for miles, gradually petering out in the distance—a supply of geo-rocks that would surely last decades. And just ahead was Bad Rock Gulch itself, a deep crack that looked like a giant had swung an enormous ax and split the hills in two. Hal flew in, his wingtips close to the glowing cliff faces on either side. The ground was sloped, and he slid sideways when he landed.

Something caught in his nostrils—the scent of blood. Whenever he smelled blood while in dragon form, it gave him a tingle of anticipation and excitement. Until now he'd stifled his urges, not wanting to delve that deeply into his dragon psyche. But now he embraced it. He *needed* it this time.

He followed the scent along the gulch, slipping on the sloping rock, his claws making noisy clicking sounds. He was afraid he'd frighten away any prey with his clumsy approach, but still the scent of blood grew stronger as he went.

Ahead he saw three large doglike animals, their heads silhouetted against a bright orange wall as he hurried along. The animals had paused in whatever they were doing, their ears pricked up. Then, when Hal was just twenty or thirty yards away, the animals turned and bolted—and it was then he realized with a shock that it was actually *one* animal, a massive dog with three heads.

He came across its victim, another of those mountain goats with enormous curved horns. It was moaning softly.

Hal stood over it, fighting a compulsion to snap his jaws together and chew on the warm flesh. Part of him relished the idea, made him drool and long for a taste . . . but mostly he was filled with horror and disgust.

Would this half-dead animal do? Hal thought it might. It was big enough and still alive—just. He gingerly clamped his jaws over it, trying to pick it up without injuring it further or giving it a heart attack on the spot. Hopefully it would survive long enough for Jolie to do her thing.

With his wings scraping the walls and the limp animal dangling, he shot up out of the gulch and circled around. He could feel warm blood seeping into his mouth, and the taste both excited and repulsed him. The goat made no sound. It had probably fainted, which was for the best as long as it stayed alive.

Hal had no time to go hunting for Robbie. He returned directly to the cave entrance on the beach. Luckily, Robbie was nearby and turned to watch him land. As Hal shuffled inside, he faced another problem: his dragon form was too big to fit in the tunnels, which meant he'd need to drag the goat in his small, human form. He dropped the animal, transformed quickly, and rushed to climb into his clothes, ignoring his tattered shirt. Moments later, Robbie shambled in, bumping his head on the cave ceiling.

Thoroughly disgusted with the sight of the limp goat dribbling blood all over the floor, Hal grabbed it by its horns and tugged. He gave a shout of frustration at its weight. "How about a *break*?" There was no way he could drag this thing a mile underground.

Then he remembered all the wheelbarrows he'd seen down in the mining cavern. He started for the tunnel, then paused. There was a second tunnel he hadn't explored yet. Hurrying into it, he turned a corner and found himself in a long, low chamber dimly lit by numerous piles of geo-rocks. There were also wheelbarrows filled with them. A conveyor belt, currently inactive, protruded from a wall and ran halfway across the cave—the other end of the belt he'd seen in the drilling room where the rocks were sent up to be dispatched.

Hal picked a barrow and gently tipped out its contents. Despite his care, the geo-rocks skittered away on the uneven floor, throwing glowing orange light in all directions. Wincing, he turned and ran with the single-wheeled contraption.

Robbie was back in human form and hurriedly buttoning his shirt. Sweating, Hal drew up near the goat. Together, they hoisted it into the wheelbarrow. Once it was in, its legs sticking out to one side, the boys started down the tunnel. The wheelbarrow wobbled precariously as Hal weaved from side to side. At least the route to the Chamber of Ghosts was downhill all the way.

After bouncing haphazardly down the carved rock steps, they hurried through the mining cavern, and the goat let out a single bleat. It flopped around but made no attempt to escape. It soon fainted again. Hal felt sorry for it and knew that, under normal circumstances, he would never be carting an injured goat toward certain death. But it was dying anyway through no fault of his, and what he was doing right now was saving Emily's life.

When they reached the second flight of steps leading down to the chamber, Hal paused a moment, vaguely aware that he had no shirt on and was sweating like a pig. *Like a miner*, he thought glibly. He probably smelled like a goblin. He took a moment to catch his breath. Robbie offered to take over, but Hal shook his head and started thumping the wheelbarrow down the steps. The goat bounced and flopped all the way and started bleating again. Hal pushed harder and faster until the jerking handles hurt his hands.

When they got to the bottom, Blair appeared, a puzzled look on his face. "What's all the noise?" But as soon as he saw the wheelbarrow, he ran back into the chamber and shouted for the others, and when Hal rounded the corner and rushed in with his load, Molly was already kneeling in front of Jolie and jabbing a finger at her, clearly having serious words with her.

Emily was unconscious. "Did she ever change?" Hal panted as he wheeled the barrow close. Everyone stared at him and the goat with open mouths. "Well, *did she?*" he yelled.

"No," Molly said. "She fell unconscious soon after you left and has been that way since. She doesn't have long." She grabbed Jolie by the front of her dress and jerked her upright, then pulled her sideways until she was within reach of Emily. "Get on with it, or else."

Jolie's eyes were no longer sunken. Her skin was less pasty and her ears a little shorter. She was far from pretty, or even normal, but she had improved even in the short time since Hal had seen her last.

She stared doubtfully at the goat. "Is it alive? It has to be alive, otherwise—"

"It's alive," Hal snapped even though he couldn't be absolutely sure. It would be just their luck that the animal had died thirty seconds ago.

Jolie nodded. "Well, I'll try."

A silence fell as Jolie reached out, planted her hand firmly on Emily's head, and closed her eyes. The goat let out a moan, confirming that it was still alive.

Nothing seemed to happen. They all stood around, looking down on Jolie and the poor, sickly, unconscious Emily. Lauren let out a sniffle. To Hal's right, something moved on the far wall—*within* the wall—but he failed to see anything once he focused on it. He shook his head irritably and put it out of his mind.

Abigail approached and looked him up and down with distaste. "You stink," she whispered.

"Thanks."

"So where did you find the goat? Did you, um . . . ?"

"Don't worry, it was already dying. I found it outside. A giant three-headed dog was munching on it."

"Ah. I was just curious," she added.

The silence continued. Then Jolie frowned and opened her eyes. "I can't. I don't think I have enough magic."

Molly spoke in a low, matter-of-fact tone. "It's quite simple, Jolie. If Emily dies, so do you."

Her threat certainly sounded genuine. Hal believed she meant it. And apparently Jolie did, too, because she nodded and closed her eyes again.

Abigail turned and spoke to Hal in a volume that suggested she wanted everyone to hear. "Molly suggested *she* take Emily's sickness."

Hal blinked. "Molly?"

"Temporarily. Just to save Emily. That would have given Jolie more time to recover and for you to get back with an animal."

Digesting this news, Hal slowly nodded. "Makes sense. Any one of us could have taken the sickness for a while."

"Only it wouldn't have worked," Abigail said, disbelief in her voice. "Jolie says the sickness is so bad now that it would have been too much for Molly to bear all of a sudden."

"But the woman she took the sickness from in the first place—"

"Was in the same sort of state as Emily is in now," Abigail finished. "I know. That's what we were all arguing about. That's why nothing got done while you were gone. Jolie was probably lying to us. Again." she said, her voice hardening.

Molly turned her veiled face to them. "Well, now she has no choice. I mean it. If Emily dies, I'll make sure Jolie becomes part of the landscape—as soon as I get my own magic back."

A gasp drew their attention. Jolie snatched her hand away from Emily's head, looking shocked. Whatever magical enchantment she had gained in the last few hours had reversed itself; now she was once again the hideous, bitter, twisted creature that had traveled with them in the wagon, her eyes sunken and her uneven, protruding teeth bared in a snarl. She was having trouble breathing, and her forehead was even slicker than usual, sweat trickling down and dripping off her chin.

And now she had the sickness inside her.

Already Emily looked different as she lay there motionless. There was a strange calm about her now.

Jolie lurched forward, falling flat on her face. She crawled, gasping, trying to reach the wheelbarrow with the goat inside. The animal's limbs were overhanging the rim but splayed upward, out of Jolie's reach. There was a long, drawn-out moment where everybody in the chamber stared, silent and mesmerized, as Jolie thrashed and flopped on the floor like a fish out of water, trying to reach the goat, the sickness causing her eyes to bulge as she struggled to breathe. Her shaking hand groped blindly for one of the goat's feet.

She was a liar. She got her kicks from upsetting people. She would happily let Emily die just to hear the others scream with anguish, for that powerful buzz of strangled emotion. It would be so easy to put an end to Jolie's miserable life right here and now—by letting her die of the same sickness she had forced on Emily. It would be a form of poetic justice, well deserved.

Just a few more seconds, and she'd no longer be anyone's problem . . .

Convulsing horribly, Jolie gave up trying to reach the goat. Instead she slowly lifted her head and tried to focus on the silent crowd. "Please . . . help . . ."

Even then nobody moved an inch. It was like they were all stuck to the floor, immobilized and breathless. A shadow seemed to flit across Jolie's face, perhaps a realization that she'd been outwitted, that everybody's intention had always been to let her suffer this way. It wasn't true, of course; nobody would be so callous. Nobody except Jolie herself, anyway.

That look of terrible despair finally broke Hal's paralysis. He darted forward and tipped the wheelbarrow over. The goat toppled out, and he dragged it closer to Jolie. Shaking, she wrapped her arms around the limp animal and held on, rolling gently from side to side as though she were hugging it with affection. It was a bizarre, crazy moment that Hal would remember forever.

It was a very long thirty seconds as Jolie lay there, her breathing ragged, eyes shut. Nobody said a word as she seemed to fall into a deep sleep. Was she . . . was she dying? Hal felt awful. Why had he waited so long? How could he have been so cruel as to make her beg for her life? No matter how mean she was, Hal and his friends were better than that. Better than *her*. If she died—

And at that moment, there was a sudden, dying gasp.

It was the goat. It managed a final grunt before slipping away, its long tongue flopping out of its mouth.

Jolie woke blinking. She pushed the goat away and lay there covered in sweat and patches of goat's blood.

Hal and everyone else turned their attention to Emily.

She was stirring. Her eyes fluttered open. She frowned.

Slowly, she sat up, blinking. Looking astonished, she placed a hand over her chest and throat, and touched her lips. Her pale cheeks flooded with color. Her life was returning before their very eyes.

"I'm cured," she said simply, her voice no longer quite as croaky. A delighted smile spread across her face as she gazed around. "I'm okay! I feel great!"

"Well, I'll be . . ." Blair muttered.

Everyone rushed forward, excited shouts from the boys and squeals from the girls. Darcy and Lauren dragged Emily to her feet and helped her for a moment as she swayed dizzily. But within seconds she was turning around and around, her hands up as if to say *look at me*. Her cheeks were flushed, her eyes bright. It had been nearly two weeks since Jolie had given Emily the terrible sickness. Now she was back to normal, the picture of health.

The tears and hugs and excited chatter lasted a few minutes. Then Hal noticed Molly pulling Jolie back over to the rounded wall of the core and sitting her up against it. With such an ugly, inhuman face, it was impossible to tell if Jolie was happy or angry or just downright miserable, but she seemed weak and dazed.

"You'll be fine," Molly assured her. "Just rest and sleep. Looks like you gave up every ounce of magic you'd absorbed, but now you can absorb some more."

"That was rough," Jolie mumbled. She looked across at Emily, who was busy skipping around in a circle with her friends. The look on the jengu's face seemed to be one of newfound respect. Perhaps, finally, she understood the pain and misery she'd put Emily through.

"Rest," Molly said again. She covered Jolie with a blanket, patted her on the shoulder, and stood to face the others. "All right, gang, listen up. Now we know for sure that this chamber—this core—can recharge us. Maybe you all have your powers back by now and maybe you don't, but rather than put it to the test and drain ourselves as Jolie just did, let's rest some more until we're fully rejuvenated. Agreed? We'll eat and settle down for the rest of the night. I'm certain we'll be ready to leave in the morning."

"Sounds good to me," Fenton said, and Hal thought he saw a flash of glowing red in his eyes. Next to him, Darcy seemed vaguely transparent although she appeared not to realize it.

Molly grabbed the bag of food and started digging through it, handing out bread rolls before emerging with a hunk of cheese. "Only a little bit moldy," she said cheerfully. "Good old Lucas."

"Want a fresh shirt?" Abigail said, tapping Hal on the shoulder.

He jumped, self-consciously crossing his arms over his bare chest. "Uh, thanks," he said, taking the offered shirt and slipping into it. Abigail peered into the sack his mom had packed for him. "What else do we have in here . . . ? Ah, spare underpants. Would you like those, too?"

Hal snatched the sack from her. "How about I rummage through *your* bag?"

Abigail laughed and wandered off to talk to Emily, who was still skipping around and giggling with Darcy and Lauren.

Molly called to Robbie. "Perhaps you'd be good enough to take the poor goat outside? Don't want it stinking up the place."

"On my *own*?"

"I'll help," Blair said. "I could do with a walk."

Molly shook her head firmly. "No, Blair. You need to stay here and recharge with the rest of us. Let Robbie go. He's a strong lad. Aren't you, Robbie?" She tilted her head. "At least I heard you were."

Robbie puffed out his chest. "I can handle it. I'll be right back."

"And bring back a mop and bucket of water," Molly added. "To clean up the blood on the floor."

Blair helped dump the goat back into the wheelbarrow. Then Robbie headed out of the chamber, and Hal watched with amusement. There was no way Robbie could handle those stairs with a fully loaded wheelbarrow.

But as Robbie was turning the corner, his skinny shoulders filled out and strained against his shirt, and his neck thickened. When Hal peered around the corner, his friend was dragging the barrow up the steps with relative ease—something he could have done on the way down if only Hal had let him.

"Help me, Emily," Molly called. "You too, Darcy—bring my bag, would you? Jolie needs some fresh clothes. She can have one of my dresses."

Surprisingly, there was no animosity as Emily helped pick up Jolie. It seemed to be all business as they carted her off to the far side of the chamber where there was a mass of dangling stalactites and weird, lumpy stalagmites. Darcy went, too, carrying Molly's bag.

Having eaten the bread and cheese, they all settled down again. Jolie was brought back to her place garbed in one of Molly's drab, unflattering dresses. It was longer than Jolie's own dress, and the lower half draped across the floor and highlighted her absent legs even more dramatically than before. Hal looked away and returned to his and Abigail's makeshift blanket-pillow. With the most serious problem of Emily's sickness finally out of the way, and the possibility of magical rejuvenation confirmed, the mood was considerably more upbeat. Just one full night in the Chamber of Ghosts and then, in the morning, they could all leave and head home as full shapeshifters. And hopefully Blair would be able to demonstrate an ability to reverse the effects of Molly's petrifying gaze.

Conversation gradually ebbed. The core's magic seeped into them all, and drowsiness overcame them in no time. At some point, Robbie returned with a bucket of water in one hand and a mop in the other. He looked around, sighed, and spent a few minutes mopping up the smear of blood on the floor.

Hal, peering through half-closed lids, smiled and drifted off.

Sometime later, he became aware of a presence in the chamber and, knowing something was wrong, forced himself awake. His back was stiff. He groaned and sat up, rubbing his eyes.

When he opened them, he nearly screamed in terror.

Chapter Eight
Ghosts and Monsters

The chamber walls were alive with shadowy figures—dozens of people of all ages pressed up against the inside of the rock, looking out at him as if squinting through glass. The walls were still orange, but now they glowed even more strongly from within, illuminating the figures from behind.

Hal gasped and reached out to shake Abigail awake, words jamming in his throat. How long had these figures—these ghosts—been there, watching silently? Some of them moved around in the background, scrambling for a space to peer out of the wall. There was absolutely no sound at all even though many of them appeared to be yelling at him, their mouths stretched open, their eyes wide.

"Abi," he croaked, shaking her harder.

She mumbled and rolled over.

Climbing slowly to his feet, Hal stood there trembling. The ghosts were all around, surrounding the entire chamber, pressed against the walls and screaming silently. It was that creepy silence that unnerved Hal the most, and not knowing what they were trying to say. They were blurred as though behind frosted glass, but it was obvious they were frantic, trying to warn him about something.

"Abi," he said, louder this time. He nudged her with his foot.

It slowly dawned on him that he might be dreaming. Or hallucinating. The chamber was deathly silent. The only sounds were the deep-sleep breathing of his friends and a gentle snore from Blair. Whether the ghosts were real or not, they didn't appear to be an immediate threat—just really weird.

Hal stepped gingerly across the floor toward the nearest wall, moving slowly, aware that the ghosts he approached grew more agitated with every step. They seemed intent on getting a message to him, and they crowded in as though drawn to him like fragments of metal to a magnet. They clamored for him, pounding the inside of the wall, mouths moving. If only he could read lips . . .

Steeling himself, he stepped all the way up to the wall and placed his right hand on it. It felt exactly like rock, only when his palm was flat on the hard surface, he felt a tingle and heard a sudden commotion—dozens of voices shouting to him from afar, barely audible, their words mingling into a meaningless cacophony. He listened hard, knowing that what they were shouting was really important. But there were just too many voices, the whole chorus too distant and muffled. "I can't hear," he said, cupping his left hand over his ear.

This proved to be a mistake because the clamor only intensified. He tried to focus on one ghost only—the one directly in front of him, who appeared to be a young woman with short hair. Her features were foggy, but Hal could see her mouth opening and closing. Her hand waved frantically. She was gesturing all around, pointing, telling him to—

Get out!

The meaning was suddenly clear. Through his right hand, which was still planted firmly against the rock, he could identify the words '*get out*' among the rest of the babble. And the word '*go*' as well.

Suddenly frightened, he stepped back, disconnecting himself from the wall. The babble cut off, and silence engulfed him.

The intensely bright illumination abruptly dimmed, and the ghosts vanished within the darkness. Gradually, the usual faint glow returned.

Shaking, Hal backed up a little more, glancing all around. The entire chamber had returned to normal—nothing more than orange glowing walls of rock, with thick columns and a dazzling core in the center.

His friends were stirring.

"What time is it?" Abigail asked as he hurried over.

"Did you see the ghosts?" he asked urgently. "Did you see them?"

She frowned at him. "The ghosts? The shadows, you mean?"

Hal nodded, then shook his head. "Sort of, but . . . these weren't just shadows. They were people. I could see them clearly, all around, banging on the wall and shouting at me."

Hal was talking so loudly that everyone came around the core to stare at him. "What are you talking about, Hal?" Molly asked gently, her head tilted.

He explained again, slower this time, and in more detail. He told them how they had been shouting '*get out*' and '*go*' over and over but that the rest of their message had been unclear. "It was a warning," he added.

Fenton raised an eyebrow. "A warning."

"Yeah."

"And what will they do to us if we don't leave?" Fenton sneered.

Blinking with confusion, it took a moment for Hal to realize that his friends were misunderstanding him. "No, not a *threat*. I mean a warning as in *danger*."

"What danger?" Darcy asked, suddenly looking nervous.

"I don't know. I couldn't hear what they were saying."

"I reckon he was dreaming," Thomas muttered.

Fenton chuckled and nodded. "All this talk of ghosts is getting to him."

"I wasn't dreaming," Hal snapped. "We should leave."

There was a long pause as everyone looked around. Hal knew what they were thinking. They were all wondering how much magic they'd absorbed and whether it would be enough. Their gazes gradually moved to Jolie, who remained propped up against the core's wall.

She was much more humanlike now. Her eyes were no longer black pits, her ears were rounded, her skin relatively ordinary compared to how slick and translucent it had looked before. Even her long, black hair had thickened and gained a bit of body.

"I think we have our powers back," Emily said, looking at Jolie with a frown. "She's normal again."

"Not yet," Fenton said. He rubbed his nose. "I mean, I don't care one way or another about her, but . . . she's not exactly pretty, and if she's not pretty, doesn't that mean we need more time?"

Molly turned to Thomas. "What do *you* think?"

"Me?"

"*All* of you boys. You'll have to be the judges here. Jolie's enchantment works more fully on boys. Is she ready?"

"I'd say she's half-baked," Robbie said flatly.

Jolie let out a laugh. "So in terms of attractiveness, I'm now on a par with you, dear Robbie?"

"Shut up."

Blair cleared his throat. "Shouldn't we just try transforming? Isn't that easier than trying to decide if this young lady is pretty or not?"

"Well," Molly argued, "Jolie's features are directly related to her magical enchantment, so if she's only, uh, *half-baked* as Robbie so eloquently put it, then I'd say we're only halfway recharged."

"But Jolie had to start over, and we didn't," Lauren put in.

That was true. Everyone stood for a moment mulling it over.

Jolie scowled. "You all leave if you want, but it's only fair that I get to stay a bit longer until I'm back to normal."

"And then you'll just walk out?" Thomas said.

Again Fenton chortled. "Wriggle, more like."

Molly sighed. "I'd rather be safe than sorry. Let's stay awhile longer until Jolie is . . . normal. Then we'll know for sure that we're all completely charged and ready to go. Don't try and transform yet. Save your energy."

Most of the group groaned. "My back's hurting," Lauren complained.

"I'm hungry," Robbie said.

Hal gave a cry of exasperation. "Did any of you hear me? We might be in danger! The ghosts told us we should get out of here!"

"The ghosts told *you*," Fenton said. "And you were probably dreaming."

"Why didn't you wake us so we could see the ghosts?" Thomas challenged.

Hal clicked his tongue with exasperation. "I was too busy looking."

Everybody began to settle down again. Hal found himself trembling with frustration. Why did nobody believe him? He glared at Abigail as if it were all her fault, and she shrugged. "What can I say? I believe you, but . . . well, nobody else saw what you saw."

"But you saw the shadows!" he argued. "Earlier—even before I did."

"I know," she said, chewing her lip. "Still, we do need everyone to get their magic back, right? That's the whole reason we're here.'

"Everyone *does* have their magic back. Jolie used hers up, and now she's half-baked again, which means everyone must be fully baked by now."

Abigail took his hand. "Just be patient. The ghosts weren't threatening you, but they weren't warning you of danger either. They're probably just worried because we're taking so much of their precious magic."

As Hal digested that, she pulled him back to their positions against the core wall. He sat and pondered while she lay on her side and peered up at him.

"There's plenty of magic here for everyone," she said. "Don't worry. Just get some more sleep. Next time we wake up, we'll be ready to go home."

It took a while for Hal to accept her logic, and even then he had doubts. The ghosts had seemed so *frantic*.

He sighed and collapsed on the pillow again. Staring up at the slab of roof above, he longed to see the sky again. Was it still dark outside? How long had they all been asleep anyway? It was impossible to keep track of time so deep in the mines . . .

* * *

He woke to pandemonium. A huge shaggy foot flailed nearby, and Abigail buzzed past. He realized he was in his dragon form, lying on his stomach and unable to stand because of the low ceiling. He thrashed his wings and brought a yell of annoyance from someone nearby.

Dewey, in centaur form, was running around, his hoofs clip-clopping noisily. Emily slithered this way and that, her black snake body making a strange rasping sound on the smooth floor. An intensely colorful phoenix, six feet tall, stood quite still amid the confusion, looking around with distaste. Next to him, yelling for everybody else to stand still, was Molly in her full gorgon form, a dark green reptilian serpent with human arms and shoulders, rather like Emily only much bigger and with a head of writhing snakes that had dislodged her hat. Her veil remained intact.

As Hal wriggled across the chamber, a long black lizard came tearing around the core. It was ten feet long from snout to rump, and its tail was at least that again, incredibly long and thin. Fenton's eyes glowed red, and he looked irritated.

Robbie was lying on his back. As an ogre, he was way too big to stand up. He flailed like a two-year-old, thumping the floor with his hands and feet as though in the middle of a tantrum. To his side, Thomas the manticore was jabbing at him with his claws, his horrible segmented scorpion tail and stinger held high. He was growling and snarling.

76

Lauren was cowering behind a column, her white feathery wings sticking out on both sides. A headless girl ran past—a partially invisible Darcy.

Hal felt a strange urge to tear into something. One of these creatures.

He knew it was wrong, that they were all his friends, but the urge was powerful. He wanted to roast someone alive. One of the snake creatures, and perhaps that black lizard, and the phoenix . . . but even as these thoughts passed through his mind, he knew he wasn't thinking straight and that he needed to get a grip or else someone might get killed. They *all* needed to get a grip.

Molly was still yelling, her head of tiny snakes hissing angrily. "Shut UP! All of you! Stand *still!*"

Gradually her voice penetrated the chaos. Still, the giant black lizard seemed ready to pounce on Hal. Fenton opened his mouth and allowed drool to spatter on the floor. Then he lowered his head and breathed on the drool, and it quickly solidified, turning into a gluey substance. It was a warning. If Fenton spat on Hal, it could severely impact his mobility, blind him, or stick his jaws together.

Hal let out a blast of fire, and the searing flames caused Fenton to retreat.

"QUIET!" Molly screamed.

This time everybody fell silent. In that moment, all thoughts of attack fled Hal's mind. Why had he shifted in the first place? Why had any of them?

He suddenly noticed Jolie. She was still sitting against the core wall right where she'd been all along, cowering under her blanket. Now, in the silence, she lowered the blanket and peered around, her eyes wide . . . and deep brown . . . and beautiful. Her complexion was pristine, her teeth perfectly even and white, the dimples in her cheeks adorable, her hair full and lustrous and shiny.

Molly was busy saying something, but Hal paid no heed. He couldn't take his eyes off Jolie. Was this the same person they'd brought along? How could someone so lovely be so vindictive and mean?

He had to consider the possibility that this person, this gorgeous creature cowering behind a blanket, was the *true* Jolie, lovely and innocent, and the hideous creature that had taken her place was some kind of demonic possession. Now it had left her alone, and the sweet young woman was back. Hal nodded, realizing now that he'd been seeing everything the wrong way around. They *all* had. There was no way—

"Hal!" Molly yelled. She was snapping her fingers in front of his face. "Wake up! You too, Fenton. Focus on me, not Jolie."

Hal blinked and shook his head. He went to say something and realized he was still in dragon form.

"Listen to me, all of you," Molly urged. "We all changed in our sleep, probably out of instinct because Hal—or maybe Robbie, or someone else—inadvertently changed and became a threat to the rest of us. Do you see? We all have our magic back, and it's making us crazy. We're overdosing on it. We need to leave this place. But before you shift back—*please check that you're attired.*"

Hal groaned. Not again! His shirt and pants lay in tatters on the floor along with several other garments. If he ever got magical smart clothes back, he would never take them for granted again!

He cast a look around. Fenton, Robbie, Dewey, and Blair were in the same pickle, currently in their monstrous forms with no clothes to revert back in. Lauren, Emily and Molly had managed to shift without completely shredding their long dresses, though Lauren's wings had ripped the fabric apart at the back. Darcy was running around with her pants and sweater on but with an invisible head, arms and legs—a very strange effect indeed. Abigail was missing, her clothes in a heap on the floor. She must have shrunk down small and buzzed away.

It seemed that Molly was dealing with the situation, though. Already back in her human form, her drab robe looking more raggedy than usual, she bent to pick up her hat before rummaging through bags trying to identify which belonged to whom and pulling out whatever was available for those who needed replacement clothes. She threw a pair of long pants at Robbie the ogre, who stared at them dumbly from his horizontal position across the floor. Then she went to offer some clothes to Dewey the centaur and Thomas the manticore. Fenton sniffed at his own clothes with suspicion, his long black snout twitching.

Finally, Molly delved into Hal's bag. "Last pair," she told him sternly. "Make them last. We *really* need to sort out this clothing problem." She stalked off toward Blair, who glared at her with beady, unblinking eyes.

Emily, suddenly bursting with energy, started ushering the other girls from the chamber. "Let's leave the boys to get dressed. Come on, girls—race you to the entrance! Where's Abi? I've got her clothes."

"She buzzed off ahead of us," Lauren said, hurrying out. As she ran, with feathers fluttering, she switched to her human form and grasped the front of her dress, which was ripped apart at the back and hanging off her shoulders.

Darcy became opaque for a second, revealing her rarely seen woody dryad features with her head of rough bark. Then she disappeared around the corner.

When Molly and all the girls were gone, Blair and the boys hurried off to discreet corners within the chamber and reverted to their human forms. For a minute or two, there was no sound at all as they dressed in whatever clothes they had left. Then, one by one, they rejoined by the chamber's exit.

"I'm so hungry," Robbie complained.

For once, Hal had to agree. He was hungry *and* thirsty.

"Well, let's get out of here," Blair said, already exiting.

Gripping their bags, the five boys gave the Chamber of Ghosts one last look and headed out. Hal caught a glimpse of something as he turned away, but then it was gone. He lingered, wondering if the ghostly figures would reappear if he was alone. When nothing happened, he sighed and left.

The group reunited in the great mining chamber. It had to be morning because work had resumed, and the goblins looked mildly surprised to see them. "Thought you'd gone," one said gruffly.

"We spent the night," Molly explained.

"You spent the night *and* day," the goblin retorted.

Molly grabbed the goblin's arm. "What? It's not morning anymore? You're saying it's the next evening already?"

"Yeah, and you're in trouble. Someone busted the gate apart, and it ain't no big mystery who did it." The goblin looked around at them all, then stomped off.

Molly turned to Hal and Robbie. "Any idea what he's talking about?"

Robbie reddened, and Hal stared at the floor. "We, uh . . . we had to get out somehow to find that goat. They locked us in."

"And you couldn't just *open* the gate?" Blair said incredulously. "You had to *break* it open?" He slapped his head and walked away. "Kids."

Molly rolled her eyes. "All right, children, let's get out of here before we're locked in for another night."

They headed out of the mining room and up the tunnel.

"What I wouldn't give to dangle my feet in the pool," Abigail said wistfully when they reached the hot spring. Hal hung back with her. A goblin sat there on the bench, his eyes closed and his boots standing neatly by his side. The hot water was bubbling and steaming around his bare feet. "Think they'd miss us if we sat for a minute?" she mused.

"Clear out," the goblin grumbled without opening his eyes.

Hal tugged on her elbow. "Honestly, I'd rather just get out of here. I think we've caused enough trouble as it is."

"*You* have," Abigail said, giving him a shove. "You're a troublemaker."

"Children!" Molly yelled down the tunnel from the top end. "Keep up!"

But before they could take a step, a rumbling started under their feet, and the ground began to shake. Hal, Abigail, and the goblin looked at one another in horror as dust began to trickle down on them.

"Earthquake!" someone screamed.

Chapter Nine
Earthquake

The goblin leapt out of the hot pool as the ground shuddered, the walls cracked, and a deep rumbling filled the air. A sudden lurch threw Abigail onto Hal, and together they fell down. They were suddenly spattered with hot droplets and steamy spray as the heated spring water slopped from side to side, hissing and spitting as it spilled out onto the cold tunnel floor.

Abigail tried to get up, but another lurch threw her back down again. This quake was much bigger than the previous one, much more violent. The goblin yelled something as he skidded on the smooth, wet floor. He reached for Hal, but a third lurch threw all three of them into the air. They slammed back down on the rock and lay there gasping as the walls shuddered around them. Cracks appeared in the ceiling and dust trickled down.

The goblin got onto his hands and knees. "Run!" he yelled, though his voice seemed eerily faraway amid the deafening noise of the quake. Running was not an option. Instead, they were tossed from side to side as the ground rose and fell time and time again. Dust filled the tunnel, slabs of rock collapsed, wooden struts splintered, and nothing made sense anymore.

Hal lost Abigail's hand in the chaos, and he was falling for what seemed like several long seconds. He landed awkwardly, twisted his ankle, slammed into a wall, and lay there dazed until he realized that someone had fallen alongside him. He reached out, groping in darkness, coughing violently with all the dust.

The earthquake ended gradually, with each rumble and shake a little less jarring than the last. The noise fell away, and eventually he heard the choking of the person next to him. It was the goblin, which both relieved and panicked him. If Abigail was not down here, where was she? Still up top? Or . . .

He shouted for her. She replied from far above. Hal squinted, seeing nothing but darkness.

"Careful," the goblin spluttered from a few feet away. "We're on the edge of something here."

Hal felt around and was shocked to find that the ground ended next to his right knee where he knelt. He pressed himself against the wall to his left. He was on a ledge of some kind, and he had no idea how deep the abyss was. He groped for a loose rock and tossed it over the edge, listening for the noise it would make as it bounced off the walls and hit bottom.

To his surprise, he heard a splash. Listening hard, he realized there was a dull roar not too far below, the sound of a waterfall or similar. A rushing torrent. Should he be worried?

He sniffed the air. It was hot and moist. He'd smelled this before— at the Labyrinth of Fire when he and Abigail had come across a pit of boiling water. Was this another such pit? If so, it could be deadly.

On impulse, he breathed fire. It came easily to him when he really needed it, an instinctive reaction in dire circumstances. The flames licked out of his mouth, and during the second that the place was lit up, he saw the goblin reeling back in fright, saw how precarious their positions were on their ledge—and how close the raging torrent of boiling, churning water was just fifteen feet below. He also saw that the walls around him were five or six feet apart. The abyss was narrow, nothing more than a crack, and his ledge was even narrower. He couldn't transform and fly out—not enough room for that. He couldn't climb the smooth wall out of this place. He and the goblin would just have to wait for help to arrive.

He lit up the place with another blast of fire, aiming upward. It wasn't too far to safety, maybe twelve feet or so. He sighed with relief, and he saw the goblin nod with approval, too. "On my shoulders," the pig-faced worker shouted above the rushing water. "Climb up."

Hal was in no position to argue. He clambered up onto the goblin's shoulders, terrified of falling sideways over the edge. He did *not* want to be boiled alive. He reached up, groping for a handhold. It was a stretch, but he found a good solid edge to grab. There was no way he was going to be able to pull himself up though. His feet scrabbled for something to stand on, but there was nothing. Beginning to panic, he was certain he would fall backward and plummet to his death . . .

He hung there a moment, and somehow his feet found the goblin's shoulders again, easing the weight on his fingers. "I can't do it!" he shouted.

The goblin gripped his feet and shoved him upward. "You have to."

With the additional upward boost, Hal was able to get his elbows under him and squirm onto his belly. As he rolled over and sat up, he bumped his head on something hard. All around he felt huge slabs of rock as if the walls and ceiling of the tunnel had collapsed inward.

He let out another burst of flame and knew immediately that his assessment was correct. Still, it was better than being stuck on the ledge below, on the side of an abyss. He had to get the goblin out of there somehow.

He leaned over the edge. "Do you have any rope?" he yelled.

"What, *on* me?" came the sneering retort.

Hal thought for a minute. "Well, you'll have to stay there until I can get some help. You're too heavy, and there's no room to change into a dragon here."

There was a long silence.

"Stay right there," Hal called, and began looking around his dark prison. There were no orange glowing walls in this part of the tunnel, so he had to belch fire and light the place up to look for a way out. If there *had* been orange glowing walls here, they might have cracked open and caused an even bigger disaster.

"Boy!" the goblin shouted.

"I'm looking!"

"No, listen—shine yer light down here!"

Hal twisted around and crawled back to the abyss. He carefully released a flickering sheet of flame—and gasped. The boiling, churning water was rising. It was almost at the ledge. Soon it would be creeping around the goblin's bare feet.

The goblin flattened himself against the wall. Not that it would help him much when the water reached the ledge and overflowed onto it . . .

Hal frantically turned and lit the place up again. He *had* to find a way out. He considered transforming. His dragon form might be strong enough to push a way out of this rock.

Only there was no room to change.

Maybe a partial transformation, then? Robbie seemed to manage them okay. Maybe Hal could grow a tail and dangle it down to the goblin. He could breathe fire while in human form, so why not grow a tail? But *only* a tail. There was no room for a full transformation.

Thinking of the goblin standing on the ledge with boiling water spilling over his toes, he knew he had to try. He steeled himself and concentrated—

—and screamed in agony as the pressing walls threatened to crush his huge, fully formed reptilian bulk. He felt his wings crack in several places and pain all over, and then he reverted back to his human form with a long, shuddering breath. Dust and small rocks tumbled down on him, and he covered his head, but more rocks began to fall behind him, bigger ones that cracked apart and made the ground bounce beneath his battered body.

The small rockfall lasted half a minute before subsiding. Shivering, Hal slowly crawled around until he found the abyss with his fingertips. He dragged himself to its edge, fearful of the rushing, gurgling water below. Its sound had changed. Now it was lighter, somehow muffled.

He lit up, and his flames danced across a pit stuffed with massive rocks. There was no sign of the goblin, nor the boiling water. The abyss was blocked.

"A-are you down there?" Hal called. "Please be down there!"

There was no answer.

Hal began to moan, tears welling up. He'd killed the goblin. He'd caused the roof fall and crushed the poor worker under tons of rock.

Whatever fighting spirit he'd had seemed to flee him in that moment, and he lay there sobbing and shaking, his arms dangling over the edge. His fingertips could actually reach one of the boulders that blocked the abyss, and he stroked it as if it were the shoulder of the poor dead goblin. "I'm sorry, I'm sorry," he said over and over.

Time stood still. He wasn't sure if he'd blacked out or just lost his mind for a while, but he suddenly realized his face was steaming hot and he was sweating profusely. He snatched back his hand and tried to focus.

The water was still rising, the air thick and humid.

"No way," he mumbled, a new wave of fear overcoming him. But it was. He could hear it trickling up around the rock. The rushing sound was reduced, but it was definitely coming, up and up, rising from deep within the earth's mantle. The earthquake had opened the floodgates. The entire tunnel would be flooded, and Hal along with it.

He didn't know what was worse: drowning or boiling. He corrected himself. The latter was far worse.

Trying not to panic, he spun around, lighting up with fire in a feverish attempt to find a way out. There was absolutely nothing except a small round hole no bigger than his head. He crawled over and peered through. Despite a cool draft and faint pools of light, he saw an impenetrable wall of rubble.

To his surprise, a buzzing thing came through the tiniest of gaps toward him. He stared at it, hardly able to believe his eyes. "Abi?"

She rushed to him. "Hal!" she shouted, her tiny voice clear in the silence of the tunnel even though the hot water continued to gurgle up the abyss behind him. What on earth was she wearing? It looked like a dirty rag pinned around her like a towel. Then he realized his own predicament. His very last set of clothes had been ripped apart and now lay in tatters around him. Even though it was probably too dark for Abigail to see anything, he pressed his face to the hole.

"I'm trapped!" he said urgently. "And there's boiling water coming up out of the ground behind me. I think it's going to flood the tunnel and—" He broke off, unable to voice the rest.

Her eyes were wide. "The others are right behind me. They're pulling the rocks out of the way. They'll be through in a minute. I'll tell them to hurry."

Now that she mentioned it, Hal could hear the soft grunts of workers on the far side of the rubble. Abigail disappeared again, and Hal called after her. "Bring me some pants!"

He was left alone to listen to the gurgling water. Maybe it would stop rising. Or, if not, maybe it would have time enough to cool so as not to boil him alive. And if the cooling water continued to rise around him, maybe his friends would drag him out of the rubble before he drowned.

The water hissed as it rose out of the abyss and started pooling not far from his feet. He swung around, lighting up for a second. His flames picked out the vicious, hungry torrent as it bubbled and swirled. It started to run away downhill, and Hal suddenly realized he was safe. The sloping tunnel was endlessly long, and the water would pour downhill *away* from him. He breathed a sigh of relief.

Then yelped as scalding hot water trickled up over his bare toes.

Why was it still rising?

Because the tunnel below was completely blocked. Sure, there had to be cracks for the water to leak through, but it was rising faster than it was draining away. Hal pulled his bare feet clear and, lighting up with fire once again, watched with horror as the water spread across the width of the tunnel and began its rapid, steaming approach up the slope toward him.

"Hurry!" Hal yelled, again pressing his face to the hole.

Abigail reappeared. "They're coming through now. Hold on, okay?"

Light appeared behind her as a boulder suddenly shifted. It revealed that the wall of rubble was at least ten feet thick. Hal gasped. It would take forever for his rescuers to get through that.

The boulders and slabs of rock were removed painfully slowly. Blinding lantern light framed a number of stout goblins working fast and hard, grunting and swearing as they fought with the heavy debris. All this was visible to Hal through a slowly widening gap.

Abigail, still buzzing around in her tiny faerie form, dragged a pair of pants through. She was red-faced and panting with the effort. "Here. These are Fenton's. Robbie had none left." She buzzed away and returned moments later with a shirt.

Hal hurriedly twisted around in his cramped prison and got dressed.

In doing so, one of his bare feet touched the rising water again, and he jerked his knees up with a shout. There was no doubt in his mind now—the water was boiling. Whether it was enough to kill him hardly mattered now. It would hurt no matter what. He was suddenly very, very glad the poor goblin in the abyss had died from a deluge of rocks before the rising water had reached him.

As he watched the goblins toil and saw the slow progress they made, a strange feeling came over him. He knew he was going to die. The water would reach him well before he was able to escape this prison.

Abigail seemed to sense his thoughts. "We'll get you out," she said shakily. But she zipped away and started screaming at the goblins to hurry.

Hal repositioned himself sideways so he had more room before the creeping death reached him. He swore it was alive, hissing and spitting at him, hungry for his life. He didn't want to look at it but could feel the heat coming off it. He was sweating profusely. He felt sure he'd sweat to death before the water got to him.

He thought frantically. Maybe there was a chance for him. Which of his friends could help in this situation? As an ogre, Robbie could easily pull these rocks aside—except that an ogre couldn't fit in the tunnel. A partial ogre, then. But he was probably a partial ogre already, helping with the rescue effort, doing the best he could in the confined space.

Nobody else?

Hal sighed with resignation. A quick death. That was all he could hope for now. But who could reach him to deal a fatal blow? Maybe Thomas with his venom-tipped tail . . . or maybe Emily could reach in with her long snake tail and strangle him . . .

Dozens of ideas raced through his head, each as crazy as the next, but the simple fact was that there was no time for anyone to reach him.

Except . . .

A huge slab of rock suddenly cracked and fell, and a crawlspace opened up. But still Hal was trapped. He was unable to squeeze through his tiny window to *get* to the crawlspace. Time had run out. "Stop!" he yelled.

Robbie peered into the gap, holding up a lantern. As Hal had suspected, he was half an ogre, his upper body shaggy and muscular. If Hal had been able to manage a partial dragon transformation, would it have helped? He doubted it. "We'll be right there," Robbie said, panting.

"There's no time," Hal said shakily. He could feel his back beginning to blister from the steamy, bubbling water that kept splashing over him. "I need . . . I need someone to kill me. I don't want to die slowly like this."

Robbie's face was a mere silhouette as he moved the lantern sideways and spoke to someone. Then, to Hal's surprise, Abigail ducked into the tunnel. She was back to full human size and dressed, her wings retracted. "Hold on, Hal, we're coming," she said breathlessly. On hands and knees, she crawled in so that her face was inches from his. Behind her, Robbie and the goblins resumed their efforts. "Don't start talking about dying."

"You shouldn't be in here," Hal told her, surprisingly calm considering how drenched in sweat he was. He was beginning to feel dizzy.

The lantern light was dazzling after so much darkness. Hal and Abigail stared at each other, inches apart. Hal kept his face pressed to the hole, not wanting Abigail to be too alarmed at the sight of the steaming water. On the other hand, he needed her to leave. Now.

"I have an idea," he said. "Tell Molly to turn me to stone."

"What?"

"Do you hear that, Molly?" he yelled. "I need you to turn me to stone. Otherwise I'll be boiled to death. Or I'll drown." He spoke quickly now, suddenly filled with hope, his voice raised so everybody could hear. "Molly can turn me to stone, and you can all dig me out when the water's gone away or cooled down, and then . . . Blair can wake me up later."

Abigail continued to stare at him, her mouth working soundlessly.

"You have to go now," Hal told her quietly. "Please, hurry."

"Come on out of there, Abigail," Molly said, appearing behind her.

She nodded, her eyes filling with tears, but still she didn't move.

Hal jerked as the steaming water began to scald his elbow. He writhed in pain, no longer able to escape it. "Go!" he urged. "Hurry!"

She let out a sob and, leaving the lantern where it was, backed out of the hole. Immediately Molly appeared in her place, leaning in.

Hal bucked and twisted and began to cry out.

"Look at me, Hal," Molly said sternly. "Hal—*look at me.*"

He was so racked with stinging agony that he almost didn't hear her. But through his pain, he glanced her way and saw her unveiled face illuminated by the lantern: her thin cheekbones and pale complexion, her thin nose . . .

And her eyes. They blazed with a terrifying fury, a pair of bright yellow orbs with a deathly gaze that drilled into his brain. In half a second, everything seemed to freeze, and the excruciating pain faded away. Rather than fearing Molly's stoning, he was grateful for it—even though he might never wake up.

The last thing he saw as he painlessly turned to stone was the glow fading from Molly's eyes. Finally, now that her magic had worked its curse on him, she was able to look at him briefly through her own human eyes.

They were filled with sadness.

Chapter Ten
A World of Darkness

Hal slowly became aware that he was drifting in darkness. He tried to look around but seemed unable to make his body work. Was he paralyzed? He had no feeling in his fingers or toes, no pressure on his limbs, no pain anywhere on his body, not even a hint whether he was hot or cold.

Panic swept over him, but even that was a strangely peripheral experience. In a situation like this, his heart should be pounding in his chest, his breath coming in ragged gasps, sweat pouring down his face. Instead he was in a dreamlike state, floating in a vast nothingness. His mind screamed with terror and revulsion at the suffocating blackness, and he fought to regain control of his paralyzed body, to wake it up and gather some sensory input from his surroundings. He wanted to touch a hard surface, smell the air, hear echoes of dripping water, feel warmth or even icy chills on his skin—it didn't matter, just *something.*

"Help!" he yelled, only his voice came not from his lips but from somewhere else, nothing more than a distant murmur.

What *was* this?

He took a deep breath—or at least imagined doing so—and tried to calm his racing, tumbling thoughts. *Think.* What was the last thing he remembered? It came to him easily. He'd been trapped under rocks as boiling water gurgled up from below, steam pushing ahead of a rising river. As it began to scald his back, Molly had pushed her veil aside and turned him to stone.

But where was he now? Was he dead? Or merely in some kind of suspended animation? Would it stay like this until Blair performed his rebirth and woke him? How long would *that* take? For that matter, how long had he been here already?

"Quit asking stupid questions," he told himself. He was sure he'd spoken the words aloud but again heard himself whispering in the distance. It gave him the eerie feeling that his mind had left his body.

With a jolt, he realized that was exactly what had happened. His body—a statue of stone—was by now submerged in boiling water beneath a rockfall deep within the mines. His consciousness was elsewhere.

"All right, then," he said.

He floated in silence. Panicking would do him no good. If his physical body was in pain, his mind was detached from it. He had no senses to rely on, and it occurred to him that this smothering blackness might not even be a blackness in the physical sense. If none of his other senses worked, it stood to reason he was blind, too. All he had was his active imagination.

The more he waited, the more bored and impatient he became. Now what? Is this what Fenton had been through? Floating around in absolute silence for a few hours? Where were the reported bright lights? The sparkling orange glows?

At that moment, Hal felt a sensation in his incorporeal fingertips. "What's that?" Again his voice was distant . . . but perhaps not as distant as before.

He focused on the tickling sensation and imagined it to be smoke curling around his hand and creeping up his legs. He forced his eyes open.

Shock almost overwhelmed him. *He'd opened his eyes!* And now he could see that this place of darkness wasn't quite as featureless as he'd thought—strange, pulsing black cloud all around, dabs of light here and there . . . He gasped and spun, arching his back and kicking his legs. As he thrashed, the billowing cloud whorled haphazardly, disturbed by his movement. Hazy sources of light flitted in and out.

He was drifting aimlessly, uncertain which way was up. As he spun head over heels, he felt sure blood would rush to his head when he was upside down. That, at least, should clue him in to his orientation. Only he found that it didn't seem to matter which way he faced. He was weightless, as if in space.

The smoky black substance was familiar. It was what formed the curious holes between worlds. And through the pulsing cloud he started to see faint orange glows just as Fenton had reported. In one direction was a hazy white light, which stood out as something important. Hal headed for it. A bright white light in a world of darkness had to be worth checking into.

Simply moving through the murk took all his concentration. He thrashed and writhed, uncertain how fast he was traveling or even if he was moving at all. The great pulsing cloud relented as he pushed through, but not without a moment of gentle stubbornness, teasing and nudging him as he went.

The white light grew more intense. Sometimes it dimmed and brightened again beyond the constantly billowing cloud. Meanwhile, the numerous orange glows scattered all around seemed to be multiplying—little balls of fire drifting in random directions, hundreds of them, flickering as they crisscrossed the void.

Something passed in front of Hal. It startled him so much that he let out a cry and windmilled his arms in an attempt to stop. It was a figure, utterly black and roughly human shaped. It sped by, angling across in front of him, apparently intent on its own journey toward the light.

The light. What Miss Simone had referred to as 'synaptic firing in the visual cortex,' something people often experienced when they slipped into death for a few minutes and returned to tell the tale. Hal didn't believe it. This was far more than some random sparks in his brain.

He saw more black figures. They darted across his path from left and right, above and below, all angling toward the light. The people—if that was what they were—had no real form. They were shadows in the darkness, apparently headed for the same place as he, with no interest in anything else. As the light brightened and grew ahead, more and more shadows appeared until there were dozens of them visible all at once.

Some of them moved the same way Hal did, with flailing arms and legs. Others simply drifted, standing motionless but moving all the same. One or two were looking around as they went.

A shadow appeared within arm's reach of Hal. He jerked in shock, but so did the shadow. They stared at one another. Even from a couple of feet away, Hal saw nothing but a featureless void where a face should be and an equally black, fuzzy, decidedly shapeless body. Despite that, the shadow person's movements were clear. It was looking him up and down. It reached out a tentative hand, and Hal stared in wonder as the appendage came close to his face. It looked solid but leaked black smoke. He flinched when the eerie hand touched his cheek and cold fingers tingled on his skin.

The creature withdrew and drifted away. It vanished into the rolling cloud and reappeared amid other shadows, quickly getting lost in the group.

Hal wondered why he was the only one with any real substance. He held up his hands to check he was still there. He was. He looked perfectly normal from what he could see. Even his clothes were intact.

Could he transform? The idea of it struck him all of a sudden. It would be nice to know that he could protect himself in the event of danger. He focused . . . and, abruptly, his hands became familiar dark green reptilian paws with curved claws. He glanced over his shoulder and saw his scaly, armored hide. Satisfied, he reverted to human form.

Still, something bothered him. His transformation had felt different, somehow without substance, as if he had only *imagined* it happening. And his clothes were intact. He fingered them with confusion. They were smart clothes, yet he'd been wearing Fenton's ordinary shirt and pants right before he'd turned to stone.

He was still pondering when the cloud cleared ahead, and the white light suddenly dazzled him. He slowed, blinking rapidly. Shadowy figures crowded together in front, shoulder to shoulder, now in sharp silhouette. Hal glanced backward, hoping to catch a glimpse of brightly illuminated faces behind him. No such luck. They were just as fuzzy and featureless as ever, the blinding light somehow failing to reflect off them. Hal felt as though he stuck out like a sore thumb among this crowd. He was surprised nobody was looking at him curiously.

The light was tall and thin. It wasn't just a light, though—it was a person, or a creature of some kind, either several times taller than everyone else or elevated on a pedestal of some sort, arms outstretched, towering over the army of shadows that crowded in from all sides.

Blinking against the glare, Hal tried to focus on the creature's face. He failed. Still, everyone was clamoring to reach it, and Hal felt the same compulsion. He wanted answers and somehow knew this *thing* could explain everything. Everyone else apparently had the same idea. Judging by the varying sizes of the shadows, adults and children alike were pressing in, trying to get closer.

Hal pushed forward, at first nervous about the intensity of the crowd but increasingly confident that he wasn't about to get crushed. The jostling was light and insubstantial. He knew he could simply turn and push his way out if he wanted. For that matter, he saw no reason not to sink downward and escape through the non-existent floor—or shoot straight upward. There was actually no reason for this crowd to be jostling shoulder to shoulder other than an instinctive urge to apply real-world laws of physics to this bizarre, weightless void.

Despite the fact that the crowd completely surrounded the creature, Hal made slow but steady progress toward the light. Ahead, dozens of silhouettes promptly vanished, allowing more to shuffle forward. It didn't seem possible. Where were they all going? And where were they coming from? Hundreds of shadows circled the dazzling center while many more floated in from all directions.

Hal kept moving, herded forward with the rest. He felt no fear but was almost overwhelmingly curious, burning with questions. What *was* that light? Who were all these people? Why were they, unlike Hal, utterly black and featureless, nothing but shadows? What made Hal different?

He began to make out a face within the glare of the light. It was a woman, impossibly tall and slender, her face long, her eyes unusually large and dark. She tilted her head and smiled as dozens of shadow people surged toward her in a frantic rush—and vanished.

The urge to hurry forward was overpowering. Like everyone else, he was eager to throw himself into what appeared to be an illuminated pit beneath the creature's feet. She was floating high above, bathed in a shaft of white light. The shadow people directly in front of Hal pitched forward into the pit without a sound, and through the glare he saw others rushing toward him from the opposite side, toppling in with obvious excitement. Then it was Hal's turn, and he pitched forward in a nosedive . . .

Abruptly, he was lifted upward by an unseen force. His faceless neighbors continued their plummet and vanished without him, and then it was time for the next row, and the row after that, dozens of figures toppling into the pit without pause—all except Hal, who found himself rising above the crowd, held in the gentle but firm grip of a pressure around his waist. He felt enraged. Why was *he* being excluded? He wriggled furiously, trying to break free.

An extraordinarily long face stared back at him. The woman's eyes were like mirrors, and Hal saw himself reflected in each. Seeing himself floating there startled him, and suddenly his desire to dive into the pit of light fled him. Now he was concerned by his recklessness and scared of this ghostly woman. Mere yards below his feet, the mindless crowd continued to surge forward and vanish.

The woman stared at him, saying nothing. Then she gave a shake of her head and flung Hal away. He hurtled backward over the teeming masses. As he went, he saw something that shook him to the core. Seconds later the light was a mere pinprick in the distance, and he was once again alone in the void.

Shaking and confused, he hung there in silence thinking about what he'd glimpsed. In some ways it made perfect sense, but at the same time it made no sense at all. He felt as though he were on the threshold of discovering something if only he could untangle his jumbled thoughts and calm his frazzled nerves.

The orange glows were everywhere, all around, drifting lazily through the pulsing black cloud. He hadn't paid much attention before. If he had, he would have noticed that there were far more orange glows around the ghostly woman and the streaming shadow figures. And more were popping into existence at the same rate those people were throwing themselves into the pit of light.

What did it all mean?

"Dead people," Hal said aloud. He liked the sound of his own voice. It was clear and sharp in the darkness. No echoes or muted whispering, just a solid, comforting voice as though he were sitting in his bedroom talking to himself. "Turning into specks of orange light and buzzing around like fireflies."

Even though he knew that was what he'd seen—what had been happening all along and was happening even now—he still didn't know what it all *meant*. Dead people turning into . . . what? Some kind of magical energy? Perhaps the same energy that powered the geo-rocks? *Sparkle*, as Lucas put it?

He floated there and wrestled with the notion of people dying in the real world and coming here to this place of darkness, heading toward the light, eager for some kind of explanation to their predicament . . . and pitching forward into the pit without a moment's thought to what danger might lie there. Hal hadn't considered the danger either. He'd just gone with it, curious at first, increasingly eager, feeding off the hunger of the mob around him.

But what if there was no danger at all? What if it was all good, what was *supposed* to happen? If so, why had he been excluded?

"Because I'm not dead," he realized. "She turned me away. I'm not dead, just suspended."

Which meant all he could do was wait.

* * *

He had no idea how much time passed while he floated there. He got to wondering what Fenton had seen while suspended by the gorgon's stony glare. Presumably he'd also been turned away by the creature of light.

That is, if Fenton had approached the light in the first place. He said he'd seen orange glows for just a second or two, sparkling everywhere, what Abigail had jokingly referred to as faerie dust. Surely he'd seen the white light, too, even just a glimpse before waking, a fleeting memory that had faded like a dream.

"Doesn't make sense," Hal muttered. "He was out of it for hours. He had plenty of time to see what I've seen. How come he only saw a bunch of—"

He froze, suddenly aware that he was now pacing back and forth instead of floating in space. Under his feet was a ground of sorts. It was soft and spongy, invisible in the gloom. He dropped to his knees and gingerly felt around, his hands disappearing into the pulsing black smoke. His fingers touched . . . *something*. That was the only word for it. It wasn't rock, grass, wood flooring, sand, nor anything else he could think of.

Still, it felt good to stand on something reasonably solid. How far did it stretch? He edged around, probing with his toes and finding that his new ground wasn't very large at all. It was like he'd found a platform hidden in the void. What were the chances of that?

Still, it was good to lift off and perform a short, relatively normal jump. Perhaps if he stumbled off the edge, he'd go tumbling into the void again. But now that he was back on terra firma, he wasn't sure his nerves could take the fright of wandering off the edge of a cliff. He vowed to watch his step.

Having ground under his feet boosted his sense of reality and gave him something to call 'Up.' He peered high into the thick, black rolling cloud and watched the flecks of orange as they moved aimlessly this way and that. He wished he could see one up close. Maybe one would float by. He half expected them to be shaped like people, the souls of dead folk, but was fairly sure they were simple glowing orbs, mindless and inanimate, part of the scenery.

But *why?*

Answers eluded him, though his mind buzzed with possibilities. He couldn't help thinking there was a connection to the faeries as Abigail had suggested, some link to the strong dawn magic the faeries reveled in.

And the Chamber of Ghosts. It, too, glowed orange. The combined energy within those walls and the dozens of geo-rocks that had been mined over the years was staggering. There *had* to be a connection somewhere.

He shook his head, tired of thinking. It was easy to make wild guesses, but what he wanted were solid answers. He felt sure the woman, the creature of light, had all the answers he sought, but asking her struck him as a supremely bad idea. He'd just have to wait some more.

The hairs on the back of his neck stood on end. He tensed, knowing there was someone watching him. He swung around, searching the pulsing, billowing cloud. A shadowy human figure floated twenty or thirty feet away, motionless, looking down on him. It started moving toward him without effort, barely altering its posture, not even bothering to paddle its legs or arms as Hal had done earlier. This shadow had mastered the art of gliding by willpower alone.

"Have you worked it out yet?" the shadow asked softly.

Startled, Hal's mouth dropped open. The voice had been clear, carrying easily across the void. The shadow was male and probably not much older than Hal.

"W-worked what out?" Hal stammered.

"Everything."

The shadow closed the gap and hovered a couple of feet above Hal's smoke-smothered platform.

Hal rubbed his eyes and squinted. The shadow was still there. "I don't know what you mean. Who are you? Where am I?"

"Huh." The shadow tilted its head again. "Funny. You've been here a while, long enough to resist the light. Were you turned away? Are you in a coma?"

"What?"

After a pause, the shadow edged closer still. It was now within reach if Hal were to extend his hand and touch the thing's featureless face. What would he find if he did? Was it pure smoke? Or something more substantial?

"My name's Chase," it said. "What's yours?"

"Uh—Hal."

The shadow named Chase nodded. "So you're a boy, then. I wasn't sure."

"What?"

"I can see you're short, but that's about all," Chase said. "Other than your height, all I see is a black smudge. I like to fill in the details as fast as possible, so tell me—are you thin? Fat? Average?"

Hal blinked rapidly. "Average."

"What color hair?"

"I don't—uh—light brown. Sand-colored. Does it matter?"

Chase nodded. "Okay, that'll do for now. I'm kind of thin with really curly dark brown hair. I wear glasses."

"Why are you—?" Hal started, growing irritated with the seemingly pointless conversation. But he broke off as something strange happened. Although Chase never moved a muscle, it was as though he stepped forward out of the shadows into whatever gloomy light there was, suddenly becoming clear to see. There he was, thin and gangly, with dark brown curly hair and glasses. "Oh."

"Now you see me," Chase said, and grinned. "Or your own perception of me at least. I've always wondered what people imagine me to look like based on a simple description. If you could take a photo right now and show it to me, I wonder how different I'd look compared to the real me."

Hal struggled for words. "What are you *talking* about?" he finally blurted.

"I see you found yourself something to stand on," Chase went on, gesturing toward Hal's feet. "I guess you got tired of floating and conjured up a floor. I've done that millions of times. So tell me, were you rejected? By the Gatekeeper?"

"The 'Gatekeeper'? If you mean the woman hovering over a pit of light, then yeah, she turned me away."

Chase frowned at this. "You see a *woman*? Funny. I see a great big demon with horns and a pitchfork. But everyone's different."

Hal threw up his hands. "Stop! Just slow down a minute. Gatekeeper? What do you mean by that? What gates? What's she guarding?"

Chase sank lower and spent a moment prodding around with his toes. He looked up and grinned. "There. I've created myself a floor as well. I reckon it's pretty much the same as yours."

Hal said nothing but put on his fiercest glare.

Laughing, Chase pushed his glasses up his nose and brushed at his shirt. His clothes, which Hal had barely noticed before, were gray and nondescript. "Okay, freshman, I'll fill you in as best I can."

Chapter Eleven
Chase

"Spill it," Hal growled. Even though Chase was taller, he seemed utterly unthreatening, even weak and feeble, a bit of a nerd. Like Robbie, only with glasses.

"I call the demon the Gatekeeper because he's guarding the way through that pit of light," Chase said. "It's where dead people go. They throw themselves in and are spat out the other end as balls of energy."

Hal mentally punched the air. He'd guessed correctly.

Chase waved a hand airily. "Of course, if you're not dead, you don't get to go through. And quite often there are people who *are* dead but don't *want* to go through, so they hold back and kind of run around the place."

"Run around the place?"

"Yeah, angry at everyone. Best steer clear of those types. That's why I waited before saying hello. Just making sure you weren't a haunt."

"A haunt?" Hal said, aware that he was beginning to sound like a parrot.

"Yeah. Those who want to return to the living. They're always trying to reach through. They just end up frightening people."

Hal blinked. "You're talking about ghosts."

Chase shrugged. "But like I said, I'm just guessing. I've seen evidence of everything I'm telling you, but the thing is, nothing in this place is real anyway. When you look at me, you're just seeing what your mind is telling you based on the description I gave you. Do you see this scar on my face?"

Looking closer, Hal searched for a scar. It turned out there was indeed one on Chase's right cheek—a small, curved line just below his eye. "Yeah, I see it."

"No, you don't," Chase said, "because I don't have a scar on my face."

Abruptly the scar vanished, leaving Hal to gape in amazement.

"I do have one on my neck, though." Chase pulled back the collar of his drab shirt to reveal the same small, curved scar on his throat. "And just to be clear, it's a really *long* scar reaching from my shoulder all the way up to my ear."

Hal's eyes widened as the scar lengthened before his eyes.

". . . And it's on the *back* of my neck, not the front," Chase teased, suddenly twisting all the way around and yanking his shirt collar down so Hal could see the knobs of his spine. The scar repositioned itself alongside.

Hal closed his eyes. "Okay, I get it. Quit messing with my head."

When Chase had finished chortling, he became serious and stared at Hal through his small round spectacles—if indeed Chase wore small round spectacles and not thick-rimmed square ones or something entirely different. "There's not much more to tell. It's pretty simple. If you're dead, you show up and head for the light. Next thing you know, you're floating around as a ball of energy. If you're dead but resist the urge to head for the light, you kind of hang around forever. If you're *not* dead—" He paused and narrowed his eyes. "You never did tell me what your deal is. Are you in a coma?"

"No, not exactly. Well, maybe. I don't know."

"What happened to you?" Chase persisted. "I've met quite a few who were laid up in a hospital after a car accident or some other trauma, deep in a coma, neither here nor there. I've even met a few who literally died for half a minute. Well, I didn't *meet* them exactly. Those people are gone almost as soon as they arrive. There was also one who hung out here for ages, and one day he must have slipped away in the hospital. Suddenly headed off to the Gatekeeper."

Hal held up his hands. "Wait. Hospitals? Car accidents? Are you from—" *My old world where I grew up? The one without dragons and faeries?* He paused, wondering how to phrase such a question.

"Place called Happy Valley Ridge in the south," Chase answered. "You?"

He *must* be from Hal's old world if he spoke of car accidents and hospitals, which surely meant he came from a time *before* the virus outbreak.

"How old are you?" Hal asked.

"Fourteen."

Hal's perception of the boy's age seemed about right. Still, something didn't add up. Time must have frozen or something. "And you've been here how long?"

Chase shrugged. "Hard to say. There's no night and day. Maybe a month?" He held up his hands and wiggled his fingers dramatically. "We have only our minds to keep us company in this world of darkness."

"Do you . . . remember the virus?"

There was a long silence. Chase frowned at him and nodded. "Yeah. I didn't see it, but it happened recently. A few weeks ago."

Hal gaped.

"When I first arrived here, the Gatekeeper just had a slow, steady stream of dead people to deal with. Then thousands showed up at once, and it's been like that ever since."

This news chilled Hal, but still it didn't add up. The virus had struck over a decade ago! "How long have you been here?" Hal asked again, his head spinning.

"I told you, I don't know. A month? Two?"

"But this doesn't make any sense! You *must* have been dead longer than that. And the virus happened thirteen years ago."

"I told you," Chase murmured, "I'm not dead."

Hal sighed. "No, that's right, you're suspended. So what happened to you?"

"What happened to *you*?"

The two stared at each other for a long while. Then Hal grimaced. "You wouldn't believe me if I told you. Let's skip that for now. I'm trying to wrap my head around how long you've been here. The thing is, the virus broke out right before I was born. Pretty much the whole world went down the drain. Most people died, some escaped underground, and there were survivors who were immune and became . . . well, crazy. So if you don't remember all that stuff, you must have come here at least thirteen years ago—*before* the virus."

Chase looked off into the swirling black cloud, lost in thought. An orange glow materialized out of the gloom behind him, not more than thirty feet away, and Hal wondered if he could grab it and get a better look.

"That's pretty much what I heard from others," Chase said eventually. "I know all about the virus. Heard it from a few of the dead."

This was hard for Hal to deal with. "You've spoken to *dead virus victims?*"

Now Chase looked down at his smoke-engulfed feet. "There's not much to do around here, so I talk to people. I try to avoid virus types now, though. It gets old hearing that story over and over. But there are others. Actually, my best friend is a haunt. She was murdered. Want to meet her?"

"Uh . . . yeah, I guess.

"Thought you might. Come on."

The orange orb was tantalizingly close. As Chase turned to leave, Hal reached out and grabbed his shoulder to stop him. He jerked back, horrified at the abnormal way his hand sank into the older boy's spongy flesh.

"Whoa," Chase protested. "One thing you learn around here, buddy, is not to touch. What's up?"

"Sorry. That—that orange thing. Have you ever touched one?"

Chase shrugged. "It's just sparkle."

Hal stared at him. There was that word again! "Sparkle?"

"Energy. Magic. Call it what you want. It's what happens to dead people when they go through the light. Dead people are recycled."

More and more questions plagued Hal. "Recycled? But . . . why?"

Again, Chase shrugged. "I can only tell you what I've figured out while I've been here. It's not like there's a book lying around with all the answers in it. What I *think* is happening," he added cautiously, "is that ordinary people die and are recycled as blobs of magic."

Hal nodded slowly, allowing that to sink in.

Chase frowned. "Wait—you believe me? You believe in magic?"

"Why did you call it sparkle?" Hal asked, diverting the question.

"Why not? It's as good a word as any."

"Yes, but why *sparkle*? It's just that someone else I know . . . Never mind."

He returned his attention to the orb, a fiery orange glow so bright that it almost hurt his eyes. It was starting to float away, beginning to fade into the black cloud, dimming as it went, becoming just another eerie smudge of orange.

Without thinking, Hal ran for it, launching off the platform and upward.

Reaching the orb was easy. He barely had to think about it. Any worries he'd had about no longer being able to float around in this world were gone in an instant as he soared through the billowing smoke after the glowing orange trail. In seconds he was upon the orb, coming up behind it with outstretched arms, his hands closing on either side.

Its aura was the size of a beach ball, but the orb itself was not much bigger than his clasped hands. As soon as his palms touched its surface, a massive jolt of energy crackled through him.

* * *

"Wake *up*," Chase called from far away.

Hal stirred. When he opened his eyes, he was surprised to see the boy inches from his face, peering down at him through his fragile glasses.

"And that, my friend, is what happens when you ignore my advice. Total brain-fry."

"Yeah," Hal mumbled. His throat felt dry, which of course made no sense since his entire physical being was purely imagination.

"Just stay away from them, all right?" Chase urged.

Hal nodded and started to get to his feet before realizing he was actually floating upside down in the void. Or maybe it was Chase that was upside down. It was impossible to tell.

Chase clicked his tongue. "What is it with newbies? They always want to touch one of those balls of light. And the same thing always happens. Brain-fry. I mean, what did you expect to happen?"

"I don't know," Hal admitted. "Didn't you try it when you first came here?"

"Well, anyway," Chase said quickly, "let's go see my ghost friend."

They hurtled through the void. Chase flew with ease while Hal flapped his arms and pedaled his legs. He was about to ask Chase to slow down when he had a spark of inspiration. Well, *duh*. He was, after all, a shapeshifter.

He transformed. As before, the shift felt different, somehow insubstantial. He flapped his great leathery wings and thrashed his tail, but he continued to trail behind Chase no matter what he did. Disgruntled, he let out a roar of disgust and blew a sheet of fire into the pulsing cloud.

Chase glanced back. "Am I going too fast? You don't need to make such an effort, you know. Just look ahead and find a point you want to aim for. Then go."

Puzzled, Hal picked up speed. Beating his wings hard and panting, he finally drew alongside Chase, who was simply standing there with his arms folded as he sped easily through the void. He looked like Aladdin standing on a magic carpet, only without the carpet.

Chase glanced at him again. "You're still trying too hard. Quit flapping your arms and kicking your legs. Just stand still. Relax."

Hal blew another sheet of fire. Chase appeared not to notice. "Can you even see that I'm a dragon right now?" Hal demanded.

"A *dragon*? Well, okay. Whatever floats your boat."

"So you can't see it?" Hal persisted. "You can't see my wings? You can't see when I breathe fire?"

"I see a short kid with sandy-colored hair just like you told me. We're not really here, Hal. Not physically anyway. We're just thoughts floating in a big fat nothingness. You can pretend to be whatever you want, but I'm still going to see you as whatever my mind tells me to see."

Hal nodded slowly. He'd already known his transformations had felt off. Now he knew why: because they weren't real transformations. And besides, when he'd spoken in dragon-tongue just now, Chase had understood him perfectly.

He switched back to his human form, staring at his hands and arms as they shrank down in size, lost their green, scaly complexion, and became soft and feeble. His clothes were intact, but again, that was simply because he imagined them to be. Because he *wanted* them to be. Nothing in this place was real.

"So how do you even know which way to go?" he asked, seeing nothing but the same black, pulsing cloud all around. The only point of interest in the scenery was the distant glow of the Gatekeeper.

"I don't really know," Chase admitted. "That's probably in my imagination as well. I imagine my ghost friend to live over there, so that's where I go. I think some stuff is just automatic. We think like we're still in the real world, and in the real world we all live in different places. There are no homes here, but people—dead or otherwise—seem to choose a place to hang out. Like your chunk of floor back there. That had become your home. After a while, you'll see more than just black clouds everywhere. You'll see floorboards under your feet, furniture, maybe shelves with books, walls and windows . . ." He paused. "There are limits, though. You can create scenery outside— forests, mountains, and so on—but it's hard to keep that imagery going. Everything goes dark and cloudy again eventually."

Hal shuddered. While he felt a certain attachment to that conjured platform, it was horrible to think that all he had in this featureless world was his imagination. "Where do *you* live?" he asked.

Chase jerked a thumb over his shoulder. "Back there. Not too far from where you ended up. I guess we were rejected and thrown in the same direction by the Gatekeeper. My place has walls, though. I built myself a cloud house." He grinned. "All in my head, obviously."

Hal wondered if Chase had actually grinned just then. He decided he had. The subtle facial twitch was simply a reflection of Chase's words and general mood. Even if Hal were blind, he would probably know when someone was smiling by the slight change in the sound of their voice. Or perhaps with Chase there was a stronger sensory input at work here—some kind of telepathy between floating minds that conveyed emotion as well as basic communication.

Or maybe Hal was imagining this entire place and everyone in it.

"Who *are* you?" he asked. "Who *were* you, I mean?"

Chase looked askance at him. "Nobody. Before I came here, I was living at a school. A private school for a small group of special kids. My dad owned the property—a great place in the valley, countryside for miles around. I was schooled there, too, but I had my own private tutor because all the other kids were much younger than me. I didn't get out a whole lot, so . . ." He trailed off and shrugged.

Hal nodded. "I know how that is. I lived on an island, cut off from the rest of the world. But I had friends my age, so it wasn't so bad."

Chase was silent for a strangely long time. Then, still moving through the void, he turned sideways and looked directly at Hal. "You mentioned being a dragon earlier. Why did you say that?"

"You wouldn't believe me," Hal said. He realized that he wasn't flailing so much now, yet still seemed to be keeping up with Chase.

"I'd believe you," Chase said seriously. He looked earnest. "Seriously. I believe in magic. Tell me the truth. *Are* you a dragon?"

It was a weird moment. How could a boy from an ordinary world seriously be asking if Hal was a dragon? "Yes," he said simply. "Not all the time, though."

"I realize that," Chase whispered, his eyes wide behind his glasses. "This place is for humans only. Otherwise we'd be overrun by squillions of dead animals. I imagine other creatures have their own endless black clouds to float around in." He nodded slowly. "You're a shapeshifter, aren't you?"

Hal was speechless.

Chase grinned. "Well, what are the chances of bumping into a shapeshifter? Don't look so shocked. I come from an ordinary world, but I know something about the other world, too. I've crossed over and seen a few things. I would have gone crazy at that school if there wasn't something to keep me occupied." He pointed ahead. "Look, there's my friend."

There was nothing to see except the endless rolling cloud. However, as they slowed, Hal spotted a fuzzy black shape hanging almost upside down, motionless. Chase approached, twisting himself around so that he was oriented the same way as he drew up alongside.

"Darlene," he called.

The shape jerked. Then it relaxed, and Hal heard a nervous laugh. "Hello, Chase. Who's your little friend?"

"This is Hal. He's like me: not quite dead. Short, sandy-colored hair."

"Nice to meet you, not-quite-dead Hal. Are you in a coma?"

"Sort of," Hal answered as he awkwardly turned himself upside down. Once he'd done so, his world instantly righted itself in his mind so that he no longer *felt* like he was upside down.

Chase gestured at Darlene. "Just so you know, Hal, she's tall, has really long, completely black hair, and is fifty-two years old."

"But picture me as *forty*-two," Darlene said.

Already Hal was beginning to visualize her. He could hardly believe his imagination so easily filled in the blanks. He assumed she was kind and motherly, not too thin or fat, and wearing—well, he wasn't sure what she was wearing, and as a result her body seemed faded out, heavily shadowed. What little he could see revealed a shapeless, dreary gown that trailed to her feet.

"What are you wearing?" he asked tentatively.

"A bright red dress," Darlene said. "I'd just come from a party when I died."

Hal saw it now—a pretty red dress that hung past her knees. He had no idea if it was the right kind of dress, but it would do.

106

"Darlene was brutally murdered," Chase said, sounding almost proud that he was friends with such a tragic figure. "A man stabbed her to death in an alley just outside the community hall. She left behind three daughters and a son, and a husband she's been trying to get in touch with ever since."

"I feel him sometimes," Darlene said softly, her hair beginning to swirl as though she were floating underwater. "He uses mediums to connect to this world, and sometimes I hear his voice. But I can never get my message through. I want to tell him I love him, but—" She screwed up her face and clenched her fists. "It's *hard* communicating with the living."

"Would you show us?" Chase asked gently. "If that's all right?"

She gave a bitter laugh. "Not much to show, dear. But yes, if you like. Come closer, not-quite-dead Hal. Step into my living room."

Hal moved in, glancing left and right to see if he was missing anything. There was nothing to see—no furniture, no walls, no floor or ceiling. He wondered if Chase saw anything. Presumably he'd visited here many times before, so he may have conjured a small house simply based on whatever description she had given.

Darlene wasted no time. She raised her arms and drew her audience in—yet didn't touch them. Hal felt a little awkward being air-embraced by a stranger like this, but she seemed nice enough, like a mother hugging her two children. As Hal and Chase were invited closer, a vibrant energy buzzed between them.

"Relax," Chase murmured to him. "This is just our minds merging. We'll see what Darlene sees when she goes in."

"Goes in?"

"Shh," Darlene said softly, and Hal fell silent.

A stillness crept over them. It had been silent in this dark world throughout Hal's stay, but this was a special kind of quiet where even the thoughts in his head were reduced to whispers. Even though his face was almost buried in Darlene's shoulder, a sort of air-hug, he quickly lost any sense of physical proximity. When he closed his eyes, he felt detached from reality—just like when he'd first arrived, only this time there was no panic or confusion. He felt more relaxed than ever before in his life.

"We're going in," Chase said, his voice strangely distant.

Hal opened his eyes—or at least imagined doing so. A scene was fading in from the blackness, brightening and becoming clearer. It was a building, a large hall with thick, horizontal wood siding, stout and weathered. Oil lamps hung outside the entrance. The moon shone above, but it was sliding fast across the night sky, causing heavy black shadows to stretch and move on the dusty ground. Even the stars were busy, traveling in formation. It was a fascinating sight, and Hal knew instantly they were seeing the land of the living in fast forward.

Something about the scene made him think of the village of Carter, or the larger town of Louis in the north. There were wheel ruts leading into a field where a cart stood on cropped grass. Everything was neat and pretty, quite unlike Hal's old virus-stricken world where things were overgrown and unkempt. Was Darlene from Miss Simone's world?

The moon made it all the way across to the silhouetted line of trees before halting. In the nearby field, three goats appeared as if by magic, munching on the grass. A flickering blur on the steps of the hall morphed into several people emerging through its double doors, laughing and waving as they headed off in different directions. They were garbed in clothes reminiscent of Carter, somehow old and quaint. Their noisy chatter seemed distorted and shallow.

People don't stand still all day long, Hal reasoned. *Nor do goats.* While time was accelerated, the living zipped about all over the place, moving too fast to see. Only buildings and the land itself remained stationary.

Hal wondered if he was looking into the past, about to witness Darlene's murder. But Chase, as if sensing what Hal was thinking, whispered that this was in fact the present—same place, and no doubt a similar party, but here and now.

"Time flies by in the land of the living," he explained. "Darlene waits until there's a party and slows things down for a while."

Hal watched the scene, fascinated. He realized he was seeing everything through Darlene's eyes as though he were hitching a ride in her head. While she stood there on the path looking up at the community hall, he might as well have been there himself.

Another couple left the brightly lit hall, pushing through the double doors and clinging to each other as they came down the steps. The woman was laughing hysterically, the man rolling his eyes and smiling as he supported her. But they stopped dead when they saw Hal—or Darlene—standing on the path before them. Their smiles faded instantly. The woman's eyes widened, the man's jaw dropped open. Hal knew they were seeing Darlene, but still he felt like they were staring right at him. He was, however, used to reactions like this when he was in dragon form. He stared back, curious about what they would do next.

The woman gasped and backed up, breaking free of her husband's supporting arm. He was so entranced by Darlene's presence that he barely moved an inch, staring in amazement and shock at what must be a ghostly apparition.

"What's your name?" Darlene asked gently. Her right hand rose into view, extending toward the man in a form of greeting.

The man found his voice. But he didn't reply to Darlene. Instead he turned his head sideways, his gaze never wavering, and whispered out of the side of his mouth to his cowering wife. "She's saying something."

"Let's just go," his wife wailed. She was behind him, clinging to his jacket, almost completely out of sight.

"But this is the Ghost of Westerley Hall," he told her, awestruck.

The scene flickered briefly, and abruptly the couple were gone. The moon slid onward and, suddenly, the sun began to rise. The sky brightened and daylight flooded the place, and a blur all around suggested that people were coming and going, tearing in and out of the hall for a morning event of some kind. As the sun moved into position high in the sky, shadows shortened and people vanished completely . . .

Then Hal was back in the void, finding himself drifting away from Darlene and Chase as though he were on a raft in the ocean. "What happened?"

"Show's over," Chase said, grinning.

"What? That's *it*?" Hal blurted.

Darlene nodded. "It takes a lot of effort to slow time and show myself like that. I always try to say hello, but people never hear me. I keep hoping my dear husband will come by. I'm always watching out for him. I've appeared enough times that word has got around that the hall is haunted, so perhaps he'll come and visit just to see if it's me. But he may have been already. He may have stopped by many times. We might just keep missing each other. Life goes by too fast out there, and I can only slow things down for a minute or two."

As she turned away, Chase whispered to Hal, "Actually, it's more likely she's temporarily speeding up to match the pace of time on the outside. It's like she's stepping onto a fast-moving train for a second or two. The thing is, her husband's probably an old man by now or passed away already."

Hal was speechless. There was so much to take in, so many possibilities to consider, so many questions to ask. As he floated there, dumbfounded, Darlene went and sat down—on thin air—and leaned back in her imaginary chair looking washed out.

"We should go," Chase said.

Questions came bubbling to the surface. Hal could barely contain himself. "Darlene, can you visit anywhere or just that one place? How long have you been here? How fast is time speeding by outside? Can you touch things? Make them move? How come—"

"Whoa, slow down," Chase interrupted.

Darlene gave a chuckle. She crossed her legs and slumped back farther in her non-existent chair as though she were performing a magic trick. "I can only visit that one place. It's fairly typical for the lingering dead to be fixated on one spot, often the place they died but sometimes a place they loved. I know of a few ghosts who move around though, following a particular person rather than remaining in one spot. They're not very nice ghosts, though."

"Darlene's not sure how long she's been here," Chase explained. "Neither am I. Time has no meaning here. There's no day or night, we don't eat or sleep, and if we get bored we just kind of drift into a stupor for a while. But if you think about how fast life is moving out there, it's about a day every six minutes."

"A day every—" Hal repeated. He stopped, flabbergasted. "A day *every six minutes*? You mean time is passing by really fast outside right now? For every six minutes I'm here, another day goes by?"

"That's what I said, yeah."

Hal immediately tried to figure out how long he'd been trapped. An hour? Maybe more. But even sixty minutes would be . . . *ten days!*

Chapter Twelve
Glimpses of Reality

Hal looked around as if he might spot some previously unseen exit from this dark, cloudy place. "I have to get out of here. There must be a way."

Chase shook his head. "You think I'd still be here if there was a way out? No, we're stuck. The only way out is if we wake in the real world. I've known a few people in comas. One fell from a bridge and cracked his skull. He remembered falling and nothing else, yet he wasn't dead because he was rejected by the Gatekeeper. Anyway, he was here for ages, and then one day he just looked at me in a funny way and said his kid was calling. Then he was gone. I assume he woke up in the hospital and returned to the living."

"Did he . . . did he remember *this*?" Hal asked, waving all around.

"How should I know? I doubt it, though. If people remembered this place, there would be plenty of stories about it after they woke. As far as I know, most people just remember moving toward a bright white light."

This filled Hal with horror. Time was rushing by outside, and when he eventually woke, he wouldn't even remember where he'd been. He'd be left with a long blank period as though he'd just woken from a deep sleep.

He rushed toward Darlene. "Is there any way I can see where I came from? To see what's happening with . . . with my body?"

Darlene shook her head wearily. "That sort of talent is reserved for the dead." She frowned. "Where *do* you come from, not-quite-dead Hal? Anywhere near Westerley? What year is it out there?"

"I live in Carter," Hal said absently. "Although I was up at Bad Rock Gulch when the accident happened."

Her eyes widened. "With the glowing caves? The Chamber of Ghosts? It's legendary. But it's a long, long way from my town. Thousands of miles."

More questions rattled through Hal's mind. If she'd lived thousands of miles away while she was alive, what was she doing here with Hal and Chase? Was distance irrelevant in this place? Did people from all over end up in this same void when they died, clustered together, marching toward the Gatekeeper? Apparently the void was for those in both Miss Simone's world and Hal's—basically anyone human—but it was hard to imagine all the dead ending up in one relatively small place. No wonder millions of virus victims were still lining up to be processed. The Gatekeeper had a backlog to deal with.

Now he had a better understanding about that, too. Although thirteen years or so had passed since the virus outbreak, it was actually a much shorter period in this world of darkness. How much shorter, though? Six minutes in here for every day outside? He shook his head. He never had been very good at math, and the answer eluded him.

"Penny for your thoughts?" Chase broke in. "What happened to you, buddy?"

"There was an accident in the mine," Hal explained, speaking to both Chase and Darlene. "An earthquake. The ground opened up, and I fell into it."

"Ah," Chase murmured. "So that's what happened? You were badly injured and fell into a coma?"

Hal shook his head. "No. Not exactly. Before that happened, my friends and I fell asleep in the chamber to absorb the magic from its walls. We're shapeshifters, but we lost our magic and were trying to get it back. Anyway, Abigail and I kept seeing movement, and later I woke and found people all around, inside the walls, shouting at me." He looked from Chase to Darlene. "Inside the walls. These people were like ghosts or something. I couldn't hear them, but they were shouting at me, trying to warn me of something, telling me to get out."

Darlene nodded slowly. "That chamber is a hotspot for lost souls. It's easy to communicate with the living there. You don't even need to be a haunt—you could manifest there yourself, not-quite-dead Hal."

"I could?" Hal said, instantly wondering if he could get a message to his friends. "How? What do I do?"

"Ah, well, it takes practice." Darlene smiled, tilting her head to one side. "I'll teach you, if you like. But I should warn you: the problem with the chamber is that hardly anyone ever goes there. It's one of the easiest places to manifest, yet one of the least visited. We never see anybody except goblins and those horrible lycans. And they can't see us. Only humans can."

"I'm only half human myself," Hal muttered.

"You're human enough," Darlene assured him. "If you weren't, you wouldn't be here. Anyway, a few of the haunts sensed you were there and knew something was going to happen. They all joined in, trying to warn you. How strange that you're here now. And unfortunate."

Again, Hal's head spun. Dead people, lost souls, haunts, ghosts, magic, energy, sparkle . . . it was all just too much. He closed his eyes tight and shook his head as if trying to shake his thoughts loose.

"I need answers," he finally announced.

"Don't we all?" Chase agreed. "I think the only one with answers is the giant demon that chews up dead people and spits them back out. Want to pop over and ask him a few questions?" He spoke flippantly, but when Hal stared at him silently and thoughtfully, Chase's smile faded. "I was kidding."

"I don't see a demon," Hal said. "I see a tall woman. Or something like a woman, anyway. She seemed gentle. She didn't look like she wanted to hurt me. She just kind of threw me aside."

Chase was shaking his head. "Hal, don't mess with the demon. I've watched him from a distance, and he just gets meaner and uglier as time goes on."

Hal had already made up his mind. He started to float away. "I have to try. You said yourself: you only see what you imagine is there. I guess we just see two different things. Maybe it's not a demon at all but . . . but an angel."

Chase snorted.

"Well, I'm still going," Hal insisted. "See you. Bye, Darlene."

"Be safe, not-quite-dead Hal."

Waving, Hal headed off in what he thought was the right direction. Squinting into the black clouds, he saw the faint white glow in the distance.

"Hal, wait," Chase called, coming after him. "I need to ask you something. Darlene asked you, too, but you didn't answer. What year is it outside?"

When Hal told him, Chase was silent. They both floated onward toward the light. "About twenty-five years, then," Chase said eventually.

"What is?"

"Twenty-five years. That's how long I've been here," Chase said.

Hal almost flipped out. He twisted around and stared at his friend as they moved through the void. "Are you kidding me?"

"Time moves at a different pace," Chase reminded him again. "I've lost track of the days and nights, but it feels like I've been here a month or two. Darlene's been here longer than me, maybe twice as long. She keeps hoping to see her husband, but I'm sure he's probably long dead."

Hal was well aware that another day on the outside had probably slipped by during Darlene's haunting trick. But what could he do about it? The sense of urgency was overwhelming, and he picked up his pace even though he was entirely in the hands of his shapeshifting friends. Hadn't they dug him out of the tunnel yet? What if Blair was unable to reverse the magic and bring him back?

"I need answers," he said again, and leaned forward as if that would somehow increase his speed further. Oddly, it helped, and the clouds rushed by.

Chase said nothing as he tagged along. Hal was glad of his company.

As the white light brightened, the army of shadows came into view around it. So these were virus victims, still being processed by the angel-demon creature? Millions of people from around the world that had only been in this strange limbo a few weeks while the years flashed past outside? It was mind-boggling.

Hal and Chase weaved in and out, but as the teeming dead organized themselves onto a flat, two-dimensional plane, the airspace opened up and Hal flew over their heads straight toward the ethereal being at its center.

Now Chase hung back, terror written on his face. "Wait here, then," Hal said.

He closed in on the giant, slender figure. Her huge, utterly black eyes gave nothing away. He had no idea if she was looking at him or not. He slowed his approach, squinting in the blinding light, until he floated fifteen feet away—what he hoped was out of her reach.

"I—I need answers," he called.

Her head lifted slightly. He felt the weight of her stare. While the black shadows all around continued surging toward her, and those at the front tipped into the pit of light below her feet, the woman studied Hal silently.

Then a voice filled his head. It was whispery and soft, but at the same time so loud it made him recoil. *Just lay him down on the ground—and gently! Wait until we're way over the hills out of sight before doing your thing. Okay?* The pitch of the voice altered slightly, becoming marginally deeper. *Fine, but I'm telling you it won't work.*

Totally befuddled, Hal shook his head to clear it. "I need to know if there's a way out of here. I'm not dead—"

Hang in there, Hal. Just another few minutes. We'll be waiting for you.

He blinked. Although the voice in his head had been just as loud and whispery as before, again its pitch had shifted, and something about the words and the way they were spoken struck him as familiar. "A-Abigail?"

A vision filled his mind. He was outside in bright sunlight, staring upward into Abigail's face. Then, abruptly, she was gone. In her place was a vast expanse of open land with hills on the horizon. Blacknail's buggy was driving away, rapidly receding into the distance, its movements jerky as if Hal were seeing a series of snapshots. He wanted to call out, but another figure moved into view—a vivid, colorful bird standing about six feet tall, staring off into the distance as the buggy reached the hills and disappeared.

"I don't understand," Hal said. "Is . . . is this happening right now?"

A barrage of new visions filled his head. He gasped and reeled.

It started with a view of Earth from high above, much higher than Hal had ever flown. The curvature of the planet was acute. He was in space.

Then he saw a meaningless flash of scenes from history: the ancient Egyptians, the Chinese military, Greek warriors, the fearless Spartans, the powerful Romans . . . Hal vaguely recognized them all from history classes with Lauren's mom, Mrs. Hunter. In fact she had talked more about ancient history than modern times. Hal watched as a series of moving images faded in and out—violent one-on-one clashes, bloody battles of armies, shielded phalanxes marching toward fortresses . . .

He didn't understand the point of it all until numerous whispery voices filled his head again. The words they spoke seemed disjointed as if full sentences had been snipped from hundreds of conversations and cobbled together to form a narrative to go with the pictures, a sort of scrapbook packed with information—but relating to what exactly? Hal

115

had to listen carefully. At first it was a senseless cacophony. After a while he learned to tune in to one or two voices at a time and let the rest sweep past, all the time watching the flicker of images. Gradually the theme of the scrapbook became clear: war, war, war—bloody battles, death and destruction the world over, from ancient times to modern day. That was what mankind did.

Hal thought this point of view was a little harsh. He'd been led to believe the world was a wonderful place despite its violent history—or at least it had been before the virus. In any case, what was the point of this lecture? People were people, and there was nothing anybody could—

An experiment.

When the thought popped into Hal's head, he wondered if the whispery voice had explicitly said so or merely suggested it in a roundabout way.

In any case, the idea of an experiment stuck. An experiment with life on Earth. Humans were violent and greedy. What if other intelligent beings were introduced? What if humans were not alone in the world and had to share? Ah, but these beings couldn't simply appear one day—it would be like an invasion, and the humans were bound to take back what they thought was rightfully theirs.

But if humans were to start afresh in a new world alongside other intelligent creatures that were considered equals . . .

And so began Miss Simone's world.

Astonished by this notion, Hal allowed the onslaught of visions and voices to continue. He was barely aware of the teeming shadow figures below. Mesmerized, he stared into the ghostly woman's huge black eyes as a new world unfolded.

How it came into being wasn't clear, but it was an overlapping copy of Earth. Yet although the continents were roughly the same size and shape, there were subtle differences to coastlines here and there. Oxygen was richer, and this led to a startling variance in the ecology of this twin world. Humans popped up as if by magic, just a few hundred thousand of them spread around this new, rich planet, with no memory of how they came into being.

And then came the others: centaurs and naga, goblins and elves, faeries and mermaids, harpies, dragons, ogres, trolls, gorgons, and many, many more. They came into being in much the same way as the humans of this world, with no evolutionary past. But they were different. Many of them required a special form of energy just to function properly. *Magic.* Such a power couldn't simply be conjured out of thin air. Still, when humans died, they released a small amount of energy that normally went to waste. That energy would henceforth be repurposed, sent back into the ground and utilized by the fantastic new creatures.

The experiment commenced. And, after a thousand years, it was considered a success. Humans behaved better in the company of equals. In the old world, they fought for territory, for power over other humans in the region; they'd been doing so throughout history, resulting in bloody battles and senseless loss of life, all in an effort to gain a bit more land even if it meant ruling under tyranny. In the new world, however, humans seemed content to live peacefully alongside other creatures of similar intelligence.

"But why?" Hal wondered aloud.

Perhaps because they all regarded each other with fear and respect. There was no desire to try and govern or enslave other cultures. Each species was proud and formidable. The centaurs, for example, would never bow to a human ruler. They would die first. And if one settlement was overrun and enslaved, others from afar would rise up in anger and come to its rescue. Conquering or destroying a mere handful of a species was a futile prospect when there was no viable way to enslave or rule the rest. It was simply too much effort for too little gain. Short of exterminating an entire species with a targeted virus, as a handful of evil centaurs had tried to do, the equal and intermingled spread of diverse cultures actually promoted peace; they all lived in respectful harmony with each other, accepting things as they were.

Miss Simone's voice suddenly filled Hal's head. "In my world there are perhaps just as many dumb animals as in yours, and these are no threat. But, unlike you, we also have a large number of *intelligent* species. In your world, humans always enjoyed being the only smart animals on the planet, but in ours, we have to share our world with numerous other creatures that are just as smart as us, if not smarter."

This all rang a bell. Hal pictured her back on the island, standing in the street one evening right before the shapeshifters had demonstrated their powers. She was trying to explain how her diverse world forced humans to be more respectful.

She stood there in the street with her cloak fluttering in the night breeze. "Sharing a world with all these smart creatures," she said, "is, frankly, very difficult. It humbles us, too. We humans strive to make peace and keep to ourselves. We try hard not to encroach or trespass on land occupied by others, even though sometimes contact is inevitable . . ."

Abruptly, Hal saw centaurs and naga dwelling as neighbors, standoffish but respectful. He saw ogres and trolls warily steering clear of one another, elves who welcomed outsiders but were fiercely protective of their humble territories, and an unexpected kinship between the creative humans and the decidedly grumpy but industrious goblins. None of these alliances exuded love and friendship between species, but there was plenty of healthy respect, and with this respect came acceptance—that they all had a right to be here, and that the world was large enough for them all. So it was the same message again: humans behaved better when they had smart neighbors.

"Okay, I get it," he said finally. "But so what? The world I grew up in has nothing *but* humans, and look what they've managed to do! It's amazing! I've seen it myself: the tallest buildings you can imagine, cars that go really fast without needing horses to drag them, helicopters that fly through the sky . . . Men have even set foot on the moon!"

"And one day, Lady Simone, your ambition will be your downfall," a familiar voice growled back at him.

Hal flinched. It was the centaur khan and a snippet of conversation played back with absolute accuracy. He remembered this conversation well, and it wasn't something he wanted to hear again. The khan's voice filled him with disgust.

"We all know about the *other world*," the centaur snapped. "The human race, left alone to its ambition . . . Inevitably they will cause their own destruction sooner or later. By forbidding the mining of precious energy from the earth, I'm not only saving our land, but *saving you from yourselves.*"

The audacity! That centaur had killed millions! How dare he!

Still, no matter how brutally this particular centaur had acted, his message was clear, and his sentiment felt by others of his kind. Humans were by nature rash and greedy. Left alone, they would eventually spoil the landscape, ruin the atmosphere, and destroy each other.

Shaking his head, Hal knew these dark thoughts weren't his own. They were being fed to him by this strange, ethereal woman as she floated before him in dazzling light. Still, the more he was fed, the more he swallowed . . .

Of course, it wasn't all roses in the new world, either. Dragons were hunters and killers by nature, a menace to all, but this was to be expected of beasts with low intelligence and a powerful hunger, and in a strange way they gave the humans, goblins, centaurs, and everyone else a common enemy that united them. Maybe that was the point. Such dangerous threats left no time for petty squabbling between rival species.

And there were other dangerous predators like manticores and harpies, both of whom were smart, conniving, vindictive, greedy, and just plain nasty. They had no aspirations of taking over the land, no ulterior motive for their hostile nature. They were just there, a darker part of the landscape, no different than deadly scorpions, snakes, and spiders—a pest problem that kept everyone on their toes.

"But *who cares?*" Hal demanded again, getting impatient. Time was flying by outside, and here he was being given a history lesson.

The relentless visions ended abruptly, and a new scene opened up. Hal let out a sigh when he saw the ocean with a rip across its horizon, a long, pulsing cloud of smoke that Hal instantly recognized as a hole. But what a hole! It had to be miles wide. A ship sailed toward it, but its crew suddenly seemed to lose its nerve, and Hal saw the sails bulging as the ship came about, trying to turn away from the hundred-foot-high wall of eerie blackness. The ocean thundered into the hole, churning monstrously, dragging the ship with it.

Hal followed the vessel through to find that the level of the ocean on the other side was somewhat lower, the result being a wall of seawater miles long pouring from the pulsing cloud. The ship tumbled with it, tiny and insignificant.

The edge of the world, Hal thought. He'd heard stories about that. Up to a few hundred years ago, people still believed Earth to be flat, that the horizon marked the edge of the world from which a ship could fall to its death. Many sailors dared to get close, to seek out the truth, perhaps view the edge of the world and return from it. Few ever did. There were countless tales of sea serpents, not to mention monsters and creatures that had gone down in history books as pure fantasy and legend. The creation of the holes thousands of years ago had allowed the two worlds to mingle.

The barrage of moving pictures began to show more and more black, smoky holes opening up between the worlds. Was this a new experiment? To see if the humans of the old world could be changed for the better in the face of adversity? Dragons, harpies, griffins, and other monsters pushed through the holes. Hal saw many creatures he didn't know existed—a one-eyed giant stamping around on the cliffs, a colossal multi-headed snake patrolling a narrow passage of sea, a powerful bull-headed man trapped in a maze of tunnels in an ancient city . . .

At first it seemed the invasion of bizarre and fantastic monsters did indeed bring humans together as one to deal with their common enemies. Great battles were fought, monstrous creatures defeated. But for the most part there was no real difference. Kings and emperors were set in their ways, and their dealings with enormous and deadly magical creatures were but temporary inconveniences. Battles continued across the globe no matter what.

You can't teach old dogs new tricks.

This bizarre saying seemed totally out of place, but its meaning was clear. Hal's old world was set in its ways and would never change. He sensed that this new experiment was a lost cause.

In any case, people all over the world—*both* worlds—continued to die no matter what, their combined energy utilized as magic. And out of this magic rose a bizarre creature. The phoenix was a magical anomaly—nothing new there, only this one despised magic, and when it began to suffocate from the stench of all that energy, it spread its wings, puffed out its chest, and burst into flames. Crackling and sizzling, its feathers curled and blackened as the phoenix quivered with the anticipation of obliterating magic from its region. When it was reborn, rising from the ashes, the surrounding land was pure.

Similar rebirths occurred worldwide over millennia, and the vast majority of holes vanished. Magical creatures were temporarily affected by these rebirths, too, but since ordinary, mortal folk in both worlds continued to die no matter what, their combined recycled energy went on seeping back into Miss Simone's land.

Most of the holes were closed, but humans had been inadvertently recreating them for centuries. Their intent was simply to perform sacrificial ceremonies, cracking open energized geo-rocks, causing tremendous explosions, and thus 'appeasing the gods' in some way. As new holes appeared—a mere side effect of the ceremonies—magical creatures continued to enter the history books from time to time, albeit in smaller doses, and in a world where humans no longer believed what they saw with their own eyes.

Hal saw another phoenix, aged and filled with loathing for the surrounding land, perform its rare regenerating trick. More holes closed, magic vanished, and the phoenix sighed with relief as it renewed its life . . .

"Who *are* you?" Hal cried suddenly. "Why are you showing me all this? I just want to go home!"

To his surprise, a familiar but decidedly unwelcome voice rang out: "Have you ever considered the benefit of having U.S. Marines standing by your side against the monsters of your world?" It was Lieutenant Briskle. Why on earth was *his* opinion being aired?

"Now what?" Hal demanded.

Another barrage of voices flooded his mind, and he decided he'd had enough. He started to back away from the alien-woman-creature. As he went, the images and voices faded, but their meaning was burned deep into his memory: *Start over. Re-open the holes. Unite the worlds. It will be different this time.*

"Yeah, right," Hal muttered.

Do it. And do it soon. Unification is inevitable. Take the first step. Invite them in before they invade.

He felt a flash of pain as if something had given him a violent shove on the chest. He twisted and tumbled backward through the air, the visions fading and leaving with him nothing but remnants of a dream. When he finally righted himself, the dazzling creature of light was just a speck in the far distance.

"What happened?" Chase said, appearing in front of him.

"I—I'm not sure," Hal admitted.

He floated there, glad to be rid of the deafening noise in his head. Everything was calm. The black cloud rolled and pulsed, and small orange specks floated around aimlessly.

"How long was I talking to her?" he asked, fearing the answer.

But Chase surprised him. "A few minutes."

"Huh. It seemed much longer."

"And you kept babbling, talking to yourself."

Hal rubbed his face. "I need to get out of here," he groaned.

"Not going to happen," Chase said, "unless you wake from your coma."

Hal sighed with frustration. "I'm not in a coma. I'm a statue of stone from where a gorgon looked at me. I'm kind of . . . suspended." As Chase stared at him silently, Hal went on with his confession. "It was deliberate. I was trapped under rocks after that earthquake I mentioned, about to boil to death or drown because there was hot water bubbling up from underground. A friend of mine is a gorgon. I asked her to turn me to stone. That would give everyone time to dig me out and get me to a safe place, then wake me up."

It was a long while before Chase spoke. "But everyone knows you can't wake after being turned to stone."

"Well, apparently you can. Another friend of mine did. A phoenix turned itself to ashes and was reborn, and that knocked out all the magic in the area—including the magic of a gorgon's stoning. My friend Fenton woke up. So I know it can be done."

Chase grabbed his arm. Hal jerked back in alarm as an unpleasant tingle shot through his body. "Then I could wake up, too! I was calcified by a gorgon myself. Her name was Molly. She was only eight at the time, but she turned me to stone, and I've been here ever since." He frowned. "Funny. I knew a phoenix as well, but he was never 'reborn' or whatever. His name was Blair. They were classmates at the school where I worked."

Hal was so stunned that no coherent words came to his lips. What Chase was saying seemed impossible. Astounding. What were the chances of meeting someone in this endless void that also knew Molly and Blair? That had been petrified by the same gorgon as Hal himself? It was true that the Gatekeeper had tossed him in this direction after rejecting him, but still . . .

"I know Molly and Blair," he finally gasped. "Molly's the one who stoned me. And it's Blair who's going to wake me up."

Now it was Chase's turn to look astonished.

"He could wake you as well," Hal said, "but it'll only work if you're within range when he does his thing. Your frozen body could be too far away."

"Then find me," Chase urged. He leaned in close. "If you get out of here, *please* find my body and release me. Will you do that?"

"Well, yeah," Hal agreed. "But where will I find—"

And, abruptly, he was awake, blinking in dazzling afternoon daylight, lying on the freezing ground in the middle of nowhere. A phoenix stood before him, a mass of blackened feathers on the ground all around, and the pungent smell of sulfur filling the air.

Chapter Thirteen
A Cold Awakening

After the initial shock of waking to blinding sunlight, the vivid colors of the phoenix, and the acrid smell in the air, the very next thing Hal noticed was the freezing cold chill. He climbed stiffly to his feet and wrapped his arms around his torso. Fenton's clothes were too big for him, and he tugged on them to close some of the gaps and prevent the frigid breeze whistling through.

There was a hard frost on the ground despite the sunshine. He shuffled his bare feet in a vain attempt to escape the ice. Then he saw two piles of clothes on the ground, both neatly folded. He reached for one, but the phoenix used an enormous wing to point to the second pile instead: a thick sweater and pants, some heavy boots, and a long coat. Winter clothes.

Hal hurriedly pulled the clothes on over Fenton's. Meanwhile, the phoenix quietly reverted to human form and reached for his own.

It was only when they were both fully dressed, coats and all, that Blair spoke. "I can't believe it worked. Molly was right all along. I *do* have it in me."

"What?" Hal said, stuffing his hands into his pockets and dipping his chin into the top of his coat.

"I brought you back," Blair said softly. "I actually brought you back."

Hal nodded. "How long have I been away?"

"Two weeks."

Groaning inwardly, Hal muttered, "Thought so. Time passes much quicker out here than it does in there."

"In where?"

"In . . . *there*," Hal said, waving vaguely. "Where are we now?"

Blair pointed to the distant hills. "The others are waiting over there, hopefully out of range. I don't have the strength of a real phoenix. I don't have hundreds of years of magic in me. I don't think my nullifying power stretches very far."

They both looked all around, contemplating the situation. Hal guessed they were at least two or three miles from anywhere interesting: hills to the west and north, forest to the east with the glittering ocean beyond, and even more dense forest to the south. "What if it does?" Hal asked. "What if you've just wiped out all the magic in this place?"

Blair shrugged. "Well, the goblins won't be happy. The mines are maybe five miles that way." He pointed toward the sea. "And as for the lycans . . ."

With a jolt, Hal glanced up at the sky. The sun was heading for the horizon, and the moon was already visible. It wasn't quite full, but it was big enough to suggest an advanced phase of the lunar cycle.

"Yeah," Blair said, nodding. "We've hung around this area way too long. Come on, let's start walking. Blacknail's watching. He'll come and pick us up, but in the meantime I'm not going to stand around freezing."

They started out across the hard-packed, frost-covered dirt. "It got cold," Hal commented.

"Winter came a week ago. Cold front just swept across the land. It was mild one day, freezing the next. Winter's here to stay now. You haven't experienced winter here yet, have you? It's going to be tough."

Seeing the vast distance ahead of them, Hal said wistfully, "If only I could just transform and fly . . . but I can tell I have no magic left in me. I feel empty." He frowned. "You do, though. How come?"

"Built-in defense mechanism," Blair said with a shrug. "I guess I keep a little magic back so I can still shift and self-charge. But most of it is used up during the rebirth."

"So . . . could you maybe transform and carry me out of here?"

Blair grimaced. "I'm tired, Hal. Rebirths are hard work, you know. Besides, I'm a phoenix, not a roc. I'm not sure I could carry you."

He stopped after a few minutes and pointed at something off to their side. At first Hal thought it was a faerie, but quickly corrected himself. This thing was smaller and, while humanoid, had blue hair, fuzzy skin, and butterfly wings. It glowed faintly even in the sunshine as it sputtered and hopped around like a tiny bird with a broken wing.

"Will-o'-the-wisp," Blair said. "You don't normally see them like this."

Hal had always imagined these creatures to be like fireflies, brightly glowing nocturnal things. "It's lost its magic," he said, feeling sorry for the poor thing.

"Actually, I'm more interested in the fact that it still has a little left. See it glowing? We must be on the fringe of my blast zone." He looked back the way they'd come and shrugged. "Pretty feeble, isn't it? Like I said, my range doesn't extend far. Looks like Molly didn't need to hide over the hills after all."

"Better safe than sorry," Hal mumbled as they continued on past the struggling will-o'-the-wisp. They saw a few more after that, though these were far more active than the last, buzzing around near the ground.

Blair pestered him with questions about where he'd been while calcified. Hal answered vaguely, his mind on other things. The idea of being unable to transform bothered him more and more as they walked, and he looked longingly toward the coast, seeing the forest and the rise of rocky hills that marked the location of Bad Rock Gulch and the mines beneath.

"How bad are the tunnels?" he asked, interrupting Blair's current line of questioning. "Did anyone else get hurt? How long did it take to dig me out?"

Reluctantly switching gear, Blair told him that the main tunnel beyond the hot pool had collapsed in places. Still, there were other ways in and out of the mine, and the evacuation had been fairly straightforward. Only one goblin had been reported missing, presumed dead, and when Blair mentioned this, he looked at Hal as if seeking confirmation.

Hal nodded soberly and explained what had happened. "He saved me. Gave me a leg up. I would have died with him, otherwise. The thing is . . ." He stalled, then shakily told Blair about his failed transformation, about how he'd filled his tiny prison and pressed up against the walls and caused a rockfall. "It was my fault that goblin died," he moaned.

Blair shook his head firmly. "From what I heard, it was either a quick death under tons of rock or a slow, painful demise in boiling water. If he could, I bet he would thank you."

Hal felt no better about it, though. He listened in silence as Blair explained how the flood of boiling water had receded over several days, cutting a passage through the tons of rock and dirt and pouring down the sloping floor of the fallen tunnel. Once it was safe, the goblins had pulled the boulders out of the way to get at Hal. They'd eventually found him there, frozen like a statue.

"We took our time getting you out," Blair said. "The last thing we needed was another roof fall. And we didn't want to break anything off you. Can you imagine waking up with a finger missing?"

Hal was horrified at the thought.

"With the boiling water, it was four days before we could even get close to you. We had to wait for it to subside on its own. Then it was another two days of careful excavation. We brought you out here, figuring this would be as good a place as any to keep you."

"I've been lying in the middle of nowhere for a *week?*"

Blair laughed. "Don't tell me you got a chill."

"Well, no, but—"

"I tried to wake you right away," Blair said. "As soon as we got you here and laid you out on the ground, I sent the others away and did my rebirth thing. It didn't work. I successfully drained most of my own magic, but not much else. You lay there unmoved by my efforts."

"Sorry," Hal said.

Blair clapped him on the shoulder. "I was right about that, at least. I told Molly it would take extra magic. Remember my demonstration back at Carter a while back? I did my rebirth thing in the street, and a bunch of nearby geo-rocks fizzled out. But I didn't affect any of my shapeshifter friends, and I wouldn't have affected any gorgon statues either. My blast zone was pretty small compared to other phoenixes, but not only that, it was *weak.* Knocking out geo-rocks is one thing. When I go up in a puff of smoke, the rocks go *pfft!* and die." He grinned. "But it takes a great deal more effort to nullify the magic of shapeshifters and even our smart clothes, and a *lot* more to bring statues back to life."

Hal nodded slowly and rubbed his hands together. Speaking of frozen, his face was so cold it felt numb.

"Normally a phoenix will absorb magic over hundreds of years," Blair went on. "It'll suck it right out of the ground, take it in bit by bit, getting heavier and heavier until, one day, it's time to lighten the load and start over." He pursed his lips. "Having said that, a few days in the Chamber of Ghosts was plenty of time. I was just doing it all wrong."

"Doing what wrong?"

"My rebirth." He looked skyward as he tried to formulate an explanation. "I heard about when you first came here and couldn't fly. It wasn't as simple as just flapping your wings, was it? It has to be done a certain way, right? When I came out here to do my rebirth trick, apparently I didn't do it right. I had to go back into the chamber to recharge."

"But you got it right the second time?" he asked.

Blair shook his head. "Nope. I went back down to the chamber convinced I just didn't have that kind of ability. Molly told me I did. She said we were going nowhere until I woke you up. Some of the others stayed in the buggy to keep watch on you—Abigail, Robbie, and Blacknail, but the rest went with the goblins to their little outpost near Landis. Safer there than with the lycans." He sighed. "The lycans are practically feral now."

"So how many times did you try waking me?"

"Five. Spent a day recharging each time. But I got it right eventually." He grinned. "It should be easier from now on."

Hal slowed and turned to look at Blair with a new appreciation. "You holed up in that cave for five days? On your own? For . . . me?"

Blair shrugged. "What else was I going to do?"

They had halted by now and were face to face, although Hal was quite a bit shorter. "Thanks," he said awkwardly. "Thanks for doing all that. It can't have been comfortable in the chamber. Did you . . . see any ghosts?"

"Not a one," Blair said, "though I did catch a few movements here and there. I figured it was bats."

They resumed their walk again. Bad Rock Gulch loomed closer now, off to their right. Their route was taking them past the gulch to the higher hills ahead. Somewhere over that way was Eastward Pass—or Westward Pass as Abigail had suggested it be called when approaching it from this side.

Blair insisted that Hal explain for a second time about his time in limbo. He wanted details, but Hal was not in the mood. Things were nagging at him. He needed to know about Chase but was somehow afraid to ask—afraid that he'd dreamed the whole experience and that his sanity would be questioned. But if Chase was real, a rescue was in order, and for that Hal would need to know where he was located. There were other things nagging at him, too, but he pushed those thoughts aside for now.

He almost stopped dead as a realization hit him: *he remembered!* Despite what Chase had warned him of, Hal remembered every moment of his stay in the eerie world of darkness. Was that normal? Or was he somehow special?

Blacknail's buggy was rumbling across the flat ground from the distant hills. "They've seen us," Blair said with obvious relief. "That saves us a walk. Good. We'll be on our way home in no time."

Now Hal stopped for real. "What? But I don't have any magic! I need to go back to the chamber and recharge!"

The barking laughter he received in reply indicated that nobody would be revisiting the chamber anytime soon or even waiting around while Hal did. "Besides, Blacknail is towing a gigantic wagon full of geo-rocks. Maybe he'll let you lie on the back of it and absorb some magic that way—if you don't drain them all in the process."

The buggy, with its steam-powered engine, rattled and clanked across the plain in the still, cold air. When the vehicle arrived, it veered and circled around Hal and Blair, and that was when Hal saw the enormous wagon hitched to the back. It was covered with a gigantic sheet and tied securely, but it bulged along the top, and Hal imagined there must be several hundred geo-rocks piled up in it. A rectangular cage was secured at the very back, almost like an afterthought, tied on with ropes so that it bounced and wobbled. It was full of clucking chickens.

Even before the buggy came to a complete stop, the small side door opened and Abigail came flying down. She hurled herself on Hal with a cry, and he was knocked backward off his feet. "Whoa!" he laughed.

Her tears dripped onto his face as she climbed off him and got to her feet. She was wearing a long, thick coat and heavy boots, an equally thick knitted hat, scarf and mittens. Her wings, now retracted, had sprouted from neatly cut holes in the back, which must let in a nasty chill in weather like this.

"It's only been an hour since I saw you last," Hal said as she buried her face in his shoulder.

"An *hour?*"

"Well, an hour and a bit. I'll explain later."

Everyone was crammed against the buggy's windows and pressed into the doorway. As Robbie started to climb down the ladder, Blair stopped him. "Stay up there, guys. There's no point coming down. Let's get inside and head home. You can all talk on the way."

"But I need my magic," Hal protested as he was ushered toward the buggy. "You said I could lie on the wagon or something."

Blair gave him an extra shove. "In this weather? It's freezing, Hal, and it'll be night soon. Worry about your magic another time. We all want to go home."

"*You* do," Hal muttered as he was herded up the ladder.

Once inside, Blacknail wasted no time in getting underway, heading across the plain to the taller hills where Eastward Pass would be waiting. Hal suddenly understood the need for chickens. They were payment for the trolls.

As soon as he got settled, everyone crowded around. Hal had a jolt of surprise when his gaze fell on the most beautiful face he'd ever seen. Jolie was back to normal—except that she still had no legs. Well, nobody but her had expected them to grow back anyway. She was perched on a seat two rows away, propped in the corner, but she seemed to be perfectly comfortable and happy. With or without legs, her presence put everyone else in a depressing shadow. Hal tried to ignore her large, clear eyes and full lips, and the way she tossed her lustrous black hair and gazed at him.

Hal was badgered with questions as his friends clustered around and pressed in so close he felt like he wanted to transform and throw them all off. Only he couldn't. Finally, Molly yelled for everyone to shut up.

A silence fell, during which Blacknail gave a single grunt of annoyance.

"Now, let's all settle down and give the poor boy some space," Molly said. She turned to Hal, her veil jiggling. He shuddered, remembering the sight of her deathly gaze. "Hal, would you like to regale us with your adventures? In your own words and at your own pace?"

He sighed. *Not really*, he thought. *I'd like some time alone to think.* He cleared his throat, wondering what to tell them and what, if anything, to omit. How much of it had been real? Should he ask about Chase? And . . . should he tell them what had been nagging at the back of his mind? It had been pushing through bit by bit, a voice of reason that made no sense whatsoever and yet seemed *right* somehow. He wanted to ignore this voice in his head—to have nothing to do with it—but the more he rejected what it was telling him, the louder the voice grew.

He frowned. A voice in his head? Maybe he was just going crazy. Or maybe Jolie was messing with him.

"Hal?" Molly said gently.

He started to speak. He told them about the initial blackness, the orange dabs of light, and the thick, rolling, cloudlike substance that looked suspiciously like pulsing portals. Fenton nodded as he spoke, and Hal knew that the boy had shared his experience thus far.

After that, Fenton began to frown with the rest of them because now Hal was getting into the crazier stuff, none of which Fenton could verify because he hadn't been in the world of darkness long enough to see any of it. Hal felt like he was edging out onto a thin tree branch, his story growing more fantastic as he went, pushing the limits of what his friends could swallow. Any moment now he was going to say something too far-fetched and ridiculous, and they'd look at him like he was crazy and say, "Uh, o-*kay*, get some rest and maybe you'll feel better in the morning . . ."

Oddly, they accepted his description of the bright white light without blinking and only narrowed their eyes when he spoke of the masses of black shadows that swept toward that light. Mouths fell open when he pushed a little further and told them of the dazzling pit these shadows toppled into, and how they somehow transformed into orange glows that swam about aimlessly in the void. At some point, Abigail's hand slipped into his, and when he glanced at her, she looked worried.

"Crazy, huh?" he said nervously, and laughed.

Nobody laughed with him.

"Go on," Molly said, sounding like she wished he wouldn't.

Hal took a deep breath. "Okay, so then I met somebody."

Blacknail, who was still driving, gave a snort.

"No, I did," Hal said. "He was a black shadowy figure, only he kind of turned into a real person when he told me what he looked like."

"I see what's going on here," Blair said suddenly. "Your mind was trying to make sense of everything, so it dreamed up this place you described. I bet most people who go through traumatic experiences see the same kind of thing—a black nothingness, a blinding white light . . ."

He went on, but Hal sank into himself, thoroughly deflated. As Blair talked, everyone else started nodding, their expressions clearing, relief showing in their eyes. They preferred Blair's version, which was simply that Hal had imagined the whole thing. He searched Fenton's face, looking for something that might suggest the big boy believed this tale about a mystical world of darkness. Maybe he did, but if so, he wasn't showing it.

Hal's nervousness slipped away. Now he felt sad and alone. His own friends didn't believe a word he'd said. Maybe he wouldn't either, if someone else had been telling the story. He remembered how skeptical he'd been when Fenton had told of his own experience.

Blair's explanation seemed to have ended the discussion. Hal said nothing as the conversation shifted to the events happening in the real world. Nobody asked him anything after that. Nobody said, "Anyway, finish your story, Hal," probably because that would have been like saying, "Go ahead and tell us the rest of your crazy dream, just for kicks." And so Hal never mentioned Chase's name, never said a word about Darlene the ghost, avoided any mention of the trapped souls that tried to warn him of the earthquake in the mines, and steered well clear of the notion that had taken root in his mind.

On the positive side, Hal was brought fully up to date with the events of the last two weeks. While Blair had camped out alone in the Chamber of Ghosts, Molly and the others had secretly stayed with the goblins just outside the lycans' village of Landis. Unfortunately, about a week later, the lycans had discovered them. The chief had been unusually livid about the whole thing and ordered them to leave and never come back. Either he was angry at being disobeyed or simply worried that his clan would accidentally hunt them down and devour them. In any case, Blacknail, Molly and the others had hightailed it out of the goblin outpost before the lycans changed their minds about the wagon full of geo-rocks.

"The goblins gave us some chickens," Molly said to Hal. "They have a *lot* of chickens because Eastward Pass is the only viable route through the mountains when towing a wagon full of geo-rocks. They breed chickens just to pay the trolls. So we have some in a cage on the back."

"Fifteen of 'em," Blacknail grunted from his driver's seat. "If the trolls up the price again, they'll regret it."

Hal immediately saw another reason to regain his magic. "I really need to sit out on the wagon," he said, jerking his thumb over his shoulder. "If I can just recharge—"

"Ain't happening," Blacknail said. "You ain't draining all those rocks."

"So take me back to the Chamber of Ghosts," Hal suggested.

There was uproar at this comment. "With those lycans running around in the woods?" Lauren said. "Seriously?"

"Fine," Hal said grumpily. "Just don't come running to me when you need a dragon to fend off a bunch of trolls."

They were already approaching Eastward Pass. Out of the window to the right was the road leading into the woods: the road to Landis, and also the way through to the mines. Blacknail trundled past it, and Hal gazed longingly over the treetops where the ocean was just visible. The sun would be setting soon, and he imagined the hills glowing orange over the mines. All that magic. All that *sparkle*.

"Molly," he said. When the gorgon looked over her shoulder at him, he hesitated a moment. Then: "Why does Lucas call it sparkle?"

She chuckled. "He always did. When we were in school, Simone scoffed at him when he talked about magic. So he started calling it sparkle instead."

"She scoffed at that, too," Blair added.

Hal let out a long breath. "So he called it sparkle even back then?"

"Sure did. Why?"

Because Chase called it that, too.

Uncertain whether or not to ask the next question, Hal hesitated again. Then he blurted it out. "Did you know anyone called Chase?"

There was a long, long silence as Molly and Blair looked at each other—or rather Molly looked at him while he stared at her veil. Oddly, it was Blacknail who answered. "Who told you about him?" he barked over his shoulder.

Hal felt a surge of excitement. He wasn't crazy! He might have written the word 'sparkle' into a dream, but he couldn't have imagined a real-life boy named Chase that he had never met nor even heard of.

Before he could answer, Blacknail swore and pulled back on the levers. The buggy ground to a jerking halt. They had just entered Eastward Pass. Its steep rock walls loomed on both sides, and ahead, on the narrow road, was a horde of trolls. There had to be twenty of them, and when Hal craned his neck to look up through the holes in the roof, he saw more clinging to the smooth cliffs.

Blacknail continued to swear as he stamped to the door and climbed down the ladder. The trolls were motionless as the goblin made his way to the back of the wagon and fiddled with the cage. There was a clang as it came loose, followed by a lot of indignant clucking. Then

Blacknail dragged the cage to the front of the buggy where the trolls stood.

Everyone watched the exchange with interest. The stout goblin was waving his arms around, clearly agitated. The troll—the same leader as before—was impassive, towering over Blacknail and looking like he was ready to brawl.

"It's not going well," Darcy murmured.

"No, it isn't," Molly agreed. "Robbie, do you think you can take on twenty or thirty trolls at once?"

Robbie paled. "Uh . . . well, um . . ."

"I was kidding. Of course you can't. A few were bad enough. Thirty? Not a chance." She looked toward Hal but said nothing.

"Bet she wished I had my sparkle," Hal muttered to Abigail.

Blacknail came stomping back to the buggy. He climbed the ladder, stepped inside, and pulled the door shut so hard that the little glass panel cracked. He was in a terrible rage. Hal wasn't sure he'd ever seen the goblin so furious.

"Did they raise the price again, dearest Blacknail?" Molly asked dryly.

"Twenty-five!" he roared.

"Calm yourself. We'll just have to trundle back to the outpost and get more."

"They said times are tough, that winter's here." Visibly trembling with anger, Blacknail's piglike face was turning a deep shade of purple. "Right, this is war. These trolls have gone too far. We'll—"

"Do nothing," Molly finished for him. "My short-tempered goblin friend, there was danger even when we had a dragon on our side. Now the trolls will be expecting trouble, and we don't even *have* a dragon with us this time. So we'll go fetch us some more chickens, pay the toll with a smile, and be on our merry way."

Blacknail glared around at them all. He was breathing hard, his nostrils flaring. "We've got an ogre. We've got a manticore." He pointed his finger at Molly. "And we've got *you*, bright eyes. You can stone the lot of 'em for all I care. Go ahead—get out there and stone 'em."

"They're just hungry," Hal said.

"What?" the goblin growled.

Hal felt everyone's gaze on him, and he shifted uncomfortably. "The trolls are just hungry. It's winter, right? They have families to feed. What does it matter if we give them a few extra chickens?"

"What does it *matter*?" Blacknail yelled.

"Blacknail, hush," Molly said sharply. "Hal's right. We'll go fetch some more chickens from the goblins." She paused. "The only problem is that we'll risk running into the lycans again. They'll hear this big machine coming a mile away."

"But we could park outside the woods," Blair said, "and send someone in on foot. Someone big and strong." He looked meaningfully at Robbie, who reddened with obvious pride.

"Or someone who can fly," Fenton suggested, pointing at Blair.

Blair shook his head. "I'm tired. I'm not sure I can make it."

"Lauren, then," Fenton said.

Her eyes widened. "What? *Me*?"

"Or Abi."

As Emily and Darcy chimed in with their own views, Molly called for silence again. "Enough! Blacknail, let's get moving."

The goblin shouted something unintelligible out of the window to the waiting trolls. The leader nodded. Then Blacknail returned to his seat and rammed one lever forward and the other back. The buggy started to turn in a tight circle, dragging the loaded wagon behind. "We ain't getting out of here before nightfall at this rate," he muttered.

"We're not staying another night, are we?" Thomas said.

The buggy rumbled back across the plain, heading directly toward the nearby woods. The sun had set, and the sky was turning purple. Overhead, the moon shone bright and almost full. When the dark forest road came into sight ahead, Blacknail veered off to one side and parked under some enormous trees on the fringe of the woods. He shut the engine off, and silence fell.

"Lauren, can you carry ten chickens in the air?" Molly asked her.

"I—I don't know," she moaned. "I've never tried. I've never woken up one morning and thought to myself, 'I wonder if I can carry ten chickens through the air.' Something like that would never occur to me."

"But you can carry a person," Abigail said. "You've done it before. I can't believe ten chickens would weigh more."

"Even if the chickens weighed eight pounds each," Molly agreed, "that's no more than eighty pounds. Plus the weight of the sack."

"A sack?" Lauren said, appalled. "But they'll suffocate in a sack."

Molly leaned across and gently touched Lauren's face. "If you're that worried, you can ask the goblins to slaughter them first."

135

Lauren looked so horrified that a ripple of laughter spread around the buggy.

Hal wasn't laughing, though. He was disappointed at not being chosen to go fetch the chickens. He could have made a detour to the mine and stayed in the Chamber of Ghosts for a full day before returning home. Sure, he would have been in serious trouble when he finally got back, but so be it. He knew Molly wouldn't let him go, and if he simply tried to walk off, he would be stopped very easily. He was, after all, the only feeble human on board. The chicken errand would have allowed him to get away without raising suspicion . . . only now Lauren was going instead of him.

Lauren removed her coat, boots, and thick socks, transformed, and launched from one of the holes in the roof. As everyone crammed against the window to watch her go, Hal tapped Dewey on the shoulder and murmured in his ear. "Hey, can I borrow some paper? And a pencil?"

"Why?" Dewey asked, automatically reaching for a hidden pocket within his coat. Hal knew he kept his poetry notebook there.

"Does it matter? I just want to write something down before I forget."

Dewey shrugged, tore off a sheet for him, and waited while Hal hastily scribbled something on it. Once he was done, he handed the pencil back to Dewey and stuffed the piece of paper in his pocket. "Thanks."

He returned to his seat, knowing that Abigail was watching him with a frown.

"What were you writing?" she asked when she rejoined him.

Hal smiled, feeling terrible for deceiving her. "A secret message."

She raised an eyebrow at him but, thankfully, didn't press him. Yet.

When Lauren was a speck in the rapidly darkening sky and everyone was deep in random conversation, Hal broke in with an announcement that he wanted to lie on top of the geo-rocks and get some of his magic back.

Blacknail shook a pudgy finger at him again and opened his mouth to retort, but Robbie broke in. "He won't drain them all. Maybe a few. Or maybe he'll take just a bit of energy from lots of them, and nobody will notice the difference."

"Can't risk it," Blacknail said grumpily. "We need—"

But now Molly interrupted him. "Oh, hush, Riley. How about while Lauren's away? Just while we're waiting, okay? There are plenty of rocks back there."

The goblin sighed heavily and buried his face in his pudgy hands.

"You're serious?" Abigail whispered to Hal.

He nodded, saying nothing. Blacknail finally threw up his hands as Molly succeeded in wearing him down with her gentle reasoning.

"You're nuts," Fenton said as Hal gleefully headed for the door. "It's *cold* out there, moron!"

"It's cold inside, too," Hal muttered, pointing at the holes in the buggy's roof. He caught Abigail's puzzled gaze, gave her a smile, and quickly descended the ladder. He raced around to the wagon and climbed up onto the huge mound of rocks. They were covered by a sheet, but it was dark now, and he could see the orange glow from beneath. He crawled around until he found a place near the rear end, the farthest away from the buggy that he could get. Lying flat on his back and staring up at the sky, he felt the gentle warmth of the geo-rocks permeating through the sheet and into his body.

Although it was feasible to recharge if left alone with the rocks long enough, he'd already guessed he wouldn't be allowed to stay there while the wagon was moving. What if he fell asleep and rolled off? Lauren would be back soon, and they'd be on their way again— nowhere near enough time to recharge. And what if he *did* lie on those rocks throughout the journey home and drained them all? What would the reaction be if they showed up with a wagonload of worthless rocks?

No, he needed to visit the Chamber of Ghosts and stay awhile. The others could go on without him; he could simply fly home once recharged.

Twenty minutes passed, and the sky turned completely black. He listened to his friends chatting while, in the subdued glow of his bed of rocks, he carefully stuffed his rolled-up secret message into a hole in the sheet so it poked out: *Gone to recharge in Chamber of Ghosts. Don't wait. I'll fly home. See you tomorrow.*

Then he quietly slid off the back end of the wagon. His friends' chatter continued as he edged along the side.

Then he darted off into the woods.

Chapter Fourteen
Werewolves

Hal was well aware that what he was doing would land him in a heap of trouble. Blacknail would be furious, but he was normally grumpy anyway. He feared Molly's sharp tongue more than anything. He wasn't sure how his friends would react. They'd certainly be more annoyed at having to wait around.

If the lycans happened across the waiting buggy, they would have to deal with a whole group of shapeshifters. Hal wasn't worried about his friends. They could look after themselves.

He, on the other hand, was vulnerable. But he was on his own and certain he could slip quietly through the woods without being seen or heard. He planned to give the lycan village a wide berth and head straight to the beach where the entrance to the mines awaited him.

The temperature had plummeted in the last hour. It was too dark to see, but he knew his breath was pluming in the air before him as he picked his way between the black, shadowy trees. It irked him that almost every step he took resulted in the noisy crunch of brittle leaves. Trying to be careful slowed him down. Well, there was nothing he could do about it.

He was cutting across the woods in a direction that he expected—hoped—would take him to the road leading to the beach. He had to trust that his sense of direction was good because he saw absolutely nothing in the darkness. The moonlight, though bright, hardly managed to permeate the trees even though the branches were bare. He stumbled and scratched himself repeatedly on brambles, already beginning to regret his bullheaded decision.

To his delight, he almost fell out of the woods onto the road. It was covered with dry leaves but ten times easier to walk on. He broke into a jog. The frigid night air threatened to freeze his nose and ears, and made his eyes water, but his body was so warm that he quickly began to sweat.

He couldn't jog forever. When he slowed to a walk, panting, he wondered how far he had left to go. The road wound on and on through the woods. He wished he'd paid more attention when they'd driven this way in the buggy. Then he might recognize something and have some clue how far along he was.

A howl filled the air. He slowed for just a second, then resumed his pace. The wolfish howl was far off. It bothered him, though. Without his magic, he could be attacked by the lycans and eaten in seconds.

Would they do that? Would they really attack him? They might be in a wild animal phase right now, but surely they weren't so far gone that they'd lost all sense of humanity? When Hal was a dragon, he knew exactly what he was doing. Even with vague, occasional urges to eat raw meat, he was fully in control. He controlled the dragon, not the other way around.

As the howl filled the air again, he remembered that these people weren't shapeshifters. Not in the sense that Hal and his friends were, anyway. According to Darlene the ghost, they didn't even classify as human.

Breaking into a jog again, he kept his eyes ahead. The road was better lit than the surrounding woods, and he could see that it rounded a bend to the left. Surely, *surely* he'd be at the beach soon.

Ahead, he saw pinpricks of yellow light through the trees. Fire? It took a while to identify what he was looking at, but when he did, he sighed with relief. Burning torches surrounded what looked like a large camp. It wasn't the lycans' village, which by his reckoning was way over to the left. This was the goblin outpost, where his friends had been staying for the past couple of weeks, and where Lauren was supposed to be collecting a sack of chickens. Now he knew for sure that it wasn't far to the beach.

Relaxing a little, he slowed and walked awhile. The torches were mounted on a tall fence. He came across the entranceway with its thick posts and heavy gate. He thought he saw a goblin watching from a tower but couldn't be sure in the darkness. He was sorely tempted to run up to the gate and ask to be let in. He was sure the goblins would allow him access. But if he did that, his entire mission tonight would grind to a halt and might not get started again.

He walked on past the outpost. The safety of the flickering torches faded into the background, and the road twisted to the right.

Had Lauren already been and gone? If so, she would be back at the buggy soon with her load, after which Molly would call for Hal to come inside so they could get on the road—and he would be discovered missing. They'd find his note, but then what? He hoped they'd just go home.

Abigail would probably be really, really mad at him. But if he'd let her in on his secret, she would have made sure he never had the chance to risk his life in the woods. She would have told Molly, told *everyone*. And she'd be right. What Hal was doing was irresponsible and foolish, and he knew it—but hey, he was twelve. Wasn't he allowed to be irresponsible and foolish once in a while? The reward was great: he'd be back to his full shapeshifter self, able to transform whenever he wanted like the rest of his friends. The alternative was going home on the buggy and being the only one without powers.

He shook his head, stuffing his hands deep into his coat pockets. He had another reason for visiting the chamber. He wanted to see the ghosts again. He wanted to get a message to Chase. Perhaps this was his primary mission tonight, and getting his magic back was merely a bonus.

A noise to his left gave him pause. He slowed and stood still, listening. The noise came again, a gentle shuffling of dry leaves. It was quite a way off but still a little close for comfort. He hurried on, walking as quietly as humanly possible on a road scattered with crunchy leaves.

The noise came again, louder this time.

Then a snarl made him gasp with fright. He instinctively ducked low as if somehow that would hide him. The snarl came again, deep and savage. Then a flurry of activity sent Hal scuttling into the trees on the right-hand side of the road while, on the left, an animal leapt out of the woods. Hal ducked behind a bush, his eyes on the large animal.

He breathed a sigh of relief. A deer stood in the road, looking confused, turning around and around. Just a harmless deer.

But what had snarled?

Hal's breath caught in his throat again as something as large as the deer but much more powerful tore out of the woods and across the road. The deer bolted into the trees, and the predator bounded after it.

The chase was too close for Hal's comfort, just a hundred feet away. He cowered behind the bush, terrified. Had that been one of the lycan villagers? One of the *werewolves* as they hated to be called? If so, it was huge, easily eight feet tall with a gigantic upper body, all hair and muscle with a thick neck, long snout, and large pointed ears. Its lower body, by comparison, was slim and gangly, its legs and paws distinctly wolfish. If it had a tail, Hal hadn't noticed. He'd been too busy gazing with horror at its long, curved claws.

In an instant, he decided to run. And as he bolted, panting hard, he listened as best he could for the sounds of the savage pursuit in the woods nearby. If he waited for the beast to either catch the deer or allow it to escape, then he'd be the next target in the silent woods. At least at the moment the werewolf wasn't paying attention to him.

Minutes later, he saw glittering ocean ahead, reflecting the moonlight. His heart soared, though his chest ached with the effort of running so hard. Behind him came the triumphant howl of the werewolf. Two more howls echoed through the woods from different directions, then another much closer.

Once more he heard a flurry of crunching, swooshing leaves in the darkness. He almost stopped dead again because this time the sound came from up ahead, just off the road to the left. He didn't know how far away the lycan village was, but clearly a number of the wolfmen were out hunting tonight. Maybe *all* of them. Maybe the woods were teeming with ferocious beasts and it was pure luck that he'd made it this far.

The thought of slowing down and tiptoeing around with all these maniacal creatures tearing through the undergrowth was far worse than sprinting the rest of the way in a blind panic. He found his second wind and put on more speed.

He reached the beach at last. Now his footfalls were silent, masked by the crashing waves, but it was twice as hard to run on soft sand. He kept glancing back to make sure he wasn't being followed. He ran for a minute or two, knowing the mine entrance had to be just around the next cliff.

A cross between a bellow and a bark sounded behind him. He was compelled to twist his head around as he stumbled on.

The creature was coming for him. Its eyes were bright yellow discs, the rest nothing but a giant, blurred figure that stood out dark and huge against the pale beach. Sand kicked up all around as the werewolf tore toward him, its panting rhythmic and heavy over the constant crashing of waves.

To Hal's horror, a second monster appeared hot on its tail.

He knew he wasn't going to make it in time. Rounding the cliff, he found the mine entrance lit up with flickering torches. But the enormous gate had been repaired. There was no way he could break in without transforming.

The first of the werewolves thudded into him, sending him into a tumble so he ended up flat on his back. The creature pinned him down, its hot, heavy breath in his face. Hal barely had time to gasp in shock before long claws slashed across his chest. He let out a cry of anguish.

But the beast wasn't done. It opened its monstrous jaws to reveal deadly fangs. Snarling, it dipped its head and tore into him. Hal screamed as a terrible pain seared his belly.

A split second later, the second werewolf arrived. It slammed into the first and knocked it flying. With a chorus of ferocious snaps and growls, the two of them went tumbling into the sand just outside Hal's periphery.

Everything seemed to pause. Hal felt hot blood leaking out of his chest and stomach and running down his sides to pool underneath his body. Oddly, he felt no pain now, only numbness. Perhaps his nervous system had shut down to block out the horror of being eaten alive.

Somewhere off to his side, the savage battle ensued. Hal felt oddly detached from it all as though he were inside a protective bubble.

He turned his face upward to stare at the moon and the stars. He knew he was dying. He didn't need to feel the wounds to know they were deep. He could still feel blood leaking out. Then again, he was still alive and conscious. His heart and lungs were protected under his ribcage. A stabbing motion would penetrate easily, but a slash? He gingerly reached up with one shaking hand to touch his chest. Not surprisingly, it was wet and warm. His raised fingers were dark and glistening in the moonlight. But maybe the wound wasn't as deep as he'd feared.

His fingers moved down to his stomach. This wound was worse. His coat was torn wide open, and his groping hand felt—

He gasped and let his hand drop to his side. *Yeah, I'm dead.*

There was a sudden yelp. One of the scrapping werewolves had been hurt. It sounded just like a couple of ordinary dogs, with one of them realizing it had met its match and needed to retreat.

Lifting his head, Hal watched as the creature loped away along the beach. When it was a safe distance away, it slowed and straightened, standing on two feet with its long arms swinging. It looked back at him before lumbering away.

The victorious werewolf approached, and Hal stared up into its baleful yellow eyes. The thing was twice his size, nothing but long black hair and layers of muscle. It had wolfish features but the posture of a man and the loping movements of a gorilla. It was compact and powerful with a sense of urgent wildness in the way it circled him, sniffing and moaning as it pawed at the ground.

Abruptly, the monster shrank. Hal's vision blurred just then, so he might have imagined it, but it seemed like the werewolf was changing, reverting to a distinctly human form. Only that was impossible for lycans, which meant—

"Lucas?" Hal whispered.

"Shh," the man said, leaning over him. "Wesley's gone. And I'm going after him in just a second to make sure he stays gone. But I gotta get you to safety first. Where are your friends?"

"Outside the woods," Hal mumbled.

Lucas grumbled a complaint and said something about it being too dangerous to carry him, but then everything went foggy and Hal blacked out.

It seemed like just moments later that he woke to the feeling of being carried and set down on a hard floor. "I don't have a key to get in," Lucas grumbled. "I'll go for help. I can move fast on my own, and it's too risky carrying you through the woods anyway. They'll sniff out your blood a mile away."

Hal became aware of the heavy portcullis gate at the entrance to the mine. He was lying outside it, bleeding all over the threshold. Dimly, he saw Lucas hurrying away down the beach, transforming as he went, his two-legged run turning into a clumsy lope before he disappeared around the cliff.

Stinging pain started soon after. Hal began to shiver, too, and somehow that was worse than the wound itself. He wished for a fire to warm him while he died. At least he'd be able to slip away in relative comfort.

His vision blurred. "Go on home," he croaked, remembering the stupid note he'd written to his friends. Why had he told them that? What if they were gone when Lucas went to find them?

He closed his eyes, wishing Lucas hadn't rushed off. What if werewolves came sniffing around? Then again, if Lucas stayed, the gate would remain locked and Hal would never make it down to the Chamber of Ghosts where he could absorb magic and eventually heal himself.

His chest and stomach ached and stung terribly. He gave way to a consuming need to sleep, and then things seemed easier, less painful.

The noise of rattling machinery woke him briefly, and the feeling of being dragged and manhandled hurt so much that he blacked out again. The next time he woke, the walls and ceiling were moving, yet he was lying still. He was in motion without being dragged. His fingers rested on something cold and metal. He couldn't make sense of it.

Time lost all meaning as he woke and slept intermittently. It occurred to him that someone had been talking to him the whole time, only he hadn't been paying attention. He couldn't understand the words but recognized a female voice.

"Abi?" he murmured.

"It's me," she said. She leaned over him and whispered in his ear, saying things he was too groggy to understand.

There were a couple of horrible moments when he was jolted and bounced around, and he cried out in pain. He heard Abigail saying, "Sorry, sorry," and abruptly the juddering motion stopped. Things brightened after the second time that happened. There was an orange glow in the room. He was still lying flat on his back on cold metal, and his entire abdomen hurt terribly, but he recognized the ceiling. He was in the Chamber of Ghosts. Somehow he had been rescued and dragged down here.

He moaned and turned his head, looking for Abigail. "Where are you?" he whispered. She wasn't there.

But he was definitely in the Chamber of Ghosts. He could see the lost souls in the walls, standing there in silence, shoulder to shoulder, staring at him. Hal found their presence comforting. He tried to smile, tried to say hello, but immediately blacked out.

She was there again. He felt icy cold water on his lips, which dribbled down his chin and shocked him awake. Abigail was leaning over him, her dark hair hanging in his face. "Abi?" he tried again.

She smiled, her features less blurred than before. "I'm here. Just rest."

"How . . . ?" he managed.

"Lucas sent me. Rest. You're really badly injured and need to heal, and you can't heal until you get your magic back. So rest. Go to sleep."

"I—" he started, but felt a finger on his lips.

He slept well after that.

* * *

"Ow," he muttered. Pain flooded across his torso, and he kept his eyes shut as if opening them would make things worse.

"Hal," Abigail said, her hand on his face. "Are you able to heal now? You don't need to transform. Just do what we did at the lighthouse after the scrags attacked us. Remember? Just use whatever magic you have to heal."

He thought about that and reached deep inside for traces of magic. He sensed something there. He gathered whatever he had and harnessed it, letting it pool in his chest and stomach. Then he concentrated on healing until he could feel a tingling sensation across his stomach. He worked at it, not quite sure how he was doing it but knowing he was knitting his skin and flesh together.

"Work on the inside first," Abigail whispered. "You don't want to trap any infection under the skin. Start healing from the inside."

He opened his eyes and blinked at her. "What?"

She held up a wriggling maggot. "I've been keeping the wound clean with these. As you heal yourself, work your way outward just in case you can't get it all in one go. If you just close up the wound, you'll trap all the nasty unhealed stuff underneath. And you'll trap these little guys under your skin as well."

He stared at her, only half understanding. He kind of got it, but . . . *maggots*? What was she talking about?

She leaned down and kissed him on the nose. "Just trust me. Okay?"

He sighed, closed his eyes again, and refocused his efforts. He worked for as long as he could. Eventually he felt empty inside, like he had drained himself of magic. He opened his eyes and saw Abigail nodding at him and smiling. "Good. That'll do for now. Go back to sleep."

* * *

145

"Try again," she said as soon as he opened his eyes.

He groaned. His entire abdomen ached. He wanted to sit up and look at his wounds, but Abigail was pressing down on his shoulders.

"I'm thirsty," he said.

She let him take a long drag of water from a metal cup, then insisted he try healing again. He nodded and got to work.

It was easier this time. There was less pain, and he felt real progress. By the end of it, when he felt drained again, the pain had subsided quite dramatically. He felt around, seeing that his hands were clean. Abigail must have wiped the blood off. His coat was wide open, and his sweater and shirt had massive holes in them. She must have opened them up to get at his injuries. Yet his skin felt normal.

Slowly, carefully, he struggled up onto his elbows. Abigail didn't try to stop him. She was kneeling there with a metal cup of water in one hand and a bloody rag in the other. "Looking good," she said, smiling. "You're gonna make it out of here alive after all."

He stared at her, and she stared back. Although she was smiling, there was a haunted look in her eyes. "I messed up," he said meekly.

"Yep."

"That werewolf could have torn me to shreds."

"It kind of did," Abigail said, gesturing to his chest and belly. "Good thing Lucas was there."

"So he found you okay?"

She didn't answer straight away. Instead she glared at him. "Molly found your note and was furious. Blacknail nearly blew up. They argued about coming after you, and Blacknail refused, saying the noise of the buggy would alert the lycans. So Molly suggested a few of us come after you, but Blair said it was a bad idea to leave the rest of the gang unprotected, and there was a big argument about who should go after you and who should stay . . ."

"Man," Hal muttered.

Abigail spoke impassively. "Then Lucas showed up. He was in a hurry. He told us where you were and said he had to go after Wesley before the chief found out there were humans in the area. That would have been bad. So he tore off, and we haven't seen him since. I told Molly I was coming after you. I can fly higher than nasty old werewolves and can get through the gate without even opening it. Robbie wanted to come, but he's too slow. Blair offered to fly, but . . ."

well, honestly, I was kind of tired of squabbling adults by this time. So I said I'd get you down to the chamber by myself and report back."

"And have you?" Hal asked. "Reported back?"

She shook her head. "Not yet. I couldn't leave you. I rolled you down here and fixed you up the best I could."

She gestured to a wheelbarrow standing nearby, possibly the same one Hal and Robbie had used to transport the injured goat. He suddenly remembered the cold metal he'd felt beneath his body as he'd slipped in and out of sleep. He was astounded. Abigail had dragged him off the beach, manhandled him into the wheelbarrow, and rolled him through a mile of tunnels—including down two flights of steps! He gazed at her in awe.

"I didn't have a key to get in," she said. "I opened it from the inside."

Hal nodded feebly, remembering the metal box on the inside wall.

"Almost as soon as you got here," Abigail went on, "the bleeding stopped. It's like you channeled the magic in this room from the very first minute. But still, healing was really, really slow."

Hal sat up straighter and pushed himself back against the sloping wall of the core. "Did I dream something about maggots?"

"I had to go hunting for them. I found that rotting goat Robbie dumped outside and stole some maggots from it."

He stared at her, appalled. "Are you kidding me?"

She shook her head. "Maggots are great for keeping wounds clean. They eat dead flesh and keep the stink down."

There was a long silence. Then Hal sighed. "I still don't know if you're kidding me. I mean . . . *maggots*?"

"It's called debridement," she said stiffly. "Disinfecting the wound. My mom's used maggot therapy before. It works."

"Maggot therapy," Hal repeated. He was about to make a sharp retort, and then realized how ungrateful he was being. "Okay," he said, nodding. "Well, uh, thanks. I mean it. You . . . saved my life."

"Again," she said, a twinkle returning to her eyes.

"Again."

She climbed slowly to her feet. "All right, here's the plan. We've been here for hours and hours already, maybe half the night, maybe even the whole night. It's hard to tell. I'm going to tell the others to head home. Then I'll fly back and wait with you until you're recharged. Then *we'll* head home. Sound good?"

147

Hal nodded.

"I guess you'll need another five, six hours? So you might as well go back to sleep if you can. I'll see you soon."

"All right." As she started to walk out, Hal called after her. "Thanks, Abi. I, uh . . . I love you."

She stared at him, and his insides churned. *What* had he just said? The words had popped out. He meant it, of course, but actually *saying* those three words out loud . . . ? It was something that moms and dads told each other. Heck, it was something Hal told his mom all the time. Or used to, anyway. It had been a while. But saying it to Abigail?

She studied him intently. "I should think so, too, after all I've done for you."

Then she blew him a kiss and sauntered off with a smile on her face.

Chapter Fifteen
Who is Chase?

Sleep came easily in the Chamber of Ghosts whether desired or not. Before he dozed off, though, he gingerly climbed to his feet and swayed from side to side, poking and prodding his chest and stomach through his tattered clothes. Apart from a bit of soreness, he was almost as good as new. Once he had his magic back and could transform, he'd be back to normal in no time.

He approached the nearest wall. It glowed softly, but there was no sign of any ghosts. He recalled there had been dozens of them watching him when he'd been at his worst—and surely Abigail had seen them, too. Unless he'd dreamed them. He'd have to ask her later.

"Chase?" he called. "Chase, are you there? Can you hear me?"

He felt ridiculous talking to a wall, but he tried again and again, louder each time. He walked around the chamber, trying to find the brightest spots as if that somehow mattered. There was no sign of Chase or anyone else.

Muttering to himself, he gave up and returned to the core. Almost as soon as he lay down, drowsiness took over, and he dozed off.

He began to dream . . .

Soldiers were wading into the water and dipping below the surface. Soon they disappeared from sight. Hal submerged with them. They couldn't see him. He was a silent, invisible watcher.

The lead soldiers wore wetsuits and carried deadly spearguns. Others followed, loaded down with canisters that were most likely packed with other weapons. The soldiers swam slowly toward a black, pulsing cloud in the murky depths. Leading the procession was an underwater vehicle, some sort of miniature submarine just large enough for a single man, bright yellow with torpedoes on the sides.

The submarine plunged through the hole. Hal switched locations so that he, too, was on the other side, watching the submarine emerge from the blackness. Soldiers followed it through, aiming their spearguns ahead.

A gigantic sea serpent appeared. It hurtled through the water toward the invading soldiers, opening its massive jaws wide, and immediately the yellow submarine began to turn. Torpedoes fired and shot through the murk in a trail of bubbles. Seconds later, they plowed into their target, and the serpent exploded into a boiling red cloud—

Hal woke. He frowned and sat up, rubbing his eyes. The dream remained in his memory, far more vivid than they usually were.

Abigail was pacing back and forth. "Morning," he said shakily.

She spun around. "Finally! I didn't want to wake you, but I'm *so* bored. Can we go now? It's probably afternoon already."

As Hal attempted to tuck in his shirt and pull his coat around him, he was aware that Abigail was looking at him as though he'd forgotten something important. "What?"

"Uh, hello? You're going to fly us home, remember? Blacknail and the others are long gone by now. So quit straightening your shirt because you're just going to have to take it off again. Come on, I'm just about pig-sick of this cave."

Hal took one last look around, wishing he'd gotten a chance to pass a message to Chase. He'd wanted to tell him to be patient, that help was on the way. Still, maybe it was better that no ghosts had showed. For all Hal knew, Chase's statue body, wherever it was, might be broken up into pieces or lost forever. There was no sense giving him false hope.

They hurried up the tunnel. When they reached the vast mining cavern, Hal was surprised to see that the floor was shiny wet. It seemed the leaking hot spring was still trickling down the tunnel into this cavern, spreading out and running off into gullies and crevices. The cavern floor was uneven, and in some places the water was knee deep, still and cold. But there were also sandbag walls to guide bubbling streams off in a safer direction.

"I guess the mine's closed," Hal said as he followed Abigail around the deepest puddles.

"For now," she agreed. "They've been busy up the tunnel, clearing the debris, but they're mostly done and are working to get the leak stopped."

"So the way out isn't blocked?" Hal asked, confused.

"Not anymore. It's been two weeks, Hal, and don't forget there are other tunnels out of the cavern. One leads out to the gulch. We could go that way, but it's a long, twisty route and I don't know exactly where it comes out. The way we came in is best. Careful—some of these puddles are hot."

The tunnel was easy-going at first but turned into a mess farther up. The roof had collapsed in many places, leaving eerie gaps above, some of them vast. The goblins had managed to remove much of the debris, leaving a surprisingly clear trail. Meanwhile, water continued to cascade down the gently sloping tunnel floor, running along one side and forcing Hal and Abigail to the other.

Eventually they arrived at the goblins' hot pool—or what was left of it. Now it was a giant crack in the ground, an abyss filled with rocks. Goblins were at work dumping wheelbarrows of rubble. "They've been filling it for ages," Abigail explained. "Trying to block it up and stop the leak."

The steaming hot water still bubbled up in various places, though it was clearly struggling to get past the debris. The flow had been slowed but not stopped, and the humidity in the tunnel was thick and clammy. Hal shuddered, trying to figure out exactly where he'd been lying when Molly had turned him to stone. Everything had been cleared away, so he could only guess judging by the location of the abyss. He paused awhile, sparing a thought for the poor goblin who'd given him a leg up and saved his life.

"Are you okay?" Abigail said quietly, slipping her hand into his.

"The goblin," he mumbled.

Abigail dropped her gaze. "They couldn't get to him."

Swallowing, he nodded and turned away, suddenly wanting to vacate this place of doom and gloom. "It's weird seeing it all cleared away like this. Seems like I was here just a few hours ago."

"It's been two weeks," Abigail said. "I've been worried sick."

Hal looked at her, at a loss for words.

Before he could formulate a coherent sentence, she smiled and tugged on his hand. "Come on. Let's get out of here."

They finally reached the mine entrance where the huge portcullis gate was neatly raised into the rocky ceiling. Goblins milled about, and they frowned at Hal and Abigail. "You nuts?" one demanded. "What are yer still doing in lycan country at this time of the month? You'll get bit, see if yer don't."

"Good advice," Abigail agreed, nodding sagely. "What about you? Aren't you also in danger of getting 'bit'?"

"We stick together."

"Aw," Abigail said, tilting her head. "How sweet."

Outside, the sun was blinding. Hal shielded his eyes. It was still bitingly cold even in the middle of the afternoon. As he moved onto the beach, his gaze fell on the patch of sand where he'd lain the night before. It was soaked with his blood.

Abigail ushered him away. "Come on, Hal, let's move before we both end up getting 'bit' by the neighbors."

He took off his coat and, shivering, looked around for somewhere to take off the rest of his things. "I hate not having smart clothes," he muttered.

"I'll go around the corner," she said. "After you've changed, I'll come back and get your pants and boots." She looked with distaste at his tattered and bloody sweater and shirt. "We'll leave those behind, though."

When she'd disappeared around the rocky hillside, Hal hurriedly removed the rest of his clothes and transformed. Only when he was standing in the sand thrashing his enormous club-ended tail from side to side did he realize how good it felt to be a dragon again. Relief flooded through him, knowing that he was now fully recharged and back to his abnormal self.

He gave a bellow, and moments later Abigail dashed around the corner to collect up his clothes. She was already wearing his coat over her own and looked strangely stout. She took a few minutes to bundle his long pants, boots and socks into a neat pile, then climbed up onto his back and into position near his neck. "Go," she called.

If it was cold at ground level, he could only imagine how icy it was higher up. He didn't feel the chill so much in his dragon form, and anyway he was busy pumping his wings. Abigail, on the other hand, had the freezing air blasting into her face. She didn't say anything, but he could feel her pressed low on his back, clinging on with her face buried in his reptilian skin.

He flew hard and fast, staying low where the air was marginally warmer. Finally able to see the lay of the land from above, he followed the road from the beach past the goblin outpost. The road was longer than he'd imagined. He veered right and flew over the lycans' village. They were down there, loping around in all directions like a bunch of confused animals accidentally released from a zoo. Two were fighting savagely, but they were alone in their aggression; the rest of the villagers clearly had other things on their minds, though Hal couldn't imagine what. They seemed to be running around mindlessly, their humanity temporarily suspended. They probably slept outside at night, hunted and foraged for animals large and small, lived like the beasts they were. What must it be like to wake from this stupor perhaps a week later when the moon began to wane?

Hal gave them one last look and forged onward, heading for the line of hills. He could see Eastward Pass already. He flew over it, spotting trolls clambering over the slopes. Less than a minute later, he was out over the plains, moving fast and heading for home.

* * *

Although he was glad to be back in Carter, his welcome was not exactly friendly.

He landed next to Blacknail's buggy, which still had the wagon hitched to the back, laden with geo-rocks. He folded his wings and allowed Abigail to dismount while he looked up and down the narrow streets.

Villagers looked at him curiously, as they always did, but walked on by without fear. They all recognized him by now. He noticed that the wagon had been uncovered and a few layers of rocks already gone. Some of the more high-tech villagers had their power and lighting back. Others probably had no interest in the geo-rocks, continuing to use fire as they had always done. But more importantly, Miss Simone's laboratory would, by now, be up and running. That had probably been Blacknail's first stop upon his return.

"Hal!" a man's voice yelled.

He turned and grunted as his parents hurried into view. He wanted to grin and hug them, but first he needed to transform and put his clothes back on.

Unfortunately, a small crowd gathered almost immediately after Hal's parents arrived on the scene. In a matter of minutes there were dozens of villagers standing around looking at him. His dad seemed angry, saying he was foolish for going off on his own like that, while his tearful mom was happy he was alive but annoyed he'd put himself in so much danger.

Then, drawn by the commotion, Robbie and his other friends started to show up. And Molly. And Miss Simone. There was a mixture of expressions between them—some stern, a few genuinely happy, one or two apparently pleased to see him getting an ear-bashing, one veiled and impassive, and another—Miss Simone—with no discernible expression at all. Jolie was there, too, in a rickety wooden wheelchair. She was smiling, but it was impossible to tell what was going through her mind. She was probably just lapping up the wave of emotions.

Since Hal was surrounded on all sides and couldn't very well transform in front of them all without his smart clothes to change back into, Abigail climbed down and tried to answer some of the questions and explain what had been happening since Blacknail had driven his passengers home. She told how Hal had used magic to heal, then recharged and healed some more a bit later on, and finally slept for one final absorption session. She looked funny with two thick coats on, and after a while she took one off and threw it down, apparently quite warm now. She was hammered with more questions, and she patiently answered them. Gradually, villagers began to drift away.

"Why won't he change?" Hal's mom asked plaintively.

"Because he's got no clothes on," Abigail explained. "He'll change if you'll all just let him go find a private spot."

Hal agreed with a throaty roar, pawing the ground a couple of times.

But his mom and dad approached. "Are you okay, son?" Mr. Franklin asked gruffly, his anger having evaporated. "I can't believe you were bitten. And by a werewolf of all things! It's like something out of a horror movie." He suddenly paled. "Wait. I hope that doesn't mean *you'll* turn into a werewolf!"

Hal wanted to tell his dad that he'd never seen a horror movie, or any movie for that matter. Movies were something he'd read about, something from the past that he and his friends had never experienced. Still, he'd read books, and he knew something about the subject. He wasn't too worried. He was already a dragon shapeshifter. How could he be a dragon *and* werewolf? Since he was in his dragon form, all he could do was offer a grunt.

Molly apparently took this the wrong way. "Hal, you have no business getting angry. What happened last night was your own fault. We would all have been fine if you hadn't run off into the woods on your own."

"Yeah, you moron," Fenton said.

"Dimwit," Thomas added.

Even Darcy seemed irritated with him. "What part of 'wild, deadly, ferocious werewolves' didn't you understand?"

"Hey," Robbie said, scowling at them all. "Back off. Hal's been through enough without you chiming in. It wasn't his fault he was nearly crushed under tons of rock and almost boiled alive. He's lucky to be alive after that. If anyone's to blame for the werewolf thing, it's Blacknail."

"Huh?" Fenton said.

The goblin wasn't around, but if he were, no doubt he would be just as puzzled by the accusation.

"If Hal had been allowed to lie on the back of the wagon and recharge," Robbie went on, "he wouldn't have needed to sneak off to the chamber, and none of this werewolf stuff would have happened."

"Blacknail *did* let him—" Thomas started.

Robbie had been waiting for a response like that. "He let him only while we were waiting for Lauren. That's not enough time. So Hal would have come home being the only shapeshifter who couldn't shift. Not cool."

There was a brief silence after this, and Hal shot Robbie a grateful smile—if a fang-filled dragon grimace could be recognized as such.

"All right, enough," Miss Simone said, speaking up for the first time. Once again, Hal was struck by how *plain* she looked without magic. Next to her, Jolie sat in her wheelchair. She had probably edged closer on purpose just to show everyone how stunning she was in comparison. "Show's over, folks. Go on home, Hal. You too, Abigail." She stared at Hal for a moment. "I'd like to talk to you later, if that's okay? About your . . . experience."

Hal nodded. That was fine with him. He wanted to talk to her, too.

The crowd dispersed. His friends gave him one last look, and his parents sighed and told him they'd see him at home. Hal stomped away, and Abigail came after him with his clothes. He chose a place outside the village fence where there were a lot of trees and reverted to human form.

As he reached for this clothes, another dream entered his head. It was a continuation of the one he'd had earlier, and it caused him to gasp and reel.

The soldiers raced up the grassy banks, shooting as they went, deadly spears whipping through the air and thudding into goblin guards stationed around the lake. Canisters were dumped and opened,

155

weapons were snatched up, and soon the dawn was filled with the rattle of gunfire. Goblins dropped face down in the grass, swords grasped in their dead hands.

One of the soldiers shouted orders: "Secure the area! Bring the troops through! Prepare to march—!"

Hal almost fell. He leaned against the tree trunk and stood there breathing hard. Earlier, he'd thought his dream had been unusually vivid. Now he was convinced there was something more to it. It wasn't just a dream. It was a vision, sent by the Gatekeeper. She'd advised him to take the first step, to 'invite them in' before they invaded.

He dressed hurriedly, thinking hard. The vision wasn't happening in real time. It couldn't be. He'd seen part of it while asleep in the Chamber of Ghosts, and another part just now, as though the events had paused in the interim. The invasion wasn't happening right at this moment, but it was *going* to happen.

When? It had looked like early morning—but which morning?

He found Abigail leaning up against a gate post. As they set off toward home, she huddled against his arm. "I'm so glad things are back to normal."

"Mmm," Hal said, distracted. When were the soldiers going to invade? Tomorrow at dawn? The next day?

"What does 'mmm' mean?"

He sighed and tried to shake off the vision. "Things on my mind. I'm going to ask Miss Simone about Chase. Did you see how Molly, Blair and Blacknail reacted when I mentioned his name? They know him."

Abigail frowned. "So who is he?"

"Come home with me, and I'll tell you on the way. But there's something else bugging me." He paused, uncertain how to explain. "It's just that . . . while I was a statue, I had a sort of . . . uh . . ." He paused again. What was the word he was looking for? "You know when something really big pops into your head and it sort of changes the way you think about things?"

"A revelation?" Abigail offered. "An epiphany?"

"I guess. Something like that. Yeah, while I was away I saw stuff that made me think. And now I'm seeing visions."

"What do you mean?"

Hal shook his head. "It's hard to explain."

She gripped his arm so tight that he winced. "Try me."

When there was a knock at the door, Hal's mom got up and went to answer it as Hal, his dad, and Abigail looked at one another. A few seconds later, Miss Simone entered, her blond hair dull and lifeless.

"Have a seat, have a seat," Hal's mom said, indicating her own vacated chair.

"No, please, I won't take your place," Miss Simone said.

Mr. Franklin offer her his instead. "Hal's got some questions to ask you. And some stuff to tell you. Stuff that, uh, doesn't make a whole lot of sense."

Hal hung his head. His parents hadn't been impressed with his *epiphany* as Abigail had called it. Nor had Abigail, for that matter. And he was pretty sure Miss Simone would take a dim view of it as well.

With four of them seated around the table and Mr. Franklin loitering in the background, all eyes fell on Miss Simone. "So tell me, Hal. What was it like being petrified by Molly's gaze?"

Hal began his story again, taking his time and not skipping a thing. "Wait," Miss Simone interrupted when he got to the bit about the ghosts in the walls. "Molly said nothing about this."

"That's because Molly didn't see them," Hal said with a shrug. "I don't know why. Abigail saw them. Sort of."

"I saw fleeting movements," she said sheepishly. "Sorry, Hal."

"It's okay. I don't know why I saw a bunch of ghosts that nobody else saw. Maybe because they were trying to warn me? Because the earthquake would trap me, and me only?"

Miss Simone pinched her nose, a sign that she was having trouble accepting this. "All right. Ghosts in the wall trying to warn you of the future. Go on."

He continued, glossing over the earthquake part but detailing the moment he looked into Molly's eyes. After that, Miss Simone's own eyes widened, and she held her breath, hanging on to every word Hal said.

He explained everything including the bright white light that seemed to be a very tall, very slim female alien creature with enormous eyes. "She hovered over this pit of white light, and all these black shadow people were just falling into it. But when it was my turn, she picked me up and pushed me away. I felt like I'd been rejected. That was when I met Chase."

Miss Simone's brow knitted together. "Chase? Who's Chase?"

Hal went on with his story, and as he filled in the details of Chase—about how he was fourteen years old with glasses and used to work at a very special school in a place called Happy Valley Ridge in the south—her mouth fell open and recognition flickered across her face. She said nothing, and for now he skipped over the part of the story where he'd seen visions of war and had his epiphany about joining the worlds. Right now he was more interested in Chase. He finished up with what the boy had told him—that he had been frozen by a gorgon named Molly.

Miss Simone slapped her hand on the table, making everyone jump. "I *knew* it. I knew you were talking about him. But . . . but this is impossible."

She looked agitated, and Hal knew why. She believed in science. Magic was an ugly word to her, and the concept of ghosts left a nasty taste in her mouth. The idea of a strange being acting as some sort of godlike gatekeeper for millions of souls filled her with angst. She would love to explain it all away as pure science, as 'random synaptic firing in the visual cortex' or 'hallucinations brought on by an oxygen-starved brain' and other such mumbo jumbo, but hearing about Chase like this stopped her dead. How could she pigeonhole Hal's fantastic dreamlike story as 'all in the imagination' if he'd somehow managed to dredge up a real-life person from Miss Simone's past?

"Tell me about him," Hal demanded.

Abigail leaned forward as well, clearly just as curious.

Miss Simone sighed. "He was a helper at the school. The entire property was owned by a very rich man by the name of Richard Stockwell, and he agreed to turn it into a private haven and fund our very secret shapeshifter program. There were twelve of us at first—twelve baby boys and girls. I was one of them. We grew up like most other children in the world, only we were restricted to the property. Our parents came and went, though. They didn't *need* to work, but they wanted to continue their ordinary lives for as long as possible."

"And Chase?" Hal pressed.

"He was the son of the owner. He was schooled at Happy Valley Ridge with the rest of us, only he was six years older." She pursed her lips. "Looking back, I guess he must have been very lonely and bored, and perhaps that explains what he did. He used to help out around the place—grudgingly, I should add—and often came along on field trips and assisted during sports and games. He would tease us a lot but was almost like an uncle to us."

"What did he do?"

Miss Simone gave a shrug. "He learned about us. At first he didn't know we were shapeshifters. He used to live with his mother, you see, and then—well, she died, so he came to live with his father, and so at first he thought we were all just ordinary children. When he found out what we were . . . well, I think he flipped out. He kidnapped two of us— the Hammacher twins, Bo and Astrid—and we never saw them again. That's why only ten of us made it through the program and came to this new world." She sighed heavily. "It's a long story. In the end, Chase was tracked down, and Molly took it upon herself to stone him before anyone could stop her. So we never learned what happened to the twins."

"I thought you and Felipe were the twins of the group," Hal murmured absently, his mind racing.

"There were two sets of twins," Miss Simone confirmed. "Bo and Astrid were identical. Uncannily so."

A long silence followed. Hal sat back and pondered. He hadn't seen Chase as a bad guy. Maybe he'd had a good reason to kidnap Bo and Astrid Hammacher, one that he never got a chance to explain. Whatever his excuse, Hal's need to find and free him was unchanged. Chase deserved a chance to make his case, and if he turned out to be rotten to the core, he would be dealt with accordingly. Again.

"Where is he?" he asked. "Where's his body? His statue?"

"In a rose garden south of here. You remember Whisper Mountain? An old woman lives on one of the neighboring mountains. Some call her a witch, and she likes to keep up that persona because it keeps people away. Anyway, she has a huge rose garden, and in that garden are dozens of statues. Many of Molly's accidental victims. They're what she calls 'keepers'—those who need to be protected against the elements and wildlife in case there's ever a chance they wake up."

Hal glanced at Abigail, and she raised her eyebrows at him, her eyes shining. "So now that Blair . . ." he said, trailing off with excitement.

Miss Simone finished for him. "Right. Molly's already trying to persuade Blair to head back to the Chamber of Ghosts to rejuvenate. She wants to take him to the rose garden as soon as possible."

"Can we come? I want to meet Chase when he wakes."

She nodded. "I don't see why not. Now, on to other matters. I sense there's something else you want to tell me."

Hal shifted uncomfortably. "Uh, yeah."

He took a minute or two to explain the visions he'd received while in the strange world of darkness: the repeated scenes of battle, the gigantic smoky portal stretching across the ocean, even Lieutenant Briskle's unexpected appearance. And of course the concept of Miss Simone's magical world being an experiment.

"By whom?" she demanded.

"Not sure," Hal said. "I . . . I saw Earth from space. So maybe . . . aliens?"

His dad gave an involuntary snort and addressed Miss Simone. "He used to read science fiction."

She closed her eyes and asked Hal to continue. He went on to tell her how the barrage of images seemed to be pointing to one thing—the unification of worlds—and how the most recent vision showed an invasion of soldiers killing the sea serpent and shooting at goblins. "I think," he said slowly, "that the Gatekeeper, whoever or whatever she is, wants me to open a bunch of holes and join the worlds. You know, let everyone come together. And we should do it *now*, invite the soldiers in before they come through in force."

Now it was Miss Simone's turn to snort. "Absolutely not. You want soldiers and scrags waltzing into our village? Millions of virus survivors taking over the land and ruining the countryside? And what about the virus? Even though the source has been eradicated, the spores are still coating every surface in the world. Doors, windows, everything. Do you want that yellow dust blowing all over us?"

"But I *saw* them," Hal said. "I saw soldiers coming through—"

She stood suddenly, her chair scraping across the floor. Coming around the table, she placed a hand on Hal's shoulder and gazed down at him.

"Hal, I'm glad you're okay. You've been through a tough time lately what with scrags and turning to stone and being bitten by a werewolf. See Dr. Kessler about your injuries, and take some time off. I have a lot of business to tend to, but in the meantime I'll see to it that Blair is fully—what did you call it? Recharged?—and we'll all go to the rose garden on the mountain and wake those statues." She paused, frowning. "We have an awful lot of geo-rocks now. What if Blair uses some of those? Maybe he can absorb their magic instead of going all the way back to the Chamber of Ghosts . . ."

Hal fought to suppress a surge of irritation. *He* could have absorbed magic that way if only Blacknail had let him. He could have avoided being bitten by a werewolf. "But what about the holes? Joining the worlds?"

She shook her head and smiled. "That's a pipe dream, Hal. I'll tell you what. If you can find an instant, worldwide cure for the yellow dust, we'll open some portals and join our worlds. Deal?"

He could tell she was humoring him, and he found it a little annoying and patronizing. He gritted his teeth and smiled back. "Deal."

As she swept out of the house, he leaned back in his chair, his mind a whirl of thoughts. He was prepared to take Miss Simone's deal seriously. What she didn't realize was that he already had the germ of an idea for this 'instant cure' she had joked about.

She wanted to strike a deal?

As far as he was concerned, the game was on.

Chapter Sixteen
Making Plans

It seemed pointless for Hal to see Dr. Kessler about his werewolf injuries when he was already fully healed. However, his mom insisted, so he trudged along to her cottage that afternoon. Abigail would have come along with him if Hal hadn't told her he'd catch up with her later.

When he arrived and knocked on the door, Dr. Kessler answered promptly, nodded, and allowed him in. "Wait," she said briskly, and disappeared down the hallway. Moments later, Hal heard her talking to a man, probably another patient.

A sign on the wall read BE PATIENT AND WAIT, so he sat and grimaced at the smell of potions wafting through the cottage, only partially masked by the heavy scent of roses. Eventually Dr. Kessler saw her patient out, a large man with a broken arm and bruises all over his face. When he was gone, she immediately sat next to Hal, pulled his coat open, and tugged at his shirt.

"Let me see," she said, peering over her brass-rimmed spectacles. She was small but stern, and Hal silently allowed her to examine his belly and chest. She huffed and frowned. "Well, there's nothing there. No trace of a claw mark or bite. Weren't you bitten on the stomach?"

"I healed," Hal told her.

"You certainly did. Well, nothing to worry about, I'm sure. You can go." And with that, she patted him on the shoulder and bustled off down the hall.

Well, that was a complete waste of time, Hal thought as he sauntered outside. He stood pondering for a moment. Villagers shuffled past, most of them bundled up in thick winter coats. He only half noticed them.

Stopping the soldiers from invading was forefront on his mind. Inviting them through, allowing them safe passage, seemed like the obvious answer. Extending a welcoming hand to them should, in theory, negate their need to use guns, and therefore it might be possible to avoid the senseless slaughter of the sea serpent and dozens of goblins, and whatever else followed.

But it made sense to eradicate the virus first. If he could do that, then he could open up many, many holes—a grand welcoming gesture rather than a halfhearted attempt. With holes all over the land, there would be no way for Miss Simone to stop the soldiers and scientists from coming through. And if trying to stop them was utterly futile, there would be nothing left for her to do but accept the situation and make the best of it. Everyone would *have* to get along.

All this made sense in his head until he started letting the details bubble to the surface. He suppressed the urge to give up on the idea and headed along the hard-packed dirt road, ducking his face whenever the icy wind blew.

It annoyed him that the adults, and in particular Miss Simone, seemed to be doing nothing about the yellow spores that smothered his old world. Sure, the source had been eradicated. The enormous pit of centaur-crafted fungus was closed for good, and the spores no longer puffed up from the pit to be sucked through nine portals and blown out into the atmosphere of the other world. But they were still *there*, a fine coat on just about every surface imaginable, lying dormant until some unfortunate man or woman came along and put a hand in the stuff. Once contact was made with human skin, the spores activated. Unlike a true virus, which would die without a living host, the deadly yellow mushroom dust was durable and long-lasting.

It had to be killed off. *Nullified.* And Hal thought he knew how.

He exited the village and headed into the woods toward the centaur shelter. It was unlikely that he would be welcomed by the stubborn, standoffish centaurs, but he had to talk to Fleck, probably the most agreeable of the equine creatures.

He followed a path through the trees. It was even colder in the depths of the woods. The branches above were completely bare, and a thick layer of leaves crunched underfoot. Ahead, he saw a patch of darkness where the impressive centaur shelter sprawled.

It occurred to him that he could have brought Dewey along to help gain him access to the shelter. He wasn't sure the centaurs would welcome a lone human. Still, Hal wasn't just *any* human.

"Stop," a deep voice ordered.

Hal halted, and a powerful, dark-skinned centaur moved into view, calmly nocking an arrow in his bow as he came. His thick, leathery tunic had large, bulky shoulders but no sleeves, perhaps to show off his rock-solid muscular arms. The centaurs couldn't have picked a better guard.

"I came to see Fleck," Hal said, eyeing the sharp end of the arrow.

The centaur stared at him long and hard. "Go home, boy."

There was a heavy trace of disdain in the centaur's voice. Hal stood his ground, thinking about the times he'd successfully stared down dragons. All it took was a bit of boldness. "I came to see Fleck," he repeated, louder and more firmly than before. "I'm a shapeshifter. Don't make me transform. Sometimes I have trouble with my temper when I'm a dragon."

A flicker of recognition crossed the centaur's face. His tone was a little warmer the next time he spoke. "State the purpose of your visit."

"I told you. I need to speak to Fleck. In private." When he received no response, he added, "I'm here on behalf of Miss Simone."

This was a half truth. In fact he *was* here on Miss Simone's behalf. She just didn't know it yet.

"If Lady Simone had intended for you to visit here," the centaur said, somewhat haughtily, "she would have come with you. Or at least sent the boy, Dewey, who is after all your centaur emissary."

Hal sighed. He really should have brought his friend along. "Look, if I can't come in, just ask Fleck to meet me out here." Again, a long silence. "Please."

The centaur gave a curt nod. "That much I can do. Wait here."

So Hal waited. He shivered, tugging his jacket around him. Then he quickly ran around gathering twigs and piling them up together. He scooped leaves all over the twigs until he had a small, neat mountain, then stood for a moment and focused on bringing up a belch of fire. The flames took hold of the dry leaves and roared into life, and within half a minute he was kneeling over the fire and warming his hands until they were toasty.

It was at least ten minutes before Fleck came trotting out. He was half the size of the guard and with a gentle, perpetually concerned expression. Over his raggedy tunic he wore a protective apron with several scorch marks and spatters of what looked like oil.

He approached Hal and bowed, apparently unconcerned about the impromptu campfire. "How goes it, young dragon?"

"I need to ask you something," Hal said, skipping the small talk. "The fog you created. Does it *kill* the spores or just sort of deflect them?"

The centaur frowned. "Mmm. It deflects them to a certain extent, yes, but it doesn't kill them. I believe I explained all this to you before. If spores make it through the fog, the fog renders them dormant. Remove the fog, and the spores reawaken. The process is quite simple. You see, the chemicals in the fog produce a temporary coating of . . ."

Hal sighed while the centaur rattled on. Now that he thought about it, he vaguely remembered Fleck saying as much the first time Miss Simone had taken the shapeshifters to the shelter. That was when Hal, Abigail and Robbie had slipped away from the group and interrupted Fleck's work. "So it wouldn't do any good if the fog covered the entire world?" he interrupted.

Fleck tilted his head to one side. "It's interesting you should ask that. No, it wouldn't, unless the fog was perpetual as it was on your island all those years." He smiled. "But I'm fairly certain we couldn't smother the world with artificial fog for the rest of time. However . . ."

"Yes?"

The centaur stepped closer and tilted forward. "Hal, the scientists in your world used our formula to create their own version of the fog, but with a few differences. Do you remember the decontamination you went through?"

Hal did. After his run-in with the scrags, he and his friends, including Ryan, had been contaminated with spores. Miss Simone had taken the group back to Carter, but before they'd been able to enter the village, she'd insisted on the usual virus clean-up involving a hose down and scrub by a team of sour-faced goblins. Clothes had been either bagged or burned. Hal and his friends had finally been allowed into the village—wrapped in blankets.

"I remember it well," he said shortly.

"Well, we saved a couple of bags of clothes," the centaur said. "It's always useful to replenish our spore samples. But we were startled to find the spores embedded in your clothing were very much dead."

Fleck crossed his arms and waited for Hal to digest that information.

"So?" Hal asked at last.

The centaur spread his hands. "So something caused the spores to die. We haven't seen that before. We've seen them dormant, but not dead. It seems that the scientists back in your world have come up with something that actually works."

"The fog-pellets?"

"You all regaled us with tales of how you escaped the soldiers and scrags, and there was mention of fog-pellets, yes. You said the soldiers had a supply of mass-produced pellets that, when soaked in water, turned into highly concentrated fog."

"Right."

"Well, either those fog-pellets have an additional ingredient or they simply produce a much higher dosage of fog than our own crude chemical mixture. In any case, it seems those pellets can successfully kill the spores."

Excitement grew deep down inside Hal's gut.

The centaur edged closer still. "Hal, many of us centaurs are indifferent about humans in both this world and the other, and hardly care if humans exist or not. Of course, being indifferent is not the same as performing acts of genocide. None of us condone what our previously esteemed leader did in creating that deadly fungus and releasing those spores into your world. Most of us feel deeply ashamed for what was supposedly done on behalf of all centaurs. The honor and pride of our entire species has been greatly diminished by the despicable deeds of a few."

Hal remained silent as the campfire continued to crackle.

"A few of us continue to work on finding a way to end the problem. The source of the spores—that awful pit of fungus within Whisper Mountain—has been blocked forever. The nine dimensional gateways have been boarded up. But the spores remain in your world, and even though they're not raining down from the sky anymore, they've already coated your world like dust."

"I know all this," Hal said, growing impatient.

The centaur nodded. "But now there are *fog-pellets*. Your human scientists are mass-producing them in factories. What they lack is an effective way to distribute them. I should think they'll consider using those incredible flying machines they have. But there's a better way."

Hal nodded. "Yeah, the nine gateways. The holes that were boarded up."

Fleck took a step backward, his bushy eyebrows waggling. "My, you're a sharp one. Did you just now figure that out?"

"I figured it out ages ago," Hal said, stretching the truth a little. Then he realized he was starting to sound like Robbie. "Well, this morning, anyway."

"Well, you were right to think of using the fog-pellets instead of the old fog-machine the goblins built," the centaur said, his eyes gleaming with excitement. "The spores are nothing but dust particles. They're light enough to travel on air currents but heavy enough to fall to the ground. If we tried to introduce our chemical-mixed fog to the atmosphere through those nine gateways using the old fog-machine, I imagine we would end up with a wispy cloud high above the Earth. It would do nothing to neutralize the layers of spores on the ground."

He clapped Hal on the shoulder. "But the fog-pellets are a different story. My friend, those pellets would fall and scatter all over, and even more so if we ground them up into particles as fine as the spores. Fog-*dust*, if you like. It would follow the same air currents and fall to Earth among the spores. After that—"

"We wait for rain," Hal said.

Fleck simply grinned and nodded. Then his smile faded somewhat. "Of course, there are many places where rain is rare. There's a desert in your world stretching six hundred miles that sees no more than an inch of rainfall a year, and in some places it's *never* rained in recorded history. So while the majority of the spores will be killed off, some will be missed."

"So we just need to make it rain in those places," Hal said.

The centaur raised his bushy eyebrows. "And you can arrange such a miracle, can you, young man?"

Hal grinned. "Yeah. I think I can."

* * *

Hal and Fleck spent another half hour in the freezing woods talking through all the details. The fire was fed several times with increasingly thick logs, and by the end of their discussion it was hot enough to smolder for the rest of the night.

The centaur bowed and trotted back to the shelter. Hal stuffed his hands deep into his pockets and headed to the village. It was late afternoon. He had to assume the soldiers would attack first thing in the

"Wouldn't have been much of a rescue if I had," Ryan complained. "There's no point dragging old Jimmy and Dot out of their home and bringing them across to your island unless I know for sure there's safe passage for them into this world. And for that I need Simone."

"Or a shapeshifter willing to go with you," Hal said.

Ryan looked up and pushed his hair aside. "What do you mean?"

Hal peered up through the broken roof to the darkening sky above. "First thing in the morning," he said, "I'm going back to the island."

"I'm listening."

"I don't need you to come with me, but you can if you want. No skin off my nose either way. But I can bring Jimmy and Dot back for you."

Ryan was quiet for a long while. "You can?"

"Hey, I'm a dragon. Anyway, even if you end up stuck there, it won't be for long. Things will be different soon."

The fire crackled while Ryan studied Hal. "What's your game, pal? Why are you going back?"

And for the next twenty minutes, Hal told him everything and outlined his plan, ending with the need to fetch a few geo-rocks.

When he was finished, Ryan cracked a grin. "If you can pull that off, kid, you'll either be some kind of quiet hero or the worst enemy a guy can have, depending on who you ask."

"It doesn't matter either way," Hal said, staring into the flames. "I have to do this. I'm *supposed* to do this."

"You feel compelled?" Ryan said. "You have voices in your head telling you what to do? Well, buddy, that just means you're insane. But I'm with you, anyway. Seems like what you have in mind is the right thing to do. Uniting the worlds?" He whistled. "Millions of virus survivors will be really happy to crawl out of their bunkers and enter a new world with unicorns and pixies and good, clean air. But the people in *this* land are going to be sore about it. Sharing their pretty world with scrags and gun-totin' soldiers?" He chuckled mirthlessly.

"They'll get over it," Hal muttered.

"Sure, right after they've strung you up by the neck."

Hal said nothing. Ryan was right, of course. Miss Simone would be livid about the whole thing. But he had to do this without her consent because he knew she would never give it. And even if she did, she'd dilly-dally until it was too late. It was easier to seek forgiveness than permission.

Ryan was looking uncomfortable. "Hey, I didn't mean to mess with your head. Like you said, they'll get over it. They'll have to. Actually I think you'll get in more trouble with the smaller stuff. Once they've blown their tops over that, they'll just go numb with disbelief at the rest."

There was some strange truth to that, Hal decided. He climbed to his feet. "Well, I'm off to Abigail's. See you in the morning?"

"Bright and early," Ryan agreed. "Actually, *dark* and early. I'll be outside your house before dawn."

"Don't forget the geo-rocks," Hal reminded him.

He headed off next to see Abigail. He was nervous about putting so much faith in her. He trusted her completely, but . . . well, she had a tendency to nag him whenever he was planning to do something dangerous, or stupid as she would probably call it. She might actually try to stop him—out of concern, she'd say afterward. But he needed to talk to her about it. The matter was too big to keep her out of the loop. She'd never forgive him if he went ahead without her.

Dr. Porter answered the door, and she immediately stood aside for him to enter. "She's in her room," she said with a smile. She turned and shouted over her shoulder. "Abigail! Hal's here." She stopped him as he went to pass her. "How's your werewolf bite?"

"Oh, it's fine. All healed up."

"Well, good. We don't want you turning, do we?"

Although he smiled and agreed, he caught something in her eye that puzzled him. Had she really been concerned about such a thing? About 'turning'? He'd read stories where people were bitten and became werewolves themselves, but usually the victims didn't have the healing powers of shapeshifters.

Abigail's room was cold. She was fully clothed and huddled under her sheets, reading a book. She seemed both pleased to see him and disgruntled about his absence all afternoon. "Why'd you want to see Dr. Kessler without me?" she demanded as Hal perched on the end of her bed. "What did she say, anyway?"

"Nothing much. Listen, I need to tell you something. You might decide I'm crazy and rat me out to Miss Simone. If you do, I'll ditch you for Darcy."

She narrowed her eyes. "Is that supposed to be funny?"

"No, but . . . ." He steeled himself. "I can't let you stand in my way, Abi."

Her eyes widened. She slowly put her book down and pulled her sheets up higher as though a chill had just run through her body. "What's going on?"

"You remember what I told you? About what I saw when I was a statue?"

She nodded.

"Well, all that stuff was true. I mean it really happened."

"I know that. I believe you."

"It wasn't just some dream," Hal insisted. "Chase is real, and if he's real, so is the rest, and if the rest is real, then I need to do as I'm told. I need to open up the two worlds so that people can cross over. We all need to live together."

"Happily ever after," Abigail murmured, turning white. "Oh, Hal."

He stared at the bed. "Tomorrow, I'm taking Ryan home. I'm going to talk to the soldiers and persuade them to hold off on their invasion—"

"That's *if* they're actually planning to invade," Abigail reminded him.

"They are. I know they are. I'll ask them to organize delivery of tons and tons of fog-pellets, as much as they can get—and to keep making the stuff and bringing it through for weeks after."

"Through where?"

"Through a hole."

Abigail looked confused. "There's only one hole now, and that's in a pond in a field. I don't see how that—"

"I mean *another* hole. One that I'm going to make tomorrow."

Her mouth fell open.

"We're going to take the fog-pellets to Whisper Mountain and let the nine gateways suck them out into the atmosphere. They'll spread across our world the same way the spores did. It'll rain, and the fog will kill the spores."

Now Abigail was thoughtful.

Hal pushed on. "And after that, I'm going to open up more holes. Lots of them, all over the world—or at least *this* part of the world."

"How?" she asked weakly.

He smiled, suddenly feeling a need to tease her the way she did with him. "I have a few ideas. The point is, the two worlds will become one like it used to be thousands of years ago." He swallowed. "It's hard to explain, but . . . it's like we've been given the chance to start over.

This wouldn't have worked before, the way the world was before the virus. There were too many people then. They'd have overrun Miss Simone's land and flattened it before stopping to look at all the different types of creatures living here. Or they'd have bombed everything to wipe out the threat of dragons."

She nodded slowly. "But now that there's hardly anyone left . . ."

Hal nodded. "Exactly. It'll be like a fresh start. People can come out of hiding and start living again, and they'll find new neighbors—the naga, centaurs, harpies, dragons, you name it."

"And they'll all just get along," Abigail whispered.

"Right." Seeing the disbelieving look on her face, he shrugged and rubbed his chin. "It won't be that easy, but it'll work out in the end."

"But *why*, Hal? Why not kill off the virus but otherwise leave things as they are? People can still come out of hiding and start over, just without the manticores and unicorns."

"And the soldiers will still try to come through," Hal insisted. "They know about this world now. If they don't come through one hole, they'll find another. They'll do anything to get here, and they'll fight their way through if they have to. If they're not invited, they'll just take it, which will be worse."

Abigail closed her eyes for a moment before trying again. "But how do you know they won't kill everyone and everything in sight and take over the land? You might just be making it easier for them to get here."

Hal shook his head. "Before the virus, people had it so good for so long, they got lazy and greedy. Look at our parents. They were always saying how easy life was back when there was electricity and phone lines. I mean, they had other worries, but they always had heat in the house and food on the table. After the virus, life was much harder for them. But I remember Mom telling me how people appreciate life much more after it's nearly taken away."

He spread his hands, watching her reaction. She chewed her lip thoughtfully but said nothing.

"Don't you see, Abi? Everything is different now. *People* are different now. The survivors appreciate life more. They're desperate to come out of hiding. The virus is fading, but it'll be a while before anyone trusts that it's really gone. This is a good time to invite them into this land. They'll be *grateful* to us, and when Miss Simone sets some ground rules, they'll listen."

"And what makes you think all these people will get along with the naga and centaurs and elves? How do you know they'll be good neighbors?"

Hal got up and started pacing the small bedroom. His gaze fell on a collection of hair scrunchies, pins and clips, and an open wooden box containing bits of jewelry. He blinked, wondering if he'd ever seen her wearing such things as rings and necklaces. He couldn't recall. But then again, he was a boy.

"Remember how we all were before we found out we were shapeshifters? Before all this started? We went to school every day and kind of argued a lot. Fenton was a bully. You know how he was, always picking on Robbie and threatening to beat him up if I didn't help out with homework. He was a nightmare. And you kept picking on Dewey, teasing him all the time, while Emily was always doing her best to get top marks, making the rest of us look stupid—"

"Wait, *what*? I kept picking on Dewey?" Abigail looked flabbergasted. "What's that got to do with anything?"

"It's a feeble example, I know," Hal admitted. "But my point is, we kind of got on each others' nerves half the time. And now look at us. We're shapeshifters and have become much . . . *closer*. Don't you think?"

"I don't follow."

"We're better friends now than we ever were. Partly because our world is now much bigger, but also because we're so *different* from one another. We kind of . . . *respect* each other more, you know?"

Abigail's frown was deepening. "Maybe."

"I have this idea in my head," Hal said slowly, "that the two worlds would have been joined long ago if it weren't for phoenixes. They popped up out of nowhere thousands of years ago, a sort of accident. Before they came along, the two worlds were joined by holes. Then the phoenixes started wiping out magic and closing the holes, and the two worlds were divided again."

"Why would the phoenixes want to do that?" Abigail asked weakly.

"I don't know. I got the impression they were an accident of nature. They just popped up out of nowhere and started doing their thing. There are loads of creatures we'd be better off without, like the miengu, harpies, manticores . . . but hey, they're just part of life, right? Like wasps and slugs and skunks. Phoenixes just happen to be more powerful. If it weren't for them, our parents would have lived quite

173

happily with the naga down the street, faeries buzzing around on the lawn every morning, griffins and flying horses giving people rides to work—"

"Centaurs complaining about pollution," Abigail broke in. "Dragons flying around causing trouble, harpies breaking into people's houses and stealing things, manticores running around in alleys—"

"Ogres helping humans to build skyscrapers, dryads supplying hospitals with healing potions made out of leaves and twigs—"

"Gorgons turning everyone to stone—"

"Don't be so negative," Hal said. "Look, we have no idea how things would have turned out, or how they might turn out in the future. But this is the perfect time to see."

Abigail threw her sheet aside and climbed out of bed, her clothes badly wrinkled. She approached Hal and stood before him, looking hard into his eyes. "Think about what you're saying, Hal. You can't make a decision like that. You can't mess with two worlds just because of an idea in your head or a vision of invading soldiers. You can't do this on your own. You have to ask Miss Simone. Even *she* can't make a decision like that. And even if she asked the council for a vote, and they all said yes, Carter is just one village. What about Charlie up in Louis? What would he think about all this? Doesn't he have a say?"

Hal shook his head. "It would take ages for them all to make up their minds, and I'm pretty sure they would say no. Why would they want a load of virus survivors coming through with their weapons and technology? I get that. But if you asked the survivors, they'd say yes. They'd want this. A big, green world with amazing wildlife and magic!"

"And dragons," she argued. "Have you thought about that? Give someone the choice of growing up in a world with or without the threat of dragons. What do you think they'd choose?"

"Dragons," Hal said promptly. "Look, I'm doing this no matter what. Even Fleck agrees with me, and he's a centaur!"

"He's just feeling guilty because his kind massacred billions of people," Abigail said, raising her voice in desperation.

Hal put a finger to his lips, and a hush fell. He continued quietly. "I'm doing this, Abigail. I wanted to tell you, but I hope you don't try to stop me."

She narrowed her eyes. "And what if I tried to? What would you do to me?"

"I wouldn't do anything to you. I'd just be really ticked off and wouldn't speak to you again."

In the silence that followed, Hal wished he could read Abigail's mind. She stared at him intensely, chewing her lip all the while. And whatever she was thinking, what was to stop her from saying one thing and doing another? She might pretend to go along with him but secretly give him up to Miss Simone before he could go too far. Still, he'd expected this. She was either with him or not. He would do this with her help or without.

"And you really think the soldiers are going to invade?"

"At dawn," Hal said, leaving out the fact that he still didn't know for sure *which* dawn.

Finally, she took a breath. "Okay, here's the deal. I'll help you with the first part of your crazy plan—persuading the soldiers not to attack, getting the fog-pellets to Whisper Mountain, and killing off the virus. That's the right thing to do. I won't say a word to Miss Simone, and I'll help all I can."

"Thanks."

"But the rest? Opening more holes and letting the worlds mix and mingle?" She shook her head. "Sorry, but that's too much. It's bad enough opening one extra hole just to get the fog-pellets delivered. As far as I'm concerned, once the virus is killed off, we should tell Miss Simone so she can close that hole again."

This time Hal said nothing, and they stared at each other for a long time.

In the end, Hal nodded. "Well, if I haven't changed your mind by the time the virus is killed off, then I won't stop you. You can tell Miss Simone anything you like, and we'll see what happens. Deal?"

"Deal," she said quietly.

Chapter Seventeen
Meeting with the Enemy

Hal barely slept. He had no clock, but it had to be past two in the morning by the time he finally drifted off, and he was so worried about oversleeping that he kept waking to peer out the window. What if the sea serpent and dozens of goblins died all because he couldn't drag himself out of bed? In the end, he got up long before dawn and dressed quietly.

He checked that his carefully worded message was propped against his pillow in full view of the door so his mom would see it immediately when she eventually came to see why he wasn't up yet:

Mom and Dad, don't worry about me. Ryan wants to go back home to fetch his friends and Miss Simone's not allowing it. Back in a day or two. –Hal

Naturally his parents would worry. Hal couldn't help that. But bringing Ryan along on his trip gave him a perfectly valid reason to disappear like this. Every written word of the note was true, but his primary mission was something else entirely, something they needn't know about just yet.

Before he slipped outside, he quietly grabbed huge hunks of bread and cheese from the kitchen. It would do as his breakfast. He quietly closed the front door and tiptoed down the path to the trail that ran through the woods, and it was there that Ryan emerged silently from the shadows.

"How long have you been here?" Hal asked, pleased his friend was so punctual. It still wasn't dawn yet.

"Hours. I don't sleep much."

"Got the geo-rocks?"

Ryan nodded and patted the sack slung over his shoulder. "Five of them. Big and fat."

Hal felt no guilt at this. The wagon full of geo-rocks was, after all, there for anyone to take from. "So we just need to wait for Abigail. She'll be here soon."

Ryan frowned. "I didn't know she was coming. Are you sure about her?"

No, Hal thought, but he nodded.

He and Ryan shared some bread and cheese. The rest he saved for Abigail in case she hadn't brought anything. She appeared soon after, buzzing lightly along the trail. She was at her full size, carrying her coat, with her wings poking out the back of her sweater and the t-shirt underneath. "I really wish we had some new smart clothes," she said, accepting her share of the breakfast.

Hal agreed. He had to face the same problem himself—starting right now. They cut through the woods and eventually emerged in a field outside the village. Hal hurried across the grass and darted behind a tree where he undressed quickly, his skin already turning icy cold in the freezing early morning air. He transformed without delay, grateful that his reptilian hide was so much more resistant to extreme temperatures, both hot and cold.

Ryan collected Hal's clothes and stuffed them into his sack with the geo-rocks. Holding it firmly, he clambered onto Hal's broad back. Abigail retracted her wings, popped the last of her sandwich in her mouth, pulled her coat on, and climbed up behind. "Let's go," she said with her mouth full.

Hal took to the air. In a matter of seconds he was soaring high into the lightening sky above the village. Dawn was now approaching, and the sunrise was spectacular as he headed south.

Finding his way to what they often called Serpent Lake was difficult. Hal really didn't recognize much of the landscape from this high up. But he eventually found the road they'd traveled a few times before and, sighing with relief, followed it until the vast lake opened up ahead, as smooth and shiny as a mirror in the morning sun.

Tiny dots were posted along its grassy banks, each with a flickering campfire. Goblins. They were set up on one side of the lake, keeping watch. Somewhere under the water was the hole, smoking and pulsing, guarded by the enormous sea serpent. A tiny ring of floating yellow buoys marked the exact location.

Hal landed heavily near one of the goblin campfires. Two guards were sitting there, and both jumped up with obvious alarm at the rare sight of a dragon in these parts. But they visibly relaxed when Ryan and Abigail climbed off Hal's back.

Abigail called out to the goblins as she approached. "Hey, guys. We're taking Ryan back home. No need to get worked up."

One of the goblins muttered something to her, and she shrugged. "I know, I know, soldiers and scrags, lots of danger, I get it. We can handle it. Don't wait up for us, though. We might be a day or two."

Time for us to do what we need to do before anyone starts to worry, Hal thought. He had to assume Abigail had left a note of her own for her mom to find. He wondered briefly how she'd worded hers.

One snag with their plan was the matter of clothing, which would get soaked as they dove under the lake and through the hole. It would be absolutely freezing when they emerged on the other side, dripping wet, to confront the soldiers. But what choice did they have? Besides, there was a lighthouse nearby containing three crates full of fresh smart clothes—and they were still enchanted. The soldiers had a fourth crate stashed somewhere, too. Hal looked forward to getting his hands on some of those garments.

The goblins' buoys were tethered to the lakebed with long lengths of string, weighted on the end. They formed a circle about fifty feet in diameter. Hal submerged as soon as he entered the circle. Ryan and Abigail held on, and Hal pushed downward as fast as he could, knowing they couldn't hold their breath anywhere near as long as he could. The morning sun only illuminated the murky depths a little, but the pulsing black hole was clear to see, about nine feet across and twenty feet down. It seemed to have stabilized since his last visit. Back then, earth and rocks had trickled through from the other world, muddying the water. Now the water all around was clear, the hole well defined.

He shot up through it and experienced a moment of utter blackness. Then everything brightened again, and seconds later he exploded out of the water.

He was in the middle of a large pond. Dozens of soldiers stood at its grassy bank, and as he splashed around, they raised their weapons toward him. The foggy air was filled with rattles and clicks, but someone shouted, "Hold your fire!"

Nice welcome, Hal thought idly. But he felt a jolt of fear and awe as he noted a bright yellow machine large enough to fit a man inside secured to the back of a trailer. An open-topped army vehicle had backed up to the pond, and the trailer was half submerged. It looked like some of the soldiers were about to slide the miniature submarine off the trailer into the water.

I'm only just in time, Hal thought with a shiver of horror. He wondered what Abigail and Ryan were thinking. Were they just now realizing how accurate his dream had been? If Hal hadn't been so insistent, all those poor goblins on the grassy banks might be dead in thirty minutes.

Seeing that the soldiers were holding their positions and awaiting orders, Hal slowly paddled across the pond and stomped up the muddy bank. The armed men fell back but kept their weapons trained on him.

Behind them were several military-camouflaged vehicles, a large tent, and a noisy portable generator. The soldiers had set up a small base here, and various bits of equipment and artillery littered the field along with the bright yellow minisub on the back of the trailer.

The pond was bigger than Hal remembered. The pulsing portal twenty feet below the ground had acted like a giant drain hole, with earth and rocks running out the bottom while water flooded upward out of Serpent Lake. The water level had equalized, finally creating a large pond in a previously dry field. This particular hole had been a landscape changer.

The fog was thick and heavy, and none of these soldiers wore biosuits. As they watched him in silence, a familiar face came hurrying through the ranks: Lieutenant Briskle—just the man Hal wanted to see.

"We want to talk," Ryan called from his mount on Hal's back. "Put those guns away. We're getting down."

Hal eased up the bank a little farther to where the grass was dry. There he waited while Ryan and Abigail, with dripping clothes, slid down from his back and approached the lieutenant, who eyed them warily.

"Hi," Abigail said, shivering. "So nice of you to welcome us. We're ready to work things out."

Briskle rubbed his whiskered chin. With a shaved head and unfriendly eyes, he was a very large, thick-necked man. He raised an eyebrow at them and couldn't help sneering. "Too late for that, missy." He nodded toward the yellow minisub as if that were explanation enough.

"It's never too late," Ryan said, stepping closer to the lieutenant. "Are you seriously thinking of invading? You'd really blow a harmless morning, in which case he planned to get an early start—which meant getting a couple of things done right now.

His first port of call was a rundown cottage on the outskirts of the village. The home had been empty for years due to the gaping holes in the roof and fire damage throughout—a tragedy from the past. But someone found it perfectly suitable. "Ryan?" Hal called through the open doorway.

"In here," came the reply.

Hal's friend, a survivor of the virus, someone who was almost completely immune to its deadly effects, actually preferred the holes in the roof. He was used to looking up at the sky. He kept reasonably warm while feeling as though he were still outside.

Ryan was in the living room surrounded by weathered furniture—a table turned on its side, a couple of large armchairs, and a chest of drawers. He'd made himself a walled shelter within a shelter, and in the middle of it all was a burning campfire much like the one Hal had built in the woods.

"How's it going, Hal?" Ryan said without looking up. He was sitting cross-legged near the fire with his gloved hands wrapped around a tankard. It smelled nasty, whatever it was.

Hal seated himself opposite. "Pretty good. You?"

Ryan's reply was laced with sarcasm. "Just fine. I'm nice and safe here in this world. Everything's great. Shame about my friends back in the dangerous, virus-ridden, scrag-infested world that I left behind."

"Still haven't persuaded Miss Simone, then?"

The young man in his late teens had straight blond hair that came down almost to his shoulders. It had fallen across his face, hiding his expression. "She lied to me," he said quietly. "She told me—she *promised* me—that she'd figure out a way to rescue Jimmy and Dot. You were there. You heard her."

"Yeah," Hal agreed.

"And what's she done about it? Nothing." Ryan shook his head in disgust. "Did you know I went back to the lake the other day?"

This was news to Hal. "No."

"Well, I did. I wanted to go back through the hole under the water. Those short, ugly goblins stood there and told me they'd let me go if I wanted, but it was a one-way trip. I wouldn't be allowed to return without Simone's permission."

"So you didn't go?"

sea serpent out of the water? And then what? Swim ashore and start shooting goblins? And after that, you're prepared to take on a land filled with dragons and other monsters? You're going to blast everything you see into a million pieces?"

Lieutenant Briskle scowled. "Watch your tongue, son."

"You can't do this," Abigail said firmly, her voice trembling with cold rather than fear. Hal had to admire the way she spoke so bravely even though the lieutenant towered over her. "Invading isn't going to work. Even if you make it past the serpent and out of the lake, Miss Simone won't just let you run around with your guns. She'll form an army of ogres and naga just like before, only this time with dragons as well. You'll never win, and people will die for nothing."

"We'll take that chance," Briskle said evenly. He gestured around the field. "This is the tip of the iceberg, missy. We're just here to clear a path. We've got troops ready to go. They're being dispatched from headquarters as we speak. Make no mistake, kids—we're taking your land."

Just like in the dream, Hal thought. He felt vindicated. He'd been right to come here, to stop this madness.

He couldn't stand not being able to speak. He backed down into the pond and transformed, reverting to his human form so he stood there chest-deep in the freezing water. A collective gasp went up. Even though many of these soldiers had seen him shift before, apparently the transformation process still shocked them to the core. Even Briskle looked unsettled, and his fingers inched closer to his holstered pistol—which was ironic since Hal was less of a threat to him now than he had been a few seconds ago.

"Let's talk," Hal said, beginning to shiver hard. "There's no need to invade. We're here to help you."

Briskle frowned. "Come again?"

"We want to invite you in."

The lieutenant stood there staring at him, his brow deeply furrowed, a mixture of suspicion and interest plastered across his face. Meanwhile, Hal slowly turned into an icicle. He couldn't decide whether to dip down lower in the water or step out a little farther; the foggy air seemed as cold as the pond itself. Standing on the grass, Abigail and Ryan looked just as uncomfortable with their sodden clothes.

"Why now?" Briskle eventually asked.

Hal let out a breath, knowing that he'd got through to the big man. "Let's sit down and talk. Get us some dry clothes, and I'll explain everything. Do you have that crate of magic clothes to hand?"

* * *

Things were beginning to happen at last. It had been six long hours since Hal, Abigail and Ryan had arrived wet and cold on the fog-covered island. They'd bundled up in blankets and sat in the tent, huddled around an actual *electric heater* of all things, powered by the noisy generator. Lieutenant Briskle made a call and arranged the delivery of a crate from the main base in the woods. It was filled with brand new smart clothes—dresses, pants, shirts—and the two shapeshifters selected three layers each to wear. Still, even with the security of magical clothing that transformed when they did, they knew they'd still need their ordinary coats, jackets and shoes to battle the weather.

Hal was careful about what he told Briskle, keeping it simple for now. He explained his plan to eradicate the spores using fog-pellets, crushed into powder and dispatched into the atmosphere where the dust would spread across the planet in much the same way the spores had. When it rained, fog would spring up and destroy any spores it came into contact with.

Briskle loved this idea, calling it 'the delivery system they'd been lacking.' He seemed vague about the cave behind the temple where the nine gateways were located, saying he'd have to see it to believe it—which Hal planned very soon.

He refrained from telling the lieutenant anything else for now.

"And we're doing all this in secret?" Briskle said. "Simone knows nothing?"

"She might know *something* by now. She'll be on our trail any minute."

"Mm. So we need to move fast. A secret operation to clean our world." The lieutenant rubbed his whiskered chin. Then he gave Hal a hard stare. "And then what? What happens when we're done? When Simone catches up? We're not leaving with our tails between our legs. Once we're in your world, we're staying."

"I . . . I have an idea about that," Hal said. "But let's figure that out later. You'll just have to trust me. We both want the same thing, though."

It was clear Briskle wasn't entirely happy with being kept in the dark, but he gruffly agreed. Ryan took the opportunity to jump in and clarify that *he* was there primarily to fetch his old friends Jimmy and Dot and bring them to safety. The lieutenant nodded impatiently. "I'll arrange anything you need."

"But the Swarm—" Ryan said.

"We know exactly where that gang is," Briskle told him. "Don't worry about it. I'll arrange a pickup."

Ryan had to be content with that. He was red with excitement at the prospect of a military escort for his frail friends—a vehicle ride from their front door to the beach, then a boat ride to the island.

But he wasn't half as excited as Briskle, who finally received a message from headquarters on the mainland and clapped his hands together so hard it sounded like a gunshot. "We're in business."

"So you're not going to invade?" Hal insisted.

The man drew himself up. "Son, I'm not an idiot. All I ever wanted was a peaceful resolution. This Simone woman doesn't own your land anymore than I do, but we're all human, and we all have a right to settle there. Anyway, it was those centaur monsters that spoiled our world in the first place. We *deserve* a piece of theirs."

"So when are we getting started?" Hal asked.

"Factory's on full alert, all hands on deck to crank out the fog-pellets. First cargo is loading up now. Chinooks will be in the vicinity within the hour, more later. Let's get this portal open."

Hal had no idea what 'Chinooks' were, but he nodded and grinned.

The lieutenant leaned across the table and affectionately patted a large plastic lidded box. It held five large geo-rocks crammed in together with an electronic device and some strange, square blocks. The whole package was very heavy and ready to go. He explained that the remote-controlled detonator within the package would, when triggered, explode and set off 'six pounds of C4,' which he assured them would blow the geo-rocks to smithereens—and in turn would create the portal.

"More effective than bashing them with a hammer," Ryan murmured.

The package looked ominous, but Briskle assured them it was safe sitting here on the table. He was more concerned about the size of the portal it would generate. "Now, you're *sure* it'll be big enough?" he asked.

"They're the biggest geo-rocks I could find, and there are five of them," Ryan said. "The one I exploded at the lighthouse was tiny, and still the hole it made was nine feet across. Five big fat rocks together?" He shrugged.

"We need *at least* sixty-five feet for the rotor span alone, and as much extra as possible for safe clearance, not to mention the payload dangling underneath."

"I'm sure it'll be fine," Ryan said.

"Well, let's get this done. Are you ready?"

Briskle gave Hal a long, questioning look. Suddenly nervous about the whole thing, Hal swallowed and nodded.

"In that case," the lieutenant went on, "someone needs to sit on your back to advise on the location, throw the bomb, and trigger the detonator." He paused. "Uh, it should probably be a soldier. Someone with experience."

Abigail rolled her eyes. "If you want to go, why don't you just say so?"

"Can I?" Briskle asked quietly, his eyes gleaming.

Hal shrugged. "Suits me."

Never in a million years did Hal think he would have taken to the sky with a soldier on his back, especially Lieutenant Briskle, who had been their enemy not so long ago. But he was competent, and it made sense for him to be the one to trigger the detonator. He could decide on the exact location and altitude as well as make a snap decision about whether to abort the mission for any reason . . .

Briskle climbed up on Hal's dragon back. But when Hal tried to soar into the foggy sky, he found that he couldn't rise higher than thirty feet or so. He flapped hard, beginning to pant with the effort.

"What's wrong?" Briskle demanded from his perch. "Am I too heavy? Am I carrying too much equipment?"

Hal thought about the man's weight combined with that of the geo-rock bomb and compared it to various passengers he'd carried in the past. No, it wasn't the weight. There was something else wrong.

When he thumped back down onto the grass, he felt a little dizzy from the exertion, not to mentioned embarrassed. Abigail came running toward him. "It's the fog!" she exclaimed. "We can't fly in fog, remember?"

Realization dawned, and Hal mentally kicked himself. The original fog over the island had included a dampening agent to prevent the shapeshifters from flying away. Since the soldiers' own fog-pellets were based on the same formula, that unnecessary agent had been inadvertently included also.

"We need to find a place that's not foggy," Abigail told the lieutenant.

The delay was annoying but unavoidable. Hal reverted to human form, and the whole group climbed into one of the vehicles to be driven across the island to the far end where there was no fog. Briskle had to climb into a biosuit on the way, just in case there were spores floating around in the air.

"It's unlikely," he said, checking his facemask and breathing equipment. "From what I understand, the air's clean now. The only yellow dust left is what's picked up from the streets in a gale. The fog you grew up with on this island filtered out all the spores, so there's nothing on the ground here." He tapped the glass in front of his face. "But you never know. I'd rather be safe."

They pulled up on a grassy field near a low cliff. This was on the opposite side of the island to Black Woods, where the soldiers' camp was located, and the fog hadn't spread this far. The sun felt warm on their shoulders as they disembarked and prepared to try again.

This time Hal had no trouble lifting off. He soared into the blue sky, leaving the island behind, and Ryan and Abigail cheered from far below. It was just Hal and the lieutenant now—and the bomb.

Briskle let out a whoop, then resorted to chuckles and guffaws as Hal swooped around. It struck Hal as funny that a big, stern man like the lieutenant could be reduced to a giggling child, but it also warmed him, gave him hope that unifying the worlds might actually be for the best. If the lieutenant could appreciate the joy of riding on a dragon's back, surely others would, too.

In the distance, the thudding of helicopters came to Hal's ears. He paused in mid-flight, gliding on his outstretched leathery wings as he circled around. There—in the distance, three dark specks against the sky.

"Here should do," Briskle called. "Go higher."

And Hal did so, climbing in circles as though he were ascending a spiral staircase. Now the pear-shaped, partially fog-smothered island was a blurred white patch against the dark blue sea.

"Okay," Briskle said. "Get clear as soon as I drop the box—but not too far away. I need to watch it fall."

Hal grunted and waited until the lieutenant tossed the box. As it plummeted, twisting and turning in slow motion, he dipped and swooped away from it.

Briskle didn't say anything, but Hal knew when he pressed the button on the transmitter. The box exploded with a tremendous flash and bang, so bright it hurt his eyes, and so loud it made his ears ring. Then he felt a shockwave that would have knocked him off his feet had he been on the ground.

Hal gasped. The small geo-rock Ryan had exploded at the lighthouse had resulted in an underwater portal, and as such they hadn't seen it form. This time Hal got to witness its creation. It appeared fairly close to the initial flash, perhaps a little lower and just a few hundred feet off to one side. It seemed closer to its source than the previous hole had been. Apparently C4 was a good way to crack open geo-rocks; the explosive was hot and powerful enough to incinerate the rocks in an instant.

But what got Hal's attention was the way the hole materialized. It started out like the vertical streak of a shooting star, only solid black, and immediately expanded, becoming almost spherical. It began its rhythmic pulsing, with eerie black tendrils leaking off its surface.

"Holy cow," Briskle shouted as Hal circled back toward it. "Go in closer. I can't tell how big that thing is."

Hal flew in toward it. There was absolutely no sign of the box or chunks of geo-rock; the debris was by now raining down on the sea in the form of tiny fragments. The hole—a brand new portal to another world—was an impressive one, by far the largest Hal had ever seen.

"That's gotta be a hundred feet across," the lieutenant said. "Incredible."

Without asking, Hal flew into the middle of the hole. There was the usual moment of blackness as he entered its heart, then everything brightened when he flew out the other side.

The scenery had changed. Gone was the ocean, the fog-smothered island, and the mainland. In its place was green and brown land for as far as the eye could see, with gigantic mountains to the southeast that

Hal recognized as the location of Whisper Mountain. They would be headed there shortly. He turned toward the mountains and gave a bellow.

Briskle grunted through his faceplate. "That's it? That's our target? Okay—take us back so we can get organized."

Hal gave another bellow and a short burst of fire for good measure. Then he turned and dove back through the hole, glancing down as he went. He could see the lake where the serpent swam, where the goblins would be camped out around the shores. The lake was tiny from up here.

When he emerged from the pulsing hole over the island, he descended rapidly—too rapidly, because the lieutenant exclaimed in pain at the sudden increased pressure on his eardrums. Hal allowed himself a soft chuckle.

Back on the ground, Briskle leaned inside the vehicle and spoke into a radio. Hal caught snippets of his barked orders: "Get the chopper in the air—stay on my tail—Chinooks are on their way."

Minutes later, he returned to Hal and climbed aboard, ushering Ryan and Abigail to join him. Hal had carried three passengers before, but this time one of them was a big, burly soldier. A little perturbed at the weight, he flapped his wings awhile, trying to evaluate the load and halfway wishing Abigail would shrink to faerie size.

"Let's go," Briskle urged. "The birds will follow."

As Hal once more took to the sky, another helicopter rose from the trees way over on the other side of the island near the lighthouse. This one would be following close behind and acting as a beacon to the three in the distance. Those three were still specks, but a little bigger now, their engines deep and throbbing.

Hal flew to the hole and through it. The moment he was on the other side, peace and serenity surrounded him. It was a huge relief—for a moment. Then the tracker helicopter burst through, its noise shattering the airspace over Serpent Lake and surely alerting the goblin guards. The hole dwarfed the helicopter, reaching out with smoky tendrils as the machine tore free.

The lieutenant whooped again. "All right. The pilot will track you and relay your location to the others. They'll be through here shortly. Let's move out."

Hal put on speed and headed for the distant mountains. It was a trek he'd made before, and while it was much faster beating his wings than floating on Blacknail's rickety airship *CloudDrifter*, there was still quite a way to go. The good news was that it would be ages before word got back to Miss Simone about the presence of the helicopters, and when she found out, it would be a while before investigators arrived—whoever she might send.

Just when Hal thought the forest below was looking particularly drab today, he noticed something curious. He realized it must be the southernmost edge of the phoenix's blast zone. The transition between the dull, lifeless terrain and the more vibrant unaffected areas was almost too subtle to see. There was still a wintry bareness everywhere he looked, but it was a little less miserable outside the zone. Maybe only magical creatures could see the difference, and probably only from this altitude when passing over the perimeter.

The southern perimeter actually wasn't too far outside Carter. Everyone had assumed that the phoenix's location about eighty miles north would mark the exact center of a perfectly circular blast zone, but in fact the zone was not circular at all. It was oval-shaped, with its 'center' to the south. Blair had surmised that Jacob, the ancient phoenix, had simply been facing north and projected most of his nullification spell in that direction—unfortunately for the village of Louis and the Labyrinth of Fire, which were caught within its fringes. The entire town had been effectively disabled, its supply of geo-rocks ruined. The dragons of the labyrinth were hopping around like their wings had been clipped.

In any case, since the southern edge of the blast zone ended just a little way south of Carter, the old stone quarry was unaffected. Hal hoped this would make things easier for the soldiers.

There were lots of stone quarries, but the one he sought came into view along with its massive wooden treadmill crane that the centaurs had built long ago. There was a deep man-made shaft under that crane, and in that shaft was a portal—which Hal guessed was still intact since it was outside the blast zone. So the soldiers could likely use it to deliver the cargo of fog-pellets to Whisper Mountain. He gave a bellow and swooped downward, trying to get his message across to Abigail. It took a few more bellows for her to realize what he was saying, and then she began yelling about it to Ryan and the lieutenant.

"Down there," she told him. "The helicopters can land there."

"What? Why?" Briskle demanded.

"Just trust me."

With some misgivings, Briskle ordered the trailing helicopter pilot to land and started badgering Abigail for an explanation. Annoyingly, she said very little, just teased him with tidbits of information that were of no use to him. Meanwhile, it occurred to Hal that the temple elves might not take kindly to a bunch of visitors traipsing in the back door without announcement. These particular elves were Miss Simone's allies now; they had opened their arms to the village of Carter. Hal was in enough trouble as it was and didn't want to jeopardize that kinship. So, with a grumble, he climbed into the sky and continued on to Whisper Mountain.

"Where's he going?" the lieutenant complained loudly. "Why does my pilot have to land here if *we're* heading on to the mountain?"

"Hal probably wants to knock on the front door and be polite," Abigail told him. "He's using his manners."

Briskle grunted something, and Hal chuckled to himself.

Whisper Mountain was still a long way off yet. They'd only traveled about halfway so far. Hal gradually rose higher, pumping his wings until they ached before cruising with his wings spread out. A dragon could fly a long way like this, just riding the air currents while resting.

Behind him, the helicopter landed and fell silent—and Hal heard the distant throbbing of more helicopters. The others were through the hole at last. What would the local goblins think when they looked up to see these three monstrous hunks of metal floating through the sky?

Hal arrived at Whisper Mountain hungry and thirsty. With his stomach growling, he descended, looking for the old elfin temple that he knew was buried somewhere within the trees. Since it was winter and the branches were bare, he found it a little easier than he would have otherwise. He grunted with satisfaction as he came down on the same slope he'd landed previously—only this time with a great deal more grace in the confined space. Trees pressed in all around.

The solid ground under his feet felt wonderful. He collapsed there, spreading his wings wide and allowing his passengers to climb off. While Ryan and Abigail looked tired and cold, the biosuited lieutenant was ready for action, standing with feet planted wide, studying his surroundings. The slope provided a good view of the land, but the helicopters were out of sight, so Briskle spoke with the pilots on his radio. "Negative to a mountain landing. Repeat, *negative*. Await instructions while I check out the temple."

The biosuited lieutenant wanted Hal and Abigail to show him the temple immediately, but Hal was too tired to care right now. Eventually he transformed and lay there in the grass in his three layers of smart clothes. The cold mountain air quickly chilled him, and he retrieved his jacket and shoes from Ryan's bag.

"All right," he said with a sigh. "It's up that way."

The four of them trudged up the hillside and into the trees. Getting the helicopters through the giant portal had been relatively easy. Now he just needed to persuade the resident elves to allow access to their precious temple.

Chapter Eighteen
The Temple

Hal showed them the way to the mountain trail. Far below was a small elfin village, old and ramshackle. Higher up was the temple.

"I remember this path," Abigail said, smiling.

"I'm still not clear about how and where we drop our cargo," Briskle said, wiping his faceplate clear.

"You will be," Hal replied. "There's a back way into the temple."

The lieutenant blinked at him through his facemask, confused.

"Just trust them," Ryan offered, clapping Briskle on the shoulder.

Still, Hal attempted to explain as the four of them trudged up the steep trail. He told the lieutenant how the old wooden crane had been used by the centaurs to deliver stone blocks to the temple—by way of a specially created portal that defied all the usual rules and allowed users to hop far across the countryside, directly into the temple. "Actually, it leads to a tiny rock island in the middle of the sea," he added, "and from there to the temple. It's hard to explain. You have to see it."

Briskle said nothing for a while. "Okay, I still don't understand exactly what you're saying, but we'll take a look and see. But if that's the way in for our cargo, why are we here, walking up this hill?"

"Because we need to ask the elves before sneaking in the back," Hal said. "They *live* in that temple. We can't just bring a load of crates in the back door without checking with them."

"And you really mean elves? Little short people?"

Abigail laughed. "They're small and blue-skinned with floppy ears."

They eventually made it to the temple gardens. The sand-colored stone walls were six feet high, and the mountain trail turned sharply to the left and skirted alongside. The group turned in through a huge, ornate archway decorated with carved stone figures.

"Oh," Abigail exclaimed.

The gardens had been in disarray last time they had been here. After more than a decade of neglect, it had been quite a task just to cut their way through the jungle of ivy and weeds. Now it had been overhauled—ivy cut back, weeds removed, branches trimmed, flagstones relaid, and everything thoroughly scrubbed to remove years of grime. It was stunning even in wintertime. Although the wisteria was brown and stringy, and the rose bushes nothing but thorns, everything was immaculately trimmed. Even the old wooden bench had been fixed up and looked brand new.

They stepped quietly through the courtyard and into the next. This one had enormous boughs overhanging the walls, almost meeting in the middle. And the next had a flowing fountain in the center with a neat trellis roof. Hal rushed to the fountain and began drinking thirstily, and in seconds Abigail and Ryan were with him, leaning in and lapping it up. Only Briskle stood back, hampered as he was by his bright yellow biosuit. But he had his own built-in drink, Hal had discovered; he sucked at a straw whenever he wanted a sip.

"I'd love to see these gardens in the summer," Abigail said, looking around at the dozens of bushes lining the walls. "Imagine all the colors!"

"Let's move on," Briskle muttered.

They passed through a fourth and fifth courtyard, increasingly awed by the exquisite landscaping even in the cold, bare winter months. But the lieutenant was growing impatient; the distant drone of helicopters was his pressing concern.

They entered the sixth and final courtyard. This one was, as Hal had said, much bigger than the others. Facing them was the temple itself—a thirty-foot facade of sand-colored stone blocks that stood under an overhanging cliff, and there were eight rounded columns that appeared to be supporting the mountain above. The doorway was seven feet tall and six feet wide, which was grand considering the diminutive size of the elves. The temple interior was cut into natural tunnels and caves within the mountain, so the frontage was literally just an impressive entranceway.

Briskle, though, refused to be impressed. He was already looking with disgust at the diagonal crisscrossing paths within the courtyard, and the dutifully scrubbed statues that Hal remembered as being covered in moss. There were also wrought-iron benches and another enormous fountain.

"There could be room for dropping the cargo here," the lieutenant muttered. "If we shifted these statues and benches . . . maybe take down that fountain . . ."

"Not gonna happen," Ryan said, speaking for the first time in ages. "Come on, man—this place is amazing. You're not demolishing it."

"Just wait until you see the back door," Hal urged before Briskle's temper flared. He climbed the steps and raised his fist to knock.

As if he were being watched, one of the doors suddenly opened. It was big and heavy but opened smoothly inward before Hal's knuckles could reach it. He stepped back as a small, blue-skinned elf appeared in the gap, looking up at him. He had white hair and a small, dark beard. "Yes?"

"Hi," Hal said, recognizing him. "Uh, you're the queen's translator, aren't you? We're here to see her. We were wondering if—"

The translator was shoved aside suddenly, and another elf appeared. This one was female, very pretty with unblemished skin and large blue eyes that took Hal's breath away. Her hair was long and pure white with streaks of the same blue.

"Hi," he said to her, suddenly tongue-tied.

Abigail nudged him sharply. Then she curtsied. "Hello, your Highness. It's nice to see you again."

Hal's stomach flip-flopped. The Good Queen Addylyn herself was right here at the door. As tiny and dainty as she was, she was the leader of this clan of elves. He'd expected a servant to take them down a grand hallway to her throne room, and instead here she was in the lobby!

"Here why?" she asked in her rudimentary second language.

"Uh," Hal said.

Abigail gently pushed him aside. "We need permission to bring lots of crates into the temple. To the gateways inside the mountain. We're going to destroy the spores for good."

The queen frowned, only marginally affecting her natural beauty. "Already killed. Gateway stopped."

"I know the gateways are blocked," Abigail said, nodding, "and the pit of fungus is closed up, but the spores are still all across the world. We now have a way to make them harmless. We just need to unblock the gateways and use them one last time. May we?"

Queen Addylyn closed the door slightly and spoke quietly to someone standing out of sight. She used her own elfin dialect, her words fast and smooth. Hal had no idea what was being said, but soon the queen returned her gaze to them and peered at the lieutenant with something close to alarm.

"No enter this way," she said, shaking her head. "Back way, yes."

Hal found his tongue. "That sounds fair, your Queen. I mean, my Highness. Um, I mean *we'll* come in this way but send the soldiers around the back. Okay?"

To his surprise, she nodded and stepped back. The door swung wide to reveal around thirty elves standing quietly in the background just inside the grand lobby in the light of dozens of flickering wall torches. The sight was so strange and creepy that Briskle let out a gasp and fumbled for his weapon—but he stopped short of drawing it.

The queen had already turned and headed off along the vast corridor with a couple of officials. The crowd opened for her, then closed again. An elf waved Hal and his friends inside, speaking fast and unintelligibly.

"We're in," Hal muttered.

"How'd you manage that?" Ryan asked.

"We're heroes to these people. We reclaimed their temple from the demon."

Ryan sighed. "Of course you did. I'll take your word for it."

The crowd parted again as the visitors entered and started walking along the gigantic corridor, which had walls of stone and a stunning, highly polished mosaic floor. There were elf statues standing along the walls, and Hal suddenly wondered if they were in fact gorgon victims. He shuddered, dismissing the idea. They were just statues, nothing more. They weren't even very realistic.

There were rooms off to the sides, many of them like miniature homes while others were conference areas, chapels, dance halls, and banquet rooms. The elves lived here permanently, enjoying the safety and solitude of the temple within a mountain, and the beauty of the walled gardens outside.

The corridor ended at a wall, previously demolished but now repaired. A small door awaited them. Hal took a flickering torch from the wall, Briskle took another, and they stepped through the door.

They were still inside the mountain, only now within a natural tunnel, dark and musty. The floor was slanted and uneven, but an iron handrail on one side helped them along. To Hal's relief, even these tunnels had been cleaned up. Previously they had been smothered with fungus; every time they'd stepped on a mushy growth, a plume of yellow spores had puffed into the air. The fungus had thickened the deeper into the mountain they went. Now it was all gone, scraped clean by the centaurs that had introduced the fungus in the first place.

There had also been bones. And layers of dried glue that had been spat from the mouth of the so-called demon—a monstrous black lizard that Fenton had called his mother.

Weird times, Hal thought as he and Briskle used their flames to light a couple of unlit torches fixed to the tunnel wall. As they sputtered into life, Hal moved on to the next and lit that, too.

He was pleased the tunnel was so clean. The centaurs were nothing if not thorough even when tasked with a clean-up chore they had no interest in tackling. It seemed to be in their nature to do a job well no matter what they thought of it. Once the job had been finished, they'd been sent to a centaur prison to await their fate—probably execution.

To their left, the entrance to another tunnel appeared. He pointed it out to Briskle. "This is where the fog-dust will be brought in."

"That leads to the back door?"

"Yes. I'll show you in a minute. But first, take a look at where you'll be delivering the cargo."

The tunnel wound to the right, and finally they arrived in a huge domed cavern with a massive split down one side that let in a flood of blinding daylight. A sturdy iron rail encircled what had once been a twenty-foot wide pit, a deadly drop into nothingness. But the pit was now blocked, boarded over and all gaps sealed. The walls and ceiling of the cavern had once been completely covered in huge, wobbling fungus, but all that had been scraped away, too. Again, the centaurs had done a good job. Most of the fungus was deep within the pit; it had been burned and sealed up forever. Whisper Mountain was clean.

By far the most interesting feature were the gateways: nine of them spaced evenly around the cavern walls, black pulsing portals that had been blocked up with sturdy boards. A dull, curious, and somewhat disturbing howl could be heard from behind the boards.

"What's holding them in place?" Briskle asked, approaching one.

"Suction," Hal said, trying to remember the details. "These holes lead out high above the planet, so high that there's hardly any pressure."

Briskle let out an exclamation. "Ah—like plugging a leak in an airplane at high altitude."

194

"Just like that, yeah." Hal shot Abigail a glance and shrugged.

"Gotcha. So we remove the boards and throw the fog-pellets out."

"Right."

The lieutenant had to see for himself. He handed his flickering torch to Ryan, approached the first portal, and began yanking on the boards. Too big to be sucked through, they had wedged firmly against the rock wall around the edges of the holes. Even Briskle couldn't shift them.

Eventually he gave up. "Need some more muscle," he muttered. "Okay, show me the back door."

They left the brightly lit cavern and headed back down the tunnel, then turned to the right when they reached the ominous opening leading to what had once been the so-called demon's lair. Once again, Hal lit torches as he went, mentally thanking whoever had installed them recently. They heard the sound of trickling water and emerged into a long, low cave where daylight streamed in through a wide, three-foot-high slit. Briskle ducked under the low-hanging cave mouth and peered out. He gave a whistle of appreciation; the view was breathtaking.

Rivulets of water ran down into a clear pool in the corner of the cave, which in turn overflowed and ran off into cracks in the rocky floor. While Abigail bent to take a drink, Briskle stepped back into the cave and looked around. "I don't get it. You said there was a back door. I see a fabulous view, but nowhere for 'copters to land. It'd be murder trying to get the cargo through this low opening anyway."

Hal smiled and pointed upward.

The next few minutes were spent trying to hoist the heavy lieutenant up through the roof where another smoky portal lurked in the shadows. As Briskle remarked, there were holes everywhere in this place. Once his boots had disappeared from sight, they waited until he reached back down with one shaky hand. He was out of Hal's reach, so Ryan went next. Abigail threw off her coat, grew her wings, and lifted Hal up through the blackness.

The blast of freezing air and icy ocean spray took Hal's breath away. They were on a small rocky island in the middle of the sea. Seals frolicked on similar isles nearby, and gulls screeched overhead.

Briskle was standing there looking astonished, his yellow biosuit glistening wet. *At least he's staying dry under it*, Hal thought as another spray of water hit him. Abigail gave a scream as she caught the brunt of it. She hurriedly grabbed Hal under the arms and shot up into the air.

The final portal was a hundred feet directly above the last. A long thick rope hung from it, and Ryan was already clinging to it while Briskle eyed it with uncertainty. Abigail left them behind. Panting a little from the effort of carrying Hal, she buzzed quickly through the pulsing cloud.

They emerged in a man-made shaft with an enormous wooden contraption towering over it. The rope hung from this, wound around a giant spindle amid a series of pulleys and handles. Gasping, Abigail continued her flight up the shaft and out into the sunshine. The two of them collapsed on yellow sand, acutely aware of a deep throbbing sound in the sky.

It was then that they saw a helicopter standing idly nearby, its rotors still and its biosuited pilot leaning against the door. Another soldier was sitting on a boulder. Both were staring in amazement as Hal and Abigail climbed to their feet.

"Where's the lieutenant?" the pilot asked.

Hal pointed at the shaft. "Pull 'em up."

The pilot and soldier hastened to winch up the rope, and a minute later Ryan and Briskle appeared.

The three gigantic helicopters were approaching. Hal thought he had seen enough of the helicopters on the island to be used to them, but these three were absolutely gigantic in comparison—and each with *two* massive engines, one at the front and another sticking up higher at the back. It seemed impossible that these thundering monsters could stay in the air, especially as they each dangled a massive metal container underneath.

"Let's get these babies down and unloaded," Briskle shouted into his radio as dust started to fly. "We've got work to do."

Hal and Abigail took cover and huddled by the low shaft wall as the machines descended.

Chapter Nineteen
Fog-Dust and Geo-Rocks

Operation Hard Rain, as Briskle had aptly named the project, got started immediately. As soon as the containers were on the ground and the giant 'Chinook' helicopters landed, dozens of biosuited soldiers poured out.

They opened the containers and started rolling out pallets of large wooden crates using a forklift. The gigantic wooden treadmill crane, originally operated by a centaur trotting around within the enormous wheel and winding a rope around a spindle, was adapted for use with one of the helicopter's winch systems. It was much more efficient that way. The first crate was hooked up to the crane and lowered into the shaft along with a string of soldiers clinging to the rope. This crew would be receiving crates in the cave behind the temple and transporting them along the tunnel to the gateways.

Ryan and Hal were enthralled by the hustle and bustle. Abigail, however, quickly became bored. "Can we go home now?" she pleaded.

Hal couldn't believe his ears. "Are you kidding? This is the fun part!"

"No, this is the bit where they lower a bazillion boxes of fog-dust down into the cave, carry them all along the tunnel into the cavern, open them up, and start emptying them into the gateways. It might be interesting to see for about two minutes, but after that it's going to get old *really* quickly."

"Well, okay," Hal grumbled. "But I want to see them get started at least."

And they did. About half an hour later, when a soldier reported that the first batch of crates had arrived, Hal, Ryan and Abigail went with Lieutenant Briskle down the winch and along the tunnel to the brightly lit cavern behind the temple. The holes were being unblocked as they arrived; soldiers were levering the wooden panels off the wall to reveal the smoky black clouds. As each was opened up, the howl of wind increased until it was hard to hear anything the next person was saying. Briskle's flickering torch was snuffed out, and everyone staggered around gripping the iron railing for support. Hal felt his feet lifting off the floor several times as the nearest portal threatened to suck him through.

The crates were stacked in the center of the cavern on top of the boards that sealed up the so-called bottomless pit where the fungus had been cultivated. On Briskle's orders, the first crate was levered open. Its lid snapped upward and shot out through a portal, and the lieutenant shouted "Whoa!"—but then everyone was lost in a haze of blue-green dust as the finely ground fog-pellets whisked around the cavern like a miniature tornado, causing everyone to cover their eyes and mouths. In seconds the crate was half empty, and as the dust clung to the inside corners of the box, squinting soldiers tilted it and moved the dust around so the howling wind could catch it. Less than a minute later, the crate was empty, every tiny grain swept up and out of the nine portals.

One crate down, only a bazillion to go, Hal thought happily.

The empty crate wobbled and bucked in the ferocious windstorm but didn't quite lift off the ground. As the next crate was levered open, Briskle yelled at his men to keep hold of the lid. "Let's try not to drop wooden lids out of the sky onto the few remaining survivors in the world."

The soldiers soon got into a routine of removing lids, carefully stashing them in the tunnel, and coaxing the fog-dust out of the crates. Although the soldiers had been pleased to throw off their biosuits upon arrival in this world, now they donned them again as protection against the ongoing dust storm.

"This'll take most of the night," Briskle told Hal and his friends as they retreated from the cavern and along the tunnel. "We've got natural daylight at the moment, but we'll need to rig up some lamps for when it gets dark, which means bringing a generator through . . ." He sighed. "Stay out of our way, okay?"

"I want to help," Ryan told the lieutenant.

Briskle looked at him and nodded. "Then fall in, soldier. When this job is done, I'll personally see to it that your old friends are escorted to safety."

With a system in place, and the soldiers working tirelessly to transport full crates into the cavern and empties back out, there was nothing left for Hal to do but wait. He and Abigail bade farewell to

Ryan and hitched a ride back to the stone quarry with the first load of empty crates.

"I need to go see Lauren now," Hal said, blinking in the sunshine.

"I'm coming with you," Abigail said.

They left in style, with Hal in dragon form and Abigail sitting astride his broad shoulders. Soldiers stopped and stared, their task momentarily forgotten.

Since Hal was unable to talk to his passenger, the flight home gave him a little time to think. It was late afternoon by now; his mom would have found his note hours ago and reported it to Miss Simone, who in turn would have . . . what? How upset would she be that he and Abigail had taken off with Ryan on a small mission to help him fetch his friends? She might be annoyed but not overly concerned. She might even be pleased that the task had been checked off her list of things to do.

But someone would have heard the helicopters arrive. The goblins back at the lake surely would have been aware of them coming through the new hundred-foot portal high in the sky. They would have rushed off to alert Miss Simone. It was no more than a couple of hours to Carter at a trot, and even though goblins didn't like riding on horseback, they might have done so on this occasion. Miss Simone must have heard the news by now.

Hal could imagine her running around issuing orders: "The soldiers have found a way through! They're invading with helicopters! Gather weapons and prepare for an attack!"

Would she guess that Hal, Ryan and Abigail were involved? It was ironic that they had in fact averted the very attack she was likely fretting about!

He needed to slip into the village undetected. If he was spotted, his parents and Miss Simone would pounce on him and ground him for a decade. He couldn't let that happen. He needed to stay out of sight.

With that in mind, he landed on a hill on the outskirts of the village. This was where the soldiers had camped after their initial visit to Carter—where Darcy had poisoned them with hemlock. After he'd transformed and donned his jacket, socks and shoes over his smart clothes, he and Abigail stood there shivering.

"Humans are so weak," Hal muttered. "It doesn't seem to matter if it's hot or cold while I'm a dragon, but as soon as I change back . . ."

She beat her arms and stamped her feet. "Well, I feel like an icicle after sitting on your back for the last hour."

"It was only twenty minutes," Hal said absently, looking around to check nobody had seen them arrive. "How are we going to do this? I need to speak to Lauren, but if anyone sees us . . ."

"I'll go. You wait here. I'll bring Lauren to you."

She removed her coat and handed it to him, revealing her three layers of smart clothes—shirts and pants of varying organic shades. After taking off her shoes and socks, she transformed with a sudden pop and buzzed around like a hummingbird. She darted away down the hill toward the village.

Hal hid in a thicket of trees, really hungry by now and wishing he'd asked Abigail to bring back something to eat. He hadn't had anything since his early breakfast of bread and cheese. He sat there with his stomach rumbling, watching a robin hop around on the grass looking for a worm.

It was forty minutes before Lauren showed up on the hill with Abigail buzzing alongside. Hal ushered them into the thicket.

"What's going on?" Lauren whispered, crouching on the hard-packed dirt.

"Why are you whispering?" Abigail asked loudly.

Lauren frowned and shrugged.

"I need your help," Hal said. "Did Abi tell you much?"

"No, nothing." She looked at him earnestly, worry written across her face.

"Okay. I need you to do something for me. It's a secret from Miss Simone, but actually we're doing something really good. So I guess it's like a surprise," he added. "You'll be part of something big."

"Like what?" Lauren asked doubtfully.

Hal explained what the soldiers were doing right now and what he needed *her* to do to complete the mission. As with Briskle, he wasn't ready to share the part about creating lots of holes for people to wander through, but he had a feeling he wouldn't be able to avoid it. Lauren rocked back and forth, her forehead and cute snub nose creased with concentration.

"So you want me to go all the way to the harpy nest near Louis," she repeated, "and persuade the harpies to come with me."

"Yeah. I hear they're being quite reasonable these days—actually trading for food rather than stealing it."

Lauren shook her head. "And what am I supposed to offer them in return for this huge favor? They won't do it for free."

"You'll think of something," Hal assured her. "You did a great job when they stole a baby. You can do it again. Trick them, persuade them, bargain with them—whatever works to get the job done."

She considered the problem. "I wonder if they'd be interested in all those empty shops and homes in the ruined cities. There's a ton of stuff to steal, and nobody would care. That could be their reward."

"Yes!" Hal exclaimed. "I *knew* you'd figure something out."

Warming to the plan, Lauren nodded slowly. "So I persuade the harpies to jump through those nine holes in the temple. But how will they get back? Those holes are way too high in the sky. They can drop through them and fall to Earth easily enough, but they'll never fly high enough to return. They might not be interested in a one-way trip."

Here we go, Hal thought. He took a deep breath. "I'm going to create lots of new holes. Once that's done, they can come back anytime."

When Lauren narrowed his eyes and glanced at Abigail, she simply shrugged. To Hal's surprise, Lauren seemed okay with that. "Okay. I'll fly as fast as I can, but it'll take half a day to get there and back."

Abigail patted her arm. "You can do it. Be as quick as you can. Go pack something to eat and head out as soon as possible. Leave a note for your mom to say you're going to help Hal and me. Keep it vague. At least Miss Simone will know we're all together. She just won't know where."

"She'll find you," Lauren warned. "She's already on the warpath. Goblins reported that new hole over Serpent Lake and helicopters heading south, following a dragon. She knows you're involved."

Hal's heart sank. "Oh. Well, I figured she'd be on to us eventually."

"She's already got goblins and centaurs out searching. They didn't see where the helicopters landed, but they'll ask around and pick up the trail."

Abigail frowned. "Ask around? Ask who, exactly?"

"The naga in the woods, a few hermits they know of, a wandering soothsayer, and so on." Lauren waved her hand dismissively. "Anyway, the point is, you'd all better lie low, or she'll put a stop to it."

Actually, Hal wondered if that was true. Would she even lift a finger to stop the soldiers from doing such a positive thing as saving their world from the remnants of the virus? And *could* she? The soldiers were armed, after all.

Lauren set off soon after. She had seemed doubtful at first, but she put on the same determined face Hal recognized from her dealings with the harpy queen. She could be a tough cookie when she wanted to be.

"Let's hope she comes through," Hal said, taking off his jacket, shoes and socks and handing them to Abigail. "Okay, I'm off back to the quarry. Coming?"

"Actually . . ." She stared at the grass for a moment, then looked up at him. "I think I'm going to head home."

"What? Why?"

"Well, let's see. Maybe because I don't want to hang around in a damp tunnel at the back of the temple while the soldiers move a bazillion crates?" She rolled her eyes. "I'll catch up with you later. I think it would be better if I went home and tried to delay things—you know, casually mention that you all went off to visit the ogres in the south because the soldiers want to recruit them to help rebuild the city back in their own world."

Hal stared at her and started to grin. "You think you can persuade Miss Simone of that?"

"I can try. By the time she sends everyone off to the ogres and finds out it's a big fat fib, then sends someone to interrogate me about it, and hightails it to the stone quarry, maybe your work will be done already."

"You're a genius," Hal said, smiling.

"I know. How long do you think you'll need?"

Hal spread his hands. "Briskle said it'll take most of the night."

"All right. I'll try and hold out until morning. Miss Simone can torture me, and I'll never tell. Not until breakfast, anyway. See you later."

She turned to go but paused and turned back. She stepped up to him and gave him a quick kiss half on his cheek and half on his mouth. When he looked into her eyes, he thought she looked troubled.

"What's wrong?" he asked.

"Nothing. I just hope everything goes okay."

"It'll be fine," he assured her.

He stuffed his shoes and socks into his jacket pockets, then transformed and gripped the jacket in his claws. Taking to the air, he grunted goodbye, and she waved back. She stood and watched him, and finally he lost sight of her as he soared over the treetops.

Heading back to the south and flying low over the naga forest, something gnawed at him. It wasn't anything Abigail had said—in fact, she'd made a lot of sense in her plan to divert attention from the stone quarry. It was more to do with that farewell. That kiss, and the look in her eyes. Like she was . . . sorry?

Not quite knowing what to make of it or what to do about it, he continued onward, determined to see the project through no matter what. He hoped Abigail would do as she said. She might not be happy about the final stage of his plan—to join the worlds—but she should be perfectly fine with helping the soldiers kill the virus. Why would she jeopardize that?

She wouldn't. Hal was certain of it. So he might as well stop fretting.

Still . . .

He looked up at the sky. It would be dark in a few hours. He'd planned to wait for the spores to be fully eradicated before joining the worlds, but now he felt he should bring the plan forward before Miss Simone caught up to him.

The last thing he wanted was to contaminate this world, this New Earth. However, although holes were nothing but clouds of smoke, they were tangible enough to keep airborne spores at bay. Besides, the spores weren't floating down from the sky anymore, so that risk was minimal. Perhaps the real danger was the possibility of residents in Carter and other villages crossing into the virus-ridden world—but everyone on this side of the fence *knew* about the danger and would never go near the holes until they were sure it was safe to do so.

What about scrags? They might come through and bring spores with them on their clothes. Unlike soldiers, they wouldn't care about contamination. But what were the chances of scrags being an immediate threat? They were so few and far between. And even if a gang came through, the amount of spores on their clothes would be negligible, almost insignificant unless they engaged in wrestling with villagers . . .

He took a deep breath. It was time to get Lieutenant Briskle involved with the last phase of his plan—exploding a whole load of geo-rocks and opening holes. It had to be now before Miss Simone caught up. If Abigail told on him, he needed to be one or two steps ahead.

He circled around and headed back toward the village.

He crouched in the darkness, stiff from cold and fatigue. It had been rough waiting in the woods for the sun to go down. On several occasions he'd considered just trying his luck and walking through the village, or perhaps donning a disguise of some kind . . . but each time he thought about it and approached the village gate, he'd seen villagers he recognized.

He'd even seen Thomas and Fenton at one point, ambling along. That had been the last straw for Hal. He'd slunk back into the shadows and waited in the trees, urging the sun to hurry up and sink behind the horizon.

When at last it did, he wasted no time. It was dusk, and not as dark as he'd like, but he was sore from shivering, not to mention starving. He'd decided ages ago to enlist Robbie's help. His best friend would be invaluable right now.

Twice he nearly bumped into people he knew. He twisted away, trying to look nonchalant, and hurried on. He saw a group of goblins loitering on a street corner and had to retrace his steps and go another route.

And he saw Miss Simone.

She looked thoughtful as she walked with another goblin—one that Hal recognized as Gristletooth. They disappeared around a corner and left Hal lurking in the shadow of an alley wondering what she was still doing here in the village. Had Abigail not managed to convince her that the helicopters had gone to ogre country in the south? That the soldiers were there trying to recruit the monsters with Hal's help? The more he thought about her story, the more flaws leapt out. How on earth would soldiers—or Hal for that matter—talk to ogres without Robbie present? Why would they bring four helicopters for what was essentially a chat? Did they expect to carry a bunch of ogres home?

Hal could imagine Miss Simone's reaction to this ill-conceived story. She'd stare hard at Abigail and challenge her about it. And he doubted Abigail would keep up the lies for long.

Even if Miss Simone had believed her, why was she still here? Had she been to check on the ogres and come back already? Or had she never left?

Hal sighed. It was pointless conjecturing. He had no idea what Abigail had told her, if anything, and what Miss Simone had done about it. He shook his head and moved on.

Instead of rapping on Robbie's front door, he snuck around to the back and tapped lightly on his friend's bedroom window. He might not be in there, but if he wasn't, Hal could see if the window was open and—

The curtain moved, and Robbie peered out.

As soon as he spotted Hal, his mouth fell open. Hal shushed him and gestured to open the window, then clambered inside and collapsed on the floor of the oh-so-warm bedroom.

"Where have you been?" Robbie whispered. "What are you doing? What's going on?"

"Stuff," Hal said. "First, get me something to eat. I'm starving."

Grumbling, Robbie went to the kitchen. Hal heard him say something to Mrs. Strickland, and she answered amiably from the living room. Then Robbie returned with a cooked but cold chicken leg and a quarter of a large apple pie. Hal fell on the chicken leg with desperation, and then tore into the pie. All the while, Robbie sat on the side of his bed without saying a word.

"Thanks," Hal said eventually, licking his fingers.

"Now spit it out," Robbie growled.

"The chicken leg?" Hal quipped. "Or the pie?"

Robbie rolled his eyes. "You know what I mean. Spill the beans."

Hal considered extending the joke . . . but changed his mind when he saw the serious expression on his friend's face. "All right. I need your help. But let's talk on the way."

"On the way *where?*"

"Not far. We need to pick up a couple of nets. You coming?"

After some more grumbling, Robbie went to tell his parents that he was going out for a while. As he left noisily through the front door, Hal climbed back out the window. They met in the street and moved fast, keeping to the shadows. It was really dark now, although the moon was full tonight, and there were great pools of light in the more open spaces.

"Okay, what's the plan?" Robbie whispered.

Hal held a finger to his lips. "Not here."

They headed for a large supply shed. It was unlocked. Nobody was rude enough to mess with this shed. It belonged to the village's odd-job man, or the wheelbarrow man as he was known, and was full of useful replacement parts—tools, nails, candles, fishing tackle, an odd collection of wheels from carts and wagons, all kinds of lumber, and other random things that people might run short of. Where he acquired it all was a mystery to Hal, but the man and his shed were the village hardware store.

His wheelbarrow was there, too, half full of glowing geo-rocks that Blacknail and Miss Simone had supplied him with after their initial trip to Bad Rock Gulch. Hal was tempted to take them but decided there was no need. "Find some nets," he said quietly.

There were quite a few fishing nets folded up on a shelf, but two in particular caught Hal's eye, roughly twelve feet in diameter with little weights all around. He didn't need the weights, but the nets were a good size.

They stole one each and skedaddled. Their next stop was Blacknail's buggy and its rock-filled wagon, still standing quietly in an open part of the village streets where people could come along and take the geo-rocks as needed.

"Spread the nets," Hal said when they got there, and that was when light dawned on Robbie's face. He looked disturbed but said nothing as they stretched the nets flat on the ground. Knowing what was needed, Robbie climbed up onto the wagon and started handing geo-rocks down to Hal, who quickly placed them in the center of the first net. The work was repetitive but fast.

Hal couldn't help noticing that almost the entire back end of the wagon had been emptied of its load. The villagers hadn't wasted any time collecting! When he commented on this, Robbie put him right on the matter. "Blair took 'em. He wants to recharge and can't be bothered to fly back to Bad Rock Gulch."

"Oh!" Hal exclaimed. "For the rose garden."

"For the what?"

"It's where Molly keeps a lot of her victims. If Blair recharges, he can go and do his thing and wake them all."

Nothing more was said for the next minute. The silence was uncomfortable. "What's going on, Hal?" Robbie said at last. "Why are we doing this?"

Knowing he couldn't put it off any longer, Hal launched into his story. Robbie's eyes grew wider and wider as he worked. Hal told him everything, even including his plan to join the worlds. At this, Robbie nearly fell off the wagon. "Are you *kidding?*" he whispered fiercely, grasping a rock in each hand.

Hal wasn't kidding, and work slowed a little while he spent considerable time convincing his friend that he was extremely serious—and that he was going through with it whether anyone helped him or not. "I hope you're with me on this," he said finally. "I could do with the support."

As Robbie handed him another rock, he gripped it hard instead of letting Hal take it. "You should have told me," he growled. "You want to *open holes*? That's crazy, dude."

Hal glanced around, making sure the streets were still empty. It broke the awkward moment between them, and work resumed.

Before long, Hal held up a hand. "That's enough rocks for this net. Can we start on the other one now?"

Robbie jumped down and, together, they tightened the net. Hal estimated fifty geo-rocks or more, a heavy load.

They laid out the second net on the other side of the wagon and resumed their nighttime task. "Have you seen Miss Simone today?" Hal asked after a while.

"She was running around like a headless chicken earlier," Robbie told him. His irritation seemed to have evaporated. "A goblin came and warned her of the helicopters, said they'd been heading south. So she sent a bunch of goblins and centaurs off to the south looking for them. They had to resort to asking old hermits in caves if they'd seen big metal machines flying over."

"She didn't go herself?" Hal asked.

"Nah. She hung around the village in case someone needed her. Abigail came home a few hours ago—" He stopped, rolled his eyes, and handed another rock to Hal. "Well, obviously you know that part."

"Did she talk to Miss Simone? What did she say?"

"How should I know? I wasn't there. But Miss Simone stopped running around like a headless chicken. She and Abigail talked for ages, or so Emily said. Then again, Emily heard that from Darcy. She also heard that Lauren went off somewhere, which got back to Miss Simone as well."

"But you don't know what Abigail told her?" Hal persisted.

Robbie shook his head.

"So where did Abi go after that?"

"I don't know," Robbie said, getting annoyed.

They continued their job in silence.

When the second net was piled up with geo-rocks and pulled tight, the boys stepped back to admire their work. "You can carry all that?" Robbie asked.

"Why? Are you offering to come with me?"

"No way." Robbie shuffled his feet and refused to meet Hal's gaze. "I can't be part of that. It's just . . . it's too much."

Hal chewed his lip. "Look, you're either with me or against me on this. You can't just stand aside and watch to see what happens."

"I've helped you so far, haven't I?"

"Yeah, you have. But don't you want to come with me and watch all these things explode?"

Robbie shook his head vehemently.

"So you're just going to stay here and bury your head in the sand?"

"I was thinking under the pillow. Look, I've done all I'm going to do to help you, and that's only because you're my best friend. And because you dragged me out here without explaining why, so I didn't exactly have a choice." He paused and stared hard at Hal. "Don't do this without Miss Simone's permission. She'll be really mad."

He looked so fierce that Hal took a step back. "But what about the dream I had? About the invasion? That was real. I stopped it from happening. Abi and Ryan will tell you—they saw what Briskle was about to do, and we got there just in time and stopped it from happening."

"So you're a hero," Robbie agreed. "And you're cleaning up the spores, so you're a *double* hero. Leave it there. Don't go behind Miss Simone's back, especially with Lieutenant Briskle."

Feeling pangs of doubt, Hal turned away. "Stop messing with my head. Look, do you really think Miss Simone will agree to what I'm talking about doing? Even if I got her together with Briskle, and they talked for hours, do you see her agreeing to open up holes all over the place and letting survivors come through?"

"No."

"Exactly. I *have* to go behind her back. Robbie, my dream about the invasion turned out to be real, and so did Chase, and I'm sure the rest is real, too. I'm doing this. It's the right thing to do. Nobody else sees it but me. And admit it—you're curious—you want to see what'll happen, right? Otherwise you wouldn't have helped me load these rocks."

"You sound like a crazy person," Robbie grumbled.

"Maybe."

They stood there for a long, awkward moment, not quite making eye contact. Then, with a deep breath, Hal took off his jacket, shoes and socks, and stuffed all of it into one of the nets. He moved into a clear spot, aware that Robbie was already sidling away. Without a word, Hal transformed.

Launching into the sky with two netloads of geo-rocks was harder than he'd expected. They threatened to drag him back down to the ground. He was aware of Robbie watching from below and was determined not to show his weakness. He fought harder, pushing away across the village and over the woods. He climbed slowly, panting, his legs aching from gripping the loads.

Once he was well away from the village and toward the southern tip of the woods, he landed in a clearing that he knew nobody would easily find. He would fly the rest of the way later. First he needed to rest.

He collapsed on top of the rocks. The twin piles flattened out somewhat, and he ended up just staying there, gripping his precious loads as if they were chests of treasure. Gasping for breath, he lay across his cargo with his snout buried in dry leaves. The evening was young but so quiet it might as well have been the middle of the night. The stars shone, and somewhere an owl hooted.

Doubt descended on him again, and he groaned long and hard. *What am I doing? My friends think I'm crazy. Everyone's out looking for me. They all think I'm about to end the world.*

What if he was wrong? What if he'd misread what the Gatekeeper had been telling him? What if joining the worlds was a colossal error?

He let out a long, mournful moan. Most of his angst was because of his friends. Both Robbie and Abigail had looked at him like he'd lost his mind.

What if he had?

He closed his eyes, suddenly unwilling to go on. Maybe he needed to spend the night right here. Maybe everything would make more sense in the morning. There was no hurry. The soldiers needed time to get all the fog-dust out of the gateways, Lauren needed time to bring her harpy friends along, and Miss Simone wasn't hotfooting it to the quarry yet.

There was time to sleep. Time to clear his head.

Chapter Twenty
Neutralizing the Spores

Hal blearily woke. It was still dark, but dawn was approaching. His bed of geo-rocks was throbbing with energy. With a shock, he saw dozens of blurry faces staring up at him as though the mound of rocks were a dome of glass with people trapped below.

He blinked with confusion, still half asleep. The faces moved closer, mouths opening and closing, eyes wide with fear. There were hands, too, pressed against the inner surface of the rocks, fingers splayed apart. The silence was unnerving. As before, these ghosts were trying to tell him something.

Hal realized he was back in human form when he reached out to touch one of the mounds of rocks through the fishing net. They were as hard and rough as they had always been, just as rocks should be. Some of them shifted under his hands, but the faces were fixed in place as though their images were being projected onto the glowing surface of the mound.

"What are you trying to tell me?" he sleep-murmured with frustration, his words coming out a little garbled.

He watched as the ghosts became more frantic, their silent screams and gestures filling him with dread. What now? The first time these ghosts had appeared to him, they'd warned of an earthquake. He'd been nearly boiled alive, and turned to stone by a gorgon. They might have warned him of the werewolf attack if they'd had the means. Now they were warning him again—but of what? It was pointless trying to guess. If only he could read lips!

They gradually faded away. Some appeared to give up early, turning away helplessly, whereas others remained to the end—right up until the moment a bright white flared in front of him.

Hal lurched and slid sideways off the netted rocks, blinking at the dazzling column that stood less than ten feet away. He could feel a wave of ice-cold air as the light expanded, lighting up the clearing. It dimmed suddenly, and he recognized the strange alien-woman-creature standing there with her hands outstretched. She tilted her head and smiled, and he saw himself reflected in her enormous black eyes.

Your doubt is understandable.

Her voice was soft and whispery, echoing through his head. He flinched, wondering if he was fully awake yet. Was this another dream?

This is an important time. What you do today affects everyone.

"Stop!" he said feebly.

I see two paths, she went on. *One is a path of destruction, more of what I showed you earlier—death and war, a struggle to claim this land. The other is a path of acceptance, the beginning of a new era.*

Hal covered his ears. "Why me?"

Because you came to me, and because you're in a position to make things happen. Don't underestimate yourself.

A human voice came to him, one he recognized: "And that's why I like you, Hal. You just seem to have a way of knowing what's right. You're loyal and brave. A little clueless sometimes, but you get there in the end. I'm way smarter than you, but I'm sure you know that already."

"Abi?" he said, looking around the clearing. He spotted a shadowy figure standing in the darkness among the trees. Yet he knew it wasn't Abigail. Her voice had been played back in his head like a recording. He remembered her saying the exact same thing while they'd been seated in Blacknail's buggy just after their run-in with the mountain trolls.

Abruptly, the dazzling shaft of light was gone, and the clearing was plunged once more into gloom.

Wearily, Hal climbed to his feet and stared down at his netted cargo. The rocks were still glowing but had lost their earlier vibrancy. They were back to their normal state, no sign of faces anywhere. And the alien-woman-creature, the Gatekeeper, had vanished. Hal shook his head, bemused.

Then he swung around. The shadowy figure was moving out of the trees, coming toward him. He couldn't decide whether to transform or bolt. Instead, he remained rooted to the spot until the person—a man cloaked in tattered robes and holding a long wooden staff—stepped closer into the dawn light. His head was bald on top, but long white hair hung from the back and sides.

One of his eyes was missing. It was just an empty socket. And immediately Hal recognized the old man as the traveling soothsayer who had shown up in Carter and told them about Whisper Mountain and the demon therein.

"You saw him," the man said, jabbing a gnarled finger at Hal.

"What? Saw who?"

"Just now. The angel of light. You saw him."

Hal opened and closed his mouth, completely befuddled. "*Him?*"

"Did he tell you about the village?"

"The—what?"

The soothsayer clicked his tongue and shuffled closer. He reeked of something rotten, and Hal took a step back. "I've been seeing things again. I've been seeing the village floating on water."

"The village?" Hal repeated. "You mean Carter?"

"Carter, yes. The village. Floating on water. And—flashes of light all across the land. Yes, yes, and the village floating on water."

Hal swallowed, trying to steady his thudding heart and ragged breathing. "Okay, wait. You saw the village of Carter *floating on water*? What does that even mean? A flood? Is it . . . is it bad?"

The old man wasn't listening. He was looking off into the trees, his single eye roving. He looked as confused as Hal felt. "Not bad," he muttered. "Just . . ."

"Just what?"

"Just . . ."

Hal fought the urge to snatch the wooden staff from the man's hand and whack him around the head with it. "Just *what?*"

After a long pause, the soothsayer started to turn away. He paused and said, "Just *different*," before shuffling off into the trees. The darkness swallowed him up, and Hal was left alone with his thoughts.

Seconds later, he became suddenly aware that he was being watched. Again. Not by silent phantoms or creepy, wizened old soothsayers, but something far more tangible. "What now?" he growled softly.

He swung around, transforming in one swift movement. In dragon form, he hunkered down and peered into the trees.

Out of the shadows came dirty, greasy harpies—hundreds of them, watching him with unblinking yellow eyes as they closed in. Others were in the trees, clinging to branches and hanging there.

Before Hal had a chance to clear his head, one of the creatures rushed toward him. She was much cleaner than the rest, her feathers pure white rather than grimy and matted, and wearing a silky green dress instead of filth-encrusted rags. Hal recognized her immediately. "Lauren!"

All the harpies flinched and took a step back, and Hal mentally kicked himself for trying to speak aloud while in dragon form.

"We're here," Lauren said. She leaned closer and lowered her voice. "And we should get this done before the queen changes her mind."

She seemed to have brought along the entire nest from the hills west of Louis. Many were chewing on little green shoots. They all had little pouches or bundles of the curious plant stuffed into belts around their waists. Lauren called it 'harpynip'—like catnip for cats, it gave them a buzz and, more importantly, heightened their powers when it came to manipulating the elements.

Hal spotted a particularly unfriendly creature that he remembered as the queen. Her scowl indicated that she was already exasperated. Patience was probably not one of her virtues.

"Let's fly," Lauren urged, jerking her head skyward. "You lead."

Hal gave a nod, gripped the nets within his claws, and launched. The furious beat of his wings caused the mass of harpies to cringe back, widening the circle—but then he was soaring upward and leaving them behind.

Lauren gave a shrill cry and came after him. Hal glanced down to see the rest of them launching in groups, led by the queen herself. Pretty soon the wintry greens and browns of the forest were obscured by a blanket of ugly gray wings.

"I promised the queen a never-ending supply of stuff to plunder," Lauren said as she came alongside. "Empty stores and houses all over the world—but only for a limited time, if she came with me now and brewed up a few storms."

Hal let out a bellow of mirth. Lauren was normally so innocent, so *girly*, and yet she could manipulate an entire nest of harpies with a few well-chosen words.

"Didn't take much to convince her," Lauren went on, sounding mildly surprised. "She's been trying to work with the local villagers, trading services for food and supplies, but it's not the harpy way. I only had to mention abandoned cities and she went all wide-eyed, begging to know where."

Hal began to tire with the weight of the geo-rocks. He took his mind off the strain by forcing himself to concentrate on what she was saying.

"We were on our way to the quarry when we saw a *really* bright light shining up out of a clearing in the trees. We came down, wondering what it was. Never did find out—it disappeared before we got here. But it led us to you. Took a while to convince the queen you were my friend, though."

So the Gatekeeper really had appeared. The soothsayer had seen her—although he'd perceived her as a *him*—and Lauren, along with the other harpies, had seen the bright white light.

Then there were the ghosts in the geo-rocks, not to be forgotten. Had they, too, really had been there, warning him of impending danger as they had the earthquake?

Lauren was still talking, wondering what the old man had meant about a flood in the village of Carter and flashes of light across the land, but Hal only half listened. Looking back at the flock of harpies filling the sky, he felt a shiver of fear. Leading these creatures into his old world was crazy. Sure, they'd create storms and flood the land with rain, thus activating the crushed fog-pellets and generating fog that would nullify the spores . . . but then what? They'd invade homes, steal whatever they wanted, maybe even stick around and set up nests . . .

But the world was a wreck anyway. Cities were deserted. What did it matter if hundreds of harpies took over? They'd give the scrags a run for their money. And besides, divided between all nine gateways and spread across the planet, the harpies would be cut down to groups of maybe twenty or thirty. If they split further, went off in different directions to explore, they would become rather sparse—a rare and strange sight for the humans emerging from hiding.

Hal relaxed. It would be all right. The harpies were the least of his worries. And besides, wasn't his ultimate plan to merge the worlds?

The stone quarry came into view, and not a moment too soon because the rocks felt like they'd doubled in weight. He saw the three giant helicopters, and the smaller one, standing under a sand-colored cliff. Hal swooped down, mindful that the soldiers scurried around like mice.

As he landed, guns came up and pointed at him, then dropped when the soldiers recognized who he was. Immediately the guns lifted again as a series of screeches flooded the quarry. Harpies rained down, their birdlike feet thudding onto the hard-packed dirt or sinking into softer dunes nearby. To the soldiers' credit, they seemed to understand that the bird-people were with Hal, and not a single shot rang out despite their obvious fear. If someone had gotten trigger-happy, things might have degenerated into a brawl.

Hal left his netted geo-rocks and strode over to the shaft. He gave a roar to get everyone's attention. Harpies fell silent and turned to look at him, some chewing on green shoots. Soldiers lowered their weapons.

Since Hal couldn't really say a whole lot without making everyone jump, he simply grunted and turned toward the shaft. The winch cable still hung there, but it had been retracted as far as it would go so its hook and rigged wooden platform swung ponderously over the shaft. Hal allowed himself to fall into the shaft. He toppled head first and plunged into the pulsing black cloud below.

He fell from the sky of a different world, with ocean all around and seals frolicking on the rocks. Then he frantically flapped his wings to slow his descent and dropped through the second portal embedded in the tiny island below. His landing on the hard, rocky floor of the dark cave was heavier than he'd have liked.

He stepped out from under the hole in the ceiling and into the tunnel. There he waited, looking back. Any second now, harpies would be coming through—assuming Lauren persuaded them to follow.

Lauren was first. She landed nimbly, her wings outspread. She moved aside, and the queen landed beside her, her ugly features screwed up in a mask of shock. The difference between the two creatures was startling—one clean and elegant, the other filthy and twisted.

The queen would have stood there dumbly looking around the cave while other harpies collapsed on top of her if Lauren hadn't pulled her aside first. More and more of them appeared, wings flapping and feathers coming loose as the creatures began to jostle for space.

"Move on, Hal," Lauren urged.

Hal hurried along the tunnel, which was still lit by flickering torches even though the howl of wind from the gateways tugged on the flames. Empty crates were stacked down one side, but the tunnel was wide. He heard screeches and arguments behind him, but also the patter of feet, the scrabbling of claws on rock. The harpies were following.

He led the way to the cavern, passing endless empty crates and stacks of lids. Hal could feel the distinct tug of atmospheric pressures out of balance. He wasn't sure if he was being pushed or pulled along the tunnel toward the cavern of portals, but the result was the same.

Feathers fluttered past him, plucked from multiple harpies that struggled along behind without a word, probably quaking with fear at this strange and bizarre place. When they rounded the corner of the main tunnel, the torches were out, snuffed by the draft.

Upon entering the cavern, the noise and ferocity of the wind increased dramatically. The daylight flooding through the split in the wall revealed four soldiers braced against the iron railings surrounding the room. They were still wearing biosuits but had thrown off their masks. They looked exhausted. Freestanding lamps had been rigged up, wired to what Hal recognized as a small generator. In the center of the cavern, dozens more empty crates stood open, their contents—fog-dust as fine as ashes—long since sucked into the portals.

"What *is* this?" the harpy queen screeched from behind him.

Lauren screeched back, trying to explain as quickly as possible what these nine pulsing black holes were and where they led. The queen, however, just ended up looking even more confused.

The soldiers moved to the farthest end of the cavern, near the vertical split that let in daylight, as dozens more of the winged creatures came into the cavern, their plumage ruffling wildly and loose feathers whipping around.

The ugly queen looked ready to bolt as she turned to them. "This is a trap!"

"No," Lauren yelled. "I told you—these portals lead to the other world. You know this. You've seen holes like this before."

"Not like these."

The howling wind snatched her hissed words away, but the look on her face was unmistakable, dominated by suspicion and fear. "Trust me," Lauren told her, approaching and shouting directly into the queen's face. "There are cities down there! Abandoned long ago, left to ruin. There's more stuff lying around down there than you could ever dream of."

The queen narrowed her eyes. "What's the catch?"

Lauren nodded as if expecting that very question. "You can't return through these holes. They're too high. You'll never be able to fly back up to them. But if you do as I ask, more holes will show up near the ground so you can come home whenever you want. Or not. You can stay there if you want. It's up to you. You'd have two whole worlds to choose from."

Hal held his breath while the harpy queen considered the proposal. It wasn't much of one, he decided, at least not to him. Harpies, though, had a completely different mindset. The opportunity to plunder vast, empty cities without fear of retribution seemed impossible to resist.

"And what do you ask of us?" the queen eventually shouted above the wind.

Lauren gripped the queen's shoulders with one hand while clinging to the rail with the other. She screamed her message to *all* the harpies. "Make it rain. If you can make it rain non-stop for the next week, my friends will be able to form new holes everywhere. Then you can pass back and forth between both worlds. If you *don't* make it rain nonstop for the next week, you'll still get to scavenge the cities, but you'll be stuck in that world forever."

She was laying it on thick, Hal thought, though her message seemed to be getting through. Despite her suspicious nature, the harpy queen seemed to find it difficult to contain her greed. Having a new world to plunder was tempting; being able to cross between both worlds was a bonus.

He suddenly wondered if there was a link between the harpies making it rain non-stop in his old world, and the mysterious flood the soothsayer had mentioned. How could there be, though? And he wasn't certain it was a flood, either. The old man had said the village would be *floating*—whatever that meant.

The queen's expression hardened. As dozens of harpies crowded the space around them and in the tunnel behind, feathers fluttering and wings ruffling, she knocked Lauren's hands aside and gave her a shove. "You go first. You go, and I'll follow."

"I can't," she said. "I need to stay."

Seeing the sneer forming on the queen's face, Lauren glanced at Hal, clearly seeking an answer. Then she waved him closer.

At first Hal tried to maneuver his bulk around the edge of the cavern past the milling harpies to reach her. Then he gave up, stepped over the railing, and squeezed past the masses of empty crates in the center. That was a much easier approach. "Give me your tail, Hal," Lauren shouted, leaning over the railing toward him. When he clumsily turned and offered it to her, she gripped his club-ended tail with one hand, then two, and her feet instantly rose off the rock floor as the closest portal threatened to suck her through. Understanding her intention, Hal carefully backed all the way up to the railing, aiming his tail into the smoky cloud. Lauren vanished from sight.

A collective gasp went up. Hal let Lauren swing around in the other world for five or ten seconds before gently pulling her back in by edging forward into the center of the cavern.

Lauren reappeared, looking more than a little ruffled. She gasped, gripped the railing, and nodded to the queen. "Take a look. You'll see."

The queen reluctantly nodded and reached for Hal's tail. Like Lauren, she gripped it first with one hand. Then she let go of the rail and threw her entire weight onto Hal. Again he backed up to the black cloud, and the queen, clinging tightly to his tail, disappeared with wide yellow eyes.

Hal waited patiently, trying to ignore the whirlwind that whistled around him. Every harpy he could see stared back with wide eyes, cringing in the shadows of the cavern where the daylight didn't quite reach. Lauren watched with a fearful look on her face.

After a count of ten, he edged forward, dragging the queen out. She tumbled from the portal and grappled for the iron railing. When she finally got her breath back, she staggered toward the cowering harpies. Her feathers, as grimy as they were, stuck up everywhere.

"We go!" she screamed. "Split up. The world is ours. We may meet again, but if not—well, who cares?" She paused, then added, "And make it rain."

With that, she turned her back on her clan and leapt through the portal.

There was a long, long pause. All at once, other harpies started rushing forward and leaping at the pulsing holes. There was no order to their exit. They hardly even bothered seeking out friends or immediate family members. Either they didn't care, or they just didn't understand that these nine portals would dump them out in completely different parts of the world and that they might not see each other again.

It was a little sad, Hal thought as he watched them tumble over each other to leave the cavern—to be so detached that companionship meant so very little, to leave everything behind with hardly a moment's pause—and for what? So they could scavenge through the ruins of cities and take whatever so-called 'riches' they wanted? Were they so lazy that being alone with a nest full of goodies was preferable to working at a meaningful relationship with their human neighbors?

They'll get along well with the scrags, Hal thought with a sigh.

The harpies were moving fast, spilling into the cavern from the tunnel and out through the nine portals. It was a mad rush as if all the best stuff would be gone if they didn't hurry. They jostled and fought each other, snarling and screeching. Minutes later, every last one of them had gone, leaving only Lauren and four dumbfounded soldiers on the other side of the cavern.

Hal steeled himself and poked his head through one of the portals.

Emerging on the other side took his breath away. It was dramatically colder, and there was very little oxygen. He experienced pain in his ears and shook his head vigorously before taking in the view.

He gasped. He'd seen this before, but still—the scene was magnificent. The curvature of the Earth was especially pronounced. He was looking down on the planet from far, far higher than he'd ever flown. No matter how hard he beat his wings, he'd never be able to pull out of a dive-bomb if he fell through the hole. At this altitude, there was very little air to push against, no resistance to tame his freefall. He would drop like a stone, straight down, just like all the harpies that had jumped through moments before, until the atmosphere thickened.

He watched them falling silently, all in a line. Hal thought he saw one of the lowest specks far, far below shoot off to the side, finally able to glide off in another direction.

As Hal held his breath and fought the pain in his ears, he tried to make sense of the continent far below. There was so much ocean and so little land. Where *was* this, exactly? For all he knew, he could be on the other side of the planet—although then it would be nighttime, so perhaps not. But he could still be looking down on another continent. Nine portals meant nine locations across the planet, and the centaurs had most likely picked the most densely populated countries for their ruthless attack.

Hal liked the notion of long, wispy clouds of fog-dust trailing through the air, but he saw nothing of the sort. That stuff would take a while to fall and would be invisible. Despite the sheer number of crates that had been unloaded and emptied, the overall quantity seemed woefully light when viewing the Earth from this perspective. Much, much more would be needed.

Then again, the centaurs had released their fungal spores in the exact same way, and the virus had spread rapidly. Hal hoped the fog-dust would spread equally fast. Maybe there wasn't enough of it yet, but with more cargoes over the next week or so . . . well, it *had* to help.

It had better. Hal planned to unite the worlds very soon.

* * *

"Take a look at this," Lieutenant Briskle shouted as he strode across the stone quarry toward Hal and Lauren. "Managed to get a signal through one of the holes and got pictures back."

He was carrying a device about the size of an open book but much flatter, with a screen on it. At first Hal thought it was a picture frame and couldn't fathom what the lieutenant was up to.

It was midday. The three enormous twin-engined helicopters had gone. After being loaded up with empty crates, the rotors had started spinning. When they were a blur, the monsters had lifted off the ground, defying gravity and causing a terrible sandstorm. They took many of the soldiers away with them, though a squad lingered in the mountain behind the temple. Only the smaller helicopter was left in the quarry, along with its pilot, a few more soldiers, and an overly excited lieutenant.

He shoved the device in front of Hal and Lauren as they leaned against the low wall of the circular shaft. The cable and rigging had been temporarily removed but would be back in action as soon as the next cargo of fog-dust arrived. "This, my young friends, must be your doing."

Uh-oh, Hal thought, wondering what he'd done wrong now.

But the lieutenant seemed exuberant. He jabbed a finger at the rectangular screen, and a picture suddenly came to life complete with sound. The moving images showed a view of a city from a high vantage point. "This is New York," he said jubilantly. "Notice anything?"

"It looks depressing," Lauren said.

Hal agreed. The skyscrapers were impressive, but everything looked still and lifeless. Clouds hung dark and heavy, casting a dull shadow, and a faint white mist crept through the streets.

"Word is that these rainclouds rolled up out of nowhere," Briskle said. "A light drizzle, but rain all the same. See the fog that's sprung up?"

"No way!" Hal exclaimed.

"The rain's spreading across the state. The city only got a light dusting on one side, so maybe half is covered with fog and probably safe, but the other half is still contaminated. It's a start, though. Early days yet. I reckon a lot of that dust is still floating around in the air, and we have another cargo on the way. Look, this is Hong Kong."

The moving pictures had changed to a different scene, this time a smudge of darkness.

"Yeah, it's hard to see," Briskle said. "But imagine a bunch of skyscrapers. It's nighttime in Hong Kong at the moment. Nothing much to see, but we've had reports of drifting fog and unexpected light rain there, too."

"Reports from who?" Lauren asked, frowning. "I thought everyone was hiding underground."

"Well, most are," the lieutenant said with a shrug. "But we have people living and working on the surface as well—including stubborn old folks like Ryan's friends. In any case, virus or not, we've maintained communications from the beginning. This is the twenty-first century, you know. You think a worldwide virus is going to shut us up? We have bunkers, sure, but we also have hermetically sealed civilian camps here and there, military and scientific bases, a number of working factories, a few oil refineries . . . We can't operate effectively without communications, power, and fuel."

"I had no idea it was all so organized," Lauren said. "We only know of soldiers and scrags. And Ryan's friends, Jimmy and Dot."

"The camps are inland away from the strong coastal winds. Along the coast it's mostly scrags. But there are civilians, yes. So we'll spend this week dumping tons of crushed fog-pellets on the world, and hopefully your bird friends will keep the rain going and people can come out of hiding." He placed a firm hand on Hal's shoulder. "Kid, you and I got off on the wrong foot, and that was my fault. I'm glad we worked it out."

"Let's hope Miss Simone sees it that way," Hal muttered.

"She'll come around. We're just making our world safe, after all. What's wrong with that?"

"It's not that part I'm worried about. It's the other part." Hal swallowed, seeing his opening. "I want to open up holes everywhere and let people come across. She's not going to like that. How do you think we should do it? Strap bombs to each geo-rock and throw them out along with the fog-dust? Or will they just explode when they hit the ground? It's a long way to fall, so—"

"Whoa, wait, wait." The lieutenant blinked a few times. "Open up holes everywhere? Are you serious? No, maybe a couple here and there, just to make it easier for troops to come across. But for *civilians*? No. First of all, we don't want other countries getting wind of this. This land"—he waved his hand around—"will become part of the United States. We don't want civilians involved yet, though. They'll freak out. We want an organized military movement. We have to do reconnaissance, check the place out, report back, and all that good stuff. We're not just going to open up a land like this to the general public. The country is still under martial law. Before we do anything, you need to talk to your Simone friend and request a meeting so we can sit down and talk this through . . ."

Hal started to realize that even the lieutenant was going to be an obstacle in his mission to unify the worlds. His heart sank. He'd fully intended to get this done today just as the Gatekeeper had suggested. Today was an important day, and he'd felt sure Briskle would jump at the chance to open holes. Now it seemed that, left to him, there would be a need to meet with Miss Simone for long, drawn-out talks, which would probably result in disagreements and ultimately an invasion of soldiers, leading to bloodshed on both sides as Miss Simone rallied armies of centaurs and naga and ogres.

". . . There are channels to go through. Protocols to follow. Opening a few portals here and there is one thing—we're saving the world, after all. But this?" He pointed to the netted geo-rocks. "No, as much as I'd love to explode the lot of 'em and have gateways everywhere we turn, unicorns galloping through and little blue elves giggling in the yard, you have to understand that it needs a whole lot more consideration than that. I have to get authorization . . ."

Hal listened silently, the feeling of intense disappointment growing heavier and heavier. The lieutenant went on about how long it would take to get proper approval for such a colossal historic event, but his words faded to a dull murmur as Hal tuned him out and stared down at his geo-rock hoard.

Briskle wasn't going to help him with this, at least not any time soon. He had to do it alone.

The soothsayer's vision of the 'village floating on water' sprung to mind, and 'flashes across the land.' Hal still had no idea what all that meant, but unlike the Gatekeeper's visions of a *possible* future, the soothsayer's usually became a reality no matter what. But was the soothsayer's vision good or bad? And was it caused by Hal's action or inaction?

With the weight of two worlds on his shoulders, he muttered something and slipped away. Briskle redirected his focus onto Lauren and continued rambling about social and political responsibilities.

Like soldiers and politicians have a right to decide what's right for everyone, Hal thought sourly. *How about letting people choose for themselves?*

Hal shut him out and worked through his plan. It was very simple: grab the rocks and go. He'd take them to the cavern where the gateways pulsed. He'd sling the rocks out, just throw them and hope for the best. They'd fall for miles and eventually smash open on the ground—if indeed there was ground below and not ocean, but even then the impact might split them open.

He chewed his lip. Hopefully the majority of the geo-rocks would explode. Holes would appear instantly. Unlike fog-dust, they wouldn't drift on air currents; they'd simply drop like . . . well, like rocks. So the holes they created would be clustered together in nine different locations in the world.

This wasn't ideal. Far from it. But what else could he do short of personally carrying them across continents and dropping them one by one?

He glanced north. Something told him a storm was coming, and it had nothing to do with rain clouds whipped up by harpies.

Chapter Twenty-One
Trap

The second cargo of fog-dust came later that evening. The sky was filled with the rumble of helicopters—this time six of them. It was an awe-inspiring sight, these massive thundering machines touching down in the stone quarry and dozens of soldiers pouring from their bellies amid a sandstorm.

As the sun descended over the horizon, the winch and platform were rigged up, and the first load of crates began their journey into the shaft. It was a well-oiled operation by now, and Briskle was confident this second cargo, despite being twice the size, would be distributed by morning.

But was it enough? This question bounced around in Hal's head over and over. The lieutenant said the fog-pellets were easy to manufacture and even easier to grind down into dust, and the factories were working overtime. By the time this second load was dealt with and the helicopters ready to return home, a new batch would be stocked and ready. In theory, this operation could go on for weeks—and probably would, just to be sure that the dust was spread all over the planet.

Hal couldn't wait that long, though. He wasn't even sure he could wait until morning. Miss Simone would be tracking the helicopters by this time. She'd be here at the stone quarry soon. He doubted Briskle would allow her to interrupt Operation Hard Rain, but she would definitely pounce on Hal and demand not only an explanation for his behavior but also the return of the stolen geo-rocks. The best way for Hal to avoid the inevitable face-off was to make sure he wasn't here when she showed.

He went to find Lauren. She was sitting on a clump of boulders well away from the noise of the soldiers loading the next batch of crates onto the platform. "Hey," he said. "I'm leaving."

She looked thoughtful. "That's probably for the best. You know Miss Simone will be here soon, right?" she said.

Hal nodded.

"And once she's here, you'll be in the doghouse and these rocks will be taken back to the village."

Again, Hal nodded.

"And if that happens," Lauren said slowly, "my harpy friends will be stuck." She narrowed her eyes at Hal. "I promised them, Hal, that if they made it rain, you'd create holes for them to come back home. Well, they made it rain."

"I know."

"So you need to keep your end of the bargain."

Hal sat next to her. "I intend to. The funny thing is, you're the only one who's with me on this."

"Well, opening holes is a pretty big deal. I'm not too worried, though."

"You're not?"

Turning to face him, she said, "That light this morning. What was it?"

Seeing no reason not to tell her, Hal explained how the Gatekeeper had urged him to proceed with his mission. He told Lauren about his dream of soldiers invading, and how that situation had come so close to becoming a horrible reality. "But the way it looks now," he said, "the lieutenant isn't going to help me unless he has approval from Miss Simone—only Miss Simone's never going to *give* approval. She'll just ask the soldiers to leave, and things will get ugly again." Hal let out a short laugh. "He'll probably be on my side then, willing to help, only Miss Simone will be on my case ordering me to stay out of it, sending me home, probably getting my parents involved . . . and if my mom and dad forbid me from doing this, then that'll be the end of it. Which is why I have to do this *now*, before they forbid me. And before Miss Simone and Briskle drive each other crazy and resort to war."

Lauren patted his hand. "Well, it turned out you were right about the soldiers invading. Because of you, the sea serpent and a bunch of goblins are still alive. I trust you, Hal, and I'm sure Miss Simone will listen if you talk to her."

He shook his head and got to his feet. "Can't risk it. I have to go *now*."

"But where? When are you—?"

"The less you know, the better. Look, thanks for your help, Lauren. The harpies came through. You did good."

She reddened and smiled. "Be careful, Hal. I'll do my best to . . . you know, fight for you. I'm sure the others will, too. Eventually."

"Thanks." He frowned. "By the way, what's the deal with you and Robbie? Are you together or not?"

She reddened further. "I'm . . . still thinking about that."

"Well, think about this: If you wait much longer, he'll be over you. He might act goofy sometimes, and yeah, he can be a doofus, but he's a good guy. And you know he'd do *anything* to protect you, right?"

He left her chewing on that and headed back into the stone quarry where soldiers milled about. The netted geo-rocks were waiting for him, glowing softly.

Then he froze. Sitting on the rocks, leaning back as though basking in the sun, was a dark-haired girl with a ponytail.

"Abigail," Hal said under his breath.

She grinned as he approached. "How's it going, dragon-boy?"

"What are *you* doing here?" he asked, licking his lips nervously as he looked around. "Is Miss Simone here, too?"

"No. But she's onto you."

"Does she know I'm here?"

She raised an eyebrow at him. "The six whopping big helicopters thundering through the air gave you away. She was already on your trail because of the ones that flew over earlier this morning. These six just confirmed it for her." She grew serious and got to her feet. "But that's not why I'm here. I want to show you something." Waving a hand toward the shaft where the soldiers were working, she grimaced and said, "Think we can slip past without getting in their way?"

"You want to go to Whisper Mountain?"

"Not exactly. It's somewhere *near* Whisper Mountain. We'll just get there quicker if we use the holes instead of flying all that way."

Hal eyed the mounds of geo-rocks. Originally he'd planned to lower them down the shaft along with the crates and drag them along the tunnels to the cavern—but that was before Briskle had made it clear there'd be no new portals created anytime soon. Now the lieutenant seemed like a serious obstacle. Hal decided it would be safer to take the rocks off somewhere and hide them out of sight until he figured out how best to deal with them.

Abigail followed his gaze. "You can leave the rocks here. What I want to show you has nothing to do with them."

"And let Miss Simone find them when she gets here?" Hal scowled. "Nice try. They're staying with me. I'm going through with this, Abi, and nothing you say or do will change my mind."

She shrugged. "Well, whatever. I'm not here to cause trouble. I just need to show you something."

"Show me what?" he asked suspiciously.

A hurt look spread across her face. She stared at him a long time before looking away toward the distant mountain range. "I just wanted to show you something," she repeated. "You'll like it, I promise."

He knew she was telling the truth, but something was still off. "I'm bringing the geo-rocks with me," he said grimly.

"Fine. I don't care. As long as you can manage them all."

"Just lead the way."

"How about you fly, and I'll shout in your ear?"

Hal nodded. He removed his coat and, as usual, stashed it along with his shoes and socks into one of the rock-filled nets, then promptly transformed.

Soldiers paused in their work as he reared up and thumped his tail. He knew this was going to be tiring work, and he had to move as fast as possible, so he stood for a moment, mentally preparing himself.

Then he hopped up onto the geo-rocks, straddling them on hind feet, one to each net. Abigail climbed up on his back and held on. Without further ado, he launched into the air, taking the geo-rocks with him.

* * *

Hal was exhausted by the time they reached the hazy peaks. Whisper Mountain loomed the tallest, but Abigail directed him toward a much smaller mountain a little to the east. He was struggling by now, weighed down by the rocks. Abigail suggested a few times that he ditch his load, but he grunted his refusal. He wasn't letting the geo-rocks out of his sight.

As he approached the wooded slopes, Abigail guided him until finally he saw what she was targeting—a mass of statues within a walled garden, nestled deep in the trees. He knew that this must be the rose garden Molly had mentioned, where she stored some of her petrified victims. And, with a surge of excitement, he remembered that Chase was here somewhere.

They came down just outside the gates as the garden was packed full of statues, elbow to elbow, and there was no room for anything but ducking and weaving between them—not even room for rose bushes. The huge wrought-iron gates were locked, and the wall was twelve feet high with spikes along the top. There was a small clearing and narrow path just inside the gates, so Hal left his geo-rocks outside and hopped over with the last few beats of his weary wings.

He transformed as soon as his feet touched the ground, and Abigail toppled backward with a scream. "Sorry," Hal said, helping her up. "Man, it's cold! Can you get my jacket and shoes? They're stuffed into one of the nets."

Abigail rolled her eyes, took off her own coat, sprouted wings, and buzzed over the gates. While she was gone, Hal looked around the shadowy garden.

Apart from a few oddities, most of the statues were human. They looked like ordinary, regular people. Each had a plaque at their feet. Ivy was coiled around the plaques and the feet of many statues, even creeping up to their waists. The entire garden was dark, silent, and creepy, rather like a graveyard at night—only these people weren't dead, merely suspended, their souls trapped in the world of darkness that Hal had visited himself not so long ago.

"I hope Blair comes and visits this place," he told Abigail when she returned with his coat, socks and shoes. He knelt to put them on. "He could wake all these people in one go."

"I know," she said, slipping back into her own coat. "He's been recharging with some of the geo-rocks we brought back. Look, come over here."

She led him along the main path and veered off to the right. She ducked under the raised arm of a woman who looked like she was warding off a demon—which probably wasn't far from the truth considering what Molly had done to her. The plaque simply gave her name and nothing else. Did Molly remember exactly what happened to these people? Each individual incident?

"How come you found this place?" Hal asked her as she weaved out of sight around an extremely fat man wearing a robe. He looked like a monk. Once again it struck Hal as odd that this man's clothes—*all* these statues' clothes—were as stiff and cold as the man himself, petrified by the same deathly gaze.

"Molly told me where to look."

"But why did you come?"

Abigail sighed. "Because I wanted to find Chase for you."

She stopped before one of many statues clustered together. It looked the same as the rest, gray and lifeless, ivy around its ankles, white bird poop spattered over its shoulders. The plaque, however, read CHASE STOCKWELL.

Hal stared in awe at the frozen figure. It—*he*—was tall and thin with curly hair. Thin spectacles sat slightly askew on his wide-eyed, slack-jawed face. "Not exactly as I imagined him," Hal murmured.

Abigail frowned. "I thought you said you'd met him?"

"I did, but I only saw what I imagined after he described himself to me."

They stood there awhile, studying the boy. He'd said he was fourteen years old, and that seemed about right. Hal couldn't wait for the day Molly and Blair showed up to wake all these people. What a sight that would be—all coming alive at once, hundreds of victims starting to move, looking around in confusion, some of them as old as the hills and with no family left in the world . . . Okay, so that was pretty sad, but otherwise it would be a wonderful thing to see, these people returning to life.

"Hal," Abigail said, turning to him. "This idea you have about creating holes all over the world? You need to give it up."

He shook his head firmly. "I told you—"

"Everyone's on edge, Hal. You've got everyone worried, and the worst thing is that you're kind of a scary guy. At first Miss Simone was just going to give you an ear-bashing for stealing her rocks, and then she realized you were really serious about this and started organizing an army to trap you."

"An *army*?"

"Yes, because you're a dragon. If you're really serious about something, you can do pretty much anything you want. There aren't many that can stop you. You've got everyone worked up. There's been talk of shooting at you with tranquilizers, trapping you in a cage, and even—well, worse."

This sounded crazy to Hal, but as she went on, he realized it made sense. He *was* a dragon, after all. The idea of a small army being amassed to combat him mortified him but also sent a jolt of pride through his body. He was a force to be reckoned with. If he wanted to explode hundreds of geo-rocks and create holes all across the land, well, he could go right ahead and do it!

"Your mom and dad are worried," Abigail said. "Your friends are worried. *I'm* worried. I don't want you going off the rails. What you're planning to do . . . well, it's like going against us all. You'd be in *so* much trouble, Hal. You might be exiled from the village. Or sent to jail."

"You're exaggerating."

"I'm not." She touched his arm and gazed at him beseechingly. "Please, Hal. Say you'll change your mind. Let it go."

Something was wrong. Her plea was earnest, that much was obvious, but there was something else. He glanced around, suddenly nervous. The garden was cold and silent, lost in shadows.

"Why are we here?" he whispered. "What's Chase got to do with this?"

"I knew you'd want to see him. I didn't lie, Hal. I told you this would be something worth seeing, and I was right."

An alarm bell rang. "Molly's here, isn't she?" he demanded. Was this what the ghosts he'd seen in the geo-rocks had warned him of? Was he about to be turned to stone again? He raised his voice. "Molly, don't try anything, or—"

"Molly's not here," Abigail said, reaching for him. "She never could have gotten here so quickly."

"How did *you* get here so quickly?" he countered, thinking of her puny faerie wings and the vast distance she'd covered traveling back and forth. Suspicious, he shook her off and started moving, getting away from this tight little corner of the garden. He needed space. Room to transform.

"Hal, please," she said, her voice wavering, "before it's too late." She slowly removed her coat. Then, abruptly, she sprouted her wings and rose off the ground.

Now Hal knew for sure something was badly wrong. Molly *had* to be here. He'd been drawn into a trap. She was going to lunge out at him and turn him to stone, and he'd be left standing here with the rest of the statues, frozen solid, completely harmless, no longer a threat to Miss Simone's precious world.

He glanced this way and that, looking for the veiled gorgon—or perhaps the *unveiled* gorgon. Then he looked for the path, knowing he wouldn't have room to transform with statues pressing in from all sides. His dragon body would likely break pieces off. He'd be better off back at the entrance gates. He could transform, hop over the gates, grab his geo-rocks, and skedaddle.

He took a step—and paused. What was that smell?

"Hal," Abigail said tearfully. She was now buzzing high over the heads of the statues, carrying her coat. "This is your last chance. If you promise me right now that you're done with your craziness, I'll carry you out of here. But you have to look me in the eye and promise."

"I'm not promising anything," Hal growled. She'd deliberately led him deep into the garden knowing he wouldn't risk damaging the statues by transforming. "I can't stop until I've done what needs to be done. The two worlds need to be together. It's the way it's supposed to be. It's the way it was *always* supposed to be. We'll be better for it in the end, you'll see. You have to believe me."

Abigail buried her face in her hands as she hovered high above.

"Abi, please," he urged. "Think about what happened this morning. We saved the sea serpent and goblins from being killed! You have to *trust* me on this."

"I . . ." She peeked through her fingers at him. "I can't."

"If you loved me," Hal said evenly, "you'd be on my side."

She burst into tears and zipped high into the sky as a strange smell hit him. It was the smell of something burning. He heard the distinctive sound of crackling flames. He turned in a circle, trying to figure it out. Meanwhile, Abigail swung around and flew back to him. "Go!" she screamed. "Fly! Get out of here!"

Her sudden wide-eyed panic confirmed that something was about to happen. But he had no safe place to transform. Seeing this, Abigail swooped lower and, dropping her coat, grabbed him in a crushing hug. Before he could utter a word, she lifted him off the ground and swept upward, higher and higher, away from the rose garden.

It was then Hal saw smoke rising from behind a group of nearby statues. Moments later, blue flames suddenly shot into the air. And suddenly he knew what was going on.

Blair.

The phoenix was here, performing his rebirth trick. Abigail groaned with the strain of carrying Hal, her face turning red and beads of sweat popping out on her forehead. She was lifting him high, straight upward as if a demon were on their tails. Hal glanced down to see a dome-shaped shockwave, charged with crackling blue sparks, spreading across the garden away from the burning phoenix.

"Whoa!" he exclaimed as it rose up under him. The force buffeted them both like a gust of wind, and he felt an electrical tingle around his toes as though he'd just dipped them in toxic water.

He recalled that a loss of magic caused unlikely flying creatures like griffins and dragons to flop around uselessly on the ground, their mundane wings not quite up to the task of lifting such disproportionately sized bodies. That almost certainly applied to Abigail, too, especially as she was carrying twice her body weight.

Yet somehow they both avoided the magic nullification spell. It spread fast, reaching out beyond the garden walls and into the surrounding forest. The blast was curiously oval-shaped, the bulk of it projecting where Blair faced. It was also shallow, hardly reaching higher than a hundred feet or so. Hal felt like he and Abigail were riding a wave, a tingling surge of static.

In a second, it was gone.

"I have to drop you," she gasped, and as she said that, her grip slipped and he started to tumble. He transformed as soon as he was clear of her. The shockwave had already moved on by now, and he fell harmlessly back into the nonmagic zone and spread his wings. Though he had numb toes, his own magic was intact, and he arrested his fall and swooped around.

The entire garden was coming alive. The grayness left the statues. Color returned. They twitched and moved, jerky at first, then slowly and smoothly as if waking from a long, long dream. Hal was too far away now to see which of the statues was Chase.

He glimpsed vivid colorful feathers as Blair spread his wings from his hiding place behind the group of statues—or what once were statues, for now they were living, breathing people, staring at the phoenix in astonishment.

Hal flew back toward the bobbing faerie, his mind reeling. Blair and Abigail! No wonder she'd got here so fast—she'd ridden on Blair's back. They'd lured him here, worked together to nullify his shapeshifting ability and render him harmless. But she'd changed her mind at the final, crucial moment.

"Why?" he asked her with a rumbling growl.

She zipped closer, flying alongside as they circled around. "I'm so sorry," she started babbling, apparently guessing his question. "Miss Simone made me. She told me this was the safest thing to do to get you under control. It was either that or Molly turning you to stone again. This just seemed like the best plan—to bring everyone in the garden back to life while at the same time disabling *you*. I couldn't go through with it, but Hal, *please* don't go off and do anything stupid. Let's land and talk about this some more."

Hal grunted and shook his head. He was done playing games now. Veering suddenly, he left her behind and swooped over the walled rose garden. Landing just outside the gates, he stared in quiet anger at his hoard of geo-rocks . . . which were now utterly dead and useless.

What a waste! Now Hal understood Abigail's suggestion to leave them behind; she'd known they'd be ruined if stored in the vicinity of Blair's phoenix rebirth here at the garden. Still, the rocks weren't important. The target had been Hal himself, and he'd escaped in the nick of time—thanks only to Abigail's last-second change of heart.

He flew back over the garden and caught Blair staring up at him, his colors especially bright and vivid in the cold, wintry rose garden. People moved around aimlessly, some talking, others looking panicked. If Blair was alone with them, he'd have some explaining to do— especially as the gates were padlocked and they couldn't escape. Maybe the caretaker, the old witch Molly had mentioned, would be along soon with a key.

Hal flew away, suddenly uncaring. He'd wanted to meet Chase, but right now he had to rethink his plan. He had two options: return to the village and steal more geo-rocks, if they hadn't been hidden away already; or go back to the mines and get some from there.

"Hal!" he heard Abigail calling. She was buzzing frantically along behind him, trying to catch up. "Stop! Let's talk!"

He stared back at her as he glided along, then turned his face to the front. He put on a sudden burst of speed and began to rise higher and higher. He heard her calling his name again, but her voice was already far behind.

At first he was angry with her, but as he flew across the land, his blood cooled and he began to calm down. He couldn't really blame her. Miss Simone could be pretty demanding at times. Abigail had definitely been the best person to trap him. He wouldn't have trusted any of the adults and wouldn't have bothered going all the way to the rose garden if any of his other friends had asked. Only Abigail could have distracted him that way.

He considered himself lucky. It could all have played out differently. If Molly had been able to get to the rose garden quick enough, she might have been there to petrify him again. She could have secured him in a cage, and *then* Blair could have woken everyone with his rebirth—including him. Hal would have been awake, caged, and powerless. As it was, Miss Simone and Molly were nowhere to be seen, probably on horseback somewhere.

And when he passed the quarry, he saw them—Miss Simone with her golden hair, seated at the front of a horse-drawn cart and flicking the reins; Molly's tall, thin frame sitting alongside, her face veiled as always; dozens of goblins marching on either side; Dewey and a small group of centaurs trotting impatiently; and even Emily with some of her naga friends from the woods near the village, slithering along, swaying from side to side.

Hal's other friends were there, too, climbing off the back of Miss Simone's cart as it pulled up near the stone quarry's shaft. They were greeted by Lauren, who sauntered over from her clump of boulders.

The 'army' had arrived, but from Hal's vantage point, it might as well be an army of ants.

Someone spotted him, and instantly all heads turned to look upward. Hal gave a bellow and released a sheet of fire, then dismissed them and continued on his way. If Miss Simone and her army were here, the village was unprotected. Maybe he could steal some more geo-rocks . . .

His journey home was short and uneventful. The village of Carter came into view among the surrounding forestland, and he swooped down to it. Villagers scattered in fright until they recognized him and paused in the streets. He ignored them and searched for Blacknail's wagon full of geo-rocks.

It wasn't there.

Hal sighed. Well, he hadn't expected it to be. He could go hunting for it, or he could find a few goblins and *persuade* them to tell him where the rocks were. But neither of those ideas appealed to him, and he circled around and flew on.

His mind was already buzzing with new ideas. He headed east, putting on speed and rising high, trying to latch onto one particular plan and flesh out the details. There wasn't really much to his plan, though. It was simple and should, in theory, be extremely effective. The more he pondered, the higher he rose and the slower the landscape seemed to crawl past far below. But in the distance he saw the first glimmer of ocean and felt that he was making good progress.

The sky was black when he arrived. This helped, because he started to see an orange glow on the hills in one particular area along the coast. He turned toward it, recognizing the line of mountains directly below and the narrow, meandering crack that was Eastward Pass. He saw the featureless plain where Blair had performed his last rebirth stunt and woken Hal from his suspended animation. He saw the expanse of woods where the lycans lived in the village of Landis. And he saw the tiny beach that marked the entrance to the mine.

He came down heavily on the sand right in front of that entrance. Everything was quiet, no miners anywhere. However, the sturdy gate securely blocked the entrance. He stomped up to it and studied the locked iron box fixed to the wall nearby. The switch to open the gate was inside.

He swiped at it with his clumsy dragon paw. The box rattled stubbornly. After a few more swipes, he succeeded in knocking it askew, yet the tiny door remained firmly locked. When the box came loose and crashed to the ground, Hal knew there was no way the switch would work with the wiring ripped out.

With a bellow, he barreled into the gate. It hurt his snout, so the next time he turned his head sideways and hit the bars with his shoulder. He hammered into it again and again, wishing Robbie were here. Eventually it started to buckle, and he worked at a lower corner, yanking it out of its vertical track until it flapped loose. He battered it some more and shoved his way inside.

He reverted to human form and stood shivering in the cold air. He had no shoes and socks anymore, nor a coat, so he rubbed his hands together and hurried down the tunnel, his smart soles slapping on the rock floor and his toes beginning to freeze. When he reached the leaking hot spring, he had to avoid the bubbling, boiling water that ran down the slope. But the farther down the tunnel he ran, the cooler that water became until it was comfortably warm. Then he was able to splash around in it and thaw his feet.

The gigantic mining cavern was silent apart from the sound of trickling water. Hal hunted for a wheelbarrow. The nearest was partially full of geo-rocks. Though he didn't really need them this time, he wheeled them over to the tunnel next to the drilling room and made his way to the storage area. He recalled seeing shelves full of dynamite there.

Feeling a little nervous about handling the explosives, he carefully loaded up the wheelbarrow with armfuls of sticks, stacking them on top of the geo-rocks. He also made sure to grab the longest roll of fuse wire he could find.

Fully laden, he headed off into the mine, down the winding tunnel that would take him to the Chamber of Ghosts.

* * *

Deep inside the mine, Hal finally rounded a bend and breathed a sigh of relief. The walls were glowing, and he knew the Chamber of Ghosts was just down this last stretch of tunnel.

Thinking ahead, he dumped the giant roll of dynamite fuse on the floor and started kicking it down the slope so it unraveled as it went. He followed on with the wheelbarrow. When he reached the stone steps, he had to grip the handles tightly to prevent the heavy wheelbarrow from running away from him. The geo-rocks and dynamite bounced alarmingly.

By the time the fuse was fully unraveled, he was nearly at the bottom of the steps, and his hands were hurting from the weight of the barrow. He grabbed the trailing end of the wire as he went and continued to the bottom, dragging the entire length with him so it snuck along the tunnel like a snake. He turned the corner into the Chamber of Ghosts and walked the wheelbarrow across to the brightly glowing core. There, he collapsed on the floor and rested awhile.

After flexing his aching fingers and getting them to cooperate, he turned his attention to his task. He knew that dynamite was supposed to be shoved into holes for it to be really effective, otherwise it just made a loud ineffectual bang. But without drilling equipment, Hal couldn't bore any holes. He searched for suitable nooks and crannies around the core, finding just a few. Maybe they would be enough. He had to hope that one decent explosion would set off the core, and that in turn would set off a chain reaction throughout the chamber. The core was so intense, so full of magic, that he expected its explosion to be a whopper.

This would be the biggest hole in history.

He had about twenty sticks of dynamite. He stuffed a couple of them into the most suitable cracks around the base of the core and placed the rest all around so they were leaning against the core's smooth, rounded wall. Then, reasonably satisfied, he pulled one free of its crack. This was the one he would detonate . . . once he'd figured out how to attach the fuse.

Was he supposed to tie it around? Jam it in the end? Logic told him that the wire needed to connect with the *inside* of the stick, otherwise the flame would just burn out against the wrapper. Licking his lips and cringing, he carefully poked the thick, slightly stiff fuse wire into the end of the stick. Would that work?

He reinserted the dynamite into its crack and backed away. Suddenly he was aware that the walls all around were crammed full of silent, ghostly figures, all staring out at him with hands and faces pressed to the inside as though looking through glass. There were no frantic gestures or panicked expressions. This time they were calm.

With a shudder, Hal left the room, wincing as his toes scuffed against hard rock. He hurried up the steps, eyeing the fuse as he went. It was very long, leading all the way to the top. Did he need all that? How slowly did it burn? He needed to give himself time to evacuate but didn't want the explosion to take forever in case Miss Simone caught up and tried to stop him. Still, it was better to be safe than sorry. A long fuse was good.

He found the end of it around a bend in the tunnel. He paused and listened hard. No shouting, no running footsteps, nothing. He was alone.

Taking a deep breath, he held the end of the wire for a second, and the world around him seemed to pause. This was it. Once he lit the fuse and started running, there was no turning back. Well, he *could* change his mind and snuff it out, but there would come a point where it would be too dangerous to go chasing after it. If he went through with this, and if all went as expected, the core would explode and—in theory—a pretty big hole would appear. Probably a *gigantic* hole.

Strangely, this felt right somehow. No doubts, no nagging voices telling him to abort the mission. He exhaled long and hard. He was ready.

He leaned over the fuse and set it alight with a small, controlled flame blown through his lips. The wire immediately began sputtering and hissing. A dazzling flame and lots of smoke started its long journey down the tunnel.

Hal watched the slow-burning flame. It was hard to judge exactly how long he had, but he guessed ten minutes. Maybe more. And maybe less.

He started running.

Chapter Twenty-Two
The End

By the time Hal made it back to the giant mining cavern, his feet were sore from the constant scuffing and scraping. Wincing, he hobbled across the vast empty space, splashing through hot and cold puddles, and onward up the tunnel to the entrance. When he got there, breathless, about ten minutes had passed. He was doing okay. He'd be outside in just a minute. Then again, what if the entire mountain came down? If so, he wasn't safe yet.

Goblins were waiting for him. Hal stopped short when he saw them. He eyed them warily, and they glared at him in return.

"What have you done?" one of them said, shuffling forward and gesturing toward the buckled gate. "We just got that fixed. What are you doing here?"

"What are *you* doing here?" Hal countered. "It's late."

Roughly twenty goblins stared back at him as the leader placed his gnarled hands on his hips and scowled deeply. "Saw you flying over. What are you up to, shapeshifter?"

Hal glanced nervously over his shoulder. "We should move out before—"

"Talk, dragon-boy, or else."

At this, all the miners pounded their fists together.

There was no sense in trying to cover up what he'd done. "I set a bomb. The fuse is probably running really short by now. I don't know how big the explosion will be, but I don't want to be around when it goes off."

"You set *what*?" the goblin exclaimed. "You set a *bomb*?" He spluttered for a moment, then shook his head. "You set a bomb where?"

"At the core. In the Chamber of Ghosts."

A ripple of concern spread around the crowd. "Are you out of your tiny mind?" the chief goblin demanded. "You'll flatten the hills! Do you know how valuable this mine is?"

"Not as valuable as your lives," Hal said quietly. He cupped a hand around his ear and pretended to be listening.

The chief moved closer, his fists bunching up. "This is our livelihood. We got wives and kids to feed. You're gonna take all that away?"

Hal said nothing. The idea of female goblins struck him as odd. He couldn't remember seeing any—or maybe he had, but they were as ugly as the men.

"One of my workers died saving your life," the chief snarled.

A ripple of agreement spread among the group. Hal opened his mouth to say something, but no words emerged. Confusion and doubt began to bubble up.

The chief moved closer. "This is how you repay what he did for you? You blow up the mines?" Shaking his head in disgust, the goblin pointed a fat finger at Hal. "You're going back in there to snuff the fuse. And you'd better hurry, 'cause if this place blows—"

"You have about a minute," Hal guessed. The place could explode in two seconds from now, or it might be another five minutes. "I'm going now. You should, too."

Several goblins rushed at him—but Hal transformed, and they bounced back off his reptilian armor. He stomped away down to the beach where his wings would have plenty of clearance, and glanced back to see goblins tearing after him. It was hard to tell whether they were chasing him or simply following his lead because their faces carried the same scowls no matter what.

The chief yelled after him, "Get back here! I'll report you to—"

He was interrupted by a deep, muffled explosion from deep below, followed by a series of booms, each one closer and sharper than the last, rising to the surface at frightening speed. The last few were deafening, and the goblins fell flat in the sand. The ground began shuddering, flinging tiny rocks into the air.

Hal's dragon instincts should have flown him to safety. Instead he tried unsuccessfully to burrow into the sand. Like the goblins, he ended up flat on his belly, clawing for a grip, his teeth chattering with the vibrations.

Then he pushed up and away, wings beating and tail thrashing, while more muffled thumps and ear-splitting cracks pummeled his eardrums.

In the moonlit darkness, he saw a gigantic column of dust rolling upward and mushrooming, moving in eerie slow motion as, below, flashes were accompanied by delayed cracks and booms. The entire hill seemed to be deflating in the center, miniature avalanches forming on the slopes, a deluge of rock and dirt pouring onto the nearby beach and splashing into the water.

Flying higher and higher, circling around, Hal watched with awe and fright as the familiar orange glows beneath the hills seemed to wink out in a series of flashes and bangs. The effect started in the center and spread outward. In the space of seconds, the entire region had gone dark. The flashes stopped even though the dull, echoing booms continued.

Hal thought he heard similar booms in the distance. Squinting into the night, he saw the black landscape all around punctuated by bright flashes, most of them clustered into groups, some solitary. The booms rumbled like thunder afterward.

Stunned, Hal almost forgot how to fly. He beat his wings and climbed higher, noting that the entire surrounding area had gone dark and quiet now, and that any further flashes came silently from far, far away.

What had he done?

He turned back to the gulch. The massive dust cloud hung in the air, clear to see even in the moonlight, but a large portion of the hills had now disappeared. The mine was no more. In its place was the biggest smoking portal Hal had ever seen, from which ocean water surged out and slowly receded, then surged again—not water from the nearby coast, but *from the other world.* Great cracks spread out from the epicenter, narrow chasms that zigzagged across the land in all directions, from which more seawater rose and fell.

Goblins were picking themselves up even as the quake continued. Likewise, the lycans in the nearby village of Landis were probably sniffing the air and wondering what was happening.

When the cracking subsided, Hal headed west, suddenly feeling an urge to get home no matter what kind of trouble he might get into. All the way there, he wondered what exactly had happened. The explosion had taken out the mine and the entire hill above, but that had come as no great surprise. What had shocked him was the number of cracks and bangs across the landscape afterward. How could an explosion at the mine have such a far-reaching effect?

By the time he reached Carter, he believed he had figured it out. The answer both terrified and excited him.

As he flew over the village, his suspicions were confirmed. The entire village was dark except for flickering fires and lanterns. He landed in a clear spot and elicited a scream from a middle-aged woman. When he reverted to his human form and stood there shivering in the cold, she looked mildly annoyed.

"Really," she complained. "I wish you wouldn't keep showing up like this. How about a warning first? Whenever you just come down and—"

"What's happened?" Hal interrupted.

"You tell me," she said, easily switching subjects. "All our power went out—with a bang, I might add. Explosions all over the village, all at once. I've already been to the store, and all the spare geo-rocks are dead, too—and the barn's completely destroyed."

"Was anybody hurt?" Hal repeated, appalled.

"Nobody killed that we know of, thank goodness," the woman said. "The geo-rocks all exploded at once." She frowned. "Noisy, but not much damage. I was in the hallway when mine went off—one under the kitchen sink, and one in the closet. The sink is cracked, and the closet door is off its hinges . . ."

She went on, but Hal was no longer listening. He backed away, then took off running toward home.

He was panting by the time he tore out of the village and onto the dirt trail outside the perimeter fence. His home came into view among the trees, dark and sinister. He ran up the short path and paused on the doorstep. Through the small glass panes in the door, he could see a light flickering. He pushed the door open and went inside. He heard voices in the living room where most of the light was coming from. He edged along the hall and peered in through the door. His parents were there on the sofa, talking earnestly, candles flickering all around. His mom looked upset, and his dad was comforting her.

". . . Whatever happens, we'll deal with it," he was saying. "Hal's a good boy. Whatever he does—or whatever he's done—he's my son, and I'm proud of him. Remember how we talked about leaving this place? To stop him from being sent off on these missions involving other dragons? I'll tell you, I for one wouldn't care if he never left our sight again. We could go traveling, just the three of us. Grab a few horses and a wagon, take off with some supplies, just move on and—"

"But his friends," Hal's mom said, wiping away her tears. "Abigail. He won't want to leave them."

"He might not have much choice if Simone has anything to do with it."

Hal suddenly noticed something through the open kitchen door on the opposite side of the hallway. He gasped in shock. The kitchen sink was in small pieces, the counter cracked in two. The doors below the sink were lying several yards away on the floor. Inside the cupboard was a twisted mess of copper pipes and huge black scorch marks.

But none of that interested Hal. The damage barely registered. What caught his attention was the black, smoky hole floating in the middle of the kitchen.

He stared open-mouthed. It was five feet across, not quite spherical, more like a fat disc, about a foot off the floor. Little tendrils of inky blackness leaked off its surface all over.

Even then, it wasn't really the sight of this hole that shocked him. He'd seen plenty, after all. What blew his mind was the idea that a hole had been created *for each and every geo-rock* that had exploded across the land. In Carter alone, some homes used two or three geo-rocks, located under sinks and in closets . . .

Hal tiptoed back along the hallway. He peered into the bathroom where he knew another geo-rock was stored under the sink—and reared back when he found himself inches from another smoky hole that filled the room.

On impulse, he stuck his head through. He had to lean in quite a way, but when he did, he suddenly received a blast of cold wind. Gasping, he backed out and stood there blinking in amazement. *No way*, he thought.

He pushed through again, this time steeling himself. He hadn't imagined it. He knew the geography of the two worlds didn't quite match up, but this view drove that fact home. He was looking out on a moonlit ocean, with just a smudge of land to the west. It was terrifying. With the lights out, his mom or dad might have walked in here, stepped through the hole, and fallen twenty or thirty feet into the middle of the ocean. And then what? They'd be left floundering in the water, unable to climb up and return. They'd be swept away, and pretty soon the hole, hovering above the waves, would be lost in the night.

Even though Hal could fly, the idea of being stuck out here was daunting. He pulled back again, relieved to be back in the comfort of his home.

His parents were standing in the living room doorway, staring at him. "You're home," his mom whispered.

Hal gulped, and jabbed a thumb at the bathroom. "Uh, I wouldn't go in there if I were you," he quipped with a nervous laugh.

"What happened, son?" his dad asked tentatively. It sounded very much like he was refraining from asking, *What have you done?*

"I . . . I blew up the core," Hal said, his voice breaking. And, in case his parents weren't sure what the core was, he added, "I blew up the mine."

His dad's eyes widened.

Hal found himself rambling. "I didn't know it would make *all* the geo-rocks explode. It makes sense, though. The core is . . . well, the *core*. The heart. Destroy the heart, and everything goes with it. I mean—not that everything is destroyed. I just mean all the geo-rocks. Right after the mine blew, I could see flashes all across the horizon— geo-rocks and patches of energy in the ground. I guess all the new rocks have blown here, too. And everywhere else."

"*Everywhere?*" his mom repeated, aghast.

"Don't know," Hal admitted. "I guess. Unless there are other cores? But definitely everywhere in this part of the world."

His dad stepped forward and paused as if uncertain whether Hal would attack him. "Son," he said awkwardly. "I don't care about how much trouble you're in with Simone. I won't let her do anything to you. And if she exiles you, throws you out of the village, your mother and I will go with you. I'm not worried about that. I'm just worried about . . . about *you*."

"Are you okay?" Hal's mom asked.

Hal cracked a smile. "Have I gone crazy, you mean?" He sobered quickly. "I tried to explain why I was doing this, but nobody believed me. It doesn't really matter now. It's done, right? So . . . yeah, I'm okay. I'm fine."

In an effort to prove it, he approached his parents and slipped into his mom's outreaching hands. She held him tightly, and Hal felt his dad's hand on his shoulder. They stayed like that awhile, and some of the tension eased.

"We're safe here," Hal said suddenly, pulling back. "All these holes? This village, and everything east of here, opens up over the ocean. We're not going to have a bunch of scrags wandering through and showing up in people's homes."

His dad shook his head. "Right. We just have to watch our step when using the bathroom." He peered down at the floor. "It's a weird feeling. The ground under my feet is solid, but it's like we're suspended over the sea."

Or floating on water, Hal thought, remembering what the soothsayer had said. He felt a wave of relief as the true meaning of the old man's words clarified. There was no real danger to the village. Things were just *different*.

Hal disengaged from his mom's pincer grip. "I have to go."

"What?" she exclaimed. "Go *where*?"

"To Miss Simone. I need to explain everything to her."

Since he was only twelve, they could have simply forbidden him to go, but in the end Hal was able to slip away. The only real danger was the sharp end of Miss Simone's tongue, and that was something he couldn't avoid. It was best to get it over with and save her a night of searching for him.

No deaths, he told himself over and over as he flew away. *No deaths, no deaths.* There had been quite a few minor injuries, and for that he felt awful. But on the positive side, after the thousand-year-old phoenix's rebirth, most other local villages—including Louis in the north—probably would have escaped damage simply because they lacked a supply of working geo-rocks.

As he rose above the village, he spotted a ring of flickering torches on the outskirts where a barn stood—or where a barn had once stood. Hal realized it must be where Blacknail had stored the spare geo-rocks brought back from the mine—stored in the barn to hide them away from plundering dragons. Villagers were gawking at the damage . . . and also the spectacle of a gigantic black hole spreading several hundred feet, half buried in the ground so it looked like a curious dome of darkness in the woods. No doubt tons of earth and several trees had dropped through the hole into the ocean on the other side.

His mind boggling, Hal headed south.

* * *

Despite the midnight hour, it was business as usual in the stone quarry, with crates of fog-dust being transported across to the cavern behind the temple. Hal thumped down near a group of soldiers, and they spun around in shock.

They relaxed once he'd transformed. "Where is everyone?" Hal asked.

"Lady Simone? She and your friends flew to the mountain."

The moonlit sky revealed hulking, silhouetted shapes on the horizon. Even in the darkness, Hal quickly figured out that the soldier pointed not toward Whisper Mountain but one of its neighboring peaks. "They went to the rose garden? But how? Only Blair, Lauren and Abigail can fly. Are you saying they carried all the others?" His mind whirled as he calculated how many trips *that* would take . . .

The soldier frowned and tipped his head toward the helicopters that stood nearby. One of the six twin-engine monsters was missing. Light dawned, and Hal was suddenly envious. His friends had gotten a ride in one of those things?

He told himself it wasn't anything special. Probably uncomfortable seats and a lot of noise, not much better than Blacknail's buggy. He transformed and took to the sky again. *This* was flying, with the wind in his face, his legs dangling free.

The journey to the rose garden was much easier without a cargo of geo-rocks. Circling high above, he saw bright white lights set up on the ground inside the fence, their power fed by a rattling portable generator. The forest was dense, and the helicopter had been forced to land some distance away in a clearing.

Descending, Hal found his friends standing near the garden gates, which were now standing wide open. Miss Simone, Blair, Ryan, Blacknail, Lieutenant Briskle, and a wizened old woman were with them. The garden seemed a little emptier than before, but Hal put it down to the fact that the statues were now shambling around in clusters, leaving large, handy pockets of space. Molly was mingling with the people, hugging some of them.

Ignoring a sudden surge of anxiety, Hal landed as unthreateningly as he could. Several shouts and screams filled the air. He transformed immediately and stood there shivering in the cold night air.

A silence fell. He seemed to be the center of attention. It wasn't just Miss Simone and his friends staring at him but dozens and dozens of recently awakened strangers as well. He peered around at them, seeing perfectly ordinary men, women, and children. Some were dazed and frightened. Others were angry. Hal had lost just a couple of weeks, but some of these people had been suspended for *decades*. He tried to imagine waking to discover that his friends had grown old, his parents long dead . . . Shuddering, he turned to face Miss Simone.

"*What* did you do?" she asked, her voice as icy as the nighttime chill. The spotlights illuminated her face, and her expression left no doubt that she was mad. If she'd had any magic in her, Hal imagined she would be bathed in an eerie glow, her hair swirling as if gripped by a breeze, a deep rumble filling the rose garden, and a piercing mermaid shriek forcing its way from her throat. Without magic, all that fury was contained within a single glare.

"Um . . ." Hal said, searching for sympathetic faces. The goblins were as sour-faced as always. No help there. Some of his friends were giving him steely looks, too, but Abigail was white and tearful, and Robbie's forehead was deeply furrowed. Lauren was biting her lip and looked like she wanted to be someplace else. Hal let out a shuddering breath. "I blew up the mine."

Miss Simone's mouth worked up and down, but it was a while before she squeaked some words out. "You did *what?*"

"I . . . I set some dynamite next to the core in the Chamber of Ghosts. I lit a fuse and ran." Seeing no change in the stunned expressions of his audience, he decided it was probably best to just say everything at once. No sugar coating, just the facts. "There were lots of flashes and bangs, and the hill sort of collapsed. And there were flashes and bangs all across the land from what I could see when I flew up high. It's like the core was the heart of all magic."

Still not a single person moved. Hal could hear nothing but the faint murmur of voices from some of the reawakened people around him.

"I think all the geo-rocks have exploded," he went on, suddenly realizing that the wizened old woman behind Miss Simone must be the so-called witch who owned the garden. "I stopped by Carter on the way here. There are a few minor injuries, but that's all. Everyone who had a geo-rock in their bathroom or closet—well, now there's a hole. The barn where the wagon was parked? All those rocks exploded at once and created one *gigantic* hole. The barn's gone."

"But—I *parked* in there," Blacknail's familiar voice sputtered.

Hal picked out the goblin from the crowd. "Sorry. Your buggy's probably at the bottom of the sea now."

For some reason, it was this snippet of news that brought the first murmurs of astonishment. And, oddly, Hal grew more and more calm. Revealing his news in this detached, matter-of-fact way seemed to boost his confidence. His audience couldn't be any more shocked and horrified than they were right now, so why not just throw it all out there in one go?

"I don't know if the core in the Chamber of Ghosts was the *only* core or just one of many," he continued. He sought Molly among the crowd of strangers. "You said this part of the world had a concentration of magic, or energy, or sparkle as Lucas called it—but you said there are other parts of the world like this as well, so that probably means there are other cores."

"Yes," Molly spoke up. "On other continents. Oceans away."

Hal shrugged. "Well, this part of the world has no core anymore. All the magic in the ground—all the mines, the glowing walls, the geo-rocks—is gone. It's all been converted to holes."

He hadn't been fully aware of this fact until now. It was as though an inner voice was quietly advising him. Before he knew it, something else became clear to him, and words that weren't entirely his own forced their way from his lips.

"The core's demise set off a chain reaction that accessed the power of the geo-rocks from within," he said slowly, unnerved by what he was spouting, "and the energy coalesced into portals with minimal destructive force."

A silence fell.

"But that means we have no way to recharge," Emily said. "What about Miss Simone? How is she going to recharge? How will the land recover?"

"It just will," Hal said. "People die all the time."

Everyone stared at him open-mouthed, and he searched his mind for the reassuring voice that had advised him moments ago. This time it fed him tiny snatches of information, annoyingly vague.

"What I mean is that . . . that whenever someone dies, their life-force becomes magic, and that magic kind of ends up in the ground, absorbed by all the amazing creatures of this world—and shapeshifters. Sometimes there's too much magic, and a phoenix will come along and mop up."

"Mop up," Miss Simone repeated dully.

"Yeah. It sort of cleans up the place." Hal hesitated, wondering if he should even mention the next part. "Because of the virus, millions of people died all at once, and there's just been way too much magic in the ground lately. Now all that magic has been turned into holes."

Another long silence followed.

Lieutenant Briskle cleared his throat. He wore his biosuit but had discarded the hood and mask. "This wasn't how it was supposed to go down. Do you have any idea what you've done, kid?"

Hal began trembling with anger. "Yeah. I've done *something*, which is more than anyone else has done. Because of me, the spores are finally being cleaned up. People all over the world can come out of underground bunkers and walk around in fresh air for the first time in years—including Ryan's old friends, Jimmy and Dot. Thousands of people get to enjoy a whole new world of magic and amazing creatures. People have something to look forward to. Something to *live* for."

"And because of you," Miss Simone growled, "the people of my world are in danger of being overrun by greedy politicians and the hotheaded military."

"Now wait a minute," Briskle said, turning toward her.

"No, *you* wait a minute," Miss Simone snapped. "Abigail told me all about your plans to invade earlier this morning. Apparently you—"

Abigail suddenly leapt between them, holding up her hands as if to break up an impending fistfight. "Wait, wait! It's probably worth mentioning, Miss Simone, that this isn't really *your* world. You came from the same place as us, and the same place as Lieutenant Briskle. And don't forget it was the centaurs that caused the virus, so if there's going to be a big argument, you could say that the people of *this* world started it. So there."

Miss Simone was clenching her fists. "Don't make light of the situation, Abigail. This is no laughing matter. It's not even something children should be getting involved with. Hal had absolutely no right to—"

"I had every right," Hal interrupted. "What am I, Miss Simone?"

"I beg your pardon?"

"What am I?" he repeated. "What are my friends? What are *you*?"

Emily raised her hand. "Oh, I know this! We're shapeshifters."

"Top marks, Em," Hal said, nodding. "We're shapeshifters. And what were we created for? What's our purpose in life?"

Robbie jumped in. "We're emissaries."

"Right. Emissaries." Hal gave Miss Simone a steely glare. "You created us to make peace between different people. Between different species. To introduce one culture to another and help them understand each other." *Ooh, that's good*, he thought. He raised his voice. "Well, I just took it a step further. Now we're here to introduce *two different worlds* to each other. You were talking about greedy politicians, Miss Simone? Well, that's what *you've* become. A greedy politician. You found this world but don't want to share it—and you don't even own it! It's not yours to keep! You're just a visitor here!"

Her fury was building again, evident by her trembling, clenched fists.

"It's fine to claim a piece of land to live on," he hurried on. "A man named Carter claimed a place to build a village, and that's where we all live now. The trolls claimed the mountains in the east, and they charge people to travel through Eastward Pass. The dragons claimed the labyrinth in the north. The miengu claimed the lake in the west. People don't really *own* anything—we just claim it before anyone else, and that's okay, all perfectly normal. But an *entire world*? Nobody has a right to claim that as their own. It belongs to us all."

The more he thought about it, the more sense it made to him, and he couldn't talk fast enough to get his message across.

"There are virus survivors back home—real survivors like old Jimmy and Dot who spend their lives in depressing sealed-up houses hiding from scrags when they could be here enjoying the countryside the way we do. Even Ryan, who's completely immune, has spent his life living rough, hunting for food every day, avoiding scrags. He could have lived here instead. Him *and* his parents. But his parents died, and he was left all alone."

As everyone looked toward Ryan, Hal raised his voice further, feeling almost indignant that he was the only one voicing this.

"Miss Simone, when you first met Ryan and we were riding home in the cart, he blamed you for the death of his parents. Remember? He wondered why you couldn't have let his parents live on the island or come across to this world where it was safe, where there was no virus and no scrags. You told him you couldn't have made that decision, that if you'd let *them* come across, you'd have ended up letting *others* across as well, and that you had no right making decisions like that. Well, guess what, Miss Simone? People died because you couldn't make that decision!"

There was a collective gasp at this. Miss Simone turned white.

"Some died because of the virus," he went on, "and others died because of the scrags afterward. But think how many would have been saved if they'd had a choice, if they could have stepped across to this world at any time." Hal waved his hands dramatically. "Heck, even the scrags deserve a break! It's not their fault they've gone crazy over the years because their skin burns and itches every day. How about asking the dryads to come up with some kind of soothing skin cream as soon as the magic comes back? Maybe the scrags can be organized to clean up the spores on the streets and make them safe, maybe even supervise some of the new holes to make sure people who cross over are properly decontaminated. Give them a *purpose*."

He sagged, finally out of steam. The silence in the garden was unnerving as though Molly had turned her death-gaze on everybody present.

"Anyway," Hal went on quietly, "now there won't be any more hiding. No more separation. It's time to share everything we have. We're all in this together, and we're going to get along. It's a new start. And . . . I think it's going to be the best thing that's ever happened to us."

Miss Simone continued to glower, but the lieutenant looked thoughtful, and Ryan was nodding furiously.

"Well, I'm done," Hal said, tired. "Ground me for life. Throw me in prison. Turn me to stone. Do whatever you want. I don't care."

Miss Simone broke from her paralysis and moved slowly toward him. She stopped and pointed at him, but it was a moment before she got her words out. "Go home. Do not leave. I don't know how I'm going to deal with you yet. Maybe I should parade you around the village and let you see the faces of those whose lives you've endangered. The enormity of what you've done . . ."

She trailed off, apparently rendered speechless. Hal sighed with relief. It was over—for now. Sure, he was in for some serious discussions over the next few days, would probably be grounded for several lifetimes. But right now it was safe to go home to bed.

Molly emerged from the crowd holding the hand of one of her awakened statues. He was a tall, slightly potbellied but handsome man. "Well," she said from behind her veil, "you can all argue and reason about this for months to come, and I guarantee nobody will agree on anything. Not now, not ever. There are just two things I know for certain."

She paused for effect, and Darcy impatiently urged her on.

"First," Molly said, "I'm as happy as can be that everyone in this garden has woken. Of course I'm sad that so many have lost so much of their lives, but there's absolutely nothing I can do about that. All *right*, Wendel?" She glanced meaningfully to her right, where a middle-aged man in the crowd snarled back at her. "You'll just have to get over it and move on. Yes, it's a harsh reality, but most of you here were careless and looked at me without my veil on. Some of you actually did it on a dare. I'm a *gorgon*, for heaven's sake. What did you expect would happen?"

A few in the crowd grumbled and shuffled their feet. Even the potbellied man to her side looked away, his face reddening.

"And the second thing?" Darcy asked.

Molly edged closer to the man she held hands with. "I get a second chance with this lovely fellow. This is Dale. My husband."

Darcy gave a squeal, setting off a round of surprised and pleased murmurs. Even Miss Simone was distracted by this news, apparently unaware her friend had been married. Then again, Molly had led a reclusive life, and when she'd returned to the village recently, it must have been heartbreakingly impossible for her to admit she'd accidentally turned her husband to stone.

As the tension broke and everyone began mingling again, Hal began to feel strangely calm and content. Things were going to be all right. Well, maybe not *all* right, but certainly interesting. A new and exciting start. Two worlds merging.

Would his actions bring a new era of peace for all? Or was he way off-base? What if his actions were a recipe for disaster?

Only time would tell.

"Hey—we need to talk to you!" Molly suddenly yelled.

It turned out she was talking to a curly-haired boy with round-framed glasses, who apparently had been trying to sneak out the gate. Hal knew instantly who he was and stepped toward the familiar face. "Chase!"

As the boy hesitated and squinted at him, Hal suddenly lost interest in the comparatively petty, insignificant matter of opening millions of holes and joining the worlds. Now he was eager to hear

Chase's story. What had it been like working at a private school in the middle of nowhere with an eight-year-old Miss Simone and all her classmates as they experienced their first shapeshifting transformations? More to the point, what about Bo and Astrid, the missing Hammacher twins? What had Chase done with them?

The boy stared at Hal. "Yes?"

"I'm Hal. Remember me?"

Chase simply shrugged. "Can't say I do." Since the gate was now blocked by Miss Simone and Blacknail, who stood there with hands on hips, Chase seemed out of sorts and nervous, looking this way and that. He kept glancing at Molly and Miss Simone, and Hal suddenly realized how strange it must be for him to see them as adults when he'd seen them as eight-year-olds just a couple of months ago. "Is there another way out of this joint?" he whispered.

"Uh, no," Hal said, disappointment setting in.

So Chase had lost all memory of his stay in the world of darkness—just like everyone else that had suffered some kind of near-death experience or suspended animation. All these people that had just woken remembered nothing after Molly had petrified them except perhaps a distant, vague recollection of being drawn toward a white light. Hal alone had retained his memories because the woman-creature had burdened him with a mission and *needed* him to remember.

Still, even if Chase had forgotten all that otherworldly stuff, he would still recall everything that had happened *before* being turned to stone. He still had a story to tell.

Hal looked for Robbie. When he started toward him, trying to shoulder his way through the jostling crowd, Robbie saw him, grinned, and gave a thumbs-up. It wasn't immediately clear why until the crowd parted a little more and revealed Lauren holding his hand. Hal stopped dead, amazed and delighted.

Then he became aware that Abigail was sidling closer. He tried to decide if he was angry with her. She had gone along with Miss Simone and betrayed him, tried to take away his magic and render him normal . . . yet she had changed her mind at the last moment and saved him.

She took his hand and dragged him away from the crowd. "Hey," she said, turning to gaze directly into his eyes.

"Hey," he said grumpily.

"I'm sorry."

"I know."

She looked miserable. "I don't know what else to say. I shouldn't have gone against you. I . . . I thought I was doing the right thing. I didn't want you getting hurt—didn't want you getting into trouble. I thought that if I went along with Miss Simone, you'd hate me for a while, but you'd still be around. I was scared you'd kill yourself in an explosion or be put in prison or sent away . . ."

Her voice broke as tears welled up.

Hal sighed and took a step closer. "I'm sorry, too. But can we please just make up and go home? I'm really tired."

Her eyebrows shot up. "So you forgive me?"

He kissed her quickly—*on the lips*. Fenton hooted derisively, and Emily giggled. The kiss was short and sweet, and it surprised Hal as much as it did Abigail. Finally, *finally*, he'd done it. And while it had been nice, he wasn't sure it warranted all the anxiety it had caused him.

"So we're good?" she said shakily, ignoring everybody else.

"For now," Hal said cagily. Then he grinned. "Yeah, we're good."

Epilogue

A month had passed since Hal had introduced the worlds to one another. The village of Carter had undergone a great deal of construction work within homes in an effort to block off holes leading to the vast ocean. Nobody wanted to step into their bathroom and accidentally plunge into icy cold seawater. In some cases, rope ladders were secured and dangled through the holes so that, if anyone fell through, they'd be able to climb back up to safety. Some residents simply relocated, but most rearranged their compromised space by moving walls and creating new door openings.

Some villagers actually liked the holes. Where else could one go deep-sea fishing without even leaving the house? Families stocked up on heavy duty fishing rods, bait and tackle, and it became routine to catch five-pound haddock while seated just inside the doorway to the bathroom.

It was said that the trolls in the east enjoyed the fish, too. The mines at Bad Rock Gulch were now one gigantic pulsing hole in the ground. The hills had collapsed and fallen into the ocean in the other world, and the sea there kept surging high and pouring through, then ebbing, leaving behind flopping fish and occasional sharks. The trolls were happy to clean up. Since the goblins had no reason to use Eastward Pass anymore, this new fish diet more than made up for all the chickens the trolls were losing out on.

To the west and north of the village, more pulsing holes opened onto land, and through these holes came 'visitors.' With the spores finally eradicated, these visitors had emerged from underground bunkers and hermetically sealed camps. Some were happy to return to their old homes and wait for power and utilities to be restored. Others had nothing to go back to and stepped through the holes to start a new life in a fantastic new world.

Scrags were chased down, gangs disbanded, and the most violent of them imprisoned. The rest were organized into groups run by soldiers. It was a struggle, but they grudgingly started to 'get with the program' as Briskle called it, and a painfully slow clean-up operation commenced on the streets of the city and nearby suburbs. Though they didn't need accommodation, the scrags accepted food and a number of rudimentary salves for their burning, itchy skin while Darcy worked with the dryads to come up with something better.

These were early days yet, too early to tell how things would work out. At the moment, everyone was behaving. Hal thought it was like a bunch of dogs being herded into a cage together; they were sniffing around, eyeing one another, some of them suspicious and hostile, with others tentatively wagging their tails and offering friendship. Nobody quite knew whether a fight would break out, who would be mauled, and who would establish themselves as top dogs.

The complete loss of geo-rocks proved to be a problem until the military started supplying generators and running power cables through pulsing holes. Once some of the old spore-covered towns were cleaned up and the electricity switched back on, suddenly a source of energy was available in Miss Simone's world. Of course, to reach Carter, this meant running power lines across the countryside . . . something the centaurs began to kick up a fuss about.

Hal kept track of the discussions and arguments with a mixture of feelings. On some days it seemed everything was looking good; on others, when certain villagers glared at him and cursed his name, he wished he'd never blown up the Chamber of Ghosts. But he noticed that soldiers and scientists never tried to muscle their way into the new world. They were respectful and mindful of the many different communities and cultures in the region—the naga, the centaurs, and the elves to name but a few. Nobody wished to encroach on their land, drive out the residents, nor even spoil the landscape.

A supposedly important politician had come through a hole in the south. He'd instructed his chauffeur to drive his shiny black limousine through the pulsing cloud, using specially rigged ramps to ensure a smooth transition between terrains. It had been strange to watch the super-sized car crawling into the dusty streets of Carter and stopping outside the community hall.

In that council meeting, the smiling politician pompously stated that the people of Earth would be sure to treat the new world as an 'animal reserve'—a place where exotic creatures would be protected and where hunting would be illegal. He thought he was being magnanimous, but instead he created an uproar. Centaurs and naga in particular were irate at being referred to as *mere animals*, and they claimed that the egotistical, insensitive humans still couldn't get it into their heads that they were not the only intelligent beings on the planet. In fact, the politician's words only served to prove that humans were as dumb as ogres.

The politician apologized and tried to retract his statement, but the damage was done. The naga even went so far as to suggest, somewhat sarcastically, that they in turn would treat the entire human civilization as a petting zoo, with government officials as the main attraction.

But aside from squabbles like this, life went on.

Chase vanished. On the night the rose garden had come alive, Miss Simone had taken him home and locked him in her guest room until morning, when she and Molly intended to have a long chat with him over breakfast. But he escaped, and with two women after him, his name suddenly seemed apt. The mystery of the missing Hammacher twins remained unsolved, and Hal never got to speak to his new friend about their time together in the world of darkness. He did, however, glean some information from Molly. Though the twins had disappeared before anyone had witnessed their first transformations, it was no mystery what they would have become had they stuck around. Both were sphinxes, part lion and part human, with a tendency to talk in riddles. Their disappearance was an enigma in itself, though Molly guessed Chase had simply tried to 'release them into the wild' rather than be part of an experiment. Hal remembered his own feelings in those early days back on the island, and could understand the sentiment. So a misguided attempt to free the twins had resulted in a very young Molly, convinced Chase was a 'mean kidnapper,' trapping and calcifying him.

Where were the sphinxes today? Everybody assumed they were simply part of the landscape, out there somewhere, blending in. Miss Simone was thinking about launching a new search; after all, she'd managed to bring back Jolie and Thomas, both of whom had been 'lost' to the wild.

Jolie, not surprisingly, stuck around. Though confined to a wheelchair, she managed to enchant all those she bumped into, especially grown men who often forgot she had no legs. She broke hearts time and time again, reveling in the anguish she caused. Yet she was useful. Miss Simone's laboratory and medical facilities, now permanently wired and powered by electricity, had gained a new member of staff—someone who could perform miraculous healings.

* * *

As Hal and Abigail wandered through the village early one evening, they found Ryan talking to old Jimmy and Dot, who had moved into the village of Carter and were now enjoying what they thought of as their retirement home. Hal and Abigail greeted them warmly and moved on; the old couple tended to talk a lot. Besides, Robbie was waiting for them in the woods outside the village.

"What's so special that he needs us to go traipsing around in the trees?" Abigail complained. "In this weather. At this hour. On a Wednesday."

"It's probably another giant bug," Hal said with a laugh.

Still, he was curious himself, and he quickened his pace in an effort to get there and back before the sun went down. The bitterly cold winter was horrible. The villagers were used to it, but even they had considered traveling south and crossing over into the old city on the coast until summertime. The weather in Hal's old world was far less frigid.

He and Abigail left the village and entered the woods to the north. This was close to where Abigail had found a 'faerie patch'—though she suspected they were probably less active in the mornings now that the magic had dwindled.

Still, magic was slowly returning over time. Miss Simone was beginning to recharge. She really wasn't interested in getting her mermaid enchantment back and seemed to have enjoyed walking about the village without attracting attention. Nevertheless, she was regaining her powers as the weeks passed, much to her dismay. So, too, would the faeries.

"There he is," Hal said, pointing through the trees.

"Right on top of my faerie patch!" Abigail exclaimed.

Robbie was sitting on a fallen tree trunk alongside Lauren. They were holding hands and talking. Behind them was a pulsing, smoking black hole, which surprised Hal to no end. What was one doing out here?

Abigail sucked in a breath. "The faerie magic—this was a hotspot for them—it must have exploded along with the geo-rocks!"

Robbie jumped to his feet. "There you are!" he exclaimed. "What took you so long? You were supposed to be here hours ago."

"Well, we were busy," Hal said, spreading his hands.

"Anyway," Abigail said mischievously, "I'm pretty sure you two didn't mind waiting. Together. In private."

"Don't know what you mean," Robbie muttered, his face reddening. He let go of Lauren's hand and shuffled his feet.

Abigail's smile faded. She looked concerned again. "I hope my faerie friends are okay. If this patch had exploded early morning when they were all sleeping off their party, they would have been killed." Then she pursed her lips and began to nod. "But it happened late at night, so most likely they were flitting around everywhere. I'm sure they're all fine."

"So this was a faerie patch?" Lauren asked. "I guess that explains where this hole came from." She smiled. "Show them, Robbie."

Intrigued, Hal stepped closer. "Show us what?"

Robbie pointed to a rope looped around the tree trunk. "Surprise for you."

The rope ran into the pulsing hole and disappeared into blackness. Whatever Robbie had tied to the trunk was on the other side—most likely dangling in the ocean. Hal sighed and approached. "Is it safe?"

"Yeah. Just hang on to the rope and climb down."

So Hal eased himself backward into the hole. The ground vanished behind him, and his legs dangled precariously in midair. Cold wind whistled around his ankles. Gripping the rope, he lowered himself through the blackness.

He ended up hanging over the ocean. It stretched on forever, though cliffs loomed in the west along with the distant buildings of a city—the same city where he'd run into scrags. There was a clear sunset and a low, full moon.

Right below him, on the end of the rope, was a raft, bobbing neatly on the water. He gasped and took it all in at once—two large, hefty doors secured to crossbeams, sturdy plastic drums all around . . . It was far superior to the raft he and Robbie had built one Saturday afternoon a while back.

Hoisting himself back up through the hole, he grinned at his friend. "That thing is *awesome!*"

"What thing?" Abigail asked.

"A raft. A brilliant one. Big enough for four." Hal looked meaningfully at Robbie and Lauren. "The four of us, right?"

They nodded in unison, looking pleased with themselves. "Lauren and I built it together," Robbie said proudly. "Took a week. It was our secret project. We could have gone for a sail if you'd gotten here earlier. Too late now, though. The moon's already out."

Hal glanced between the trees, making out the moon low in the sunset sky, as it had been over the ocean. It was strange how the sun and moon appeared to be identical in both worlds. They never faltered from their positions no matter what the terrain looked like below. Were there twin moons and suns? And if so, was there also a twin universe as well? Or was it only Earth that was divided?

The moon tonight was nearly full. Hal scratched absently at his left forearm, realizing it had been a full lunar month since his werewolf attack. He shuddered, recalling how close he'd come to death that night . . .

"Maybe tomorrow, though?" Robbie said.

With a sigh, Hal shared a glance with Abigail before looking sheepishly at Robbie and Lauren. "Actually, Miss Simone is sending me on a mission."

Abigail nodded. "And I'm going, too."

"*What* mission?" Robbie said, looking indignant. "How come I don't know about this?"

"Because I just found out earlier. I'm going after Chase."

Robbie and Lauren were silent.

"He was spotted west of here," Abigail said. "Word just came back. So Miss Simone wants Hal to go find him and bring him home. She wants to know what happened to the sphinx twins, and he's the only one who knows."

"Can *we* go?" Robbie asked, gesturing to Lauren and himself.

As Abigail answered him, saying she didn't see why not but that Robbie would need to clear it with his parents, Hal looked away into the woods. He felt strange. Something was stirring in him. Was the memory of the werewolf attack causing him to feel nauseous, or was the nausea bringing up the memory? Either way, something was wrong. He blinked rapidly as dizziness overcame him. His friends went on talking, apparently unaware that he was beginning to sway.

His arm itched again. He rubbed and scratched at it through his sweater, wondering if he'd been bitten by some kind of winter bug.

"Hal?" Lauren said. "Are you okay? You've gone pale."

Immediately Abigail was clinging to him, holding him steady while she peered into his face. "What's wrong?"

"Not sure," Hal muttered. "I just feel . . . weird."

"Why are you scratching?" Robbie asked.

Realizing that he was indeed clawing at his forearm again, Hal stopped and held up his hand. His mouth dropped open, and Abigail gasped and backed away.

He *had* been bitten, but not by a bug.

With shaking fingers, he pushed up the sleeve of his sweater. Now it was Robbie and Lauren who gasped, and Hal began to mumble under his breath.

Bitten by a werewolf. The wound on his stomach hadn't healed quite as well as he'd assumed.

With his heart hammering in his chest, Hal had the strangest feeling that he needed to set off running through the woods. He needed to *hunt*. His blood surged through his body and a craving hunger overcame him.

"What now?" he moaned.

His entire left forearm, and part of his hand, was covered in coarse, dark brown hair. As he stared, his fingers slowly began to stretch.

Author's Note

The story will continue in Book 7, in which Hal and Chase embark on a journey to find the missing Hammacher twins. Of course, Abigail insists on going along for the ride, as well as Robbie and Lauren.

Originally, *Island of Fog* was a one-book story. It quickly became obvious there was more story to tell, and so it became a trilogy with *Labyrinth of Fire* and *Mountain of Whispers*. I included an Author's Note in the third book stating that further volumes would be likely, but that they would be standalone stories. Hmm. That didn't quite happen, did it? *Lake of Spirits* ended with Hal, Abigail, Robbie and Emily stuck in a virus-stricken world, and some readers couldn't stand to wait for the next book, *Roads of Madness*, to see what happened to them. When I started *Chamber of Ghosts*, I fully intended to wrap up the second trilogy as well as the series.

Again, I've been ambushed by the characters. They don't seem to know when to quit. The immediate story has ended, and I'm now done with everything to do with geo-rocks and phoenixes, but there's more to tell—specifically the story of eight-year-old Miss Simone and all her classmates when they first developed their shapeshifting tendencies. This is obviously a prequel story, and I intended for this to be an add-on book, not really part of the series. Funny how things turn out! As it happens, Hal now has a bit of a hairy problem that he needs to deal with, and it would be nice to find out where those twins are today, so the 'add-on prequel' has turned into a full-fledged Island of Fog Book 7.

What's interesting about Book 7 is that a sizeable portion of it will be told from Chase's point of view (in first person) as he recounts his story along the way. Other than prologues and epilogues, this will be the first time in the series that the reader experiences the story outside Hal's point of view.

A quick note to acknowledge a slew of beta readers and proofreaders, without whom these books would be very sloppy indeed. There are too many to name, but you know who you are. Thanks!

—*Keith Robinson, April 24, 2013*

The ISLAND OF FOG series

If you enjoyed this book, the author would greatly appreciate your review. Thank you!

The popular Island of Fog series follows the adventures of Hal and his friends as they harness their shapeshifting abilities and settle into a world vastly different from their own. If you want more, there are also short stories known as the Island of Fog Chronicles (ebooks only) as well as the Island of Fog Legacies, a spin-off series that takes place twenty years in the future with a new generation of shapeshifters.

Please visit the author's website for more information and to keep up to date with the latest releases.

http://www.unearthlytales.com

Printed in Great Britain
by Amazon

62095411R00159